# PRAISE FOR HILARY DAVIDSON

## *ONE SMALL SACRIFICE*

"Davidson's latest novel is her best work yet. *One Small Sacrifice* is a fast-paced winner. Highly recommended."
  —Harlan Coben, #1 *New York Times* bestselling author of *Run Away*

"Fans of Karin Slaughter, Tana French, and Lisa Gardner will devour this new police procedural, which boasts a strong female detective and an intriguing antagonist. Sheryn [Sterling] will draw in readers, and Davidson's complex storytelling will keep them wanting more."
  —*Library Journal* (starred review)

"Davidson has crafted a tightly woven mystery. Each thread of the intricate plot draws you toward one surprising revelation after another."
  —Sandra Brown, #1 *New York Times* bestselling author of *Tailspin*

"A thoughtfully plotted and skillfully characterized procedural mystery . . . it's easy to get drawn deeply into the various motives and secrets of each character because it's so perfectly human for all of us to keep things hidden, even from those we love."
  —*Kirkus Reviews*

"Hilary Davidson's *One Small Sacrifice* is both a heart-pounding procedural and a rich, mesmerizing tale of the weight of trauma and the elusive nature of memory. Twisty, absorbing, and deeply humane, it's a thriller you won't want to miss."
  —Megan Abbott, *New York Times* bestselling author of *Give Me Your Hand*

"Packed with secrets, lies, and surprises, *One Small Sacrifice* kept me guessing to the very end. A gritty kaleidoscope of a thriller."
—Riley Sager, *New York Times* bestselling author of *Final Girls*

"Davidson's stealthily plotted, rapidly deployed, multistranded mystery encompasses the most intimate of brutalities—including domestic abuse and postbattlefield PTSD, a solid handful of dodgy characters, and, in the most humane of touches, a dog named Sid."
—*Seattle Review of Books*

"A taut, compelling narrative with a nerve-tingling climax. Davidson turns clichés of the contemporary novel on their heads to create a wholly believable cast of characters. I hope we'll see more of Detective Sheryn Sterling."
—Sara Paretsky, *New York Times* bestselling author of *Shell Game*

"*One Small Sacrifice* is a terrific thriller with a big heart. A smart, compelling examination of guilt, blame, and responsibility that will keep you turning the pages. Hilary Davidson is a rising star of suspense."
—Jeff Abbott, *New York Times* bestselling author of *The Three Beths*

"The story line veers between alternate points of view with Traynor and Sterling, and their perspectives on the same information provide different results. Writing the novel in this fashion amps up the suspense while also giving the narrative a complex and compelling flair. In addition, Davidson does an admirable job of making a complicated issue such as PTSD relatable."
—*Associated Press*

"Hilary Davidson is one of the best crime writers on the planet. This novel is a dazzling work by a master operating at the height of her abilities. Dark, twisty, and psychologically complex, *One Small Sacrifice* kept me guessing and gasping until the final page. I couldn't put it down, even though I didn't want it to end."

—Chris Holm, Anthony Award–winning author of *The Killing Kind*

"*One Small Sacrifice* hooked me hard. Hilary Davidson has written a riveting and beautifully layered thriller that satisfies on every level. The characters surprise, the plot twists, and the pages turn themselves."

—Lou Berney, Edgar Award–winning author of *November Road*

"I tore through this book! Hilary Davidson is at the top of her game with this masterful and twisty new novel that's jam-packed with suspense. Filled with wonderfully diverse characters, breakneck pacing, and surprises at every turn, this modern mystery will thrill even the most old-school crime fiction lovers. This book satisfied me on so many levels."

—Jennifer Hillier, author of *Jar of Hearts*

## PREVIOUS PRAISE FOR HILARY DAVIDSON

"Hilary Davidson is the master of plot twists!"

—Tess Gerritsen, *New York Times* bestselling author, on *Blood Always Tells*

"Hilary Davidson delivers the goods—an exotic, atmospheric setting, a rocket-paced plot, and . . . a top-notch mystery—exciting, harrowing, and smart."

—Lisa Unger, *New York Times* bestselling author, on *Evil in All Its Disguises*

# DON'T

# LOOK

# DOWN

# OTHER TITLES BY HILARY DAVIDSON

## Shadows of New York Series

*One Small Sacrifice*

## Other Novels

*The Damage Done*
*The Next One to Fall*
*Evil in All Its Disguises*
*Blood Always Tells*

## Short Stories

*The Black Widow Club: Nine Tales of Obsession & Murder*

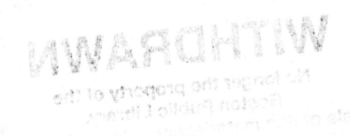

# DON'T LOOK DOWN

## HILARY DAVIDSON

Text copyright © 2020 by Hilary Davidson
All rights reserved.

Published by Thomas & Mercer, Seattle
www.apub.com

Amazon, the Amazon logo, and Thomas & Mercer are trademarks of Amazon.com, Inc., or its affiliates.

ISBN-13: 9781542092036 (hardcover)
ISBN-10: 1542092035 (hardcover)

ISBN-13: 9781542092012 (paperback)
ISBN-10: 1542092019 (paperback)

Cover design by Christopher Lin

Printed in the United States of America

First edition

*For Stephanie Craig, Ilana Rubel, and Trish Snyder*
*With love, friendship, and admiration*
*And because you know where the bodies are buried*

Never regret thy fall,
O Icarus of the fearless flight
For the greatest tragedy of them all
Is never to feel the burning light.
—Oscar Wilde

# MONDAY

# CHAPTER 1

## Jo

Jo Greaver was ready to kill someone. There were a dozen reasons why, starting with the fact that her shoulder felt like it might break under the weight of the black duffel bag she was lugging across West Forty-Ninth Street. It was unusually cold for the end of November, and a blustery wind hit her face, making her eyes tear up, even behind her black cat's-eye sunglasses. She'd figured her best disguise would be gym clothes, and she'd picked the oldest, most nondescript outfit she could find: black Pumas, black leggings, black long-sleeved tee, and a waterproof black jacket over it all, with its hood pulled up over her shoulder-length dark hair. If it weren't for the leaden weight of the bag, she would've jogged to make it look legit.

*No one is staring at you,* Jo reminded herself. It was a freezing Monday afternoon. Everyone on the street was huddled in their own misery, taking no notice of hers.

As she crossed Eleventh Avenue, a gust of arctic air struck her hard enough to make her teeth ache. She hadn't expected it to be so cold. Her breath visibly fanned out in the air in front of her. She couldn't feel her face.

*You'll get through this,* she told herself. *You're going to fix this.*

That brought a tough little lump into her throat. She'd worked so damned hard.

*Don't be a useless crybaby,* hissed a voice in the back of her head, slapping Jo back to reality.

When she found the right building on the north side of the street—number 631—she eyeballed it for security cameras. The only one she saw was a broken black shell with a missing lens and a shredded electric cord hanging down like a forlorn tail. The apartment block was a run-down eyesore, with wooden boards covering the first-story windows and a fire escape that looked like it might blow away in a gust of wind. She opened the first door with a gloved hand; inside, she found two rows of rusty buzzers with faded numbers beside them. She crouched down so that the bag rested briefly on the cracked linoleum, and she swapped it from her right shoulder to her left. She kept her head down, like a turtle, and made sure her hood was pulled up, in case she'd missed a camera. When she was ready, she pressed the buzzer for apartment 402.

"Hello?" The voice that answered was male. No surprise there.

"I'm downstairs," Jo said. "Let me in."

"Who *is* this?" The voice was gruff, biting off each word angrily.

Jo paused, unwilling to say her name in case there was audio to go with the camera. Her blackmailer had enough on her already; she didn't need to hand him more material. "You *know* who this is," she snapped. "Open the door."

There was a soft chuckle on the other end. "You're a tough little cookie, aren't you?" The voice was still a growl, but a note of amusement had crept into it.

"I've got the money," Jo answered flatly. "Do you want it or not?"

There was a heavy pause. It was long enough for Jo to wonder if he was toying with her like a cat with a mouse. He'd made it clear exactly what he knew about her, and Jo hadn't had a peaceful night's sleep since. Her blackmailer could tell her to go away and come back tomorrow, and she'd have to do it. He could order her to do just about anything, and she'd have to obey. She found herself holding her breath as she waited for him to answer.

"Come on up," he said finally. "The lock on that door's broken anyway."

There was no elevator inside. Jo pushed her sunglasses up so that they lay under the hood like a plastic headband. She was no stranger to walk-ups, but even the worst of the cockroach-infested dumps she'd seen looked better than this one. The staircase banister had been ripped off, leaving a few wooden spikes behind. The stairs themselves were sagging and crumbling. The walls were so badly damaged that they looked like they were melting, with big holes punched out of them. There was so much plaster dust in the air Jo could feel it scratching at her throat. On the second floor, there was a marshal's notice from the City of New York evicting a tenant. One of the doors was boarded up. Still, there was one sign of life as she approached the third floor: behind one of those cracked doors, someone was loudly playing a TV.

*This would be a great place to get murdered,* Jo thought. It was a sardonic aside, just her dark sense of humor kicking in, but she shuddered anyway. The strangest thing was that, in spite of the noise, it felt like there was no one else in the building. She paused on the third-floor landing to steady her nerves. Over the blaring TV, there was the sound of metal scraping against metal; Jo dropped the heavy bag and spun around, but no one was there. She studied each door; maybe someone was watching her through a peephole. *If I lived in a place like this, I'd watch everyone who came in.* Still, it was unnerving. No one knew she was there. If she died, no one would know what had happened to her.

*Maybe you should run while you can,* she told herself. But where would she go? The life she'd built for herself was in New York. She'd founded her own company when she was twenty-one; five years later, thanks to private investment and Jo's own savvy for free media coverage, it was an international business. No one was going to take that from her. She had no choice but to face this trouble head-on.

5

Finally, in front of apartment 402, she removed her gloves and balled them up in the left pocket of her jacket. She didn't know how this was going to go; she had to be ready. With her left hand gripping the bag and her right hand deep in her jacket pocket, she lightly kicked the door with the toe of her sneaker. Inside the apartment, someone opened up the peephole and stared at her for what felt like a very long time. Jo wanted to snap at him to hurry it up—she didn't have all day. She had a life to get back to; this was a brief detour from the path she was on, a wrong turn she'd made. Finally, she heard a single lock turn.

The door opened a crack, then widened.

"Hey there," said the man who answered it. He was tall and casually dressed in jeans and a white shirt; he wore a black ball cap that cast the top part of his face in shadow and made it hard to figure his age. "You must be Jo."

"You never gave me your name," Jo said. She had wondered for the past weeks what her blackmailer looked like. Her greatest fear had been that it was someone from her past, nursing a grudge that ran valley deep. A close second was her fear that it might be one of her sister's seedy associates, bitter and vicious and desperate to sell her out for their next fix. Instead, she found herself staring at a man she'd never laid eyes on before. She didn't feel relief, exactly, but there was something reassuring that this torment was only about money. An old acquaintance might be hard to placate; a fresh face who only cared about cash presented a different set of problems, but they felt slightly less dire.

"Guilty as charged," he answered. "Come on in."

He sounded casual, perhaps aiming for friendliness, but his low voice came out as a snarl, as if his teeth were gritted behind the tight smile he gave her. Jo froze in place, every nerve in her body telling her not to step inside.

"You're looking at me like I'm the big bad wolf. I don't bite," the man added with a contemptuous chuckle.

*You useless crybaby,* hissed the voice in the back of her mind. *Get inside and get this over with.*

"I've been bitten by guys who gave me that same line," Jo answered, swallowing her fear and stepping over the threshold.

The man moved to one side, holding the door for Jo. Her head swiveled as she took in her surroundings, her right hand tensing, but no one else was inside. The apartment was a small studio, well kept and decorated with pops of color. The building itself may have been desolate, but this small corner of it verged on cozy. A framed painting of the Holy Family caught her eye. She was familiar with religious imagery from her childhood, but this image was a departure from the blond, blue-eyed version she knew; in this case baby Jesus, Mary, and Joseph were black.

The man closed the door with a sharp bang and double-locked it behind her. Jo tried not to flinch, but a chill ran down her neck and through her body. For the first time, she was genuinely afraid. The apartment was clean and smelled of bleach, but for all she knew, this man was a meticulous serial killer who didn't like a mess.

"You want something to drink?" the man asked her. "I've got scotch but no ice."

"No. I just want to talk," Jo said. She cleared her throat; it felt like sandpaper from all the dust she'd inhaled on the climb up. "I want to know about that video."

"It's pretty shocking." He was relaxed as he spoke, like he was talking about a cartoon. "You've seen it before?"

"I didn't even know it existed." That was a lie, but she didn't owe him any explanations. "How did you get it?"

The man smiled wider; he was obviously enjoying himself. "I'll tell you what I wonder about," he said. "Do you ever feel guilty for what you've done?"

Jo didn't answer that, but her stomach churned.

"I want to know," he added, the wattage of his smile dimming. "Most people would feel bad, I bet."

"*How* did you get that video?" Jo repeated.

"It was part of a package deal," the man said. "It came with these."

He handed a couple of glossy photographs to Jo. She glanced at the one on top, and bile crept into her throat. She had to look away.

"You had one hot little bod, didn't you?" The man was openly leering at her now. "I've gotta say, first time I saw those, I thought, *Wow.* But then, I also thought, *Where were that girl's parents?*"

"Dead," Jo said.

"Huh. I guess that explains it." His deep voice rasped. "How old were you then?"

Jo barely heard him; the sound of her own blood was beating in her ears. She'd had a vision of what she needed to do: march in, gather information, secure every copy of the video, and hand over the cash. Everything had gone sideways fast, with this smarmy creep's hot eyes on her. She found herself gazing at the Holy Family again. There were so many colors swirling in it, but what stood out to her were little drops of red; at that moment, they looked to her like blood. The photos slipped out of her left hand. They fluttered to the floor as she clutched the duffel bag; her right hand, deep in her pocket, gripped her gun. She slid the safety off with her thumb.

"Don't take any of this personally," the man said. "We've all gotta do what we've gotta do, right?"

Jo suddenly realized he was as sly an animal as she'd ever encountered. For while he'd kept chatting, his voice low and gravelly and calm, he'd made his way over to the kitchen counter. His eyes stayed on hers while his hand darted out and reached for something. It was the hallmark move of a predator, and she noted—with searing regret—that talking herself out of her fears had only left her vulnerable. She pulled the gun out of her pocket and fired at him, but not before he raised his gun and fired at her.

# CHAPTER 2

## SHERYN

It didn't matter that she was a cop. When Sheryn Sterling came up against the gray stone facade of the NYPD's First Precinct, her stomach lurched. It wasn't fear so much as dread, a creeping knowledge in her bones for the past fourteen years that this day would come. She took a deep breath and walked inside, the soles of her black leather boots announcing her entrance as she approached the sergeant on duty at the desk.

"I'm Detective Sterling, from Midtown North." She flashed her badge at him. "I understand that you have my son in custody."

"Name?"

"Martin Sterling Hartwell. He's a student at Hunter College High School." When the sergeant failed to respond, she added, "He's fourteen years old."

Finally, the man gave her a tiny nod of acknowledgment. "Found him. Have a seat. Someone will be with you shortly."

It took all Sheryn's discipline to follow that simple command. Every nerve in her body was quivering. She wanted to storm into the precinct and claim her son. But she wasn't there as a cop; at that moment, her only role was as a mother.

The man they finally sent to speak to her looked as if he'd recently been discharged from the military. His iron-gray hair was cut like a marine's, his face was set in a forbidding frown, and his pale-blue eyes pierced right through her. "Mrs. Hartwell?" he asked.

"It's Sterling. My husband's last name is Hartwell," Sheryn corrected him. "Where's my son?"

"He's fine," the man answered, even though that wasn't what she'd asked. "I'm Detective Byrne. Let's talk in private."

"I want to see my son."

"Sure you do. But first we need to talk." He led her down the hallway. "Did anyone tell you why he was arrested?"

"I was told he attended some type of rally." The last word stuck in Sheryn's throat. At breakfast that morning, Martin hadn't dropped any hints about his plans; he'd groused about his upcoming math test.

"Your son was protesting the work of federal agents," Byrne said. "With all due respect, I have to tell you I was shocked the son of a cop would do such a thing."

He gazed at her with cold eyes, and Sheryn stared back. "No one bothered to tell me what this rally was about," she said.

"Deporting illegal immigrants. Your son was protesting the work of some of our country's brave federal agents."

Even though he spoke only a few words, Sheryn took the measure of the man in an instant. With his name and fair coloring, he was clearly of Irish descent. She wanted to ask him whether his family had come to America to escape the Great Famine, but she couldn't, not without risking her son's safety. *Follow your better angels,* her mother liked to tell her when she was growing up; the problem was, at that moment, the angels were as pissed off as she was.

"Kids these days," Sheryn said, desperately scrambling for some common ground. "They follow the news like forty-year-olds. You have any kids, Detective?"

"No," he answered curtly.

"Ah." *So much for empathy,* she thought. "Well, at our church, we talk a lot about how to help immigrants." Sheryn's voice was careful and measured. "My son's very involved at our church, you know. He's in the youth leadership program. He must've thought what he was doing today was meant to help people. Like Jesus said, 'For I was hungry, and you gave me something to eat; I was thirsty, and you gave me something to drink; I was a stranger, and you invited me in.'"

The man's mouth pressed into an even grimmer line. Sheryn had grown up in a home where quoting Scripture was normal, something even her hard-to-please mother applauded. Detective Byrne was clearly not cheering.

"Can you tell me exactly what my son did to get arrested?" Sheryn added.

"He was blocking the sidewalk."

"Did he refuse to move?"

Byrne turned his remorseless stare on her again. The air between them was thick with unspoken hostility. She knew, in that moment, that this man, or one of his close colleagues, had arrested Martin for nothing worse than setting a foot outside of the limited space protestors were allowed. She could almost hear the gears turning in his cruel little brain, the enjoyment he would take in keeping Martin in custody.

She moved her mouth into a semblance of a smile. "I just realized . . . Detective Byrne, you're in the Emerald Society, aren't you? My old partner, Sandy Reilly, loved that group."

For what seemed like the first time, he blinked. "*You're* Sandy's partner?" Byrne stared as her as if she'd beamed in from another planet.

"That's right." Sandy was a legend in the department; everyone knew him, at least by reputation. He would've been proud of her in that moment. *Play the game,* he liked to say. By that, he meant figure out the rules and use them to your advantage.

"*You're* the one who kicks his ass at poker?" Byrne's disbelief was palpable.

"I'm surprised Sandy admitted that," Sheryn said. "He's the one who taught me how to play. Stole my lunch money for about a year until I figured the game out."

"I've lost to him a bunch of times," Byrne admitted. "Always figured that old buzzard had an ace or two up his sleeve."

"He probably did." Sheryn smiled for real for the first time since she'd set foot in that building. "He's sneaky as hell. Taught me to be too."

"Serves him right." Byrne's frosty demeanor was melting. "Hold on—let me get your kid." Whatever storm was brewing between them had petered out, but the air in the precinct still felt heavy. Sheryn had to remind herself to breathe in, breathe out.

When he brought Martin out and voided his arrest, Sheryn told her son, very seriously, "You have a lot of explaining to do, young man." The words didn't feel natural on her lips; she knew they were what Byrne expected her to say. She was playing a role to shield her son from danger, and it was an audience of one that would determine its success.

"I bet he's learned his lesson," Byrne said genially.

"I certainly hope so," Sheryn added.

Sheryn kept her facade up until she got Martin out of the station house and into her car. "What. Were. You. Thinking?" she demanded, staring straight ahead.

"I can explain." Martin's voice was weak.

"You know better." Her hands gripped the wheel, even though the car was still parked. "We talked about this."

"They're rounding up immigrants, Mom. Ezra and I . . ."

"Ezra!" The name flew out of her mouth like a curse. "Your friend Ezra is white. The police are not going to treat him like a black boy. Where is he now?"

"I don't know. We got separated . . ."

Sheryn exhaled a long breath. "I don't want to hear another word out of you. Believe me—we'll be talking tonight." She turned on the engine and eased into traffic. They took the FDR north. Martin's head swiveled toward her when she exited at East Ninety-Sixth Street, an unspoken question hanging in the air between them. She stopped the car in front of the school on Ninety-Fourth Street. It was a massive redbrick building with few windows, and it always made Sheryn think of a medieval fortress. She'd thought he was safe there. But she couldn't blame the school for not protecting her son that day; he'd left of his own accord.

"I have to go back to work," she explained, her voice still sharp. "And you still have school and then band practice."

Martin slunk back in his seat. "I'm sorry, Mom."

"Do you need me to talk to your principal?"

"No, thanks," he murmured. "I'll be okay."

Her eyes burned when she looked at him. "None of this is okay," she said. "We're going to have a conversation tonight. Do you understand?"

Martin's eyes were downcast, and he gulped a little at that, but he nodded and opened the car door.

"What about your math test?" she asked.

"It was first period this morning." He gave her a shy smile. "I think I aced it."

"You better have," Sheryn said. "I love you."

"I love you, too, Mom," he answered. He shut the door and headed for the steps. Sheryn watched him until he vanished from sight. She'd known this day would come ever since he was born, but that didn't make it any easier to bear.

# CHAPTER 3

## Jo

Jo reacted instinctively, shielding her torso with the bag. His first shot went wide, but she felt the impact of the second one: it ripped into the flesh of her left arm and knocked her back. She caught herself against the front door, dropping the bag with a heavy thud.

The man reeled back, slamming his head on the countertop as he went down. She watched him fall as if he were in slow motion. A giant red stain bloomed across the front of his white shirt. Improbably, his cap stayed glued to his head, and under its brim, his eyes were wide open. For a split second, she thought he was dead.

"Moth . . . rrr . . . fuck . . . ," he groaned, clutching at his stomach and chest.

He'd dropped his gun. Jo rushed over and kicked it to the other side of the room.

The man convulsed violently. He wasn't dead, but he would be soon.

"No," Jo whispered. "This can't be happening."

Her upper arm was filled with a searing, white-hot pain; the lower part was tingling, as if the nerves were firing off random signals. She wanted to stanch the bleeding with her right hand, but she was still holding her gun. She turned back to the front door and reached for the first lock, but there were footsteps in the hallway.

Someone banged on the door with a fist. "Tony!" a male voice yelled. "Are you okay?"

"Bitch . . . shot . . . me," the man on the floor gasped. Jo looked over her shoulder. His eyes were rolling back in his head, and his breathing was ragged and labored.

There were steps from the hallway again, but they seemed to be moving away. Did she have time to make a run for it? If he had a gun, he could kill her as she made her way down that rickety, narrow staircase.

Jo held her breath, her eyes darting around the apartment. Was there anywhere to hide? She could call the police, but would they get there in time? Even in her frantic state, she realized that it had never occurred to her to call them when her blackmailer first contacted her, or in the weeks since. *The cops can't help you,* she warned herself. She was on her own, as always. Besides the front door, there were two doors, both shut. She ran over to the one farthest from the man bleeding on the kitchen linoleum. She opened it and found a closet stuffed to the gills with boxes and clothes. *Dead end,* Jo realized.

The man she'd shot was making terrible sounds, interspersed with cursing. She could see his feet moving, pedaling against air, like he was trying to get up except he'd forgotten where the floor was.

From the hallway, there were footsteps again. They stopped, and there was a loud crack of a gunshot. Jo jumped back as a bullet whizzed by. Flakes flew into the air like miniature bits of confetti. Part of the wooden door had turned into powder from the force of the blast.

"Stop," the man on the floor croaked.

The one in the hall wasn't listening. He fired again. This shot went wide, soaring above Jo's head. She shrieked and dropped to the floor in a crouch.

There was nowhere to hide. She was trapped and wounded. The only route out seemed impossible. She was four stories up; it wasn't as if she could jump from the window. But she remembered the rickety fire escape. It was her only chance at that moment. She made a break for the window, unlocked it, and pushed up the sash. It opened only a foot or so, but that would be enough.

The front door rattled on its hinges. As quickly as she could, Jo eased her wounded arm and her left leg out first. Her whole body felt like it was on fire. The metal of the fire escape was rusted and scaling, but it held her weight. She clattered down the skeletal stairs, clutching the railing with both hands, never looking back.

There was an elderly man on the block who stopped and stared at her as she dropped from the second story to the sidewalk. "Where's the fire, lady?" he called, laughing.

Jo didn't give him a second look. She ran and ran and ran until her lungs were about to burst.

# CHAPTER 4

## SHERYN

When Sheryn walked into the squad room at the Manhattan North Precinct—her home base—her partner was the first person she laid eyes on. It had only been a month since he'd been injured in an explosion, and a week since he'd come back to the job. Rafael Mendoza looked as darkly handsome as ever, with his brilliantined hair and sharp suit, gold cuff links dazzling at the wrist. But the purple circles under his eyes were more pronounced than ever, and his skin had an unhealthy, sallow cast. Those differences might not have been obvious to anyone else, but even strangers would've taken note of the cane. It was an elegant, carved mahogany, and Sheryn liked to tease him that it was perfect for a movie mafioso. At that moment, its gleaming, polished handle was resting against the side of his desk. What Sheryn hadn't told him was that the sight of it made her heart squeeze tight. It was a reminder that—stylish as Rafael was—he'd been badly wounded by a blast she'd walked away from.

"Hey, how did it go?" Rafael asked in a low voice when she came closer.

"The arresting officer was . . . bracing," Sheryn said, her voice soft so that none of the other people milling around could overhear. "Military haircut, snarky attitude. He was shocked—shocked!—the son of a cop would ever be out in the street protesting anything."

Her encounter with Detective Byrne had left her with a simmering anger that had no place to go. It was like stormwater building up behind a dam. She was upset about how he'd treated her son, and how he'd treated her. It grated on her that she'd had to maintain a veneer of civility, keeping her tone light and wearing a neutral expression like a mask. Ultimately, he had let her son go because Sheryn was close friends with a man he respected. He was racist *and* sexist, and yet he was allowed to carry the same gold shield she did. In his mind, Sheryn didn't count at all, and she was torn between kicking a wall and going back and punching his head.

"How's Martin doing?" Rafael asked, shaking her out of her own head.

"He's grounded until the End of Days," Sheryn answered. "But he's okay. He and his best friend thought it would be cool to cut school and protest something. That didn't go so well." It wasn't that she didn't want to tell her partner everything—she trusted Rafael, and he would get it—but there were enough other cops in the vicinity who she didn't have the same confidence in. Some might hear about her son and think that *he* was the problem, not the system he was protesting.

"Martin's what, all of fourteen? Speaks well for him that his heart's in the right place," Rafael said.

"Even if it makes him act like he doesn't have a brain?"

"My parents would've loved for me to get involved with a cause when I was a teenager. When I was your son's age, all I cared about was sports, video games, and Sigourney Weaver."

Sheryn raised an eyebrow.

"You don't have to be straight to appreciate Sigourney Weaver," Rafael muttered.

"When I was fourteen, I wanted to join the military," Sheryn said, glad to shift the topic from her son. She could tell Rafael the rest of the story later. "Anything I was interested in reflected that. Martial arts. Running. Even the books I read. You know what my favorite book was?"

"Knowing you, probably Sun-Tzu's *The Art of War*."

"Didn't read that until later," Sheryn admitted. "I was obsessed with *The Guns of August*."

"It rings a bell," Rafael said. "I think my parents tried to make me read it."

"It's about World War One."

"The war that made no sense."

"It does it you look at it as a bunch of privileged men who made one fatal miscalculation after another. They thought the war would be short. They were overconfident, unaware the ground was shifting under their feet."

"Was that one of the books your father gave you?" Rafael asked.

"It was. He was always trying to get my brothers into this stuff, but they resisted. I was the only one who gravitated to it." She paused. "How are you feeling? Be honest."

"I'm good." Rafael shrugged. "Mostly I wish the ringing in my ears would go away. It's like being stealth-attacked by an invisible drone all day long."

Before Sheryn could formulate the question she really wanted to ask—which would include a gentle hint that maybe he needed a little more time off the job—he moved on, snapping his fingers.

"Hey," he said. "What are you and your husband doing a week from next Saturday night?"

She regarded him suspiciously. "Why?"

"Some organization's giving Brett an award," Rafael explained, keeping his voice whisper quiet, as he always did when talking about his husband if other cops were around.

"Congratulations. What for?"

"Who knows. Bankers *love* to give each other awards." He sat back in his chair. "When you win an award, you have to buy a table. So . . . we have tickets. Please come. I'm going to be all alone at this stupid table if you don't."

"It sounds like an extortion racket," Sheryn said. "Brett's getting an award, so he *had* to buy a table?"

"It is." Rafael rolled his eyes. "I told you they're bankers. They know what they're doing."

"Hey!" their sergeant called, striding toward them. "You two catching?"

"We are," Sheryn said.

"Gunshot victim dead on the scene at West Forty-Ninth Street." The sergeant handed her a slip of paper. "All yours."

"Elevator or walk-up?" Sheryn asked.

The sergeant paused, and she knew he was about to bite out a snappy return. Then he glanced at Rafael and had a eureka moment, realizing why she was asking that question. "Walk-up," he said, turning away.

"I'll take this," Sheryn announced, before realizing that Rafael had already grabbed his cane and struggled to his feet.

"Let's go," he said. "You're driving."

# CHAPTER 5

## Jo

Jo couldn't stop shaking. She ran west to Twelfth Avenue, zigzagging down to cross the West Side Highway. She reached the edge of the Hudson River, where she ran south until she found a clear spot to throw the gun away. The wind was even harsher by the water. Jo's eyes wouldn't stop tearing, and she couldn't tell if it was because of the cold or if she was actually crying. She barely heard the splash the gun made as it hit the water; she was already running again. She knew it was a dangerous thing to do during the day, when anyone could be watching, but she didn't see how she could wait.

Half a mile away from that decaying building, Jo finally stopped running and remembered to pull up her hood. She reached for the sunglasses she'd pushed up above her forehead, but they weren't there anymore. She hadn't noticed them falling off, but they were gone all the same. She found her gloves—they were still tucked into the left pocket of her jacket, just where she'd left them. *My lucky day,* she thought grimly.

She thought fleetingly about calling 911, but she was sure the man she'd shot was dead already. She wouldn't be able to save him now, not that he even deserved to be saved. She could still feel the crackling desire in his voice as he'd said, *You had one hot little bod, didn't you?* But he had photographs of her, and that video. She'd need to find a lawyer—fast—because the cops would have little trouble connecting them.

*It was self-defense,* Jo told herself. *I only shot him in self-defense.* But that cruel voice in the back of her brain heckled her. *With you, it's always self-defense,* it hissed. *When they find the video, they'll know you're a liar.*

Jo pushed herself to keep going until she reached the edge of Times Square. She hadn't fled there by design, but it was the perfect place: even wild eyed and in shock, with a bullet hole in the arm of her jacket, she could blend in. Every few steps, she glanced behind her, certain that someone was following. No one was.

*JoJo, you won't believe it, but I saw a ghost today.* For some reason, her sister's voice floated into her head at that moment. She pushed it away because thinking about the last conversation she'd ever had with Lori was the least helpful thing she could imagine doing at that moment. But she kept catching glimpses of herself in mirrored doors and windows, and she realized she looked like a ghost—a lurching, staggering specter trying to disappear into her own hoodie. She needed a plan. She stopped moving for a moment and took stock of her situation.

Her arm hurt like hell, but it wasn't a sharp, shocking pain anymore; it had morphed into a searing ache, as if someone were slowly sawing at her arm with a dull saw. She took off one glove and poked at the wound. Was there a bullet trapped under her skin? She couldn't tell without removing layers of clothing. All she knew for certain was that it took no time at all before her hand was sticky with blood.

Jo was aware she couldn't walk into an emergency room; a gunshot wound would be immediately reported to the police. Desperate, she looked around, taking in the cheery families and wandering cartoon characters, all of whom seemed impervious to the frigid weather. Times Square was like one big, open-air mall now, but no store would let her use its bathroom in this state. She could walk to the Port Authority Bus Terminal, but there would be plenty of police officers around, more than when she'd first arrived in New York on a Greyhound bus more than a decade earlier. Her safest bet, she realized, was heading back to her health club, the place where she'd started out on this sordid errand.

Reflexively, she reached for the duffel bag. It was the first time she'd thought of it since she'd dropped it. With a sinking heart, she realized she'd left the bag behind in that apartment.

"Fifty thousand," Jo said aloud. "Fifty fucking thousand."

She gulped. The bag had shielded her from the gunman's first shot. Without it, she might've died. *Maybe fifty thousand dollars is the price of being alive,* she told herself. It didn't make her feel any better. She'd raided her own savings and her company's rainy-day fund to come up with the sum. It was gone, and there was no way to get it back.

*Move,* she told herself as her brain was trying to tally what it would take to make up the money. *You don't have time to think about it now.*

She took the eastbound shuttle—a one-stop train between Times Square and Grand Central—across Forty-Second Street. Then she caught a 6 train uptown, disembarking at East Fifty-First Street. She was feeling light-headed, but it was only a couple of blocks to her club from there. She breezed by the receptionist with a big smile and made it to the changing room, where she allowed herself to collapse onto a bench. Someone was in one of the showers—Jo could hear the water running—but otherwise, the area was empty. Midafternoon was a quiet time at the health club. The hardcore types got their workouts in by nine, and the designer-clad mom squad gravitated to midmornings. The lunchtime crew was drawn from nearby offices, but they were gone now. Jo was grateful for the privacy. She peeled her jacket off, gasping at the pain in her arm. Blood was everywhere: it had soaked through her long-sleeved top. It was black enough to hide the red stains, but the texture was slick and glossy. When she shed that layer—slowly, painfully, because she could hardly lift her arm—she discovered there was blood even on her white sports bra.

"Shit," she muttered, staring at herself in the mirrored wall. She looked like she'd walked away from a car crash. She tried to remove the bra, but she couldn't get her left arm behind her. Finally, she gave up on that, grabbed the top, and threw it into an open trash bin.

Jo had planned to take a shower, but she realized that was impossible. Blood was still oozing out of her arm, and she had to make it stop. Touching it made her flinch, but she forced herself to probe at it, terrified that there was a bullet inside. But when she examined it closely in the mirror, she realized that the bullet had gone through her, ripping a chunk of flesh out of her arm. Since she couldn't go to a doctor, she had to find some way to stanch the bleeding herself.

She rooted around in her locker. There were a few toiletries in her gym bag, none of them useful. Finally, she put her hands on a pair of pantyhose. The health club stocked all manner of amenities for their members—antiperspirant, dry shampoo, tampons—and Jo knew there was a sewing kit with a pair of scissors inside one of the drawers beside the sinks. She had just found it when a voice made her jump.

"What happened to you?" the woman squeaked. Jo sized her up. She was a petite platinum blonde with lash extensions and diamond earrings. Her golden tan was streak-free, either the result of too much time in the sun or too much time on a tanning bed. Jo had never met her before, but she felt like she was looking at a younger version of herself.

"My stitches came out," Jo improvised. "I had a biopsy, and I was supposed to be careful about working out. I guess I'm an idiot." She held up the pantyhose. "Can you help me make a tourniquet so I don't bleed all over the place on my way to the doctor's?"

To her credit, the young woman moved closer. "Sure," she said. Quickly and neatly, she cut a leg off the pantyhose and tied it tightly around Jo's upper arm. Jo winced in pain, but the benefit was immediate; the flow of blood out of her body went from a rush to a trickle.

Jo was impressed. "Are you studying to be a doctor?"

The woman giggled, as if this was a hilarious idea. "Nah. My mom's a nurse, though."

Jo wanted to say something to her. *Be careful. Save the money you're making; don't spend it.* Her sister used to laugh at the girls who spent their money as soon as it came in. *Save something for a rainy day,* Lori liked to tell them, but nobody ever listened. Jo realized it wasn't fair to make assumptions about this woman's life. But Jo had spent enough time around expensive escorts to recognize the type.

"It's really kind of you to help me. Thanks," Jo said.

She found some bandages, slapped them on, and struggled into her black cashmere sweater. *At least it won't show the blood,* she thought. She dug through her gym bag for ibuprofen, took a couple, and then took a couple more. *One problem down, only about a million to go.*

# CHAPTER 6

## Sheryn

The address Sheryn had been handed was for a four-story apartment building on West Forty-Ninth Street between Eleventh and Twelfth Avenues. There was a single police car parked in front, but no one stationed at the entryway.

"Is it just me, or does this place look haunted?" Rafael asked.

Sheryn assumed that the apartment block had started its life with a redbrick facade, like so many of its brethren in Hell's Kitchen. But over the decades, it had faded to gray with patches of rust. To Sheryn, it looked as if the lifeblood had been drained out of the place. The boarded-up windows on the first floor only added to the air of forlornness and failure.

"You're a big chicken," Sheryn answered. "Graveyards freak you out. You're scared of your own shadow."

"It's entropy in action." Rafael stood on the sidewalk, balancing on his cane and craning his neck to gaze up. Sheryn's eyes followed her partner's. "It's like Poe's House of Usher. It's about to collapse in on itself."

Truth was, it *did* look cursed, even to Sheryn. Whoever had built the place had graced it with decorative moldings over each window and a cornice of stone garlands. Most of the detail was gone; the bits that were left behind had a ghostly quality, hinting at what once was. Not that she was planning on confessing that to Rafael. She preferred to keep her teasing rights.

"Whoever owns this place needs to be hauled into court before someone gets hurt," Sheryn said. "There should be scaffolding around it."

They went inside. "Oh, look, the lock's broken," Rafael said.

"I'd be shocked if it weren't," Sheryn said.

They headed up the stairs. The building was a disaster zone, about ready to tumble down into a pile of bricks and grit. It was also eerily silent; her own footfalls echoed in her ears, even as they left indentations in the plaster dust coating the floors.

"It feels like everyone who lives here has been raptured," Sheryn whispered.

"Now who's a fraidy-cat?"

Sheryn rolled her eyes. "Who said I was afraid? If they have been raptured, there are no bodies to clean up. Look on the bright side." Rafael sometimes reminded her of her brothers and male cousins, and she felt the need to swat at him.

By the time they arrived at the third floor, there was one sign of life: someone had their television turned all the way up; it sounded like a football game. Sheryn was halfway up the next staircase before she spotted the uniforms guarding the crime scene. She recognized Pete Carpacelli, a doughy-faced flatfoot she'd known for years; he was old enough to retire from the force with a full pension, but she didn't see him going anywhere soon. She vaguely recognized his partner, a slender young brown-skinned man with a serious face and a rapidly bobbing Adam's apple. He was a new recruit, fresh out of the academy.

"Damn, we are so glad you're here," Pete called out, his voice loud. "Naveed and me were wondering if anybody was ever coming."

"There's no bus here yet?"

"Nothing," Pete said.

"Who called it in?" Rafael asked.

"Neighbor across the street. She heard gunshots. Lady named . . . um, I forget. It was a weird name."

"Gamon Srisuk," Naveed filled in. "That was the first 911 call anyway."

"The first?"

"The second call came in three to four minutes ago," Naveed said. "A man saying a man was shot and a woman went down the fire escape with a gun in her hand. He didn't identify himself."

Sheryn raised her eyebrows. Two emergency calls, only one with a name attached. That was an interesting detail. She looked around; there were six apartments on the fourth floor, same as the others she'd passed. "You start a canvass yet?"

Pete nodded. "We knocked on every door. It's like a ghost town. Even the guy playing the loud TV didn't answer the door. It's spooky as hell in here."

"There are eviction notices on several doors," Naveed added.

"The whole place looks like it should be condemned," Rafael said. "Where's the victim?"

"Through here." Pete gestured at the lone open door on the floor, which was already festooned with yellow police tape. "One victim, a black male in his late twenties or early thirties. He was shot in the chest. Dead when we got here, Detectives."

"We believe his name is Andray Baxter," Naveed added. "There's an award with his photo on the bookcase."

He gestured through the door, and Sheryn's eyes followed. She ducked under the tape and carefully stepped inside the apartment. Her partner followed, only he peeled off the tape. On the bookcase Sheryn noted a framed photograph of a handsome young man with bedroom eyes and a wicked smile. Underneath the image, there were a few words: *Andray Baxter, winner of the Kenneth Lee Spencer Musical Theatre Award.*

Her gaze shifted to the apartment's front door, which was flush against the wall. She tugged on a pair of latex gloves and nudged the door gently to examine the other side. Rafael whistled when he took a look.

"That's a big exit wound," Sheryn said.

The uniforms looked at each other. "What's that, Detective?"

"The front door," Sheryn clarified. "It's got a chunk knocked out of it, and there's sawdust on the floor. It looks like someone fired a gun through it," Sheryn said.

"With hollow-point bullets," Rafael added. "That would explain why there's this much damage."

Sheryn nodded at that. "Why don't you try canvassing again?" She told the uniforms. "There could be someone around who works here. Maybe a superintendent."

"There's a buzzer for the super in the foyer," Pete said. "It wouldn't budge when we pressed it."

Rafael sighed. "Let's be real. There's no super. This place is on its last legs."

The linoleum of the kitchen floor was coated with blood. The dead man in the center of it resembled the exuberant photograph on the bookcase, but it was a painful contrast. His dark eyes were wide in sightless horror, blank and empty. His mouth was open in what must've been a final cry. The gunshot wound in the center of his chest was messy, and the metallic tang of blood suffused the room. Blood had pooled underneath him, surrounding his body like a furious halo.

"For such a shitty building, it's a really nice apartment," Rafael murmured. There was something haunting in the silence of the building that made them lower their voices, and the spectacle of death in front of them reinforced that.

Sheryn knelt and reached her hand to touch the man's neck. She knew he was long gone before she did it, and she wasn't surprised by the absence of a pulse. What shocked her was that the man's body was stone cold. "He already feels like ice."

"The window's open, and the room is freezing," Rafael pointed out.

Carpacelli had said the victim was in his late twenties or early thirties, but to Sheryn he looked a decade younger than that. *This is somebody's child,* she thought, as she often did when seeing a victim; the young ones were particularly tough to take.

"The place looks tidy," Rafael observed. "Doesn't seem like it was tossed, unless the killer knew exactly what they were looking for."

Sheryn stood and turned in a circle, taking in every detail. It was a small studio, with few spaces where anyone could hide. She strode to a closed door, drawing her gun before turning the handle and letting it fall open. A quick glance at the bathroom showed it was empty. A sheer plastic shower curtain was pulled back to reveal an alcove with a porcelain bathtub. The cracked black-and-white tiles on the floor were arranged in an old-fashioned honeycomb pattern. Several were missing, and the replacements looked like nothing more than brown putty. The room reeked of bleach. She'd caught that scent when she'd walked into the apartment, but in the bathroom, it was overpowering.

"Anything interesting?" Rafael called out.

Sheryn opened the medicine cabinet. There was an electric toothbrush inside, along with pomade and Tiger Balm and a host of fancy toiletries. "No," she answered.

"I'm opening the closet," he called back. "Fingers crossed it's not booby-trapped."

That felt like a dig to Sheryn, but she could hardly blame him. When she exited the bathroom, she got an eyeful of the apartment's lone closet. It was stuffed to the gills. There was a rack of shirts and suits and colorful costumes; the rest of the space was filled with boxes.

Rafael lifted a hanger with a red bodysuit and yellow cape. "Superman?" he asked.

Sheryn was usually as good as her partner at keeping the tone light, but not that day. "We need backup," she said.

"I'll call it in," Rafael offered.

"Thanks." That made sense; it was far easier for her to move around the apartment than it was for him. Sheryn's eyes swept over the walls, lingering on the print of the Holy Family and a portrait of the dead man with three women she took—by their ages—for his mother, grandmother, and sister. Rafael's voice broke into her thoughts. "Far as we can tell, the cause of death was a single shot to the chest." He glanced at Sheryn. "Anything I should add?"

"He died in the last two hours," Sheryn said. "He's not even in rigor yet."

Sheryn took dozens of photos. The killer had shot Andray Baxter at close range; even without a forensics team, she could see the burns around the wound. Her eyes lingered on the victim for a full minute before she turned her focus to his surroundings, cataloging the apartment with a dispassionate eye. It was only a little bigger than a shoebox. Calling it a studio was too grand. To her left was the "kitchen," merely a wall fronted with a fridge, sink, and cooktop; above them were open cabinets with neatly stacked dishware. There wasn't room for a table, but she noted two stools next to the counter, a makeshift breakfast nook. There was a red love seat that reminded her of an IKEA sofa bed she'd once owned, a couple of carved wooden chairs, and a wooden chest standing in for a table.

There was a cable for a laptop on the kitchen counter, but the computer was nowhere in sight. The techs at TARU wouldn't be happy about that. She opened the drawers, but there was nothing inside but silverware and towels, candles and a wine-bottle opener. Nothing you wouldn't expect to find in a young man's kitchen.

"Where's his phone?" Rafael asked, interrupting her train of thought. She glanced at him; he was half-crouched beside the body, latex gloves on, balancing on his cane.

"It would be hard to lose it in here," she said.

"It's not on his body, and I don't see it lying around."

People kept their phones close at hand. That wasn't to say it couldn't be charging up somewhere, but it was odd that it was out of sight. "There was a laptop here, but it's gone now," Sheryn said.

"Looks like the killer made off with the tech," Rafael said.

Sheryn moved toward the window. Her eyes traced the frame and the sill. "There's blood here," she said. "The mystery woman who went out the window may have been shot too."

"You think this is her?" Rafael asked, holding out a couple of photographs.

Sheryn stared at them, her heart in her throat. The girl in the photographs was white, with dark curly hair and anxious eyes. She was wearing about a pound of makeup, but her body was naked.

"She looks like a teenager," Sheryn said.

"I don't know what this guy was into," Rafael said. "But my money's on nothing good."

# CHAPTER 7

## Jo

Jo's office was on Broadway, a few blocks below the Flatiron Building. Normally, she felt a surge of pride when she walked through its glass front door stenciled with a crow that had glittering eyes and the words *Corvus Alchemy* around it. Her office was just a small suite on the fourth floor of an aging building, but it was hers, and it was no longer the fledgling cosmetics start-up she'd built from scratch but a growing company beginning to soar internationally.

But that day, she wanted to slink in and hide. She had no one she could call for help. She would have to take care of everything herself—and fast. Fortunately, most of her staff was in Dubai for a makeup and skin-care trade show; that was where she should've been herself, but her blackmailer had forced her to change her plans. The receptionist was out on maternity leave, replaced by a temp whose name Jo couldn't remember, but that was fine since she wouldn't care that Jo breezed by her. However, there was no avoiding the vivacious Peyton Chin, who'd started at the company as an intern and was now vice president and Jo's right hand. Peyton was barely five feet tall, but she wore platform heels to make up the difference. Her straight hair was dyed navy blue and cut in an angular bob that was lower on the left than the right. She wore red eye shadow and skull-printed tights and some kind of black tunic fastened with boxy steel clasps that would've set off a metal detector. She was the most down-to-earth, organized, and thoughtful person Jo knew, in spite of the fact that she dressed like a time traveler from the future who had misplaced her jet pack.

"I'm so glad you're back. Today is out of control," Peyton said. "Did you know we're in *Vogue*'s holiday guide? I don't want to knock a gift horse in the mouth, but half our product line is already back-ordered. We're never digging ourselves out of this hole."

"Let's take it one disaster at a time." Jo tried to smile, but her teeth were gritted.

"I made up a list of suppliers we should be able to get extra stock from," Peyton said. "I don't think the Korean or Canadian ones will be a problem, but the Italian one is already ducking my calls."

Jo had trouble focusing on what Peyton was saying. Her immediate crisis made her head pound. She had a law firm on retainer for her business, but they specialized in patents and trade; they would be of no use on a criminal matter.

"Jo?" Peyton prompted her.

Jo knew she had to act normal. She gulped her fears down. "The Italian one makes the best lipsticks."

"They do, and I hate them for it. They're like the siren who keeps luring you in. You know you shouldn't do it, but they're *so good*." Peyton sighed. "Sorry, I shouldn't hold you back. Annabelle's waiting."

"She's on the phone?"

"No, in your office."

"What?" Jo froze in place. There were no in-person meetings on her calendar for that Monday; she'd made absolutely sure of that. "We didn't have an appointment."

"Annabelle Davies doesn't need one," Peyton said. "At least, that's what you always say."

Jo fought her urge to flee. Annabelle Davies had been an icon in the 1980s, a Texas blonde who'd graced magazine covers, rocked the runway, and made movie cameos. When she'd aged out of that business at the ripe old age of twenty-nine, she'd started a modeling agency and a chain of beauty salons. She was basically retired now, but she liked to dabble as an angel investor. To Jo, she literally *was* an angel. She'd helped Jo expand her company so that she was able to ramp up production and begin exporting to Europe. It wasn't that Corvus Alchemy would've failed without Annabelle, but it never could've grown so fast. She was also the last person in the world who Jo wanted to make a bad impression upon.

Too late, Jo realized that the always-perceptive Peyton was watching her closely, and that she must've read the panic in Jo's face.

"I didn't know there was a problem," Peyton said softly. "I left her in your office. I thought that was what you'd want me to do. But I can get her out of here just as easily."

"No, you did the right thing." Jo felt the corners of her mouth wobbling. "It's great she stopped by. But I'm not feeling my best today." *A man tried to shoot me dead, but never mind about that,* Jo thought. Part of her wanted to confide in Peyton, the way she did about all the nasty little digs her boyfriend's mother made at her. But she knew that was crazy; it would only make everything worse. The last thing Jo wanted to do was drag Peyton into this mess. She rubbed her temple with her right hand. *Think, brain, think.*

"Oh, no." Peyton's mouth formed a precise O of horror. "Not one of your headaches."

"What? No." Jo belatedly realized Peyton had handed her a great excuse. "Actually, yes. It's bad."

"Your headaches are serious," Peyton said, her blue bob swishing to one side emphatically before landing perfectly in place. "Is it an aura migraine or the regular kind?"

"The regular kind," Jo said. "I should go see what Annabelle's up to."

"You do that," Peyton said. "After that, I'm talking you into trying acupuncture."

Jo moved toward her office. The door was ajar, so she couldn't see inside. When she pushed it open, she noticed Annabelle standing in front of her floor-to-ceiling window.

"You have one of the best views in the city," Annabelle said. "You know that, right?"

Annabelle was in her sixties, Jo knew, but she looked like she had stopped aging somewhere around forty. She was still rail thin, with a puffy halo of pale-blonde hair calling even more attention to her chiseled features. She wore a powder-blue Chanel suit and gray Ferragamo pumps with a scaly pattern that matched her handbag. To Jo, Annabelle was the epitome of success.

"It's only the fourth floor," Jo said. "It's nothing spectacular."

"On the contrary, you're at exactly the right altitude to see the incredible detail at the top of all of these grand buildings," Annabelle said. "The builders didn't put these details in for the hoi polloi below. They were for insiders." Annabelle came closer to kiss Jo's cheek; she was wrapped in scents of oleander and nicotine and musk. "I love an interesting view. When I first came to New York, I lived at the Barbizon Hotel for a year. You know, the place Sylvia Plath wrote about in *The Bell Jar*. I didn't care for it, but there was a sundeck with the most magnificent view. Access to it was the greatest luxury in the world."

"What brings you here today?" Jo asked, hoping she didn't sound abrupt. She deeply admired and appreciated Annabelle, but she was desperate to get her investor out of the office as quickly as possible.

"There are a couple of things." Annabelle perched on the velvet sofa, crossing her long legs. "One of them is our China problem. I think I've finally found a solution."

"There's no solution," Jo said. "We've talked about it for months. It's binary. You have to test products on animals to get into the Chinese market. There's no other way in. I won't do it."

"I agree with you. You know how much I love animals. If it weren't for my son and his allergies, I'd have a whole menagerie of them in my apartment, you know. That's why I've been looking for loopholes in the Chinese law."

"I'm intrigued but dubious," Jo said. She felt faint; there was no way she could focus on an extended conversation about Chinese mercantile law. She could live with the throbbing pain in her arm for a couple of days if she had to. It was the question of legal jeopardy that terrified her. She knew she'd acted in self-defense; she'd shot her blackmailer when she'd realized he was about to kill her. But would the cops see it that way?

"Ye of little faith," Annabelle said. "I think I found one. It's relatively new."

Jo's eyes stayed on Annabelle's, but her mind was circling her own desperate situation. She knew the fact she'd brought a gun to the meeting was a huge problem. The cops might view that as intent, as if she had planned to murder her blackmailer. She'd been shot, so she didn't have to prove the threat to her life. But it would be up to the cops to interpret the facts.

*You had one hot little bod, didn't you?* She heard the echo of her blackmailer's voice again. She still didn't know where he'd gotten the video, and that uncertainty was the worst thing of all.

"Jo? Are you taking this in?"

Annabelle's voice brought Jo's mind back into the room. "Tell me more," Jo said, wondering what she'd missed.

"China's been modifying its own mandatory animal-testing laws," Annabelle said slowly. "Because Chinese consumers aren't happy about harming rabbits and guinea pigs either. The law is being relaxed for companies that make their products in Chinese factories."

Jo sat back in her chair. Her throat still felt tight and dry, exactly as it had in that airless little apartment. "That's great."

"Obviously, we have to think about the implications for your man-ufacturing here and abroad. I know you don't want to lay people off, so we need to keep the production facility upstate separate. But perhaps some of the international contracts . . ."

"Do you have anything I can read?" Jo asked.

"Of course I do. I know you." Annabelle handed her a thick manila envelope. Jo tucked it into the huge leather tote bag parked next to her desk; it was what she always used to schlep samples between office and home.

"You know you're brilliant, right?" Jo said, feeling guilty that her main investor was doing all the legwork on a major deal that could dou-ble Corvus Alchemy's bottom line in a year. "Thanks so much for this."

"You're welcome." Annabelle cocked her head, as if mentally review-ing what she wanted to say. "That wasn't the only reason I wanted to stop by. I wanted to make sure you're doing okay."

"Why?" Jo was startled. Her mind immediately went to her black-mailer. Had he started shipping tidbits about her to the people in her life? Who else had seen those photographs and the video?

"Cal phoned me over the weekend," Annabelle said. "He said he hadn't seen you in days, that you were either holed up in your office or running around frantically. He thought something might be wrong with the business. I told him everything was wonderful with Corvus, but I started wondering if everything was good with you."

"I can't believe Cal bothered you." Jo tried to keep her voice even, but her insides were churning. She hadn't told her boyfriend that she was being blackmailed, and while Cal knew about her hardscrabble past, she'd never admitted that she had been trafficked as a teen. She was aware he'd noticed things going awry in the past few weeks, because he'd confronted her about them. Jo had believed she'd convinced him everything was fine, but she had been wrong. She was horrified that he'd reached out to Annabelle.

"It's no bother," Annabelle said. "Cal is my godson. I know how anxious he gets. He wasn't like that as a boy. He was a golden child. But after everything that happened with his father when he was a teenager . . ." Annabelle fiddled with the chunky gold bangle around her wrist. "He stresses about everything. He's so good natured, and he tries to hide it, but . . . well, men are like hothouse flowers. They wilt into oblivion when they don't get enough attention."

Jo stared at her. "Poor Cal." She hoped her sarcasm wasn't obvious. *I've been stressed for weeks and have barely slept because I felt like my world was caving in,* she thought. *But sure, Cal needs sympathy because I'm preoccupied.*

"Maybe you could do a special dinner this weekend," Annabelle said. "Mind you, I always hated cooking, myself. When my second husband felt neglected, I'd buy a new negligee. But I ended up divorcing him, so don't take any advice from me."

"I hate cooking too."

Annabelle laughed. "I'll get out of your hair. I know you're busy." Annabelle stood and crossed the room to hug Jo. Then she stepped back slightly, still touching Jo's shoulders. "You know you can come to me about absolutely anything, right?" Annabelle squeezed Jo's shoulder. The pain in her injured arm was so intense that Jo almost shrieked. Instead, she gasped.

"What's wrong?"

"I had a biopsy," Jo said quickly, cradling her upper arm. "I have a few stitches. Ow. It's no big deal."

"I'm so sorry, Jo." Annabelle looked horrified. "I always mess things up. I just wanted you to know I'm here for you. I didn't mean to cause you pain."

"It's fine," Jo said, smiling at Annabelle even as she willed herself not to throw up or pass out or both. Her office walls were swirling around her, and the floor no longer felt solid under her feet. "Everything's fine. I promise."

# CHAPTER 8

## SHERYN

"There were multiple shots fired," the CSU investigator said to Sheryn. He was a slender man in his early sixties with coppery skin, pomaded silver hair, and a small, impeccable mustache that looked as if it traveled with its own gilded comb. Sheryn had crossed paths with him for years and only knew him as Florian, which she took for a surname, though she couldn't be sure. There were rumors that his family had fled Argentina and that he'd been detained and forcibly interrogated on another continent, but all Sheryn knew for certain about his past was that Florian had once worked for Interpol. He was the most matter-of-fact person Sheryn had ever met, one who wasted absolutely no time with chitchat but was delighted to spend hours analyzing forensics and debating evidence. "Only one bullet went into your victim, but it was a direct hit to his heart."

"Wouldn't he have died immediately?" Sheryn asked. "I don't understand why there's so much blood."

"Sometimes the heart takes its time to stop pumping. I know of one case where a man dragged himself sixty-five feet after being shot in the heart. I'm not saying that's the world record, of course." If there were such a thing as a Guinness World Record book of incredible deaths, Sheryn was certain Florian had a copy.

"You're as bad as the medical examiners," Sheryn said. "They love to compete for freaky records."

"Death as a competitive sport." Florian shrugged; the NYPD Crime Scene Unit was entirely made up of cops, unlike similar units in most cities. It made for a double dose of gallows humor. "Your shooter is either a serious pro or else had amazing beginner's luck. A shot through the heart is not an easy one to make."

Sheryn stared at the spot where Andray Baxter had died. His body had been taken away on a stretcher by a couple of burly EMTs, but she could still picture him there, eyes open, brow furrowed, surprise etched into his face.

"I can't prove anything right now, but the bullet trajectories make it look like a shoot-out," Florian added.

"Excuse me?"

"They strongly suggest that there was more than one gun fired in the apartment. We won't know until we dig out all the slugs. There's a bullet in your corpse; that'll be extracted at the lab. A couple of bullets came through the door from the hallway. Then there's this one." He paused dramatically.

"Yes?"

"I pulled it out of the wall next to the door," Florian said. "I believe I found a little bit of blood splatter around it."

"So we've got a perp who could be bleeding?" Sheryn asked. "I was wondering about that. I noticed blood on the windowsill."

"I haven't even taken a sample over there yet," Florian said. "I'll get samples from all over the scene. It's possible that some of the blood you see around is your shooter's."

"We can hope," Sheryn said.

"If the shot was a through-and-through, no organ damage, your perp might be able to self-treat, at least until the wound gets infected."

"Because any hospital would have to report it," Sheryn mused. "I'll call that in." She glanced over at her partner. Rafael was in the hallway, gripping his cane and leaning against a wall. His expression was hard to read, but she detected elements of fury and exhaustion in it.

"Thanks, Florian. Let me know when you're done." Sheryn moved in her partner's direction. The mother in her wanted to take his temperature and find him a chair. The cop in her wanted to kick his ass for dragging the team down. The cop won out. "You want me to call the EMTs to carry you out in a stretcher?" she asked. "Because you look about as right as the last body they took."

"You try getting blown up sometime—see how you like it," Rafael muttered.

"You want to sit down?" she asked quietly.

"No." He closed his eyes and took a couple of deep breaths. "The building's not spinning around, right?"

"Right."

"That's the tough part," he said. "Sometimes it feels like it is."

Sheryn moved closer so that no one else could overhear. "You're not doing anyone any favors, coming back to the job too early. Least of all yourself."

"You sound like Brett. Just give me a minute."

She didn't want to argue with him, but she didn't see how she was supposed to work the case with an injured partner. It was one thing when they were piecing together a case against, say, a former investment banker running a drug ring; both of them were welded to their desks poring over financial records and prescriptions and written correspondence. But working a crime scene was different. Sheryn knew it. They both did.

"CSU thinks there was more than one shooter, but there's no sign of a gun," Sheryn said, by way of filling the time, giving him some space. "The uniforms got residents to open their doors, but nobody saw or heard anything. There's one elderly man on the third floor, Wilbur

Bowen, who speaks English and knew the victim. He's eighty and half-deaf. His TV was the one that was blaring. Naturally, he didn't hear anything."

"As a recent veteran of a blown-out eardrum, I sympathize with him," Rafael said.

"How's your hearing now?"

"Okay." He shrugged. "If you like the sound of ringing bells."

Sheryn tapped her foot, unsure of what to say. "You ready to head downstairs yet?"

"For what?"

"You know what? Let me talk to the neighbor," she said. "How about you let everyone know our perp may be shot. We need hospitals to be on the alert. I'll be back in a few."

Sheryn headed down the stairs. It was tough being angry at her partner when she still felt guilty. She'd been with Rafael moments before the explosion went off, but she'd run down a path, curious about a possible lead. While Rafael got shredded by the blast, she'd escaped with cuts from flying glass. At first, it seemed like he wasn't injured that badly—cuts, burns, a couple of broken bones, and a burst eardrum he could survive. But he'd gotten sicker as time went on, and doctors discovered some internal bleeding that had somehow been missed before. It wasn't fair, as her eight-year-old daughter, Mercy, often said. *Nothing is fair in this world, baby,* Sheryn would tell her. *Well, that's not right. We should fix it* was always Mercy's response. But there was nothing Sheryn could do to fix this.

It was clear which door it was: the television was roaring again. She rapped on the door, to no avail. Then she kicked it a few times. A gruff voice responded from inside, "Keep your shirt on." A lock turned a minute later. The man who opened the door looked ancient, his tanned white skin turned to leather, one eye an electric blue and the other a milky marble. He was bald and he had a tattoo on his neck that slithered under a striped crew-neck sweater.

"Wilbur Bowen?" Sheryn asked, getting a curt nod in response. "I'm Detective Sheryn Sterling. I wanted to ask about your neighbor upstairs."

"Hold on," he yelled, pulling a device out of his pocket and pushing a button. "Okay, say something," he instructed her, more quietly.

"That's your hearing aid?"

He nodded again. "I don't like to waste the battery."

Sheryn blinked at that. "I wanted to ask you about your neighbor upstairs."

"You're not here to screw him over, are you?"

"Excuse me?"

"You know, evict him." Bowen looked her over. "They've tried a couple times."

"I'm here because Andray Baxter was shot dead today," Sheryn said.

Bowen stared at her. "Dead?"

"That's right."

Tears welled up in Bowen's eyes. "But he's such a good kid. Always trying to do the right thing for all of us here."

"The right thing?"

"Fighting that shitbird slumlord who destroyed our building," Bowen said, wiping his eyes and snuffling.

"The what?"

"Andray gave him that nickname. His real one is Westergard. He's a lying, thieving scumbag. He turned off the heat in the middle of winter last year. He acts like we're rats. Andray wouldn't put up with it." He wiped his nose on the back of his hand. "Sorry, I need a Kleenex."

He walked away, and Sheryn followed him inside. His apartment was roughly the same size as Baxter's, but it was packed to the rafters with newspapers and magazines and sports memorabilia. There was a narrow pass to follow through the mess, and Sheryn trod along it carefully. Bowen blew his nose and wiped his eyes.

"What kind of *fighting* did Mr. Baxter do with your landlord, exactly?" Sheryn asked.

"He was the one with the smarts and the balls to take him to court," Bowen said.

"He filed a lawsuit?"

"Yeah, in housing court. I don't know the ins and outs of it. Andray'd come by and tell me; I have trouble keeping track. My memory's not what it used to be."

"Did you hear any shots fired? Andray died in the last couple of hours."

"No." Bowen eyes darted toward his massive wall-mounted television. "I hate quiet, so I keep it on a lot. I'm sorry."

"Did you see anyone in the building this morning or early afternoon?"

"I had a doctor's appointment this morning," Bowen said. "I only got home around twelve thirty."

"Did you ever see Andray with any female visitors?"

"Oh, yeah, all the time. Andray likes the ladies." Bowen cocked his head thoughtfully. "Not in a while, though. There was a girl he was crazy about, but I think they called it quits. It's been quiet since then."

"Do you remember the girl's name?"

Bowen considered that but shook his head. "Sorry."

"Did she have long, dark, curly hair?" Sheryn asked.

"No. She was a blonde. Pretty. A big-boned gal, if you know what I mean." He mimed an hourglass figure with his hands.

Sheryn ignored that. "Do you have any idea who might want him dead?"

"Westergard," Bowen answered decisively. "He did it. Or his evil henchman."

"Who's that?"

"Andray calls him GI Joe. He trails after Westergard and glowers at everybody."

"Okay, thanks for your time, sir." Sheryn handed him her card. "If you think of anything that might be important, call me."

She hurried up the stairs. Rafael hadn't moved an inch from his perch against the wall, but he was on the phone.

"Bet you haven't had the chance to check your messages yet," Rafael said. "Listen to this 911 call about this shooting." He held up his phone and put it on speaker.

"A man has been shot at 631 West Forty-Ninth Street. Apartment 402," a male voice said, speaking quickly. "A woman ran down the fire escape. Late twenties, brunette, long curly hair, about five foot five, slim. She had a gun in her hand."

"What's your name, sir?" the operator asked, but the man hung up.

"That's a lot of information coming from a casual bystander," Sheryn said.

"Same thought I had," Rafael said. "You gotta wonder at that guy's motive. The first 911 call was from a lady across the street, Gamon Srisuk. We need to talk to her."

# CHAPTER 9

## Jo

After Annabelle Davies left her office, her perfume lingered in the air. Feeling sick and exhausted and dizzy, Jo dropped onto the sofa.

*I'm not going to be able to keep this up,* she thought.

*Don't be a useless crybaby.*

That was the voice in the back of her head again. It had an accent that could've been her mother's or sister's. Jo's mother hadn't been the nurturing type any more than Lori had been; she'd generally neglected her younger child. But that wasn't to say her mother was abusive. Her own personal problems drained her to the point that Jo had had to take care of her, borrowing frozen peas from a neighbor whenever her mother had another black eye from a bad boyfriend. *Don't let this be your life,* her mother used to warn her. *You're meant for better things, like your sister.*

That memory made Jo shudder. Her sister was the last person in the world she'd ever want to be like.

Jo forced herself to go back to her desk. On her way from the health club to her office, she'd stopped at a drugstore for gauze pads and surgical tape. She tried to roll up the sleeve of her sweater, but she couldn't push it high enough. Instead, she pulled the collar of the V-neck down over her shoulder and slipped a gauze pad onto the wound. It burned so hard she wanted to cry.

The physical pain was only one side of her torment. Part of her wanted to call Cal and scream at him for dragging Annabelle into her personal business. She knew that wasn't fair—Cal had no clue what he was meddling in—but she wanted to vent at someone. Instead, she took a deep breath and typed *Best criminal defense lawyers in New York* into a search engine and started to skim over the results.

There was a tentative knock on her door. Jo knew it was Peyton. There was no way to hide from her.

"Come in," Jo called, shifting her computer screen to something innocuous. At least she was facing the door; Peyton couldn't surprise her the way Cal had in her home office a couple of weeks earlier.

The door opened, and Peyton's blue-hued head popped in. "I brought ibuprofen, the quick-dissolving kind," she said, her voice softer. She set a thermos, a vial of pills, and a flat, rectangular cardboard box that was a little over a foot wide on Jo's desk. "Also, green juice. You look like you could use a boost."

*Green juice* was a Peyton-devised concoction of kale, green tea, carrots, ginseng, and another herb called rooibos. To Jo, it tasted like sewer water smelled, but she didn't have the energy to refuse. She figured it might even kill some of the germs breeding in her wound. "Thanks. I'll try to choke it down." She smiled.

"Are you okay, Jo? You look . . . kind of pale."

"I forgot to eat lunch," she admitted; at least that was true. "Maybe that's why."

Peyton's eyes widened. "That's so dumb! I'm getting you some snacks from the break room. I'll be right back."

Jo reached for the thermos, took a sip, and shuddered. It might be tolerable if she added some whiskey to it, but she was afraid to head down that road. She badly wanted a drink, but it would be so easy to let her nerves take over and turn one drink into five. She had to keep her mind clear. She needed a lawyer. She couldn't relax until that got sorted out.

Knowing Peyton would be back in a minute, she picked up the box. *Ace Computer Repair* was hand-lettered in black marker on the top-left corner. It was addressed to Jo Greaver.

*I haven't taken a computer in for service,* Jo thought as she opened the box and extracted a battered laptop. When she opened it, the screen was black; what Jo noticed was the keyboard. She stared at it, hoping she was delusional. That couldn't be blood. Could it?

As she took a closer look at the stains, the screen hummed and came to life. The screen saver took Jo's breath away. It was an image of her sister in her modeling heyday, her blonde hair curled and blown out for some shampoo ad, her slender body poured into a revealing pink top and strategically torn jeans. Jo felt as if all the air had been squeezed out of her lungs.

"Here you go," Peyton said, setting some almond packets on her desk. Jo hadn't even heard her come back.

She slammed the screen shut. "Where did this package come from?" Jo demanded.

"The guard gave it to me when I came back from the drugstore."

"Who gave it to him?" Jo didn't care that she sounded desperate. She felt like the walls were closing in on her. She hadn't seen a computer in her blackmailer's apartment. There was no way his blood was on the keyboard. That was impossible. But—whoever it belonged to—what was Lori's image doing on it?

"What's wrong?" Peyton's expression was serious.

Jo's heart skipped a couple of beats and started tapping out an irregular rhythm, as if it wanted to communicate in Morse code. "Nothing," she muttered. Had her blackmailer handed her the laptop at their meeting, she would've taken it as a sign of good faith. But it showing up mysteriously at her office was nothing short of menacing. Seeing a smiling image of her dead sister was too much.

"Was that your sister's face I saw on the screen?" Peyton asked gently.

Jo nodded.

"Is that—was that—your sister's computer?"

Even in her panic, Jo realized Peyton hadn't seen the blood, only a semifamous shampoo ad.

"I forgot all about it," Jo said. "I took it in months ago, hoping they'd find something on it. But there wasn't much, I guess."

"I'm sorry, Jo. That's incredibly disappointing. I know a girl who's a computer genius. I can ask her . . ."

"It's okay. I don't even know what I thought there was to find." Jo reached for the box and tucked the laptop inside. She studied the block print on the box.

Peyton's phone buzzed. "That's the alarm for your conference call."

"I can't do it," Jo said softly. "Would you take it for me?"

"Of course." Peyton gave her a long look. "Jo, I don't want to pry. You know I'm here for you if you want to talk, and I also totally get it if you don't want to."

"Thank you," Jo whispered. "You're a better friend than I deserve to have."

When Peyton left and closed the door behind her, Jo slid the computer out of the box again. When she opened the laptop and scratched at the small rust-colored streaks, she was positive: they were blood. She'd thought her biggest problem was that she needed a good lawyer, but she'd been wrong. Her biggest problem was that her blackmailer hadn't been working alone.

# CHAPTER 10

## Rafael

Gamon Srisuk wasn't exactly what Rafael expected. From her surname, he wondered if she might be Eastern European, but she was actually Thai. Srisuk was in her late seventies, under five feet tall, and nursing a cup of tea she kept spiking with gin.

"Everybody think Thai names so long, but that only Chinese-Thai. Ethnic Thai, we have short names," Srisuk explained, pouring more booze. "You want some?"

"No, thanks." Alcohol was one of a long list of forbidden items for Rafael. In theory, his wounds would heal, and he'd be able to enjoy spices and meat and cocktails and everything else that made life pleasurable again. In the meantime, he was stuck on a diet of carrots and rice that made him feel like the world's saddest bunny rabbit. He glanced at his partner, but Sheryn's eyes were on the elderly woman. It wasn't that he expected a pat on the head for struggling up and down four staircases in the first building and another four in this one, but some acknowledgment would've been welcome. All he was sure of since he'd come back on the job was that Sheryn didn't think he belonged there anymore.

"Too bad," the woman said, shrugging and sitting back in a throne-size gold-upholstered chair. "My English is so-so," she warned them.

"That's okay," Sheryn said.

*"Mai pen rai,"* Rafael added, hoping he didn't sound completely ridiculous.

Gamon Srisuk clapped her hands delightedly while his partner swiveled to stare at him as if he'd sprouted a second head.

"I went to Thailand on my honeymoon," he said. "The only phrase I learned was that one: 'No worries.'"

"Where you go there?"

"Bangkok and Phuket."

"Okay! We from Chang Mai." The woman was still beaming at him. "My husband, he police too."

"With the NYPD?"

"No, back home. Here, waiter."

His partner was seated next to him on a small wooden love seat carved out of rosewood. The apartment, to Rafael's keen eye, was like a tiny jewel box, with a single red-painted wall separating the kitchen from the main room. That wall was dotted with white shelves, each of which held a tiny green plant. He had to focus his attention on the conversation. The nonstop ringing in his ear was like a tiny mosquito slowly driving him mad.

"You called 911 today because of what you saw," Sheryn said. "Can you describe it to us?"

"I did not *see* a lot," Srisuk said. "I hear a shot—pow! I go to my window. I look and look, but I see nothing. Later, I hear more shots—pow, pow, pow—and I watch but see nothing. Then two more—pow! pow!—and I see hands. They push the window up at Andray place . . ."

"Hold on," Sheryn said. "You know Andray Baxter?"

"Sure, sure. He famous actor someday." The old lady smiled, revealing gold teeth. "Sweet boy."

"You know which apartment is his?" Sheryn asked, getting to her feet. "Show me."

Gamon Srisuk rose as well. *Dammit,* Rafael thought, realizing he had no choice but to follow suit. Leaning heavily on his cane, he followed them to the window.

"That one," Srisuk said, pointing. "Those metal blinds on the window. See?"

Rafael took in the view. Gamon Srisuk's apartment was diagonally across the street from Baxter's; it was at an angle that gave no view of the apartment, except for a sliver in front of the window. Srisuk would've had a solid view of his neighbor's apartment if that neighbor didn't have what looked like garbage bags taped over the window.

"Okay, you saw hands pushing the window up," Sheryn prompted.

"Yes, white hands. Not Andray," Gamon said. "I watch, and this girl, she crawl out. She run down fire escape. She look scared."

"Can you describe her?" Sheryn asked.

"Dark hair." She thought about it some more. "All in black."

"Was she carrying anything?"

"No."

"How can you be so sure?" Rafael asked. Both of the women turned to look at him; it was as if they'd forgotten he was there.

"She grab railing with both hands when she run down." Srisuk held up both of her hands for emphasis. "She fall on the street, but she get up and run."

"Which way?" Sheryn asked.

"West. Toward Twelfth." The woman's eyes were serious. "Is Andray okay?"

"No, I'm sorry to say he isn't," Sheryn said. "He was shot in the chest. He's dead."

"Oh, no." The woman collapsed into the big chair again, her hand over her mouth. She murmured something in Thai; Rafael took it for a prayer.

"I'm sorry," she added. "I should have call 911 first time."

"First time?" Sheryn asked.

"I thought maybe it was a car," the woman answered. "Because nothing happen. Pow! But all quiet. Then I make tea; I read magazine."

"How long was it before the next one?" Rafael tried to keep his voice low. The louder he got, the more the sound echoed in his own head.

"Half hour?"

Sheryn glanced at him, her brow knitted together in consternation. "So there was a big gap between the shots?"

"Maybe? Maybe not a shot?" Srisuk said. "Later, definitely shots. Five." She counted on her hand. "Pow-pow-pow, then pow-pow. Five." She looked down, twisting a gold ring on her fourth finger. "I should have call first time. I am sorry I wait."

Sheryn's phone buzzed. "The landlord's on the scene now," she told Rafael. "We need to talk to him." She turned back to the woman. "Thank you for your help. If there's anything else you think of, please contact us." She handed her a card and shook her hand.

"You think I make mistake?" the woman asked. She stared at Rafael.

He couldn't tell her *mai pen rai*. But if she had made a mistake, he didn't think she deserved to suffer for it. "No," he said. "You did the right thing."

Rafael left the apartment feeling unsettled. It wasn't simply because he had to make it down four flights of stairs again, a task he was dreading. Even tougher was watching an elderly woman carrying a burden of guilt for not acting quickly enough.

"Maybe she should've called us sooner," Sheryn said quietly, as if reading his mind.

"She's beating herself up over not saving him," Rafael answered. "That's pointless." You couldn't save everyone. Rafael knew that all too well.

"Maybe if she'd called earlier we would be dealing with an injury instead of a corpse," Sheryn said.

"You know the philosophical argument about guilt being as non-existent as witchcraft?" he asked.

"That's ridiculous."

"That's Nietzsche." He wanted to elaborate, but each step was a chore. Rafael had liked quoting him as a teenager, but he had to admit that Nietzsche was wrong. Guilt was real, and it was a force to be reckoned with.

He felt paranoid that his partner was behind him, watching him struggle.

"Hey, Mr. Worldwide," Sheryn said finally. "You told me you went to Bali on your honeymoon."

"Brett arranged it." Rafael kept one hand on the banister and set his cane down before he put his foot on the next step. It wasn't unlike using crutches. "So you know it was elaborate. We went to a few different places."

"That explains it," Sheryn said. "You want me to wait, or get a head start on talking to the shitbird slumlord?"

"The *what*?" Rafael was startled. Sheryn didn't often swear, so it was odd to hear a phrase like that roll off her tongue. He was so surprised that he forgot to be annoyed that she wanted to ditch him again.

"That's what the neighbor on the third floor called him," Sheryn said. "Andray Baxter was suing him in housing court. I can't wait to hear his alibi."

# CHAPTER 11

## SHERYN

"Going down the stairs is the worst," Rafael muttered. "You'd think *up* would be the pain in the ass, but no, it's down." He glanced at Sheryn. "Are you even listening?"

"You hate stairs. They are your mortal enemy." Sheryn tried to keep her tone light, but it made her cringe to watch him move in such a painstaking way. *That could be you. Maybe that should be you,* she thought.

"Smartass." Rafael winced and kept going.

Finally, they made it to street level. The block was a mess of emergency vehicles now, but even so, the large black SUV stood out to Sheryn. The flatfoot, Carpacelli, was on the sidewalk with a lanky man in an expensive camel-hair coat who was in a heated conversation with the SUV's driver. Sheryn could hear them even before she crossed the street.

"This is incredibly poor service," the man said. "I'll call your supervisor."

"Look, my job is to get you from point A to point B," the driver said. "I can't hang around and wait for you. I have to pick up other fares."

"I don't normally *hire* cars, because I have my *own* driver." The remark was delivered in a snarky tone that raised Sheryn's eyebrows.

"Well, then, call him," the exasperated SUV driver said. "I can't help you. You need to use the app for another car when you're ready to go." He powered up his window and drove off.

"Can you believe that?" the man in the camel-hair coat asked Carpacelli.

"Hey, Detectives," Carpacelli said, waving anxiously. "This is Elliott Westergard. He owns the building where we found the body."

"It's such sad news," Westergard said. "Tragic. I had to come as soon as I heard."

Sheryn studied him closely. Elliott Westergard was a handsome man—of that there was no doubt. He was tall, well over six feet, with sandy-brown hair and a close-cropped beard he'd probably grown for gravitas. He was somewhere between thirty-five and forty, with vivid blue eyes that peered back at her calmly. He smiled at her. His demeanor was markedly different from what it had been a moment earlier.

"Did any of the officers mention why we called you here?" Rafael asked.

"They told my assistant someone was killed," Westergard said. "They didn't say who. Was it one of my tenants?"

"Yes, a man by the name of Andray Baxter in apartment 402," Sheryn said. "I take it you know him."

"Andray." The name slowly escaped from Westergard's lips, like air from a deflating tire. "That's *horrible*. What happened to him?"

"He was shot," Sheryn said. "We're looking for anyone with a motivation to harm him."

"Shot? I can't imagine anyone wanting to kill Andray," Westergard said. "He was the most charming man I ever met."

"That's interesting," Sheryn said, noting his odd choice of words. In all her years on the NYPD, she'd never heard a person react to news of a death by calling the victim *charming.* "Because we heard that he had you tied up in housing court with a series of lawsuits."

"I hope you're not suggesting I had anything to do with his death," Westergard said. "There's a difference between having a legal dispute with a man and wanting him dead, Detective." He looked at Sheryn and Rafael in turn. "There are a number of unfair laws on the books, laws that give a tenant, even an illegal tenant, more rights than a building's owner. None of that was Andray's fault. I understood his position, why he was suing me."

"And that was . . . ?"

"His uncle had an apartment in this building for three decades," Westergard said. "It was rent controlled, fair and square. But when he died, Andray moved in, expecting to pay the same rent. Claimed he'd lived there with his uncle. Succession rights, they call it in the law. It's ridiculous. Do you have any idea how far below market value his uncle's rent was? It was a tenth of what the rent should've been."

"Excuse me, Mr. Westergard," Sheryn said. "But we've been inside your building and talked to some of your tenants. Condition it's in, I'm not sure why anyone would pay a dime to live there."

Westergard didn't seem perturbed. "It's a catch-22 situation. My father let his tenants get away with far too much. They'd withhold rent over the littlest thing. The result was that there wasn't any money for upkeep, and it went downhill from there. I've been trying to right this ship since I took over." He stared up at the building, his expression lavishly admiring, as if there were a glamour about it that showed it in its former glory and not as the wreck it currently was. "You'd be surprised what a building like this is worth, even in its current condition, now that Hudson Yards has opened up. I'm currently in negotiations to sell the property."

"Congratulations," Rafael said drily. "But in the meantime, we're going to need your assistance solving this murder. What kind of security does the building have?"

"Security?" Westergard looked blank, as if this were a foreign concept.

"The lock on the front door is busted," Rafael said. "Anyone could get in. Are there any cameras?"

"Not anymore. There used to be one, but someone stole it."

"We saw eviction notices from the city marshal on some doors," Sheryn said. "What happened to your other tenants?"

"They left," Westergard answered. "I'm not afraid of using the law to get them out. Quite honestly, if I'm going to sell the building, it's better for them to go now. Less of a headache for my buyer."

"How long did Andray Baxter live in your building?" Rafael asked.

"He claimed five years. It was really more like two and a half years. Maybe three."

"When's the last time you saw Mr. Baxter?" Sheryn asked.

Westergard didn't stop to think about that. "It was in housing court, almost a month ago. I had an eviction order for him, and he was fighting it."

"How did that go?"

"He got his way yet again," Westergard answered grimly. He stared up at the building once more. "At the time, I thought he was lucky. He'd charmed another judge. Only I guess it wasn't a lucky decision for him after all, was it?"

Sheryn paused for a moment. Every word out of Westergard's mouth seemed false, and it was clear he despised the dead man. "We'll need a list of everyone who lives in the building and everyone who has access to it," Sheryn said.

"I will have my assistant email that to you as soon as possible."

"We also need to know where you were between twelve and two this afternoon."

"Are you asking me for an alibi?" Westergard smiled. "I had breakfast early this morning at Loews at Sixty-First and Park. I ate alone, but I like to go there for the view—it's an incredible power-breakfast scene."

Sheryn cocked her head, thinking how interesting it was that Westergard had started his alibi well above and beyond what she'd asked for. "And after that?"

"I had appointments with a couple of different real estate agents to look at properties. I'm expanding my little empire."

"Good for you," Rafael said. "But we're not up to twelve o'clock yet, are we?"

"Oh. I had lunch at Nobu Fifty Seven. That was at twelve thirty. I had a reservation."

"Who were you eating with?"

"No one. I was at the hibachi counter. I'm sure they'll remember me. I tipped very well," Westergard said. "Then I went back to my office and found out the police had called."

"What about your . . ." Sheryn remembered Wilbur Bowen using the word *henchman*. That wasn't an appropriate way to phrase it, she knew. "Your associate? Your tenants said you always have a male employee with you."

"My driver?" Westergard frowned. "He's in Florida this week."

"We'd like to access the other apartments on the floor," Sheryn said. "Can you open them up for us?"

For the first time since the driver took off, Westergard's genial, confident front wavered. "*Why* would you need that?"

"We've tried knocking on doors, but we can't tell which apartments are occupied and which aren't."

"Again, *why* would that matter?" Westergard raised an eyebrow. "You're not suggesting that the killer is another tenant, are you?"

"We can't rule anything out."

"Because the median age in the building is probably ninety-five," Westergard said. "I don't want to be ageist, but no one in that building except Andray would be able to shoot straight." He looked at his watch. "I'm so sorry, Detectives, but I have an appointment I simply cannot miss."

"Mr. Westergard, a man was murdered in your building," Sheryn said. "There is no meeting more pressing than solving a crime."

But Westergard was already moving away. "You'll have to talk to my lawyers about that," he called over his shoulder.

"I don't want to keep reminding you of this, but I can't chase him down," Rafael said quietly.

"I'd like to, but it wouldn't help right now," Sheryn said. "I know we need to find this mystery woman who was on the fire escape, but my gut's telling me the landlord is mixed up in this too."

# CHAPTER 12

## Jo

Seated at her desk, Jo stared at the laptop as if she could will it to unlock. She'd cleaned the blood off as best she could with water and tissue. The screen saver had floated in front of her eyes several times, but the lock-screen name simply read "AB's laptop," as if her blackmailer wanted to exhibit a singular lack of creativity. Jo tried typing the alphabet into the password box, but that got her nowhere. She tried her own name, but that failed too. She picked the computer up and turned it over, wondering what she was missing. It was an older laptop, its silver casing banged up and dented.

*You don't know that it's his,* Jo thought. Still, who else would send her a laptop? There were two possibilities, as Jo saw it. One was that the man she'd shot was still alive and determined to torment her. The other was that it was his partner in the hallway, who was following up. For the tenth time, she shook the cardboard box the laptop had been delivered in, hoping to find a clue. Even a demand for more money would've been reassuring, because she would've known where she stood. Instead, there was nothing, and Jo was terrified.

She set the box under her desk and leaned forward, rubbing her temples. She didn't have a headache, exactly; it was more of a full-body ache that made every inch of her throb in pain. The fact her blackmailer handed her those old photos disturbed her more than she could've imagined. It wasn't that they were a surprise; early in their correspondence, he'd attached them to some of his emails. Jo had been angry when she'd see them, and defiant. Her fourteen-year-old self was easily recognizable: orphaned, hungry, desperate to please. She'd come to New York with a dream of life in the big city, and it had turned out to be light-years from the reality. But she wasn't ashamed about that. What choice had she had?

The first message from her blackmailer had come in a month earlier, and it was unforgettable. Dear Jo, You don't know me, but I know all about you. You've done horrible things and you've never been punished for them. All of that is about to change.

She'd ignored it at the time. Jo herself avoided the spotlight, but Corvus Alchemy reveled in it, and the company had received hate mail for campaigns and causes it supported, from celebrating trans people to advocating for human trafficking victims who'd been jailed. It wasn't until the second message came in from the same account that it became clear this was personal. Dear Jo, You were never a successful model like your sister, but I suppose you had your moments. Do you think your boyfriend and your investors and your customers would like to see these? Attached were disturbing photographs that a teenaged Jo had been forced to pose for.

But even that hadn't broken her. It was the video that had shamed her. Even the thought of it made Jo want to drown herself in whiskey and pills.

Jo got up from her desk, stuffed the laptop under a cushion on the sofa, and went to the kitchen. There was a bottle of champagne in the fridge, stored for some impromptu celebration at a future date. Jo itched to open it at that moment, but she knew she'd finish the whole bottle. Reluctantly, she closed the fridge and retreated to the bathroom.

Under the harsh fluorescent light, she looked like hell. Her eyes were puffy, with bluish half-moons underneath them, and her skin was washed out. She reapplied her lipstick, as if that could fix her problems.

Her blackmailer had made it clear in their email correspondence that he had all the information he needed to destroy Jo's life. Her business would be ruined, her boyfriend would abandon her, and she would go to jail. She'd gone to the address he'd given her, expecting to make a trade. Instead, she'd found a man toying with her as a cat would with a mouse. *Do you ever feel guilty for what you've done?*

Jo hadn't answered him, but she knew what her answer was as she stared into that unforgiving mirror.

*Yes. Every day.*

Her sister never allowed her to forget her guilt. If Lori had still been alive, Jo would've wasted no time in identifying her as the blackmailer, but Lori had been dead for eighteen months. As much as Jo had hated her, Lori's death had opened up a void in her world; there was no one else who knew what she had been, only what she'd willed herself to become.

*Except my blackmailer,* Jo thought. *He knows all about me.*

She wanted to blame one of her sister's friends, but Lori had none; by the time she'd died, she'd burned every bridge. Lori had been alone with her drugs and her ghosts.

Jo could feel her body shaking, and she was afraid she'd burst into tears. *Everyone is going to know something is wrong with you,* she warned herself. *Get it together.*

When she returned to her desk, she opened a new tab for local news, searching for any mention of a death in Hell's Kitchen. There was nothing. Not yet, at least. How long would it take the police to find a dead man in that crumbling building? Maybe a few days, if no one was looking for him. Or maybe he'd already been found.

For a moment, Jo felt like she was fourteen again, right after her mother died. She'd known the same sheriff's deputy who'd given her candy and a Coke was going to hand her over to foster care, and that had terrified her. The only thing she could do back then to save herself was to run. In a heartsick instant, Jo realized nothing had really changed; if she was going to save herself now, she had to flee.

# CHAPTER 13

## SHERYN

"Butter wouldn't melt in Elliott Westergard's mouth," Rafael said. "It's not like I expected him to admit how much he hated the victim, but it was weird to hear him praising Baxter to the skies. What did you think of him?"

"Phony, pretentious, obsessed with impressing people," Sheryn said, keeping her eyes on the road. She was driving them back to the precinct, but in Rafael's car, a Mercedes that cost more than she and her husband made in a year. She treated it with care.

"You're telling me you don't care that he normally has his own driver? That he eats at fancy places by himself? That he tips well and wants everyone to know?"

"The weird part is that he clearly thinks he's one smooth dude," Sheryn said. "I bet if anyone asks him, he thinks he pulled a fast one on us."

Rafael shook his head. "That guy's a walking, talking cartoon. He's Elmer Fudd's good-looking city cousin."

"I love that sometimes you're full of philosophy, and other times it's Bugs Bunny references," Sheryn said. "You keep it fresh."

"The question is, if someone's so transparently dumb, is he capable of committing a crime?"

"No matter how dumb he is, the math comes down to basic addition and subtraction. If Mr. Westergard gets rid of a troublesome tenant who won't move out, he'll stop bleeding money in housing court. Plus, he's clearing the way to sell."

"Westergard clearly has the means," Rafael agreed. "He's got the keys to all the apartments, which means something because there was no forced entry into Andray Baxter's place. Either he knew his killer, or his killer had access. Maybe both."

"Means, motive, and opportunity. Congrats. He wins the trifecta, no matter how much he tells us he admired Mr. Baxter. But there's one problem."

"Shoot."

"Mr. Westergard isn't a man who'd do this himself," Sheryn said. "Those soft, manicured hands of his aren't going to test positive for gunshot residue. If he's our man, he's got someone else working with him, someone capable of pulling a trigger."

"The mystery woman," Rafael suggested. "The one who went out the window, according to our witness."

"But *think* about it." Sheryn arched a brow. "You're the owner of the building, you've got the perfect setup for murder, and you have your button man—or button woman—call attention to themselves by running out a fire escape at the front of the building? There's something wrong with that plan."

"We agree he's a dum-dum," Rafael said. "His plan doesn't need to be good."

"It feels like we're missing something. I wish I could say what."

"The mystery woman could be a girlfriend who walked into the apartment at the wrong time," Rafael said.

"We really need to talk with her. Even if there's no security cam in the building, there's got to be something from the street."

"I'm already on it," Rafael said. "I know you think I'm a bundle of uselessness right now, but while you were talking to the neighbor, I got uniforms looking for street cams. We'll have a lot of tape to dive into."

"I don't think that." Sheryn gave him a sidelong glare as she pulled up in front of the precinct and parked. "I'll give you a head start. We've got an address in Harlem for Mr. Baxter's mother. I've got to head up there."

"You want to do the next-of-kin notification alone?" He looked incredulous. "That's the worst part of this job."

"You're not feeling well. Don't argue. I'm a mom and I know." Sheryn glared at him. "Do us both a favor and start hunting down the documents filed in housing court. That's going to give us a better picture of the not-so-talented Mr. Westergard."

"I'll do that on the drive up."

Sheryn tried to stare him down.

"I refused desk duty," Rafael added. "You know why. Even if you've been blown up, you're a cop, and a cop doesn't hide behind a desk. If you're trying to help me out, I appreciate it, but that's not going to fly. I'm your partner. We're going to deal with this case together."

"Those are words to live by," Sheryn said, pulling into traffic again. "Please don't make me regret this."

# CHAPTER 14

## CAL

When Cal McGarran arrived at his apartment building on Hanover Square—a stone's throw from Wall Street—he gave the doorman a big smile and friendly wave. He hoped he looked like a man who didn't have a care in the world as he headed to the apartment he shared with his girlfriend. Upstairs, he unlocked the door, shut it behind him, and took a deep breath.

"Jo?" he called out. "Are you home?"

There was no reason for Jo to be there, of course. Her office was in the Flatiron District, her gym was in Midtown, and he knew enough of her schedule to expect her to work late. He didn't want to see her because he would owe her some explanation for abandoning work to rush home in the middle of the afternoon.

*I don't want to lie to her,* Cal thought. *Even though I know she's lying to me.*

He listened for the telltale clip-clop of the furry pink slides Jo wore at home. They were a dead giveaway, even when she sat at her desk in the windowless, airless den she called an office, because she had a habit of tapping her foot impatiently. But there was no sound, only a silence that stretched on until it sounded like noise in his ears. Jo was out, of course. He had the place to himself.

He slipped out of his shoes, padding down the hallway in sock feet, and glanced at his watch. Four o'clock. He wanted to strip off his suit, but he knew he'd have to head back to work in twenty minutes if he didn't want to lose his job. He had to move fast. The door to Jo's office was ajar. He pushed it open and stepped inside.

Jo was an extremely organized person, and her office was spartan. There were boxes filled with makeup samples—an occupational hazard, Jo always joked—but otherwise just a desk, a chair, and a bookcase. Jo had never bothered to decorate her office much beyond adding a series of framed photographs of her icons: Helena Rubenstein, Elizabeth Arden, Madam C. J. Walker, Estée Lauder, Bobbi Brown, Lisa Price, Marcia Kilgore. Cal wouldn't have recognized any of them without the little nameplates attached. There were no pictures of friends or family . . . or of him. Cal didn't let that fact ruffle him. Jo got to see his mug every morning and night.

He woke the desktop computer and entered Jo's password. The screen shook as it rejected it. He tried again, wondering if he'd screwed it up. He hadn't; Jo had already changed it.

It was a small detail, but it felt ominous. Jo kept a plastic figurine of a crow on her desk, and its eyes seemed to gleam knowingly. *She changed it because of the video,* Cal realized. *Whatever the hell that was on her screen, she didn't want me to be able to find it.*

It had started so innocently. Three weeks earlier, Cal had made coffee one Saturday morning and delivered it to Jo. She was sitting in her tiny office with the door shut; when he opened it, she was watching a video on her computer. He couldn't see the full screen—her head was in front of it—but it looked like a man sexually attacking a woman. The sound was turned down low, but Cal could hear the woman's voice. "Stop! Please stop!" she shrieked.

Jo had become flustered when she realized Cal was there, immediately switching the screen to something innocuous. *Was that rape porn?* Cal had asked her.

*Of course not. It's a stupid thing Peyton sent me,* Jo had responded.

Cal knew Peyton Chin well enough to realize she had an offbeat sense of humor, but it didn't sit right with him. *Why would she send you that?* he'd asked.

*One of our competitors used a clip from it in an ad on social media,* Jo had said. *Can you believe it?*

Cal would've forgotten all about it, but a couple of odd things had happened since then. The latest was on this past Thursday, when he'd gotten an overdraft notice on their shared account. When he'd asked Jo about it, she'd told him that one of her suppliers was in trouble and she'd had to front him money. She'd promised to put the money back into their account over the weekend, but she hadn't. Cal wasn't naturally inclined to be suspicious, but he was starting to have doubts about Jo's story.

He kneeled down to tackle the safe under the desk. He'd never invaded Jo's privacy like this before, but the events of the past few weeks had him worried about her. The lock was a combination one that turned, and Cal tried the numbers that came to mind: Jo's birthday, his birthday, the day they met. Nothing worked. He leaned close to the lock, following the instructions he'd looked up online. There were little clicking sounds, but no matter how closely he listened, he couldn't crack it.

When his phone rang, his whole body jolted, and he hit the top of his head against the underside of the desk. He backed away, pulling the phone out of the inner pocket of his suit jacket. His mother's number flashed on the screen.

"I think I'm having a heart attack," his mother said immediately when he answered.

"Have you called 911?" Cal asked, alarmed.

"No, I'm calling you."

"If you're having a heart attack, you need an ambulance," Cal said, getting to his feet.

"I had to drop some things off for a client downtown, and I started feeling dizzy and having heart palpitations," his mother said. "I don't know if it's really a heart attack. If I call an ambulance and it's a false alarm, my insurance isn't going to pay . . ." Her voice trailed off, and he heard a snuffling sound. He knew his mother wasn't crying—she never cried—but she seemed afraid.

"Where are you?" he asked.

"Outside Trinity Churchyard."

"I'll be there in five minutes," Cal promised.

He was good to his word. As he turned from Wall Street onto Broadway, he caught sight of his mother. Her head was bowed as she leaned against the low wall, but Priscilla McGarran was hard to miss. She was wearing a Vivienne Westwood tartan suit he remembered her buying when he was in high school, before disaster struck his family.

"Does your chest hurt?" Cal asked as he approached her. "Should I call an ambulance?"

She shook her head. "I think I overreacted. I started feeling dizzy, and I couldn't find my pills . . ."

"Are they in your bag?"

"I can't find them."

Cal took the black crocodile Birkin bag from her and rooted around inside it. His mother was tidy, but the bag ended up as a repository for small items for clients. He found a small box from Cartier and a couple of vintage Lucite bangles and a dozen small bottles of moisturizer and primer and other magic potions before he found her medication.

"Do you need water?" Cal asked. "I can buy a bottle at the corner."

"No, it's fine," she answered before palming the pills and tossing them down her throat. She grimaced, then sighed and rubbed the bridge of her nose with her thumb and forefinger. "I wish I could lie down for a few minutes."

"Come to the apartment. You can rest there."

Her mouth quivered. "I wouldn't want Jo to see me like this. I'm a mess."

"Jo's at work."

"Maybe we could have a quick drink somewhere," his mother suggested.

Cal sighed inwardly. His mother had quietly depended on alcohol after his father's scandal and the ensuing divorce. She'd righted herself eventually, and while he saw nothing wrong with her having a glass of pinot grigio, he didn't like her mixing meds with booze.

"I need to go to the apartment," Cal said. "You can rest there for a bit and lock up when you're done."

"I don't have the key with me today."

"No problem. I'll walk back with you, and we'll find an extra one, okay?"

"All right." She sniffed.

She refused to take a taxi, insisting that the air would do her good. She leaned heavily on Cal's arm on the walk to Hanover Square. He'd made it over in five minutes, but walking with his mother in her state—and in her towering heels—took four times as long.

*So much for my stealth search,* Cal thought, glancing at his watch once they were in the elevator. *And so much for getting back to work any time soon.*

"How is Jo?" his mother asked.

"Fine," Cal answered automatically, unsure whether it was a lie.

"I asked her to lunch a couple of weeks ago, but she hasn't gotten back to me," his mother said. "I suppose she's very busy."

"She's always busy," Cal muttered.

She gave him a curious look. "Is everything all right with you two?"

"She's such a workaholic. I wish she'd calm down." Cal hated himself for answering in such a clichéd way. He admired Jo's ambition and drive; what he couldn't stand was her lying to him. But Jo's relationship with his mother had gotten off to a rocky start. It had improved lately, but Cal felt like it would be a betrayal of Jo to voice his fears.

When they finally arrived at the apartment, Cal's mother moved quickly from the foyer to the pale-gray sofa. She set her expensive bag on the coffee table and kicked her heels off.

"I'll get you some tea," Cal offered. "Maybe a side of Advil?"

"Not with the blood thinner I'm on. Tea would be lovely." She twisted a ring on her right hand. "Did you know your father had another baby with that Lolita of his?"

Cal knew he could be honest with his mother and reveal that he stalked his father on social media, reading his news but never following or liking or commenting. If he chose that path, he'd have to reveal that he knew about the new baby a month ago. He didn't want to do that.

"Please tell me you're joking."

"I wish I were. Congratulations. How many twenty-seven-year-olds have a newborn brother?" She settled back against the cushions, her mouth set in a grim line. "I know it shouldn't bother me, but it does."

Cal went to the kitchen. It was a small galley that lacked any windows, which was hardly surprising, given that the Financial District building was constructed for offices, not apartments. He poured water into a stainless steel kettle, thinking of how news about his father had bothered him for years, but now it was like learning about a stranger in a distant country. That cord had been cut a long time ago. Cal's father had gone to jail when Cal was seventeen; his only contribution to Cal's life since then was his name, which allowed Cal to follow in his footsteps and attend Harvard as a legacy. His father had sent a strange letter when Cal graduated—he was out of jail by then and basking in Florida sunlight—and Cal could quote it. *By now, your mother has undoubtedly turned you into her own creature, but you should know my side of the story.*

Cal hadn't bothered to respond. He knew that his father had married and divorced and married again since leaving Cal's mother, and Cal didn't feel any connection to his new family in West Palm Beach.

"Is this the week Jo goes to Dubai?" his mother called.

"No, she decided to skip it. Most of her staff is there," Cal said. It was strange, now that he thought about it; Jo didn't like to fly, but this trade show was hugely important for her company. As he turned it over in his mind, he realized he was deeply worried about Jo. She played things close to the vest, but he'd never known her to flat-out lie. He didn't want to be petty about the money in their joint account, but it was out of character for her to take any cash out without warning.

As he poured his mother's tea, he heard the rattle of keys; a moment later, the front door slammed shut. For a split second, Cal wondered if his mother had fled from the apartment. Before he could check, there was a scream from the foyer.

# CHAPTER 15

## SHERYN

Andray Baxter's mother lived in a low-rise apartment building on Bradhurst Avenue, overlooking the eastern edge of Jackie Robinson Park. Sheryn knew that when people thought of Harlem, they pictured the bustling, lively 125th Street, with the Apollo Theater and restaurants like Sylvia's and Red Rooster. Hamilton Heights was different: quiet and residential, a place for families to retreat to but without much in the way of amenities. Sheryn and her husband had actually considered renting an apartment there after their first child was born.

Rafael rang the bell. It took a long time for anyone to answer, but Sheryn heard movement inside, soft footfalls approaching slowly. When the door finally swung open, there was a tiny woman behind it. Her black hair was pinned back, with a stray streak of silver in it. Her brown skin was virtually unlined, and her eyes were huge and serious.

"Are you Ornelle Baxter?"

The woman nodded.

"I'm Detective Sheryn Sterling of the NYPD. This is my partner, Detective Rafael Mendoza. We're here about your son, Andray."

"What's happened?" Ornelle Baxter's voice was soft, barely above a whisper. Her face was frozen in fear, as if she already knew what they were going to say.

"Could we come in?" Sheryn asked. "We don't want to trouble you, but we need to ask a few questions."

The woman's expression hardened. "Is my son in some sort of trouble?"

"No, ma'am," Sheryn said, aware she'd awakened the suspicions of a mother lion. Parents of black boys were often too familiar with the fact that the police took their sons for criminals. "May we come in?"

"I'm sorry, but no."

Sheryn hated to deliver the awful news like this, standing in a doorway, but she had no choice. "Mrs. Baxter, I'm very sorry to have to tell you that your son, Andray, has passed away."

The woman made a sound as if she'd been punched in the stomach. She stared at Sheryn with eyes wide with shock. "But . . . how?"

"He was shot," Sheryn said as softly as she could, as if that would deflect the blow. As a mother, she knew there was nothing more awful you could tell a parent.

"By the police?" Ornelle Baxter asked, an edge as sharp as a knife under her words.

Sheryn blinked at that, and her heart squeezed inside her chest. "No, ma'am. No. Andray was shot and killed in his apartment by an unknown assailant or assailants. We are investigating."

The older woman's head bowed, and her small body seemed to shrink into itself. Sheryn could hear her whisper something that she took for a prayer, even though the words were indistinct. "Come in," she said finally.

The main room was airy, with crown molding around its edges and gauzy curtains over the windows. The furniture was dark wood, well loved but also well kept. There were framed photographs on every available surface; Andray Baxter's image was everywhere, alongside a beautiful young woman with a bright smile. Between two tall, rectangular windows hung a wooden cross, easily two feet tall. The room smelled faintly of violets.

"Sit down, please," Ornelle Baxter said. "Tell me how my son died."

"He was at home in his apartment on West Forty-Ninth Street," Sheryn said. "He was shot once in the chest at close range."

"He died quickly," Rafael added. "He wouldn't have suffered."

Ornelle Baxter bowed her head. "My flesh and my heart may fail, but God is the strength of my heart and my portion forever," she murmured, briefly closing her eyes. Then she stood ramrod straight again, staring into Sheryn's face. "My son was robbed, wasn't he?"

"His computer is missing, and so is his phone," Sheryn answered. "Aside from that, it didn't look like his apartment was ransacked. Why would you think it was a robbery?"

"Andray had come into money in the past few months. He wouldn't tell me the how or why of it." The woman's head drooped, like a sunflower on a broken stalk. She blinked back tears, but one slid down her cheek.

"I know this is the worst possible time to be asking you questions," Sheryn said. "We wouldn't do it if it weren't important . . ."

"I understand. Ask me whatever you need to."

"What kind of work did Andray do?" Sheryn asked.

The older woman took a deep breath. "He's an actor. And a writer. But he paid the bills as a fitness instructor. He taught at a couple different places. I don't remember the names."

"That's all right," Sheryn said. "But unless he landed a starring role in a show, I'm going to guess that his work wasn't bringing in a lot of money."

"It kept the wolf from the door, but not much beyond that. Andray's always been independent. He's been giving me money since he turned sixteen, trying to help out. But he's never made a lot."

"When did Andray tell you he was coming into money?"

"He didn't. He showed up here with a bag of cash five months ago. Ten thousand dollars." She considered it thoughtfully. "He was all excited about being able to help pay my medical bills. I have a brain tumor. I've got some insurance, but it doesn't come close to covering treatment."

"I'm so sorry," Sheryn said. "Andray's your only child?"

"Only son," Ornelle Baxter clarified. "My daughter, Audra, is at Stanford University on a scholarship. She's studying biomedical computation."

"That's fantastic," Rafael said. "You must be very proud."

"I am. I've been blessed." Her eyes started to fill again.

"Did Andray have any conflicts or disputes with anyone?" Sheryn asked.

"Oh, yes, that landlord of his," Ornelle Baxter said. "Not the older Mr. Westergard, but his son, Elliott. I could never forget, because every time I see Andray he's got a list of new horrors from living in that man's building. My brother-in-law, Lord rest his soul, lived there for years without any problems. Mr. Westergard was a kind man, and he liked his building neat and tidy. But in the last while . . ." She wiped her eyes. "It's gotten really bad. Andray took him to court. Not poor Mr. Westergard, bless his soul, but his son. When Mr. Westergard died, Elliott inherited everything, and he could give the devil himself a run for his money when it comes to being petty and mean. Last winter, there wasn't even heat in the building. The city told Elliott he had to turn it on—that it was his obligation and responsibility—and he ignored them."

"We met Elliott Westergard," Sheryn said. "He acted as if he admired your son."

Ornelle Baxter made a dismissive noise from the back of her throat. "An act is all that would be. The man is trying to empty the building by cutting off essential services. Andray wouldn't stand for that. He said nobody was forcing him out of his home. Andray told me a few things about him that made my hair stand on end."

"Like what?"

"Elliott was spying on him." Ornelle Baxter said this decisively.

"Spying? How, exactly?"

"I don't know the ins and outs of all this new technology. But there was something in his apartment, something the landlord put there. Andray was furious when he discovered it. I know he confronted Elliott. Almost got into a fight with the man's bodyguard over it."

"Bodyguard?"

"Some jarhead Elliott keeps around so he can pretend he's a player. I think he drives his car."

That was an important piece of information, to Sheryn's mind. Elliott Westergard made it seem as if his battle with the dead man was simply a legal formality. If there had been personal confrontations between them, that would point the investigation even more strongly at him. Also, Westergard had made it ostentatiously clear that his driver wasn't around that day. To Sheryn, that felt suspicious.

"Do you know if Andray ever contacted the police about this harassment?" Sheryn asked.

The older woman gave her a long look. "The police? I don't believe that ever came into his mind," she said, her voice low and cautious.

Sheryn understood what she was saying without the woman spelling it out. The line between them had been clear from the moment Ornelle Baxter had asked if it had been the police who'd shot her son. There were a lot of black men who never expected the police to be on their side, even if they were the victim of a crime.

"Has your son been harassed by police?" Sheryn asked.

"Constantly, since he took Elliott to court. There's been nothing but trouble since that started. It's been awful this year. Elliott told the police my son was selling drugs out of his apartment. They got a warrant based on an anonymous tip—how do you like that? Of course, they found nothing."

"Andray knew it was Elliott Westergard who called the police?"

"There was no one else it could've been," Ornelle Baxter said. "Elliott denied it, but he's called the city marshal's office to evict Andray. He's had cops of all stripes there to harass my son."

"It would be helpful if I could speak with your son's friends. Would you have any names and numbers?"

"Sure." Tears were trickling down her cheeks, but she smiled softly. "Some of them are real characters, but I mean that in the best way."

"Was there anyone besides Elliott Westergard that your son had a conflict with?"

Ornelle Baxter shook her head. "No. Andray was easy to get along with. He was the type to make a joke when there was tension. He didn't fight with people, and he never held a grudge."

"When he told you he was coming into money, where did you think it was coming from?"

"Work, I figured. Andray could surely keep a secret. He was in a few TV commercials. You can make good money from those."

"What about his personal life? Was your son dating anyone in particular?"

"That I don't know." She wiped her eyes with the back of her hand. "He was always very private about dating. A little while back, he told me he'd met someone special. Whenever I asked about having her over to dinner, he'd get all coy and say, 'Not yet.'"

"Did he say anything else about this person?"

"Not really. I'm sure she's a nice girl, though."

Sheryn's first thought was about the woman who'd gone out the window and fled the scene. "Has he introduced you to his other girlfriends?"

"Not really. He hadn't mentioned anybody special for a while."

Sheryn's phone interrupted them. "I'm sorry; I should get this," she apologized, recognizing the number from the medical examiner's office. She stood and moved to the foyer. "What's up?"

"This is Florian," the voice on the other end said. "We were examining your victim, before we hand him over to the ME, when we found a business card in a hidden pocket in Baxter's pants. The name on it is Jo Greaver, with a business address for something called Corvus Alchemy at Broadway and East Twenty-First Street."

"Hold on," Sheryn said into the phone, then turned to Ornelle Baxter. "Does the name Jo Greaver sound familiar to you?"

The older woman shook her head. "No."

"Okay, go on," she said into the phone.

"There's more. Handwritten on the back of the card is today's date and a time: one p.m."

"You're telling me our victim had an appointment with her when he died?" Sheryn asked.

"Exactly," Florian said. "If you're looking for the shooter, you might want to start there."

# CHAPTER 16

## Jo

Jo clapped her hand over her mouth. She hadn't meant to scream, but she'd been astonished to find her boyfriend's mother reclining on her sofa when she walked into her apartment. It was exactly the worst possible moment to encounter Priscilla McGarran.

"What are you doing here?" Jo cried. She realized too late that her tone had come out brittle and sharp. She couldn't even hide how upset she was.

"I'm sorry if I startled you," Priscilla said, her voice soft but certainly not kind. "You look like you've seen a ghost. Are you all right, Jo?"

"Of course," Jo snapped. "Why would anything be wrong?"

"I was just . . . I'm sorry . . . I'm still dizzy," Priscilla said. "You look gorgeous, as always. I only meant that I didn't mean to surprise you."

"Jo!" That was Cal's voice; he was walking out of the kitchen with a steaming mug in his hand, which he handed to his mother. "You're never home this early. Is everything okay?"

Jo tamped down an acid response. "Everything is just fine. I have to fly to Chicago for a business dinner. I was going to toss a couple of things in a bag. I wasn't expecting a greeting party."

She rushed down the hallway and into her office, shutting the door behind her. *Of course Priscilla is here,* she thought. Cal's mother was like a spidery shadow she couldn't escape. She'd been frosty to the point of rudeness when Jo had started dating Cal, but Jo preferred that to the fake geniality she'd exhibited lately. Jo was certain that Priscilla had decided she wasn't good enough for her son, and no forced smile could prove otherwise.

Jo shoved those thoughts aside. She didn't have time for them. She set her tote bag and her purse on the chair, then ducked down, kneeling in front of the safe under her desk and extracting her passport and the cash she'd stored for a rainy day. The storm was on her doorstep.

She relocked the safe and ran into the bedroom, grabbing her carry-on bag from the closet. She threw it onto the bed and unzipped it, then turned back to the closet.

"Jo."

She caught a glimpse of Cal standing in the doorway. He stepped inside and quietly shut the door behind him.

"What's really going on?" he asked.

She didn't have time for his concern. "I'm fine. Honest. This came up suddenly, and I'm kind of frantic." She stopped, realizing how odd it was that he was standing there. "Why aren't you at work?"

"My mother called me because she thought she was having a heart attack, and she didn't want to call 911." He shrugged. "She was close by, so I brought her here to rest for a bit. I was going to head back to the office."

She stared at him, unprepared to deal with anyone else's bad news. "Is she sick?"

"She found out something about my dad that sent her for a loop. That's her usual reaction to news about him." Cal winced, but he kept his tone light. "He's got a new baby boy. I guess this means I owe him a gift."

Jo stared at him. She thought of Cal as her polar opposite. He'd grown up in privilege in the elegant enclave of Gramercy Park, and he'd attended private schools that had paved his way into Harvard. He had a network of wealthy connections from knowing the right people and belonging to the right clubs. It was easy to forget that his family had lost their money while Cal was still a teenager and that his parents had divorced; his father had gone to jail.

"That's . . . bizarre," Jo said. "Did he get in touch to tell you?"

"Of course not. Everything my mother and I learn is from orbiting him on social media."

"I'm sorry."

"Don't be," Cal said. "His first son didn't work out so well for him. I guess he finally got the nerve to try again."

Jo wanted to help him, but she didn't know how. The pain in her arm throbbed through her body, and she didn't know how much time she had before the police found her. "I should get packing," she said.

"Where are you really going, Jo?" Cal asked. He sounded calm, but his deep-blue eyes were focused on her like lasers.

"I told you. Chicago." She didn't make eye contact with him; instead, she pulled a navy dress out of her closet.

"Is this about the supplier you had to loan money to?"

"No," Jo said. "Different issue."

"Because you haven't put the money back into our account yet," Cal said.

"Really? You want to nickel-and-dime me about that? I already told you I'll put the money back in." Jo's voice was heated, less because she was angry and more because she was on the defensive.

"This isn't about money," Cal said. "It's about you lying to me."

Jo stopped what she was doing and gazed at him. What could she say? *Honey, I shot my blackmailer dead this afternoon. Let's fly to the Caymans because there's no extradition treaty.* She was used to brazening out most situations. She was tough. She never would've survived otherwise. But those skills weren't helping her at that moment, and she knew it.

Jo took a deep breath. "Look, I get where you're coming from," she said. "If I had a business partner and they emptied out an account, I'd be freaking out too. You have every right to be upset."

"It's not about the money. It's about trust. Clearly, you don't want to tell me what's going on. I wish you would just say that instead of lying."

"I'm sorry," Jo said. "Because you're right. I can't talk about what's going on right now."

"Are you in some kind of trouble?"

His concern was palpable. Jo could feel it. She cared for him more deeply than she ever had for anyone, and at that moment, she couldn't decide whether she was making a terrible mistake by withholding the truth from him. She was light headed and dizzy and almost inclined— almost—to tell him a version of what had happened that afternoon that glossed over the goriest details.

There was a soft knock on the door. Cal turned to open it.

"I'm sorry to interrupt," Priscilla said. She was in her stockinged feet, holding her stiletto heels in one hand. No wonder they hadn't heard her, Jo thought. She was creeping around the apartment like a rodent. "I wanted to apologize to both of you for being a bother. I thought I'd let myself out and head home."

"You should rest a little longer, Mom," Cal said.

"I'm fine. I think what I had was a panic attack. I should be smarter at my age." Priscilla gave them both a smile. "Good night, you two."

Neither Jo nor Cal spoke for a moment. It was quiet until Priscilla put on her shoes, and then the tapping was audible. It sounded to Jo like Priscilla had gone into the kitchen, but she wasn't sure.

"I hate how she pretends to tolerate me," Jo muttered.

"She does care about you," Cal whispered back.

Jo rolled her eyes. "Do you need to talk to her? Make sure she's okay?"

"Is that how you're going to drop this conversation?" Cal asked. "You're not going to tell me the truth?"

Jo decided she couldn't risk revealing anything. It would put Cal in danger, and he wouldn't even see that.

"I think your mother needs more attention than I do right now," Jo answered coolly.

"Are you high?" Cal asked.

"Of course not. Why would you even ask that?"

"You're pale and sweaty. You're tightly wound up. You don't seem like yourself."

"Is that an accusation?" Jo demanded.

"An observation," Cal said.

"I'll be fine."

"I hope so," Cal said. "Because I don't think you know how to ask for help, no matter how much you need it." When she didn't answer, he stepped into the hallway. Jo heard his footfalls as he went to the foyer. "Let me get you a taxi, at least," he said to his mother. She couldn't hear Priscilla's muffled reply. The front door of the apartment opened and shut, and Jo was finally alone.

# CHAPTER 17

## Rafael

"Do we have enough for a warrant?" Sheryn asked Rafael as they headed back downtown via the FDR Drive.

Rafael was glued to his phone, typing away rapidly. "Very funny. Like anything's ever easy in this life."

"Don't ask, don't get. I figured it was worth a try."

"Finding Jo Greaver's business card on Baxter's body is suggestive, but it doesn't carry that much weight. Not enough to convince a judge, anyway. Even so, it led me to find this." Rafael held up his phone.

"I'm driving, you might've noticed," Sheryn said.

"Fine. Let the record show I'm holding up a photo of an attractive woman in her midtwenties," Rafael said. "She's got long, dark, wavy hair. If I'm being honest, she looks like a grown-up version of the woman in those kiddie-porn shots we found in Baxter's apartment."

"We don't know for certain that girl was underage."

"We have eyes," Rafael said.

"You're suggesting our victim was taking pictures of underage girls?"

Rafael heard the defensiveness in her voice. In the short time they'd worked together, he'd noted that Sheryn resolutely took the side of the victim, whether dead or alive. Rafael's worldview was darker: he saw an endless cycle of victims becoming abusers themselves and creating a new generation of victims to repeat the cycle all over again. He'd seen that play out time and time again when he was on the LAPD. He didn't have any illusions that things would be different in New York.

"I'm not saying that, because Baxter and Greaver appear to be about the same age," Rafael said. "If he took those photos, he was a kid when he did it."

"It feels wrong to find them at the crime scene, especially with his computer and phone gone," Sheryn mused. "Like they were meant to be found."

"Maybe. In any case, Jo Greaver also fits the description Srisuk gave us, as well as the mystery 911 caller. We've still got video coming in. We're going to have a busy night."

When they got down to the Flatiron District, Sheryn parked on Broadway, a couple of doors down from the building listed on the card. Rafael felt like crossing his fingers until he got inside and discovered there was an elevator. Old and rickety as it was, he was grateful, not least because he was sure that Sheryn would rather mothball him than continue waiting for him to make his way up and down staircases. When she teased him, he felt like there were teeth in it.

The Corvus Alchemy offices were on the fourth floor, with lacquered red and black walls that made Rafael think of a 1980s Robert Palmer music video. The receptionist was on the phone and barely glanced at them as they walked in.

"I'm a temp," she was telling someone. "I have no idea how to answer that. I can transfer you to voice mail." Without waiting for an answer, she pressed a couple of buttons and switched to another line. "Corvus Alchemy, how can I help you? Sorry, Ms. Greaver isn't in. Let me transfer you to Ms. Chin."

Finally, the receptionist looked at them. Her hair was auburn, and her face was blotchy, and she looked to Rafael as if she were about to explode. "It's insane here," she said.

Sheryn held up her badge. "I heard you say Jo Greaver is out. Which office is hers?"

"It's at the end of that hallway," the receptionist said, pointing to the right. She didn't seem to care who they were or what they were there for.

They strolled down the corridor. "So far, so good," Rafael said.

"Just so long as nobody starts asking for paperwork," Sheryn murmured.

The door at the end of the hall was closed but not locked. When he stepped inside, Rafael noted that the most stunning feature of Jo Greaver's office was the view. The windows were high enough to have a panoramic view of the Flatiron District but low enough to appreciate the intricate details of the surrounding buildings. It was a stone-carved menagerie of griffins and gargoyles and cherubs.

"Wow," Rafael said, taking it all in. "They put the best stuff up top, didn't they?"

"I'm sure it was something executives back in the day competed over. You know, who's got the biggest gargoyle." Sheryn looked around the office and headed straight for the glamorous Art Deco desk. Rafael noticed a laptop peeking out from under a sofa cushion, as if it were halfheartedly attempting to hide. He took a seat next to it.

"You getting comfy over there?" Sheryn asked, jiggling the mouse to wake the desktop computer.

Rafael pulled on a pair of latex gloves and reached for the laptop. It was banged up and looked out of place in the sleek office. It took a minute for the screen to come on.

"How's that for a coincidence?" Sheryn said. "Jo Greaver was searching for a defense attorney."

Rafael found himself staring at a blandly pretty blonde woman when the computer's screen lit up. He pressed a key, and the screen saver disappeared, replaced by a log-in box that read *AB's Laptop*. There was a blinking cursor in the space for a password.

"If you found a computer labeled *AB's Laptop*, do you think it's crazy to assume it was Andray Baxter's?" Rafael asked.

Sheryn's eyes popped. "You're kidding me."

"Excuse me—are you two actually cops?" asked a voice from the doorway.

Rafael looked up. The woman was young and navy haired, with a round face and meticulously applied makeup that made her look ready to appear on camera.

"Hi, I'm Detective Sterling," Sheryn said. "My partner, Detective Mendoza, and I are looking for Jo Greaver. You work here?"

"Yes. I'm Peyton Chin, Jo's assistant. What are you doing in Jo's office?"

"Like I said, looking for Jo Greaver," Sheryn answered smoothly. "Is she around?"

"I think Jo went out for a little while." The woman stepped into the room tentatively, as if she were walking on glass. "Is this about her sister?"

"Why would you think that?" Sheryn asked.

"Because whenever the police called, it was always because of Jo's sister. She died of a drug overdose."

"How long ago?" Sheryn asked.

"About a year and a half," Chin said. "It was a really tough time for Jo." She stood a little straighter. "If you're not here about Jo's sister, what are you doing with her sister's computer?"

"I wonder if there's some kind of mix-up," Rafael said. "Because this laptop actually belongs to someone else. Did Jo bring it into the office today?"

"No, a guy delivered it this afternoon."

"What guy?"

"I didn't see him. It was at the guard's desk downstairs."

"I didn't see anyone when we came in," Rafael said.

"Yeah, he disappears for long stretches," Chin said. "Calling him a *guard* is an exaggeration."

"Was it delivered in a box or a bag?" Sheryn asked. Rafael admired his partner for always being on point. He knew he could get distracted—especially these days, with an attention span that flickered like a candle—but she never seemed to.

"A brown cardboard box. It's probably around here somewhere . . ." The assistant moved around the desk. "Here it is." She pulled a cardboard box from under the desk and handed it to Sheryn.

Rafael got to his feet and crossed the room to examine it. *Ace Computer Repair* was handwritten in the top-left corner of the box, with an address of 600 West 42nd Street in New York, which Rafael was almost positive was the location of a shiny new condo and not any kind of repair shop.

"We need to dust it for prints, inside and out," Sheryn said.

"Did your boss tell you this was her sister's computer?" Rafael asked.

The assistant cocked her head, considering the question. "Yes. I saw Lori's photo on the screen and asked her about it."

"This shot?" Rafael asked, opening the laptop and waiting for the screen saver to return.

As soon as it did, Chin nodded. "That's Lori. Probably her most famous ad." She frowned. "You still haven't explained what you're doing here."

Rafael admired her tenacity. She was smart, and she wasn't going to let an unanswered question slide by.

"We think your boss was injured in an altercation today," Sheryn answered evenly.

The assistant's eyes widened. "Jo hasn't been herself today, especially since she came back this afternoon."

Ringing be damned, Rafael's ears perked up at that. "When was that?"

"Around two, I guess. She was pale. She hadn't eaten," Chin explained. "You think she's hurt?"

"We're going to need Ms. Greaver's home address," Sheryn said.

"I can't give out personal information like that . . ."

"It's okay," Rafael said. "I've already got her driver's license. She lives in a swanky building downtown."

"We should get over there now," Sheryn said.

The assistant walked out of the office.

"We've got more than enough for a warrant now," Rafael said quietly. "Can you do the honors? I want to ask the assistant something."

When he found Peyton Chin's door, it was ajar. Rafael read the nameplate and let out a whistle. "I thought you told us you were an assistant. That nameplate says vice president. Nice."

"Titles don't mean much around here." Chin hid her hands under her desk; Rafael was positive she was holding her phone. "There's a lot of work to go around."

"It's obvious you care about your boss," Rafael said, nudging the door wider and stepping inside. "Don't text Jo right now. That could be considered obstruction."

"There's a lot more to this than you're telling me," Chin said. "What's really going on?"

"Do you know an actor named Andray Baxter?"

"No. Who's that?"

"He was badly injured today," Rafael said. "We're trying to figure out how he's connected to Jo Greaver. They might've been dating."

"Definitely not. Jo's been with her boyfriend for over a year. She hardly ever dated before she met Cal."

"How long have you known Jo?"

"Five years," Chin said. "I can tell you she's a good person. I don't understand why bad things keep happening to her."

"What do you mean?"

"I've been working for Jo since she founded Corvus. When we started making money, her sister started coming around, looking for money. Lori was. . . not a good person, let's put it that way. She was downright mean to Jo." Chin paused for a moment. "Even so, Lori's death was hard on Jo. Her sister was her only family, and Jo was the one who found her body. After Lori died, there were maybe a few months that were drama-free, but it started up again a year ago. Someone sent an envelope with white powder in it. I know that probably doesn't sound like a big deal to you, but there's weird, low-grade harassment going on all the time. There have been anonymous complaints about Corvus to regulatory authorities so many times I've lost count."

"Was there anything suspicious about her sister's death?" Rafael asked.

"Lori overdosed every other week. She'd call Jo to help her, to inject her with . . ." Chin's voice trailed off.

"Naloxone?"

She nodded. "That's it. The only person who thought her death was suspicious was Jo."

"What did she say?"

"Her sister was raving about seeing a ghost." Chin leaned forward, spreading her hands wide. "I know that doesn't make any sense, but Jo kind of believes in ghosts. She'd deny that, but she's superstitious. Her sister claimed that she'd seen the ghost of her old boyfriend, some guy who OD'd years ago. Jo went to the police, because she wondered if this guy was really dead. He was some kind of sociopath, to hear her tell it."

"What happened?" Rafael asked.

"Nothing." Chin looked him in the eye. "Jo said the cops never bothered to follow up."

# CHAPTER 18

## SHERYN

Jo Greaver wasn't at her apartment, but she had been. "She was here a little while ago," said the floppy-haired blond man who answered the door. To Sheryn, he looked like he belonged in a toothpaste commercial, maybe with a golden retriever bounding along beside him on a beach. "She had to go to Chicago for an overnight trip."

"And you bought that line?" Rafael asked skeptically.

"Why would Jo lie?" The man's voice was firm, but his expression was deliberately blank, a look Sheryn had seen plenty of criminals wear in interrogation. She had the distinct feeling that this man was paranoid about giving anything away, which meant he knew there was *something* to hide.

"What's your name?" Sheryn asked.

"Cal McGarran."

Sheryn handed him the warrant. "We need you to stand back and keep out of the way, sir."

"You can't just barge in here," the man said.

"That warrant says we can, Mr. McGarran," Sheryn answered.

He unfolded it and started to read it. "I can't believe this." He stared at Sheryn. "Is this some kind of prank?"

"Do you live here?" Rafael asked.

"I moved in six months ago," McGarran said.

"Well, Cal, why don't you take a seat," Rafael said. "Because we might be here for a while."

Sheryn suppressed a smile. She's been raised in a military family, where everything was *yes, sir* and *no, ma'am* and where everyone was addressed as *Mr.* or *Mrs.* or *Miss.* Rafael's laid-back swagger would not have been appreciated by her parents, but she figured it had its uses.

Sheryn swept into the apartment, four uniformed officers trailing in her wake. "Where's Jo Greaver's computer?"

"In her office," the boyfriend said. "That's her desktop."

Sheryn headed inside, donning a pair of latex gloves. There was a large leather tote bag on the chair. She riffled through it and found a thick manila envelope full of information about cosmetics-testing laws in China, lipstick samples, and an assortment of tiny perfume bottles with code names like *XCX-76-W* written in fine black marker. Sheryn excavated it all slowly and carefully. At the bottom of the bag was a gray T-shirt with a Corvus Alchemy logo in red, black, and white; when Sheryn reached for it, she realized it was wrapped around a heavy object roughly in the shape of a triangle.

Her heart began to race.

With painstaking care, she freed the edges of the T-shirt. It was folded in half. Once the corners were untucked, she lifted it away, feeling like a magician about to pull off a trick. At the bottom of the bag was a handgun.

"I've found a weapon!" Sheryn called out. She lifted it and sniffed at the barrel. "It's been fired recently."

A uniformed officer rushed to bag it.

"Let me see," Rafael said, limping as he hurried in. The uniform handed him the bag, and Rafael held it up to examine it. He frowned. "Is that a .38 Special? What century is this?"

"It's only the most reliable revolver ever made," Sheryn said. "You know the NYPD only stopped using them a couple of years ago."

"You're kidding? The LAPD stopped in the eighties." Rafael turned to Cal McGarran, who'd followed him into the office. "You have any idea how your girlfriend got ahold of this?"

"That's not Jo's," the boyfriend said.

"I found it in her bag, wrapped in a T-shirt from her company, inside her home office," Sheryn said.

"Maybe it's a gift from the Gun Fairy," Rafael suggested. "We hear about her all the time from people who don't know how they got their guns."

"Jo doesn't own a gun," Cal McGarran insisted.

"There's a safe under the desk," Sheryn said. "You happen to know the combination, Mr. McGarran?"

"I have no idea."

"That's fine. We'll crack it." She nodded at one of the uniforms. "You feel up to that?"

"No problem, Detective."

It took a few minutes. When Sheryn looked inside, she saw a stack of folded pages. She pulled them out and stared at the one on top: it was a printout of an email from a month ago. She read it aloud. "Dear Jo, You don't know me, but I know all about you. You've done horrible things and you've never been punished for them. All of that is about to change." She looked at the boyfriend, who was staring at her with an expression she could only describe as thunderstruck. "It sounds like someone had a grudge against her. Who would that be?"

"I have no idea. Jo does so much to help other people. I can't imagine . . ." His voice trailed off.

Sheryn wanted to read more of the messages, but the rest of the contents of the safe were more pressing. She dropped the pages into a large clear plastic bag that a uniform handed to her. The next thing she pulled out of the safe was a rectangular device that was charred black and obviously broken. "Is this . . . from a computer?" she asked.

No one answered. Sheryn knew it was hard to get rid of old hard drives, but this one had its guts hanging out. It went into a plastic bag too.

Only one item remained, a cardboard box tucked into the back. Sheryn pulled it forward, then froze as she did a double take.

"What's wrong, Detective?" asked the uniform who was bagging evidence.

"This is 9-millimeter ammunition," Sheryn said quietly. "It doesn't match the gun."

Briefly, she considered asking the boyfriend if Jo Greaver had a second gun, but she knew that was pointless; McGarran was still in denial about the one they'd actually found. Instead, she handed the box to the uniform to be bagged as evidence. Then she turned her attention to the desktop computer. It blinked at her, asking for a password. Sheryn knew better than to mess with that. *Let the folks at TARU work their magic,* she thought.

There didn't seem to be much point to sifting through the cosmetics samples. Instead, Sheryn made her way to the bedroom. There was a tang of something metallic in the air. Blood. She was sure of it. "Mr. McGarran?" she called down the hallway. "What did your girlfriend do when she came home?"

"Packed an overnight bag and changed her clothes," he answered. "Why?"

Sheryn moved toward the closet, but the harsh scent wasn't any stronger there. Sheryn followed it into the bathroom, where she found a black cashmere sweater in the trash. She fished it out. It stank of congealed blood; one arm was stiff with it.

"Mr. McGarran," Sheryn said. "Was this what your girlfriend was wearing when she came home?"

"It could be." He shrugged. "She wears a lot of black."

"Sure. Typical New Yorker," Sheryn said. "Take another look. Anything about this seem strange to you?"

Cal McGarran came closer. As he did, his face registered distaste, then shifted to worry. "Is that . . . blood?"

"It is. Your girl's in serious trouble, Mr. McGarran."

"What do you mean?"

"We believe she may have been shot this afternoon," Sheryn said. "That means she's been bleeding for hours. She's probably in shock and struggling. Losing blood doesn't help your brain function."

"How could she have been shot?" He was incredulous. "That's impossible. She couldn't hide that from me. Could she?"

Sheryn studied him closely. "Has she hidden other things from you, Mr. McGarran?"

He didn't answer, but the way his face fell told Sheryn exactly what she needed to know. "Help us find her," Sheryn said.

"She told me she was flying to Chicago. But I had my doubts about that. She hates airplanes."

"I don't think she'd fly," Sheryn said. "Too much risk of discovery. Plus, there's a lot of security, and if someone sees blood, she's going to be hauled aside."

"Besides, we've got the airports on alert," Rafael added. "They're looking for her. Try again."

"You *don't* think she's going on a business trip?" Cal McGarran's expression was pleading.

"I do not," Sheryn said. "Who would she turn to for help?"

"No one," he said. "Jo doesn't have any family. Her parents died years ago, and her sister died before I met her. She doesn't have any close friends, outside of her staff. They're a really tight group."

"Where's Jo from?"

"Kentucky. But she hasn't been back there since she left on a bus when she was a teenager."

"She's going to need urgent medical care, Cal," Rafael said. "I bet she hasn't sought it out already because she knows gunshot wounds are automatically reported to the police."

"She might take a train," the boyfriend said. "Last year, we took the Surfliner from Los Angeles to San Diego. She likes trains, except . . ."

"Focus, please," Sheryn said. "Where would she *go*?"

"I have no idea."

Sheryn believed him, but that didn't make her any less frustrated.

"But Manhattan's an island," he added. "It's tough to escape an island."

"Mr. McGarran, you're zeroing in on *how* she would leave," Sheryn said. "We have an APB out on her, so she can't use her credit cards, but she probably hired a gypsy cab and paid cash. We're not going to catch her at one of the tunnels. That's why we need to figure out where she'd be heading."

"Jo won't take any of the tunnels, ever. She has claustrophobia. It's why she won't fly unless she absolutely has to."

"What are you saying?"

"She takes Xanax if she has to fly. And she didn't bring it with her. I checked."

Sheryn and Rafael looked at each other. "Did you notice anything else?"

Cal McGarran looked down, and his mouth quivered. "Dramamine," he said. "She took a bottle of that with her."

"Thank you, Mr. McGarran," Sheryn answered. "That's actually very helpful."

# CHAPTER 19

## Jo

Jo knew it was only a matter of time before the police found her. When she'd left her apartment that morning, she'd been hopeful about paying her blackmailer to go away. But there had been a fear lurking in the back of her brain that she might end up dead.

*JoJo, you won't believe it, but I saw a ghost today.*

That was one of the last things her sister had said to her, and it haunted Jo. Normally, when her sister got in touch, a cash infusion was involved, but for once, Lori had wanted to talk about something other than money.

*What are you talking about?* Jo had asked her over the crackling phone line. *What ghost?*

*I saw the man I love,* Lori had said. *The one you destroyed.*

That had taken Jo's breath away. *You saw Dom?* she'd asked, her voice choking on the name.

*I did. He's as handsome a devil as ever.*

*This isn't funny,* Jo had pleaded. *You told me he was dead. He is. Isn't he?*

Lori had laughed at that, a sly, malicious laugh that sent chills down Jo's spine. She'd hung up on Jo without another word. Jo had raced over to Lori's apartment to find her sister comatose. The naloxone hadn't brought her back. When Jo had called 911, her sister was already gone.

In the days and months afterward, Jo tried to tell herself that Lori had been raving. Her sister had seen someone who looked like her dead love, and it had set her on a fatal path. Jo herself saw no evidence of ghosts, or that Dom was anything but dust at this point. But a seed of doubt was planted in her brain. After years of certainty that her sister's monstrous boyfriend was gone from the face of the earth, the specter of his reappearance suddenly felt like a possibility. The suspicion ran deep in her bones, no matter how much her conscious mind rejected it.

That was why she'd bought a gun. It was a doubly foolish thing to do, she knew, because it was against the law, and anyway, what ghost was ever stopped by bullets? Jo wasn't sorry she'd brought it with her to meet her blackmailer. She hadn't meant to kill anyone. That had been self-defense. But in the end, that fact didn't matter: she was a murderer, and when people found out the truth about her, her life would be over. Her brain was spiraling, and she couldn't come up with a plan. She had to buy time.

She'd retrieved her passport to give her options, but she knew she couldn't fly anywhere in her current state. She needed to get out of Manhattan, and she was aware her options were limited. Briefly, she considered taking the ferry to Staten Island—South Ferry was walking distance from her apartment—but she knew she'd be stuck without a car once she landed there, unless she wanted to give away her location by using a credit card. Getting across the Hudson River to New Jersey was her main concern. The easiest route would be to take the PATH train from World Trade Center Station to Hoboken or Newark; that trip was fast and easy, and she could use her MetroCard to do it. But the risk was huge: WTC Station was crawling with police, and she knew she'd be conspicuous with her bag. She went with her last option.

New York Waterways had ferry service between Pier 11, at the foot of Wall Street, and several New Jersey cities. She paid for a ticket in cash and waited. Unlike summer, it wasn't crowded or even busy. Her plan was simple: get to New Jersey, then take SEPTA down to Philadelphia and head south. She'd bought her gun in Virginia. If she got that far, she figured she could chance seeking treatment for her wound at a hospital; even if they had a mandatory-reporting rule, she wouldn't be connected with any shooting in New York.

All of this made sense until she was actually aboard the boat and it pulled away from the dock. She'd already been feeling light-headed, and she'd bought a bottle of orange juice to keep her going. But on the boat, she started to feel ill. It was as if her insides were churning in concert with the water. The Dramamine did nothing to quell them.

*Do you ever feel guilty for what you've done?*

The dead man's words popped into her head, jolting her as if they were tinged with electricity. What right did he have to ask her that? She'd never met him before—she was certain of that—but he'd stared at her with a dead certainty, as if he'd known her inside out. She'd been a victim, but she'd also made an awful lot of decisions that she wasn't proud of. *You were just a kid,* she reminded herself, but there was no comfort in that thought. She had been a kid with unusual drive and fierceness. She had been a kid willing to do anything to survive.

Jo got up and slowly made her way to the back of the ferry, looking for a portal that would lead out to the deck, like the Staten Island Ferry had. Too late, she realized the boat had no external deck. That made sense with the wintery chill, but it was a nightmare for someone desperate for a breath of fresh air.

She sat down again and bowed her head, hoping she wouldn't throw up. When she realized that she was definitely going to, she stumbled to the toilet, vomiting before the door closed behind her.

When the ferry finally pulled into the dock at Port Imperial/Weehawken, Jo tried to exit on rubbery legs but found she couldn't stand without the support of a wall. When all the other passengers had gone, she decided she had to follow them out before the staff threw her on the dock. Moving carefully, she clutched the railing, but she was so dizzy and disoriented that she tripped and fell. Lying on cold metal, Jo realized she'd been so desperate to run away from what had happened that it never occurred to her that her own body might fail her.

It was almost a relief when she opened her eyes and saw two pairs of ugly black cop shoes in front of her. She couldn't even lift her head to see if they wore New York or New Jersey uniforms.

"I've been shot," she mumbled, her mouth still tasting of bile.

If one of the cops answered, she didn't hear it. Scenes from the day were flashing in front of Jo's eyes: her blackmailer's cruel mouth as he mocked her, his astonished expression as she shot him; her terror as she ran, directionless, through Hell's Kitchen and Times Square; Peyton's kindness; Cal's real concern for her and his mother's phony platitudes. But it was Annabelle's agonized face saying *I didn't mean to cause you pain* that stayed with her until she passed out cold.

# CHAPTER 20

## Cal

After the police announced that Jo was in custody and being brought back from New Jersey to Manhattan, they finally left the apartment. Their parting shot was that Cal wouldn't be allowed to see Jo that evening, because she'd be under arrest but in a hospital for medical treatment and observation. Cal paced through the rooms, uncertain what to do. He'd never encountered a situation like this in his life. Even when his father had been arrested, he'd been allowed to surrender himself to police custody in the company of his lawyer. If uniformed officers had carried items out of his parents' apartment as they had out of his home with Jo, he hadn't seen it happen.

*I don't even know how to help her,* he thought.

Her office didn't really look that different: the police hadn't touched the boxes of makeup samples, which were still neatly stacked. Jo's icon wall was intact, and her desk and chair were in place. The police had left with her desktop computer and the contents of her safe. Jo's black tote bag was gone too; Cal supposed that made sense, since it was where they had found the gun. Or so they claimed; Cal still had doubts.

He hadn't seen them remove anything from inside the desk, but that didn't mean they hadn't. He picked up the little crow figurine Jo kept on her desk. It was cheap black plastic with fake feathers and eyes that gleamed ominously. Aside from the icon wall, it was the only hint of personality in the room. Cal turned it over in his hand; it was virtually weightless.

*Why wouldn't you tell me what's wrong?* Cal wondered, staring at the bird as if it could answer for Jo. *Why wouldn't you trust me?*

He knew he wasn't going to find any answers in that room. After changing into jeans and a casual shirt, he pulled on a jacket and took the 5 express train up to Union Square. It was a quick trip up, but there was a foul-smelling homeless man screaming at everyone trapped in the metal carriage. He had barely registered on Cal. All that was running through his head was what Detective Sterling had read aloud from the pages she'd extracted from Jo's safe. Dear Jo, You don't know me, but I know all about you. You've done horrible things and you've never been punished for them. All of that is about to change. Cal couldn't even imagine who could have written that. But he thought he might know someone who would.

He exited Union Square Station into a cold, dark night. The police hadn't given him any details about Jo, except to say that she likely had a bullet wound. Where had she been and what had she done?

Cal didn't want to be the suspicious type. He knew enough men who fit that description, men who expected to know exactly where their girlfriends were and what they were doing at any given time. But he felt desperate to get to the truth. If the police were right, Jo had stood in their home with a bullet hole in her arm and lied to his face.

*Jo wouldn't buy a gun,* Cal kept telling himself as he walked toward his mother's apartment. It was several blocks east of Gramercy Park, where he'd grown up. *Jo wouldn't buy a gun.*

*Do you think the police planted that gun they found?* asked a voice in the back of his mind. He didn't have an answer for that. He trusted the police yet couldn't accept what had happened. There had to be another explanation.

There was no doorman at his mother's building—it wasn't that kind of place—but he had his own key. He took the stairs up to the third floor and let himself into her apartment. The lights were off, indicating that his mother had probably gone to bed early—hardly a surprise, given how she was feeling that afternoon. He turned on the hallway light and another in the living room. His mother's gray Persian cat, Sukie, dozed on a vintage Louis XV chair, one of the family treasures his mother had managed to hold on to. The cat lifted her head and gave Cal the evil eye before closing her eyes again.

The fact that the cat was in the living room and not the bedroom suggested that his mother had gone out, but Cal padded down the hall to her bedroom to be certain. The door was open. He flicked his hand against the light switch on the wall, briefly illuminating his mother's personal sanctuary, where the walls were wrapped in pale-pink damask silk like an opulent cocoon. The bed was topped with a billowing canopy, and its legs were hidden by a flouncy skirt. She had re-created her old bedroom almost perfectly, even if the scale was off. He was close to his mother, especially after what happened with his father. He found it disconcerting that his mother clung to the past, dreaming of the days when she was a lady who lunched rather than one who had to work for a living to support herself. Cal flicked off the light quickly.

He sat quietly in the living room, patting the imperious Sukie; she accepted some of it as tribute but occasionally reached out to swat at him. Finally, he heard a key in the lock of the front door. He didn't want to startle his mother. But he was the one who was surprised, because there was a peal of laughter that rang out, loud and delighted.

"Mom?" he called out.

The laughter stopped abruptly. The front door closed, but he didn't hear the lock turn.

"Calton?" his mother called. "Is that you?"

Cal closed the distance between them. The first thing he noticed was that his mother was dressed up for a Monday night. She was shrugging off her fox-fur coat, revealing an oyster-gray jacket and skirt. Odder still was there was a man beside her who looked about Cal's age. He was tall and dark haired, with his broad-shouldered frame tucked into a charcoal-gray suit. His eyes were blue and his skin lightly tanned, as if he'd been on a beach earlier that month. Cal stared at him, aware he knew the man but confused because he couldn't quite place him.

"Hello, Cal!" The other man extended his hand with a lopsided but delighted grin. "It's been forever since I saw you. How are you?"

It hit Cal in an instant; that smile hadn't changed. He had known Zachary Lytton-Davies for most of his life, on account of their mothers' friendship; Zachary was a couple of years younger than Cal. Zachary had disappeared for a while when his mother had remarried and moved across the country. Back then, Zachary had looked like the *before* image in one of those old Charles Atlas ads with a beanpole getting sand kicked in his face. Since then, Zachary had doubled in size.

"I'm fine," Cal lied, shaking his hand. It didn't matter that his girlfriend was in police custody; it was the only answer he had been raised to give. "How are you doing?"

"Keeping out of trouble, mostly," Zachary said. "Where are you working now?"

"Asmodeus Capital."

Zachary blinked at that. "They're naming hedge funds after demons now? Did they run out of ancient monsters?"

Cal's boss *was* almost supernaturally bad. He remembered that Zachary had been a nerd, eager to show off his command of trivia. "Most people have no clue. They think my boss must be a rabid Mozart fan. What are you up to?"

"I'm working for Serge's dad. It's a little weird, but it's okay."

It was Cal's turn to blink. His friend Serge Severight had died in an accident in college, and the last time Cal had seen his father was on the day of the funeral.

"Would you like to stay for a drink, Zachary?" Cal's mother asked. "You two could catch up a little."

"I wish I could, but I have such an early start," Zachary said. "It was truly a pleasure to see both of you, though. Night, all."

Cal waited until his mother had shut the door and turned the lock. "I didn't realize that you and Annabelle had buried the hatchet," he said hurriedly. "Look, I'm sorry to show up like this, but something terrible's happened to Jo."

"What do you mean?" Sukie gave an insistent meow, and that grabbed his mother's attention. She strode into the apartment, picked up the cat, and sat down, cradling the furry creature in her lap.

"The police came to our apartment this evening, and they . . . they were looking for Jo. With a warrant. And a gun." The words were tumbling out of him in a jumbled torrent. "I mean that they found a gun. At least, they claim they did."

His mother was watching him closely. "What's that supposed to mean?"

"They went into her home office and went through all of her things. There was a gun in her bag," Cal said. "But the more I think about it, the more impossible it seems. Jo doesn't have a gun. Someone had to have planted it there."

"Oh, no." Her cheeks colored, blooming poppy red on her carefully powdered face. "That's horrible. Poor Jo. I've always been afraid . . ." She took a deep breath and shook her head. "How can I help?"

Cal sank into a chair, trying to gather his thoughts. "Something's going on with Jo. Things have been strange with her for weeks. She won't tell me anything."

"What did the police say?"

"They wouldn't tell me what had happened, except to say that she had been shot," Cal said.

"Shot?" His mother repeated in astonishment. "Is she . . ."

"They said she'll be okay, but they wouldn't give me any other details. They took some things out of the apartment—her computer, her bag. She's in custody now."

"I can't believe this is happening." Her hand floated to her forehead. "It's like . . . it's like the situation with your father all over again." She massaged her temple. "Can you see Jo? Ask her to explain?"

"No, she's at a hospital tonight. I can't see her until court tomorrow morning." Cal took a deep breath. "I need to talk to your private detective."

"Why?" his mother asked. "I've already told you everything he told me."

"I need to talk to his sources."

"How would that help anything?"

"I need to understand what's going on," Cal said. "Jo won't tell me. I don't see any other way."

"You wouldn't believe me when I told you what he'd found." His mother's voice was soft, but there was reproach in it. "I warned you about Jo's past. She worked as an escort. I didn't want to believe it, but . . ."

"It's not that I didn't believe him," Cal said. "But I decided that I didn't care."

"No one can ever run away from their past. Not for long, at least." She folded her hands in her lap. "I objected to your relationship when I found out about Jo's past. I regret that now, because I can see that she's a good person. Has Jo ever admitted anything about her past to you?"

"No, and I've never asked."

"You're a good man. I'm proud that you're my son, Calton," she said. "But you can't be in a relationship with a person who deliberately lies to you."

"Jo's not."

"Well, she isn't being honest with you."

Cal couldn't argue with that. Jo had told him stories about her past—her mother's drinking and black eyes, her sister's casual cruelty when an orphaned Jo came to live with her in New York—but she'd never mentioned anything more about her early life than family drama. Cal never felt he had the right to ask about it. After all, he'd told her something of his father's crimes and his own shame—details about his father's case were a mere click away—but he'd never revealed the whole story. It was buried in the past, and Cal wasn't one who wanted to exhume history. He kept moving forward, and he believed Jo preferred that too. For the first time he was wondering if he should have pressed for a deeper conversation, for some sort of reckoning of their respective pasts.

"No one tells you everything about themselves," Cal said. "Do you tell every man you date about your ex-husband?"

"Your question presumes that I am dating." His mother's voice assumed its usual hauteur again. "I can assure you I'm not."

"Would you want your friends to know every last detail about you?"

"That's not the same thing."

Cal knew it wasn't, and he was too tired to argue the point anyway. "I need the name of the investigator you hired."

"I don't think that's a good idea," his mother answered. "Jo wasn't out robbing banks. Unless you want to torture yourself with all the gory details of Jo's days as an escort, I suggest you drop this. It's not going to help you, and it won't help Jo now."

"I still wish you hadn't done it," Cal said. He understood where his mother was coming from—after her experience with his father, of course she was suspicious of everyone—but he couldn't condone her meddling.

"One day, when you have a child of your own, you'll understand. There's nothing more important than protecting your child."

"Do I need to remind you that I'm twenty-seven years old?"

"When you get to my age, that will sound like a baby."

"I should get going," Cal said. It embarrassed him to talk about Jo with his mother, as if he was proving that she had been right all along.

"What's going to happen to Jo?" she asked quickly. "You said she had to go to court tomorrow."

"That's what the police said."

"*Why* does she have to show up in court?" his mother asked. "That's what I'm asking. Just because of a gun?"

"I don't know the full story yet," Cal admitted. "The police wouldn't tell me much."

"Have you found her a lawyer yet?"

Her question made him feel stupid; of course Jo needed a lawyer. That should've been his first thought. "Not yet."

"I can help with that. I know some people." She patted Cal's cheek, as if he were still a child. "Jo's a tough creature. She always lands on her feet. She'll get through this. You have to trust in that." She glanced at her watch. "I'll make some calls right now."

"It's late."

"Criminal defense attorneys never sleep," she said. "Let me help you with this. I know Jo and I aren't that close, but she matters to you, so she matters to me. I'll do everything I can."

# CHAPTER 21

## SHERYN

"You know what's completely unsatisfying?" Sheryn asked her partner.

They were sitting side by side in a corridor at Bellevue Hospital, waiting for a signal from the doctors. "I'm assuming that's a rhetorical question," Rafael murmured, his eyes on the screen of his phone.

"There's no joy in arresting somebody who's basically passed out. I think we need to Mirandize her again."

"We can do that when we arrest her for murder," he said. "Right now, she's only up for illegal possession of a handgun."

"One felony down, a few more to go," Sheryn quipped.

"You're assuming the ADA will charge a wealthy white lady with felony possession. That's anything but a done deal."

Sheryn sighed. "If I'm being honest, I don't think she's in this alone. I was just looking at the housing court records. You remember what Ornelle Baxter told us about Elliott Westergard harassing her son? It's worse than that." She held up her phone. "At least six times, Andray Baxter found equipment illegally set up in his apartment to spy on him. Video and audio. Gizmos that looked like a transformer you'd plug into the wall for a computer." She set the phone in her lap. "I'm not saying it makes him a killer, but Westergard needs to be locked up. He's in this somehow."

"You must really be mad," Rafael observed. "You didn't call him *Mr.* Westergard."

"My temper's getting the better of me," Sheryn deadpanned.

"Did you read all the emails Baxter sent to Greaver?" Rafael asked.

"I only saw the first one."

"Right. 'Dear Jo, You don't know me, but I know all about you. You've done horrible things and you've never been punished for them. All of that is about to change,'" Rafael read aloud. "Greaver didn't respond to that one. Then he emailed, 'Dear Jo, You were never a successful model like your sister, but I suppose you had your moments. Do you think your boyfriend and your investors and your customers would like to see these?' That's when he attached some photos."

"How would he have gotten his hands on those?" Sheryn asked. "That's a detail that bothers me."

"Maybe TARU can figure that out," Rafael said. "They're working overtime matching up their correspondence. Baxter clearly knew secrets about Greaver's past. He wasn't explicit about it, but there's definitely a sexual overtone to it. Listen to this: 'Dear Jo, You were never innocent. You were always a disgusting whore who enjoyed being degraded.'"

Sheryn winced. "He starts every message 'Dear Jo.' It's . . . oddly formal, especially when he's calling her a whore."

"That *is* weird."

"Do you think she was trafficked? That's what those photos look like."

"That's what it sounds like. Baxter uploaded a video at one point, but it was to an outside source. TARU says the video's gone. It wasn't downloaded on Greaver's computer, but they're positive she viewed it. The email with it said, 'Dear Jo, Do you ever feel guilty for what you've done? You must. Imagine what the police would do if they found out . . .'" Rafael shook his head. "That got a reaction from Greaver. She wrote back, 'Tell me what you want.' He said a hundred thousand. She said that was impossible. Then they haggled to fifty thousand."

"Blackmailer's not a good look," Sheryn said. "I can't help but think what Andray Baxter's mama will feel when she finds out. She talked about her boy like he's a saint."

"Isn't that what all parents think about their kids?" Rafael asked.

"You've never met my mother. She's my biggest critic," Sheryn said. "But I take your point. My kids are the best, and that is that."

"My mom loves me, but my dad is another story," Rafael admitted. "When I was a teenager, he used to call me *peuchen*. Think of it as the Chilean version of a shape-shifting vampire."

"Clearly a reference to the hours you keep," Sheryn said. "*Peuchen*. I'm gonna remember that one."

"Please don't," Rafael said. "He only started calling me that after I came out. He wasn't thrilled."

The sound of footsteps on the white tile floor caught their attention. There was a doctor coming toward them, her gold-framed glasses glinting under the fluorescent light. Her dreadlocks were pulled up and fell in an elegant cascade.

"Jo Greaver lost a lot of blood, and her heart rate's still on the high side, but she's in stable condition," the doctor said. "If you want to speak with her now, you can. She's legit exhausted, though, so I don't want you talking for long."

"That's fine," Sheryn said. "How bad is her wound?"

"The bullet passed through her arm—she's lucky it didn't hit bone—but it tore out some flesh. She'll be on antibiotics for a few days."

Sheryn and Rafael followed her back to a private room with its walls painted a sallow yellow. Jo Greaver lay in bed with her long, dark curls fanning around her face like a mermaid's hair. The upper third of the bed was in the up position. Greaver's right wrist was shackled to the metal railing with handcuffs.

"Good evening, Ms. Greaver," Sheryn said. "I'm Detective Sheryn Sterling. This is my partner, Detective Mendoza. How are you feeling?"

Jo Greaver blinked at her. "Peachy. Obviously." She sounded breathless, as if she'd run a marathon.

"You understand that you're under arrest for possession of a firearm?" Rafael asked. "You have the right to remain . . ."

"Not again. I've heard all this already."

"We need to ask you a few questions about a man named Andray Baxter," Sheryn said.

"I don't know who that is," Greaver said.

"I don't believe he ever gave you his name when he was sending you those threatening messages," Sheryn said. "From an online account called 123ABJG666 . . ." She stopped reading the long string of characters, figuring the first half was enough to be recognizable.

Greaver pursed her lips and sighed, but she didn't answer that.

"Here's a photograph of Mr. Baxter, to help you put the name with the face," Sheryn said. She held up her phone so that the woman could see the screen, and she watched her closely for her reaction.

"Who's that?" Greaver looked puzzled.

"You encountered him early this afternoon," Sheryn said. "Let's not be coy here, Ms. Greaver. This is the man you shot."

"No." Greaver leaned closer to the screen; the effort made her paler. "That wasn't the guy."

"You *admit* you shot a man this afternoon?"

"I'm not admitting anything," Greaver said. "Except that if I *did* encounter a blackmailer today, he was white. That's definitely not the man."

# CHAPTER 22

## Jo

Jo's head had been swirling since before she'd set foot on the boat. Part of her wondered if she was trapped in a nightmare. A man had lured her to his apartment—well, someone's apartment—and tried to murder her that afternoon. She'd been trailing blood since then, trapped on every side and waiting until it was too late to run. Now, there was a pair of cops showing her a photo of a handsome black man who looked absolutely nothing like the creep who'd handed her pornographic photos of her teenage self and then fired a gun at her.

"*This* is Andray Baxter," the female detective, Sterling, was saying. "You went to his apartment today."

"I went to an address," Jo said. "No name, just an address. The man who answered the door was white. He was wearing a ball cap. I didn't get a great look at him, but he was definitely not black. I can tell you that for sure. But . . ."

"But what?"

"There was a painting of baby Jesus and Mary and Joseph on the wall, and they were black," Jo said. "I remember noticing that. It was . . . odd, I guess? I mean I'd never seen a painting like that before. Everything happened so fast. When I looked at it . . ." Her voice trailed off. *I thought I saw blood.* But that made no sense, even to her. There had been a kaleidoscope of colors on that canvas. "I got scared because I thought I saw blood."

"Blood? On the painting?"

Jo nodded.

"Why were you at that particular apartment?" Sterling asked.

The question hit Jo like a hammer. *Never talk to the cops,* Lori had warned her when she'd first come to New York. *They are not your friends.* And there she was, faint headed and spilling her guts to them. "Who says I was?" she challenged, aware that she couldn't take back what she'd already tacitly admitted.

"Well, there was an eyewitness who saw you," Sterling said. "But the fingerprint and DNA evidence are what's really conclusive."

"You just took my prints," Jo said. "You're going to pretend you matched them already?"

The cops gave each other a quick but sharp look.

"I mean, those fingerprints could've been left at any time," Mendoza added. "But the blood? That was fresh. And you have a matching wound. There's no point denying you were there."

Jo closed her eyes and tried to steady her nerves. In spite of her bravado, she was genuinely terrified. She had no idea what to do.

"Look," Sterling said. "You have no reason to trust us. We get that. But right now, it's looking like you went to that apartment to commit murder. Give us another reason."

"I need to talk to a lawyer," Jo said.

"Sure. You should know that our technical unit has been going through your email," Sterling answered. "Also, we found Andray Baxter's laptop in your office."

"It was delivered to me this afternoon," Jo said softly. "I have absolutely no idea who sent it. My assistant brought it in."

"That would be Peyton Chin?" Mendoza asked.

"Yes. I guess you talked to her."

"We did. She had a similar story," Mendoza said.

"It's not a story," Jo answered. "I don't know why it was delivered to my office."

"We were wondering about that too," Sterling said. "A witness saw you go out the window and down the fire escape. That witness said you grabbed the railing with both hands. You weren't carrying off the victim's computer. It seemed like someone else must've carried it out and sent it to you."

Jo was afraid to say too much. On the one hand, the police could be screwing with her. *The cops are allowed to lie to you long and loud,* Lori had always warned her. *They play games with your head.* Even so, it was hard to figure out why they were showing her some random man's photograph. She'd shot her blackmailer in the chest; she was almost certain he was dead.

*Almost* wasn't good enough, though.

"Maybe you're not alone in this?" Sterling added. "If you're not, why should you take the fall for it? You should help yourself."

"I need a lawyer," Jo said. "I shouldn't be talking to you without one. I'm exhausted and confused, and I really need to sleep."

"Sure," Sterling said. "But I should let you know we also found your gun."

Jo felt like she was going to choke. "What?"

"It was in your tote bag," Sterling said. "In your home office."

"But I . . ." *But I threw it away,* Jo's mind screamed. *I threw it into the Hudson River.*

"Don't worry—we'll get this all sorted out," Sterling said. "Sleep tight."

# TUESDAY

# CHAPTER 23

## SHERYN

It was long past midnight when Sheryn finally arrived home that night. Mentally, she'd been rehearsing what she wanted to say to her son. She wasn't any less upset with Martin than she'd been that afternoon, when she'd collected him downtown from the First Precinct. She'd left a long voice mail for her husband, Douglass, explaining what had happened, but they hadn't had the chance to talk about it. The late hour meant that everything would be tabled until tomorrow; that left her feeling unsettled and unhappy. She'd never been a person who put off until tomorrow what she could take care of today. But a conversation with Martin would simply have to wait.

What caught her attention, after she came inside and locked the door, was a note on the kitchen table in Douglass's elegant handwriting.

> *Took the kids to my parents' for the evening. Leftovers*
> *are the blue-plate special. Love you.*

There were only a few words, but Sheryn stared at them for a long time. She loved her father-in-law, but Douglass's mother was another story; the woman never passed up the opportunity to criticize Sheryn, particularly for her career choices. *Don't overreact,* she warned herself. *Your mother-in-law would* love *that.*

To calm herself, Sheryn opened the fridge and discovered there was indeed a blue plate waiting for her with Sunday's pork loin, garlic mashed potatoes, and glazed carrots neatly arranged on it. That had been a joke, early in their marriage, about the blue-plate special. But she and Rafael had grabbed sandwiches at the hospital after Jo Greaver had been brought in; it had been a woefully spartan dinner by her standards. Still, it was too late for Douglass's blue-plate special, unless she wanted a worse case of indigestion than she already had. She closed the fridge and went to check on her kids.

She slipped into Mercy's room and kissed her daughter's forehead. Her eight-year-old's face was beatific; to Sheryn, she really did look like an angel. When Sheryn stopped at Martin's door, she raised her hand to knock. It was tricky having a fourteen-year-old: he was adult enough to know his own mind—most of the time—but enough of a child still not to think out all the consequences. Instead of knocking, she gently eased his door open, just as she had with Mercy's. Martin was asleep, but there was a flashlight—still on—beside him and a paperback book unceremoniously plopped in front of it. Sheryn walked in and picked up the book, recognizing the copy of Octavia Butler's *Survivor* that she'd given him for his last birthday. Her love of science fiction was one trait she'd passed along, at least. She closed the book and set it on his night table, leaned in to kiss his cheek, and turned off the flashlight, setting it on his desk on her way out of his room. She closed the door behind her.

Her husband was in bed, too, but he was still awake, with a copy of *Americanah* in his hands. "Late night," he said quietly when she walked into their bedroom. "Must be some case you're working on."

"It is. There's a young man shot dead, and I can't figure out whether he was a victim or a criminal," Sheryn said, slipping off her suit jacket. "None of it's sitting well with me, truth be told."

"Good thing you're on it."

She didn't answer that, instead pretending to focus on undressing. She pulled a robe on while her back was still to her husband, as sure a sign she was disgruntled with him as anything.

"How was it you decided to take the kids out to your parents' on a school night?" Sheryn asked.

"Well, I figured after the day Martin had, he needed a break," Douglass answered.

"I'm sure your mother had some choice words about the NYPD."

"About the failures of the justice system in this country, yes. But she was upset with Martin too. He's pretty shaken up by the whole experience."

"Shaken up enough not to do something that stupid again?" Sheryn asked.

"He understands that he needs to be more careful," Douglass said. "But I think his moral compass is working just right."

Sheryn didn't answer that. Barefoot, she padded to the bathroom. She carefully unpinned her hair and wrapped it in a silk scarf. Then she brushed her teeth and washed her face and massaged some marula oil into her skin. She decided that was enough for one day.

Douglass was still pretending to read when she got into bed next to him. "You going to turn off that light?" she asked.

"I can't. That would break the rule."

"What rule?"

"We're not supposed to go to bed angry," Douglass said. "You know that."

"I'm not angry," Sheryn said. "I'm worried. I'm fearful. I'm concerned that my son is going to end up a statistic."

"Martin's not a little kid anymore. We raised him right. He cares about justice. He wouldn't be our kid if he didn't."

"This isn't about his *heart* being in the right place," Sheryn said. "This is about *him* being in the wrong place at the wrong time."

"You can't think only about what-ifs. Not if it's going to keep you from doing the right thing."

"You think it's fine that he ditched school for this?" Sheryn knew that would hit a nerve. Douglass taught high school English to kids considered at risk, which meant they'd gotten into trouble already. She was well aware that he impressed upon them that there was no such thing as an acceptable reason for cutting his class.

"No," Douglass said seriously. "Not at all. I told him literally nothing in life is more important than his education right now. I talked to him about that the way I talk to my kids." Sheryn knew by *my kids*, he meant his students, the teenagers who'd been in and out of foster homes and state care so often it must've felt like their lives were playing out in one big revolving door. "But this isn't really about cutting school, is it?"

"It's bigger than that," Sheryn said.

"You have to trust that we raised him right."

"You could raise the best boys in the world, and some of them will still be cut down by bullets." Her chest felt heavy, as if there were a stone pressing on her heart.

"You can't expect him not to move forward in this world because of what other people might do," Douglass pointed out.

"I really need to get some sleep."

"Not if you're still mad."

"I'm not angry at you," Sheryn said. "I'm angry that there's an additional set of rules my son has to follow, that he doesn't get to make innocent mistakes. I'm angry that the stakes are always so damn high."

"I know," Douglass said, turning out the light and leaning close to kiss her. "I am too."

# CHAPTER 24

## Jo

Jo lay quietly in the darkness. Sleep wouldn't come. Her brain was going full tilt, whirling like a pinball from past to present. She was determined to make sense of the madness she was caught up in.

The problem was she didn't even know where to begin.

Jo was positive she'd never so much as laid eyes on Andray Baxter before. *Why would the cops show me his picture?* she asked herself. There was no good reason for it. She wasn't crazy, and she wasn't drunk or high. The man who'd shot her—the man *she'd* shot, the one she'd left writhing in pain on a linoleum floor—had vanished like a ghost.

Fear coursed through her body. The man she'd shot was out there, somewhere. The police didn't know where he was—or who he was.

Jo opened her eyes and stared at the ceiling, trying to conjure his face from memory. When he'd opened the door, the stupid ball cap parked on his head was the thing that really stood out. It had been black. The man's skin had looked deeply tanned, but she hadn't taken him for anything other than white.

*You must be Jo,* he'd said. When she'd pointed out that she didn't know his name, he'd smiled. *Guilty as charged. Come on in.*

She wished she could get another look at the photo the police had shown her. She didn't want to be in fear for her life; it would be easier if she knew the name of her assailant, if she understood why he'd wanted to torment her. *Maybe I made a mistake,* she thought. Lighting could make a person's skin lighter or darker, she reasoned. But it couldn't make the grim lips of the man she'd met transform into the full mouth of the one in the photograph. The body the police had found belonged to a different man.

That raised terrifying questions in Jo's mind, starting with where the man she'd shot had gone. Was he still alive? What if he was quietly recuperating in a safe house, planning to finish what he'd started and murder her?

She tried to keep her breathing steady. Her mouth was dry as bone, but she didn't want to ring for a nurse. She needed to be alone to piece everything together.

The man's face was fuzzy in her memory, but his voice wasn't.

*I'll tell you what I wonder about,* he'd said. *Do you ever feel guilty for what you've done?*

Jo remembered how he'd eyed her. Time had slowed down, and the walls had moved closer, boxing her in so that there could be no escape.

*Most people would feel bad, I bet.*

Jo had assumed he was talking about the video, and then he'd handed her those awful photographs.

*You had one hot little bod, didn't you? I've gotta say, first time I saw those, I thought,* Wow. *But then, I also thought,* Where were that girl's parents?

Was she supposed to feel bad about something she'd had no choice in? It wasn't as if she'd had parents to protect her. She'd never known her father, and her mother had perished from a fatal combination of bad drugs and bad boyfriends. Getting on that bus to New York when she was fourteen hadn't been a choice; it had been her only hope of survival. She'd gone straight to what she thought was her sister's apartment, only to discover it was a post office box. Not knowing where else to go, she'd waited there for seventeen hours, hungry and fearful and afraid to stop moving. She hadn't done that because she'd had options. Her sister hadn't been happy to see her . . .

Jo's thoughts came to a screeching halt. Her sister. She could feel bile rising in her throat. It was almost as if Lori were stretching one bony arm out to wave at her. *Miss me much, JoJo?* Lori would ask whenever they hadn't seen each other for a long time.

*Not one bit,* Jo had always wanted to answer, but she'd never had the nerve to say that to Lori's face.

*Miss me much, JoJo?* That was how Lori had greeted her when she'd shown up at the Corvus Alchemy office out of the blue three years earlier.

*What are you doing here?* Jo had demanded.

Lori had been a beauty once, but years of substance abuse had left her wan and wraithlike, and her sly smile had felt like a threat. *Imagine my surprise when I heard my baby sister is running her own company. Who ever imagined you'd be the successful one in the family? You were always so shy.*

Lori had made it clear that day that if Jo wanted her to go away, she'd have to pay her. *Don't think of it as blackmail,* Lori had said, her eyes gleaming like a crow's. *Think of it as helping out family that's down on their luck.*

Jo had gritted her teeth and paid her to go away. It wasn't the last time Lori had shown up on her doorstep, and it wasn't even the worst, but it was the first step down a path Jo never wanted to take.

She didn't understand why the memory made her hot under her skin. Her sister wasn't her blackmailer this time. Lori had been dead for a year and a half, her emaciated pincushion of a body cremated out in Queens. Lori hadn't faked her death; Jo had touched her cold skin and understood that the last bit of family she'd had in the world was gone. But Jo found herself wondering if one of Lori's shady friends had picked up where Lori had left off. It was a solid theory, except for one detail: Lori had no friends and no one she trusted. The junkies she knew would never have waited months to contact Jo. Besides, Jo had gotten her sister's laptop and flash drives when Lori had died.

*Don't take any of this personally. We've all gotta do what we've gotta do, right?*

That was what the man who'd shot her had said, but that didn't make it true. There was one other detail that bothered Jo: her blackmailer had referenced Lori in email, but he'd never mentioned her when they met. If he'd known Lori—if Lori had somehow sold Jo out yet again—what was the connection between them?

*You want to pin this on me, you useless little fool,* Lori's voice hissed at her. *But this is all on you. You're the killer in the family, not me.*

Jo blinked back tears, and she was grateful for the blanket of darkness that meant no one else could see. She was alone in the room, but she'd been in enough places where she was filmed against her will; she expected there was a camera trained on her whether she spotted it or not. She didn't understand what was happening, but deep down she worried that she deserved it. She'd done terrible things, and the fact that they weren't of her own free will didn't make them any less awful.

She knew it didn't make sense to blame some drug-addicted associate of Lori's. Anyone who fit that description would want to find their own golden goose, and they weren't going to come at it with bullets. Her blackmailer hated her—of that much she was certain. His messages to her weren't filled with curses or insults, but they seethed with a quiet contempt that always made her feel like she needed to shower after reading them. His first message replayed in her mind on a loop.

Dear Jo, You don't know me, but I know all about you. You've done horrible things and you've never

been punished for them. All of that is about to
change.

He hadn't been joking about punishing her. She didn't know what
she'd done to spark his rage. Her business had taken off in the past year,
but Jo had always been careful to keep a low profile; her name was in
legal filings for Corvus Alchemy, but there wasn't a single photograph
of her on the company's website. Jo was aware her past could catch up
with her at any time, and she didn't want to give it a running start. It
would take nothing more than a light breeze to knock her off the high-
wire perch she occupied at that moment. Jo was given to superstitious
wariness—she'd been raised by a mother who believed that a crow caw-
ing three times over your house meant there would be a death in the
family—and in that dark hospital room, handcuffed to the bed, she felt
in her marrow that she'd brought this curse on herself. The rational part
of her brain kept looking for a pattern in the madness, but she couldn't
make it out.

# CHAPTER 25

## SHERYN

Sheryn had always been an early riser, and she woke before her alarm went off on Tuesday morning. The clock blinked 5:20, and she slid the switch back so that it wouldn't wake Douglass. She got into the shower and stood under the hot water for longer than usual, aiming to sort her thoughts. She'd had a strange dream that tugged at her, even though she couldn't remember it clearly. In it, she'd been following a teenaged white girl through a house that appeared to have an endless series of doorways, letting the girl remain just beyond arm's reach as she vanished and reappeared. It made little sense, like most of her barely remembered dreams, but it left her feeling disconcerted. It wasn't exactly the girl in the photographs they'd found at Andray Baxter's apartment, but Sheryn felt an instinctive connection. No matter what Jo Greaver had done, someone had preyed upon her as a child.

When she stepped out of the bathroom, Douglass was already up, pulling breakfast together in the kitchen. While she got dressed, the door opened. "Good morning," Douglass said, setting a mug of black coffee on the dresser. Sheryn took it for a peace offering. They hadn't exactly gone to bed angry, but nothing felt like it was resolved either.

"Thank you," she said.

It was her job to get the kids out of bed. Technically speaking, they had alarms, but they were often set to snooze after they went off. She started with Mercy. "Five more minutes," her precious eight-year-old said, falling back to sleep immediately. Sheryn knew they'd go a couple of more rounds like that. She went to Martin's room, expecting to repeat the routine, but he was already up. He was sitting in bed, writing in a notebook.

"Morning," Sheryn said, eyeing him. "You're up early today."

"I woke up at five," Martin said. He didn't make eye contact. "I figured it was easier to stay up."

Sheryn stepped into his room. "Lucky you. Sounds like you got my early-bird genes."

Martin shrugged a little. "Maybe."

She sat on the edge of his bed. "We need to talk about what happened yesterday."

"I'm sorry I cut school," Martin said. "I won't do that again."

"Good, but this isn't just about cutting class." Sheryn took a deep breath; there was a lot to get into, and she didn't feel ready at that moment. "I don't want you to put yourself in a situation where you could get hurt. That's how every parent feels about their child. But it's not the same when you're black. You know that."

"You put yourself in a situation where you could get hurt every day," Martin said.

Sheryn was taken aback. She'd expected an argument, but not along those fault lines. "When you're older, if you want to become a cop or join the army, I'll support you one hundred percent," she said. "I'm not trying to wrap you in cotton wool to keep you from living a full life. But I want you to have clear eyes and a cool head. I'm trying to tell you what's out there waiting for you in the world."

"Things are changing, Mom," Martin said. "They really are."

"The arc of the moral universe is long, but it bends toward justice," Sheryn said. "We keep forgetting how long that arc is, and how slowly the world moves. Do you remember when your uncle Marcus was in the service?"

"A little. He always showed up at Thanksgiving in his uniform."

"He loved that uniform. Strangers would come up to him and thank him for his service. If he had to fly somewhere, he was treated like gold. Thing was, he had to take that uniform off sometime, and when he did, he was just another black man. The same people who thanked him for his service . . ."

"I know," Martin said quietly.

"Most of the officers I work with would give their life to save a civilian. But not everyone walking around with a gun and a badge is like that. A few of them are wrong in the head. All it takes is you crossing paths with one . . ."

Martin nodded somberly. "I know," he repeated, his voice barely a whisper.

Sheryn got to her feet, feeling like there was so much more she wanted to say that she couldn't find the words for. "I wish we had more time right now, but I've got to get your sister up."

She had one foot out the door when Martin called, "Mom?"

She looked back at him.

"Did you never once ditch school?" Martin asked.

"Never. My father would've . . . he would've been disappointed. We were a military family. He was strict. I was the eldest, and it was my job to set a good example. I took that seriously."

"I thought Grandma was the tough one," Martin said.

"Oh, she is. Now get going." She shut she door. Martin had been born long after Sheryn's father had died; the boy knew stories about him, but Sheryn had always been careful about how much detail she doled out. Douglass knew how long years of military service had broken her father's mind, but that was something she still kept from her kids.

While she was waking Mercy up, she heard her phone ringing. "Come on, sleepyhead," she told her daughter.

132

"Five more minutes," Mercy answered, repeating her early-morning mantra.

"Sheryn?" Douglass called. "That's your phone."

"Thanks," she called. To Mercy, she added, "This is a temporary reprieve. Up, now!" She picked up her phone from the night table.

"This is Florian," said a smooth voice on the other end of the line. He was, like her, an early riser. "I wanted to let you know as soon as I had the forensics on the guns."

"Guns, plural?" Sheryn asked.

"Yes. There were two different guns used: the .38 Special you found, and a 9 millimeter."

Sheryn took that in silently. It meant that Andray Baxter had had a gun, too, not just Jo Greaver. For some reason she couldn't quite pin down, that made her heart sink. "I'd like you to walk me through it later, okay? I'm not sure I could take all the details right now."

"Sure," Florian said. "But you should know the weapon you found in . . ." There was the sound of paper shuffling. "Jo Greaver's apartment? It matches the bullet that killed Andray Baxter."

"You're running tests on the ballistics?"

"That's the next step," he said. "One small detail that's probably not a big deal: there are no prints on the gun."

"Not even on a bullet? No one's ever as good as they think they are at wiping prints off a gun."

"Whoever did this did it perfectly," Florian said. "I only mention it because the gun was found inside Greaver's apartment. Why wipe the weapon down yet keep it? It's a strange thing to do."

# CHAPTER 26

## Jo

Jo woke with a jolt. Somehow, in the dark hours of the morning, she'd managed to fall asleep, but suddenly there was a nurse beside her bed. "Your lawyer is here," the young woman said. There was a question mark looming over her words, as if she wasn't quite sure what was going on herself.

"My . . . what?" Jo rubbed her eyes and sat up.

"Your lawyer." The voice that answered her was a commanding baritone. Standing at the foot of the bed was a tall, heavyset man. He was pale and bald with lashless eyes and a lipless slash of a mouth. To Jo, he looked for all the world like a raisin-eyed snowman poured into a bespoke suit. "Jon Urraza, Casper Peters McNally. I've been retained to represent you, Ms. Greaver."

"Retained by who?"

Urraza turned to the nurse. "You can go now," he said. She gave Jo a look, as if to make sure this was okay with her, and vanished, closing the door behind her.

"The McGarrans are paying my bill, if that's what you mean," the lawyer said to Jo. "My time is worth a fortune, so I suggest you not waste any of it. Let me explain your options to you." Urraza's dark eyes were baleful. "You have no options."

"Excuse me?" Jo said. She'd encountered men like Urraza in the past—arrogant and contemptuous, their default mode one of domination—and while there had been a time in her life when she'd had no choice but to comply, that was long past.

"Do as I say, and you'll be fine," Urraza said. "Possession of a gun can be treated as a misdemeanor or a felony in New York. That's up to the district attorney's office, but I'm certain I can get them to go with misdemeanor—with this being a first offense—but you will have to plead out."

"No," Jo insisted. "That gun isn't mine. Look, can I tell you what actually happened? This is entirely confidential, right?"

"We have attorney-client privilege. You can speak openly."

"Okay, here's the truth," Jo said. "Yes, I had a gun. I bought it at a gun show in Virginia and brought it back with me to New York. But I threw that gun into the Hudson River yesterday."

"Where were you standing?"

"The pier above the *Intrepid*," Jo said.

Urraza closed his tiny eyes briefly and shook his bowling ball of a head. "That's a terrible defense. All it proves is that you're the kind of person who'll skirt state firearms law. That only makes you look guiltier, Ms. Greaver."

"Are you listening to me?" Jo tried to keep her voice quiet. "I had a gun, and I threw it away. I don't know how the cops got the gun they found, but someone either pulled it out of the river, or they planted a different gun."

"This isn't helping your case. If you refuse to plead out, here's what's going to happen," Urraza said. "There will be a jury trial. You'll swear you're innocent, that you never laid eyes on the gun before, and then the detective who found it will testify about finding it in your apartment. Guess who the jury's going to believe?"

Jo narrowed her eyes at him.

"You already know that answer," the lawyer continued. "Juries believe the police every time, unless there's video evidence that contradicts the testimony. That's the hierarchy now: video, then the word of a police officer. You'll lose."

"I'm *not* going to swear that a gun I've never seen before is mine," Jo said. She hated to be ordered what to do or pushed around; if someone she trusted told her this was the only option, she might've considered it, but there was no way she'd take the word of this smug overstuffed suit.

"Look, I'm doing this as a favor for a friend, and you're not making this easy," he snapped back at her. "You can go rot in Rikers, if that's what you want."

"What friend?"

"Priscilla McGarran."

That was all Jo needed to hear. She pressed the button next to her bed, and the nurse opened the door and poked her head inside, as if she'd been listening at the door. "We're done here," Jo said. "Please escort Mr. Urraza out."

That cracked his composure. "What are you doing?"

"Thanks for coming by," Jo said. "But I don't need bad advice."

"Don't be stupid. You . . ."

"In case it wasn't clear, you're fired," Jo said. "Now haul your ass out of here."

The lawyer took one last look at her and stormed out. He barged past the nurse, forcing her to jump back to get out of his way. His heavy steps echoed on the tile.

The nurse stepped closer. "He's a real charmer."

"He's not used to people saying no to him," Jo said. "Bless his heart." She was afraid and alone yet absolutely certain of what she was doing. Cal's mother was too sweet to be wholesome, to use a phrase Jo remembered her mother saying. She'd been cold and rude to Jo until she realized Jo wasn't going away, and then she'd tried to charm her.

All Jo knew was that if Priscilla was involved, she needed to run in the opposite direction.

"Do you need anything?" the nurse asked.

Jo shook her head. "Nothing except a lawyer who talks sense. I don't need one who tells me to plead guilty when I'm not."

"That's their standard line," the nurse said. "Plead out. Admit guilt whether or not you did it. There was a girl I grew up with who got into some trouble. Her public defender told her the same thing, plead out, but you know what? It messed up her life. You plead guilty, that's on the record forever."

"I can't imagine doing that," Jo said.

"She's not the only one I know," the nurse said. "The justice system is broken. Sometimes the only way to get out is to say you did something you didn't. Honestly, I thought shitty advice like that was what black folks got. I'm kind of surprised a fancy lawyer in an expensive suit would say the same to you."

Jo thought about that. As her sister liked to say, *You're not paranoid if people really are out to get you, JoJo.*

"Do you know how that guy got in here?" Jo asked. "I thought no visitors were allowed."

"There's an exception for lawyers," the nurse said. "But we don't see many traipsing through here. Most of the folks in here will only have a public defender, and they've got no time for their own mother."

Jo rested her head on the pillow and stared at the ceiling. Satisfying as it had been to listen to her gut and kick out the arrogant ass, it meant she was going to be left with a public defender. Jo had always managed to get herself through the worst, but she feared she hadn't even seen the worst yet.

# CHAPTER 27

## CAL

"What about this one?" Cal held up a white dress. He was pulling outfits out of Jo's closet, desperately hoping to find something appropriate.

"That looks kind of . . . virginal," Mike Nakano said. "It *could* work, I guess. Jo's what, twenty-six? Maybe she's a bit old for it. Hey, does she have a cross she could wear? Paris Hilton did when she went to court. Juries love that."

"This is just the bail hearing, remember?" Cal reminded him. He was starting to regret asking his old pal Mike for help. It hadn't been a deliberate decision; Cal had called him because Mike's father was a formidable defense attorney, only to learn that he was away on a cruise. When Mike volunteered to help, Cal hadn't felt like he could say no. Mike had been a party animal when they were in prep school, and his tastes had gotten harder since the years when he and Cal were hanging out every day. Somehow, Mike had managed to get through law school in spite of—or perhaps *because* of—his cocaine habit. Cal wasn't sure he believed that Mike had actually passed the New York State Bar. It wasn't clear whether he'd be employable at all if he weren't working for his father's firm. But at that moment, Cal needed a lawyer for Jo, and he didn't have time to spare. Cal figured he'd find a real lawyer if the case went any further; he was desperately hoping it wouldn't.

"A suit would be a good look for Jo," Mike said. "You can't go wrong with something professional." He glanced into the hallway. "The police actually put crime scene tape on the door to Jo's office? Are they even allowed to do that?"

"They took her computer already," Cal said. "They warned me about going in. They don't want my prints messing it up."

"Seems like that ship already sailed," Mike said. "You have any idea why Jo had a gun?"

"No. But I still think it was planted by the police."

"That . . . that's not really something that happens outside the movies, Cal."

"Of course it does!" Cal was angry. "Didn't you see that cop in Baltimore who forgot to turn off his body cam when he was planting evidence on a dealer? The police aren't above that."

"Point one, that guy was a known drug dealer," Mike said. "I'm not saying it was okay, but it's not like the cop picked some random dude off the street to frame. Point two, that guy was black."

"Meaning what?"

Mike held out his phone. It started playing "This Is America" by Childish Gambino.

"Point taken," Cal said, depressed that his hard-partying pal was more woke than he was. Worse, he was finding it hard to evade the fact that his girlfriend wasn't a stranger to firearms. "Jo once told me she'd grown up with guns. Her mother had a shotgun and at least one handgun."

"That's freaky. Is she from Florida?"

"Kentucky."

"Ugh, that's just as bad," Mike said. "Hillbillyland. You ever watch *Justified*?"

"No," said Cal, frustrated by Mike's crude characterization; so much for wokeness. He knew that Jo didn't like to talk about her background, and this was precisely the reason why. "Do you think it's time to check in with the police, see what's going on?"

"I'll have to meet Jo at the Tombs," Mike said. "I've always wanted to see it."

Cal felt exhausted; anxiety was wearing him down. He hadn't slept at all. "She's not at the Tombs. She was in a hospital overnight. Bellevue, I think? I have no idea how this is supposed to work."

"Oh, that's different." Mike looked at his watch. "There's no time to get uptown to Bellevue and back downtown to court. That's okay, though. We'll meet her at the courthouse. Let me make a couple of calls." Mike headed out of the room with a little too much bounce in his step.

Cal lightly thumped his head against the wall. Deep down, he knew he was obsessing about what to bring to court for Jo to wear because he couldn't do a damn thing to control the situation. Worse, he had no idea what Jo was really up to; her secretive, sketchy behavior of late was giving him an ulcer. He didn't think she was guilty, exactly, but he knew she was involved in something she didn't want to talk about. Somehow, she'd gotten a gun, and she'd also gotten herself shot. Was that connected to the money she'd taken out of their account? The odds seemed high that it was.

He picked a navy suit for Jo, pairing it with dark heels. Stockings, he thought, opening a drawer. The chaos inside it unnerved him; the police had picked over every corner of the apartment like street mutts hunting for scraps. Jo was always so organized, and they'd pulled everything she owned apart, even her underwear.

"Cal?" That was Mike, standing in the doorway, nervously chewing on a thumbnail. "I've got some news."

"What is it?"

"Do you know what a GSR test is?"

"Never heard of it," Cal admitted.

"It stands for gunshot residue," Mike said. "The cops tested Jo for it in the hospital last night, and it came back positive."

"She was shot," Cal answered defensively. "Obviously there's residue from that."

"No, Cal," Mike said, not unkindly. "What they found was on her right hand. They know Jo fired a gun yesterday." He cleared his throat. "You told me this case was about possession of a firearm."

"That's what the police said."

"That's what the police told you," Mike said. "You know there's got to be more to this case, don't you?"

# CHAPTER 28

## SHERYN

Watching Ornelle Baxter identify her son's body was one of the most painful things Sheryn had done in a long time. The woman let out a long, low wail that became a series of racking sobs. Sheryn wanted to comfort her, but the friend of her son's she'd brought with her stepped in, hugging Ornelle close and sobbing with her. Sheryn and Rafael stood there, shooting each other helpless glances.

"I can't tell you how sorry we are," Sheryn said.

Ornelle's breathing was ragged. "I would . . . like to take . . . some time . . . to pray over my son."

"Of course. We'll be upstairs, whenever you're ready to talk," Rafael said.

"Take your time," Sheryn added.

They settled into a room upstairs that looked like a wood-paneled home library, only with an oval conference table in the center. "That was brutal," Sheryn said.

"Wait until we tell her what her son was into," Rafael answered.

Sheryn's phone buzzed, and she looked at the screen. It was the ADA, Vedika Iyer, wanting to know when she'd be in court.

"For the arraignment?" Rafael spluttered when Sheryn showed it to him. "What the hell?"

"She's an eager beaver," Sheryn said, tapping out a quick response— At ME for vic ID—before turning off her phone.

"Hey, guys." Pola Ostrowska stuck her head in the door. She was a medical examiner, but to Sheryn she looked like an Eastern European supermodel, with her green eyes hidden behind cat's-eye glasses and her pale-gold hair up in a bun. "Mrs. Baxter will be up in a minute. I was going to start straightaway, unless you think that's a problem."

"Sure. I appreciate you waiting, Pola," Sheryn said. She knew the New York ME's office was excellent at what they did, and they fully stitched up a body after an autopsy. But the standard Y-shaped cut across the chest and down the torso wasn't a sight a grieving mother should risk encountering.

"We already know exactly what killed him, and we have the bullet that did it," Pola said. "But the devil is always in the details. I'll let you know as soon as I have something for you."

"Thanks."

"There was one thing I . . . ," Pola started to say, but a door opened and she turned her head quickly. "Mrs. Baxter," she mouthed at them, backing away gracefully.

Sheryn and Rafael got to their feet. A young technician escorted Ornelle Baxter into the office. Sheryn noticed that while the older woman looked more frail than she had a day earlier, she'd clearly decided to dress for the occasion. She wore a black wool bouclé skirted suit; her hair was hidden under a glossy black turban adorned with a mother-of-pearl brooch in the shape of a bird. Its seed pearl of an eye seemed to glare at Sheryn.

"Mrs. Baxter," Sheryn said. "We are so sorry for your loss. I hope you know that."

"Thank you."

There was a young man beside her dressed in a black suit. His dreads were pulled back, and his youngish face was aged up ever so slightly with a goatee. Sheryn took him for roughly Andray's age. When they'd first come into the morgue, Ornelle had introduced him as Yousef Terris, adding that he'd been Andray's best friend since first grade. She'd also mentioned that her daughter was flying in from California, but she wouldn't land until that afternoon.

"Let's sit down," Sheryn said. "Can we get you anything to drink?"

"No, thank you. I want to do whatever I can to solve my son's murder."

Sheryn and Rafael glanced at each other uneasily. "We have a young woman named Jo Greaver in custody," Sheryn said. "I mentioned her name to you yesterday, but I wanted to check again. Does that name sound familiar to you?"

"Not at all." Ornelle Baxter glanced at her young companion. "Do you know her?"

"I never heard that name before," Yousef said. "You got a picture of her?"

"We do." Rafael held up his phone.

The grieving mother's jaw dropped when she saw the photo. "Some white actress shot my Andray? Why would she do that?"

"We're still working on that, but we have evidence that your son may have been blackmailing this woman," Sheryn explained.

"What *evidence* are you talking about?" Ornelle Baxter demanded.

"We have their email messages," Sheryn said. "They corresponded for the past month. They negotiated an amount. Jo Greaver was supposed to deliver it in person to your son's apartment. They had an appointment yesterday."

"Your son seemed to know a lot about this woman's past," Rafael added. "He had naked photographs of her that appeared to be taken when she was a teenager. He may have possessed a video of her, though we haven't seen it yet."

Ornelle Baxter stared at him, then slowly turned her head to Sheryn, as if she'd decided Rafael Mendoza didn't exist. "Where is this woman now?"

"In the hospital. She was shot, too, but not critically."

"You trying to sell me a story that my son was carrying a gun around and blackmailing people? No. No. No. That's the craziest thing I ever heard. That is nothing but a dirty lie."

"With all due respect," Rafael said, "yesterday you told us your son had been getting money from some unknown source for months. He was helping you with medical bills."

"You think that money came from Andray blackmailing folks?" Ornelle Baxter's voice rose in fury.

"Mrs. Baxter, we're not trying to disrespect your son," Sheryn interjected. "Clearly, he had good intentions. He wanted to help you."

"What does this Jo woman say?" Ornelle Baxter's voice rose in frustration. "Does she admit she shot Andray?"

"No," Sheryn admitted. "She claims she's never seen him before."

That gave the older woman pause. She cocked her head, like a bird. "She's *not* saying Andray shot her?"

"No, she says she met a different man in your son's apartment."

"Well, then!" Ornelle Baxter slapped the table. She looked at Yousef for confirmation, and he put his hand on her thin shoulder and nodded his head. "You haven't figured it out. You still have to do your job. What kind of investigation have you really done?"

"A gun was found in her apartment. It matches the weapon that killed Andray."

"Listen to me. My son is a good man. *Was* a good man. He took care of his family. He was kind to everyone. He helped people. He loved Jesus. I don't know this woman. I don't know her story. But anything that tells you Andray was a blackmailer is a filthy lie. That is all I have to say to you."

She got to her feet and so did Yousef. She took his arm to steady herself.

"Mrs. Baxter, I'm sorry, but we need to ask you these questions," Sheryn said. "If you would just . . ."

"Shame on you." Ornelle Baxter turned abruptly to face her. "The police don't do enough to harm hardworking folks when they're alive? You got to do a character assassination when they're dead too?" With that, she fled the room.

# CHAPTER 29

## Jo

When Jo was brought to the courthouse on Tuesday morning, the first person she saw was Cal. He looked good in a slim-fitting navy suit, with his longish hair combed back, like a rogue aiming for respectability. She watched him hurry over, his expression a mix of relief and trepidation.

"Jo!" he called. "Are you okay?"

Her smile fell. There was an echo from the day before, the man in the hallway calling to the man she'd shot, *Are you okay?* She hadn't really thought about him at all; her mind had been preoccupied with the man she'd met with.

"I'm fine," Jo said.

A uniformed female guard stepped between them before Cal could reach Jo. "No contact allowed," she said sharply. She wasn't tall, but she had fifty pounds on Cal. Her nails were bright orange, but they were short, and her knuckles looked calloused. In any fight, Jo would put her money on her.

"But she's my girlfriend," Cal said.

"No contact with *any* prisoner," the guard repeated. "You'll see her in the courtroom."

"What about her lawyer?" Cal persisted.

Jo scanned the hallway for Urraza, whose big head would be hard to miss, but she didn't see him.

"That's different," the guard said. "Where's her lawyer?"

"Right here."

That was when Jo noticed Mike Nakano. He was a slender guy with slicked-back hair and alert eyes that exuded the nervous energy of a meerkat. "Hi, Jo," he said with a little wave. He held up a garment bag. "I've got my client's outfit," he told the guard.

"There better not be stiletto heels in there," the guard muttered. "Department of Corrections won't let the accused wear those anymore."

Jo stared at Mike in disbelief and despair. *This* was who Cal had dug up to be her lawyer? The last time she'd seen Mike, he'd been drunkenly stumbling around her apartment, looking for an exit before passing out in a coat closet. She had the sudden feeling that she should run to the police and tell them everything she knew. "You've got to be joking," Jo said.

The guard misunderstood and nodded her head. "No lie. We had too many incidents, folks wielding stiletto heels like weapons."

"Is there a room where I can speak privately with my client?" Mike asked the guard. At least he sounded polished when he wasn't drunk, Jo noted.

It frustrated her that she wasn't even allowed to touch Cal's hand, but having a lawyer who wasn't a public defender improved Jo's conditions immediately. After the outfit was inspected for contraband, she was allowed into a bathroom to change. It was a little awkward to slip the sleeveless white shell on, since it involved lifting her bandaged arm, which was stiff and sore and actually in a sling to remind her not to use it. She couldn't get her injured arm into the suit jacket, so she put her sling on again and draped the jacket over her shoulder.

Cal hadn't thought to include makeup, but there was a comb. She fixed her unruly hair, taming it and tying it back. After that, she was allowed to meet with Mike Nakano in a miniscule office that smelled like sweat socks.

"What's going to happen in court this morning is pretty simple," Mike said. "You'll be called up in front of the judge to enter your plea. Then the judge will set bail. That's it. This is arraignment court, so there's no jury, only the judge, though there will be plenty of other people in the courtroom: lawyers and clients, media, the curious public. Be prepared for a busy courtroom, with people coming and going all morning."

"Okay."

"I'm not going to lie to you," Mike said. "I think the ADA might be kind of a hard-ass. She's charging you with felony possession of a handgun. I called her office, because you've got no prior offenses, so she should only charge you with a misdemeanor. But she's, um, sticking to her guns, I guess?"

"Now is not the time for bad puns, Mike."

"Right. Sorry. Don't worry. It's your first offense, so nothing really bad will happen. Probably some probation, maybe you have to do some volunteer work—you get the idea."

"Here's the thing," Jo said. "The gun they have isn't mine."

Mike shook his head and laughed awkwardly. "You kind of sound like me when I was fourteen and my parents found my stash of magic mushrooms," Mike said. "They did a test on you in the hospital, looking for gunshot residue, and they found it. They *know* you fired a gun yesterday."

"That's true. I did," Jo said, remembering how her conversation had gone with her first lawyer. "But I threw the gun into the Hudson River immediately afterward. I don't know where, exactly, but I could see the *Intrepid*. It was at the next pier."

"I'm not sure that's a great excuse. It's kind of like, 'Oh, I used my *other* gun.'" He was watching her closely. "At some point, we'll have to talk about what happened yesterday. The ADA's office has been tight lipped, but I know there's more to this story."

Jo grudgingly admitted to herself that telling the truth about the gun she'd had might not win her any points. She leaned forward.

"Here's the thing," Jo said. "I have more experience than you can imagine with the New York criminal justice system. Not personally, but because of my sister. Anyway, here's my point: your job is reasonable doubt. That's what a defense lawyer is there to plant."

"Today's just the bail hearing, Jo."

Jo leaned back in her chair. "I don't think you really know what you're doing, but you're a big improvement over the lawyer Cal's mother sent over."

Mike frowned. "Who are you talking about?"

"Jon Urraza. He came to see me in the hospital. He said that Priscilla was footing his bill."

"Wow. He's kind of a legendary shark."

"That's why I fired him," Jo said. "That, and the fact that Priscilla can't stand me. Why would she help me?"

"Because of Cal," Mike said. "Priscilla's hated the whole world since her husband went to jail. She's lost a lot. Cal is everything to her."

# CHAPTER 30

## SHERYN

"I want to tell you something, and I need you to hear me," Sheryn said. She and Rafael were still sitting in an office at the morgue. They hadn't moved since Ornelle Baxter had reamed them out. Sheryn felt like she was sitting in a blast zone. Her ears were still ringing.

"What's that?" Rafael asked.

"Don't say 'With all due respect' to a grieving mother. Not to anyone, really, unless it's a perp you want to piss off."

"Why not? That was me being polite."

"It's what people say when they're pretending to be polite. They're putting up a front so you can't call them on their bullshit."

There was the sound of a man clearing his throat, and Sheryn looked up. Yousef Terris was standing in the doorway, tugging awkwardly at his tie. "Hey. Can I talk to you?" he asked.

"Please do," Sheryn said.

"Unless you're here to yell at us for Mrs. Baxter," Rafael added glumly.

"Nah," Yousef said, sitting down with them. "Auntie Nelle's heart is broken. You know that, right?"

"Yes, of course," Sheryn said.

"I left her in the car for a few minutes to gather herself. She understands I need to tell you a couple things." Yousef paused for a moment. "There's no way Andray blackmailed anybody, okay? He's, like, the best man I know. Known. Andray was always the kid who did everything right. My gran used to say to me, 'Why can't you be like Andray?' all the time. You'd think I would hate him for that, but I loved him. He never put me down. He'd tell my gran she should appreciate me more." He stared directly at Sheryn. "My gran never even smacked him down for that."

Sheryn nodded in tacit acknowledgment.

"I've known Andray my whole life," Yousef went on. "We went to school together, until he got into the *Fame* school . . ."

"LaGuardia," Sheryn filled in.

"Yeah, but we'd still hang out. Andray was always making new friends, but he still had time for his old friends, you know? Andray's got the biggest heart of anyone I ever met. I know Auntie Nelle's describing him like he was a saint, and nobody's a saint in real life, but Andray's always been a good person."

"How was Andray *not* a saint?" Sheryn asked.

Yousef raised an eyebrow. "Andray was always good with the ladies, you know what I mean? He was always busy."

"He liked to play the field?"

Yousef smiled at that. "Yep. A *big* field."

"He use any drugs?" Rafael asked.

"Andray was never into anything illegal," Yousef said carefully. "But if it was legal in Colorado, he might go for that."

"You have the names of the girls who were around the most?" Sheryn asked.

"Only a couple," Yousef said. "There was a Russian model named Olga for a while. Also, an actress named Tamika Weller. But I'm not saying they had anything to do with Andray's . . . with his death. Both of those relationships ended a while back. What I'm saying is, the last year was kind of a strange one for Andray."

"How's that?"

"He always has a girl around, and suddenly he didn't. He used to joke about all these rich ladies throwing themselves at him at the gym when he worked. Auntie Nelle doesn't know this, but Andray got fired from that job."

"Because a client complained about him?"

"All he'd say was, 'I guess I crossed a line.' He never explained." Yousef looked at the table. "That was six months ago. He got a job at another fancy gym, but he hasn't had any girls around. He doesn't—*didn't*—even joke about the rich ladies anymore. He changed. Deep down, I wonder if it was on account of a girl, or if it was the way his landlord was treating him. It was like that man wanted to mess with Andray's mind."

"We've talked to the landlord," Sheryn said carefully.

"Elliott. That freak is sick," Yousef said. "Andray took him to court because of the state of the building, but that guy wanted to mess up Andray on a personal level. He set up spy cams in the apartment. He got this GI Joe knockoff from a dollar store to harass Andray."

"We saw some of that in the housing court filings."

"It was way worse than any filing would show. Andray kept finding them. At least one of them was, like, a computer adaptor, but it was transmitting sound and video. There were others too. Andray was all, 'Can you believe this shit?' But it didn't stop there. Sometimes he'd wake up Andray early in the morning. I mean, like four or five a.m."

"The landlord did this?" Rafael asked.

"No one would be there when Andray answered the door," Yousef clarified. "But it had to be Elliott or someone working on his behalf. Andray had a tough schedule, because he'd be up late doing a show and then getting up early for his job at the gym. It was like someone wanted to mess him up on every level."

Sheryn mentally filed that away. "Did Andray ever confront his landlord?" she asked.

"One time that I know about. He went to his office to dump the spy cams in front of him and demand an explanation," Yousef said. "Andray said the landlord acted like he'd never even seen this shit before. Said Elliott was a better actor than he was."

"What about the money?" Sheryn asked. "Andray's mother told us about that. Where did it come from?"

"I don't know. I asked him. He was like, 'I gotta keep my mouth shut. If I say anything, the golden goose is cooked.'"

"Someone was paying him off for his silence?" Rafael asked.

"I figured that's what he meant, but he wouldn't tell me."

"Could the money have come from his landlord?"

"I don't see how," Yousef said. "They were still duking it out in court. And he complained about Elliott all the time. Nobody was paying him to keep quiet about that."

"Could Andray have seen something . . . ?"

"Ma'am, I do not know. I swear on my mother's grave, I don't. Andray wouldn't explain." Yousef stared into Sheryn's face again. "But if I'm being completely honest, I was kind of worried for him. Somebody was giving him ten thousand a month. I know Andray turned around and gave it to Auntie Nelle, but unless you believe in Santa Claus, you gotta think about who'd be handing him a bag of cash like that."

# CHAPTER 31

## Jo

As Jo's new lawyer had warned her, the courtroom was bedlam. She sat next to Mike Nakano, taking it all in and trying to crush the panic that kept threatening to swallow her up. Her arm ached terribly, and she was on an antibiotic that made her stomach queasy. Every so often she looked around, catching sight of Cal. She was grateful that he was there, but at the same time she wished she could make him keep his distance. She never wanted him to find out what her past had been really like. The hardscrabble history she'd told him about was enough.

When Jo finally heard her name called, every nerve in her body vibrated; she was filled with a keen terror. All she wanted was for this to be over with, but—in spite of Mike's assurances—she didn't feel like that was going to happen any time soon.

It didn't help that the assistant district attorney stared at Jo with contempt. Vedika Iyer was petite—a couple of inches shorter than Jo, maybe all of five foot two—and a couple of years older, but she looked like a powerhouse who felt pity for no man. Jo couldn't help but notice that the ADA was wearing stiletto heels. After the lawyers' brief introductions, the judge turned to Jo.

"On the charge of illegally possessing a firearm, how do you plead?" he asked. He was a bored-looking man with wispy gray hair. The deep lines etched into his forehead and sizable jowls gave him a hangdog appearance.

"Not guilty, Your Honor," she said.

The ADA raised an eyebrow. "This is no longer a case of simple gun possession, Your Honor," Iyer said. "I learned moments ago that the weapon found in Ms. Greaver's apartment has been conclusively tied to the murder of a young man in Hell's Kitchen. The facts of the case are still being gathered, but I can tell you that on Monday, Ms. Greaver went to see a man named Andray Baxter, a successful young actor, at his apartment. She brought a gun with her, and she shot and killed Mr. Baxter and subsequently fled the scene. The People expect to add a charge of murder in the first degree as well as other charges. The grand jury is in session now."

"Objection, Your Honor," Mike said. "None of this was communicated to defense counsel."

The judge gave the ADA a long, searching look. "Let me see if I understand this. The grand jury has these details in front of them, but the defense does not?"

"I don't know how that happened, Your Honor," Iyer responded. "The investigation has been moving very quickly."

The judge rolled his eyes and sighed. "Care to change your plea, Ms. Greaver?" he asked.

For a moment, everything around Jo ground to a halt, and she felt as if she had been released from her body to observe herself. There she was, wild-eyed but primly dressed, a creature that had been trapped but never quite domesticated. Everyone in the courtroom stared at her, surely realizing what Jo herself had known all along: she was an impostor in this world, a fraud who clung to the shadows so no one could examine her in the sunlight. She had climbed higher than anyone could've imagined, only to crash exactly as everyone had expected. It had been a matter of time. Jo's panic in that moment was drowned by her sense of shame. She wasn't guilty of doing exactly what they said, she knew; she was guilty of much worse.

"No, Your Honor," Jo said. Her gun was in the Hudson; the one the police found wasn't hers. She had to hold on to that fact as if it were a rock in a stormy sea; otherwise she'd be swept away.

"Of course not," the judge said. "The People on bail?"

"The People request remand, Your Honor," Iyer said. "Ms. Greaver was apprehended by police while attempting to flee. She had her passport and almost one thousand dollars in cash. She had a GSR test that was positive. She is a person of considerable means and poses a serious flight risk."

"Attempting to flee? That's quite a stretch," Mike said. "Jo Greaver took a ferry from New York to New Jersey, something thousands of people do every day. Are they all fleeing New York?"

"How many of them have their passport with them?" ADA Iyer countered. "That makes her intent clear."

"Jo Greaver is an entrepreneur who frequently travels for business," Mike improvised. "Carrying your passport is normal when you fly at a moment's notice."

Jo touched Mike's arm, and he leaned in to hear what she had to say. "Fingerprints," Jo whispered to him. "I probably left them all over that apartment. But they can't possibly be on that gun."

Her lawyer turned back to face the judge. "Your Honor, it's extremely confusing to be given important forensic information at the last possible second by the ADA," Mike said. "Obviously, they've had time to analyze the fingerprints they found on the gun, but we haven't received that information either."

"Ms. Greaver's fingerprints were found in the victim's apartment," Iyer said.

"But not on the gun," Mike asserted.

"No," Iyer admitted. "Not on the gun. It's been wiped clean."

"It sounds like you have some work to do," the judge said. "Ms. Greaver will surrender her passport immediately. Bail is set at fifty thousand dollars." He struck his gavel. "Dismissed."

Jo looked around the courtroom quickly before sinking into her chair.

"You've got to get up," Mike said, pulling at her sleeve. "That's it for now."

Jo's legs felt like jelly, and she didn't trust them to get her out of there. "I don't have any money."

"Don't worry," Mike said. "It sounds huge, but you only have to front part of it. As soon as you put up the bond, you'll be free."

"I don't have any cash," Jo said. "It's all gone."

"Well, Cal has money," Mike said. "Don't worry about it."

His words didn't soothe Jo's mind. She'd caught sight of Cal's face when she'd turned around, and it was grim. She felt her hold on her rock slipping. If Cal was ready to believe the worst of her, there was no hope at all.

# CHAPTER 32

## SHERYN

"I don't like this case," Sheryn said to Rafael as they walked out of the medical examiner's office and onto First Avenue. It was another cold day, and the sky was gray and forbidding.

"You mentioned that," Rafael answered.

"I mean that I *really* dislike it. If it were going door to door, handing out free Bibles, I'd still punch it in the head."

After Yousef Terris had left, Sheryn had checked her phone and found a message from Florian saying that ballistics had matched the slug that killed Andray Baxter with the gun found in Jo Greaver's bag. There was no doubt about it, yet Sheryn couldn't take comfort in that certainty.

"It's not really that complicated," Rafael said. "Look at the basic facts: We have the gun that killed Baxter. It was in Greaver's apartment. She's guilty. It's really that simple."

"Is it?" Sheryn asked. "Because Jo Greaver's prints aren't on that gun."

"She was smart enough to wear gloves."

"Yet dumb enough to hold on to the gun and leave it in her tote bag with a bunch of lipstick samples?" Sheryn shook her head. "There's more here than meets the eye."

"You feel bad because of what Ornelle Baxter said." Rafael regarded her seriously; the sardonic edge he usually wore as armor was missing. "Nobody wants to believe that their son or their friend or their spouse is a criminal. We make excuses for people we love all day long. From her perspective, she had a wonderful son who gave her every cent he could to help with her medical bills. That's her truth. But let's be honest here: Andray Baxter wasn't picking up that extra cash by being an upstanding citizen."

"Everything you're saying makes sense," Sheryn agreed. "But everyone who knew him can't be wrong. It's not just his mother and his friend. His downstairs neighbor started crying when he heard Andray had died. Everybody loved him. Obviously otherwise-great guys do shady things. We see that all the time. But . . ."

"What is it?"

"The forensics say there were two guns in play at the scene. Jo Greaver was shot. That would mean Andray shot her, but there's no gunshot residue on his hands."

"You know how flaky the GSR test can be," Rafael pointed out. "People who never went near a gun can test positive. There are false negatives. We know this."

"We believe the test when it's convenient," Sheryn said. "What about Jo Greaver not recognizing Andray Baxter in the photo we showed her? Doesn't that give you pause?"

"Of course she's going to say that."

"I watched her," Sheryn said. "Perps work so hard to stay cool. They see a photo of someone they killed, and they're using every ounce of energy so their eye doesn't twitch. Jo Greaver wasn't like that. She seemed baffled."

"*Seemed* is the key word in that sentence," Rafael said. "Because hiding your emotional reactions is easy when you don't have any because you're a psychopath."

"She was being blackmailed," Sheryn reminded him. "She's the CEO of a growing business, and something from her past is tripping her up."

"Not for nothing, did you know that CEO is the profession with the most psychopaths?"

"You made that up, didn't you?"

"Look it up," Rafael insisted. "CEO is number one, followed by lawyers. The world makes a lot more sense when you realize it's run by psychopaths."

"I don't believe half the shit you say, you know."

"Fine." Rafael shrugged. "But cops are on that top-ten list for psychopaths. I forget what number we are, but we're on there."

"You are a ray of sunshine today," Sheryn said. "And every day, if I'm honest."

"I try. Look, literally everything points to Greaver shooting Baxter because he was blackmailing her. It's Occam's razor. When solving a puzzle, go with the option that contains the fewest variables. The simpler answer wins."

"Not when you're dealing with people. Humans are messy," Sheryn said.

"We've got DNA, fingerprints, the gun, the surveillance cameras . . ."

"I never saw any of the footage. Did you?"

"Sure, last night at the hospital. Didn't TARU send it to you?" Rafael pulled out his phone. "It's definitely Greaver."

They were stopped at a red light, so Sheryn studied the image. In it, a petite woman in sunglasses and a hoodie had a big bag hanging off one shoulder.

"Okay, that's Jo Greaver, off to deliver cash to her blackmailer," Sheryn said. "So, where's that big bag of cash now?"

Rafael frowned and looked at the photo again. "Holy shit."

"According to our witness, she wasn't carrying it when she went down the fire escape," Sheryn said. "Honestly, with the bullet wound in her arm, it's hard to imagine her carrying off anything. I don't think she or her assistant were making up a story about that laptop mysteriously showing up yesterday afternoon."

"I didn't think Peyton Chin was lying," Rafael said. "I figured Greaver had an accomplice who'd sent it to her."

"We've got evidence, but it feels cherry-picked," Sheryn said. "If we hadn't been pointed at Ms. Greaver, we'd still be talking to people Andray knew. We never reached out to his friends. We never even followed up with the landlord."

"We've got a lot of evidence. You think we really need to retrace our steps?"

Sheryn was quiet for a moment. "Look, you've got your car, so you can head back to the station."

"Where are you going?"

"If you think about the timeline, Andray started getting cash payments around the time he lost his job at the fitness center," Sheryn said. "I'm going to find out why he was fired."

# CHAPTER 33

## Jo

"Thanks for coming to court," Jo said quietly. "I can't even tell you how sorry I am to be putting you through this."

She and Cal were standing in a tiny alcove outside the courtroom. The guard was pretending not to notice; from what Jo could tell, she wasn't quite so concerned about following the rules to the letter now that Jo only needed to post bail.

"Just tell me this," Cal said. "Who is Andray Baxter, and why were you at his apartment?"

Guilt weighed on Jo's shoulders. She could tell herself she hadn't directly lied about her circumstances to Cal, but she'd hidden the truth from him and committed so many lies of omission that it made her sick to think about. She'd spent her adult life swimming forward like a shark, abandoning the parts of the past she didn't want to take with her—which, really, was pretty much all of it. She'd rewritten so much of her history that revealing the truth to Cal now felt like trying to build on top of quicksand. She'd always thought that if she could stack up enough accomplishments, her past wouldn't matter, but that was a lie. The leaden heft of it was pulling her down.

She took a deep breath and looked Cal in the eye. "I was being blackmailed. I never told you, and I should have."

"Blackmailed?" Cal repeated. He didn't look surprised; there was a grim acceptance in his manner that alarmed her. Maybe he had always expected the worst.

"I told you when I came to New York, I had nothing," Jo said quietly. "My mom had just died, and I hopped on a bus to Port Authority because my sister was here. But nothing worked out like I thought it would. I ended up being forced to do some bad things to support myself."

"You've got a couple more minutes," the guard said. "Then I have to take you back while he arranges your bail."

Jo took a deep breath. It was humiliating to ask Cal for money, but she didn't see that she had a choice. "You can get the bail money?"

"You still haven't explained who Andray Baxter was to you," Cal said. "How were you involved with him?"

"I wasn't. I don't know him."

"But you went to his apartment anyway?" Cal's voice was quiet, but his expression was stony. "You can see how none of this makes sense, can't you, Jo?"

"Someone was blackmailing me. That was the address I was given to deliver the money." Jo swallowed hard. "My sister was an escort, and she made me . . . she made me do that kind of work too."

She had never told anyone about her past, and she watched Cal's face, hoping for a sliver of warmth. She would understand if Cal hated her, but she needed him to know that she hadn't had a choice in everything that had happened.

"Was that the video?" Cal asked. "Was that what he was blackmailing you with?"

"Please don't ask me about that."

"What was it?"

"Time's up," the guard said. "Let's go." She looked at Cal. "I hope you're good for the bond. If you're not, your girlfriend will be spending the night in Rikers."

164

# CHAPTER 34

## Sheryn

Sheryn walked into the Sculpted Goddess Health Club on East Fiftieth Street like she was strolling into a nightclub with every eye on her. It was reflexive with so many mirrors and strobe lights around. Her spine straightened and her chin lifted. There were blonde women everywhere, all of them uniformly lithe and, yes, sculpted. The only other black woman was sitting behind the reception desk. With her high cheekbones and doe eyes, she looked like a supermodel waiting to be discovered.

"Hi, I'm Detective Sterling," she said, holding up her gold shield. Suddenly, the blondes were silent; Sheryn was tempted to pull a hairpin out of her bun and listen for a sound when she dropped it. She leaned forward and lowered her voice so that the blondes couldn't hear. "I'm looking to talk with anyone who worked with Andray Baxter."

The receptionist's eyes widened. "Is he okay?" she whispered back.

"No, he's not. He passed away yesterday. We're investigating."

The receptionist's eyes filled with tears. "He's dead?" she whispered.

Sheryn reached forward and gently touched her wrist. "Please don't tell anyone. That makes it harder for us to get to the truth."

The receptionist nodded in understanding. "How did it happen?"

Before Sheryn could answer, a broad-shouldered white man in his early forties approached them. He wasn't particularly tall, but he was built and wearing a turquoise dress shirt that was at least two sizes too small, to emphasize his muscles. His expression was tight, like he'd dropped a bag of bricks on his foot and was trying not to cry out.

"I'm Peter Landau, the manager here. Please come with me," he said to Sheryn.

"I haven't even had the chance to introduce myself yet," she said.

The receptionist inclined her head slightly. Sheryn followed the trajectory and saw a glossy black dome in the wall. A camera. A quick glance around showed her that there were at least two in the lobby. You were under surveillance the moment you walked in, Sheryn realized.

She followed Landau, who held a glass door open for her with exaggerated politeness. He ushered her into an office that might kindly be described as cozy.

"I saw you flash your badge at the reception desk," Landau said. "I don't know what would bring the police here, but I know our clientele won't like it. What do you want?"

"I'm here to talk about Andray Baxter."

Landau crossed his arms. "This club has not been associated with him for a long time."

"You mean that you fired him six months ago," Sheryn said.

"I'm sorry, but I'm not at liberty to discuss personnel matters."

Sheryn shook her head. "Look, there are two ways for this to play out. One is that we have an open and frank conversation right here in your office, just you and me. The other is that I come back with a warrant and a six-pack of New York's finest, and we turn your club upside down."

Landau's eyes registered shock, but his face barely moved. Botox, she realized, gazing at his virtually unlined face. The upkeep to work in a place like this had to be rough, even for men.

"The good news is that you have a choice," she added. "What will it be?"

There was no contest. Landau had broken out in a sweat when she'd announced she was a cop in reception. Harming the club's reputation in any way put him into mortal terror.

"What, exactly, do you need?" he asked.

"Let's start with details on Andray Baxter's employment here."

"That's in the computer." He typed in a few commands and turned the screen so that Sheryn could view it as well. There was Andray Baxter's face on the screen, youthful and grinning.

"You took that when he started working here?" she asked.

"Yes. Almost three years ago."

Sheryn scanned the screen. There was the victim's address and social security number, Pilates certification, and references. There were time sheets and paychecks: a long history that showed he'd worked at the club roughly twenty hours a week, almost all of it training sessions with private clients. There were a few well-known surnames in the mix but nothing that really stood out to Sheryn. Finally, she got to a document with NOTICE OF TERMINATION spelled out in big letters at the top. Sheryn read it over. There was a nondisclosure agreement attached, with Andray Baxter's bold signature on it.

"There's no reason given for firing him," she said.

"New York is an employment-at-will state," Landau answered.

"It also has laws to protect workers from harassment and discrimination. Why did you do it?"

Landau crossed his arms. "It wasn't just one thing. Andray didn't like authority. He would break rules and get upset for being reprimanded."

"I heard that he was very popular," Sheryn said. "People seemed to love him."

"Andray *was* popular here—that's true. But we have protocol and procedures."

"You're making a fitness club sound like the army." Sheryn glanced back at the screen. "One thing about Mr. Baxter: he wasn't afraid of getting into a fight when he felt he was in the right." She pointed at the screen. "You gave him roughly six months' pay as severance. That's pretty generous, given how long he worked here."

Landau was sweating in his too-tight shirt. Of that she was sure.

"Why did you give him so much severance?" she asked.

"Everyone liked him," Landau muttered.

"Did some people like him too much?"

Landau nodded and looked down at his desk. "That's completely against club policy. We had to let him go."

"Were there complaints?"

Landau nodded again.

*This is like pulling teeth,* Sheryn thought. "Who were the complaints from?"

"I'm sorry," Landau said. "I can't give you any information about our clients. I want to help, but I can't do that."

Sheryn understood that she'd pushed him as far as she could. Even if she came back with a subpoena, she couldn't make him talk, and it didn't look like any of the complainants were named in Andray Baxter's file. "I understand," she said. "I appreciate your time."

On her way out, Sheryn made eye contact with the receptionist. Outside, she crossed the street and waited. The receptionist came out five minutes later, looking to the right and left. When she spotted Sheryn, she jerked her head to the side and headed up the block. Sheryn caught up with her a couple of minutes later.

"Hi, I'm Sheryn," she said, extending her hand.

The receptionist shook it. "Tracie. I told them I had to run out to the bank." She took a gulp of air. "Was Andray murdered?"

"He was."

Tracie shook her head. She walked quickly, taking off one glove to brush away a tear. "He was amazing," she said. "The life of every party. He lit the place up."

"Peter Landau wouldn't tell me why he was fired," Sheryn said. "Except that Andray didn't like authority."

"That's a lie," Tracie said. "Andray never had a problem with anyone there. Everyone loved him. Even Peter. Honestly, I think he had a crush on Andray."

"Then why'd he fire him?" Sheryn asked.

"Sofia Severight," Tracie said.

Sheryn frowned. The name was familiar, but she couldn't place why. "Who's that?"

"Daughter of a billionaire," Tracie said. "She was Andray's client for a year. We all had to pretend not to know who she was when she came in. Never talked to anyone except Andray. I thought it was going well. She really got into shape—must've lost thirty pounds. Then, just like that, Andray had to be let go. Because of her."

"Did you ever talk to Andray about it?"

"I tried. He wouldn't talk about it, except that it wasn't really Sofia's fault." Tracie's eyes flashed. "Can you believe it? This rich bitch gets him fired, and he still wouldn't say a bad word about her."

# CHAPTER 35

## CAL

When Cal walked out of the court building into Foley Square, he took a deep breath. The air was frigid, but the day was sunny and clear, and he was tempted to pick a direction and keep on walking without a backward glance. Part of him felt churlish for deciding not to post Jo's bail; it was an unkind move to make, no matter how he looked at it. But a bigger part of him was angry. Jo had lied to him again. She'd played him for a fool.

He followed Broadway south until he came to his office building. He'd spent all morning trying to help Jo, and he couldn't think of any other place to go at that moment where he wouldn't be reminded of her. The apartment on Hanover Square was hers; if he called his mother, she'd ask what was happening with Jo. That was likely true for any of his friends, who would see the news about Jo; from Cal's experience with his father, he knew that word of a fall from grace spread like the plague through his social stratum. Everyone loved watching that spectacle.

Cal took the elevator up and strode into his office purposefully, as if he had important work to take care of. He shut the door and sat down behind his desk. He'd gotten a couple of texts on the walk over from acquaintances asking about Jo, and media queries about her were starting to trickle in. Cal typed her name into a search engine and stared glumly at the results. There was one tabloid piece with the title "You Give Love a Bad Name," which made Cal cringe. The main photo was of the dead man, Andray Baxter, possibly because there weren't any public shots of Jo. Cal realized there was an entire image galley dedicated to Baxter, and he clicked through it, feeling more despondent with each shot. Baxter was a handsome man who was obviously a gym rat, and it wasn't hard to see why Jo would've been attracted to him.

*You don't know that,* he reminded himself. *Jo said he was blackmailing her.* Only that didn't make much sense. If the hushed confession Jo had made to him was to be believed, she'd been *forced* into prostitution as a teenager. Since Baxter was a little younger than Jo, it was hard to figure how he could've known about that. Cal had a dismal sense that Jo had probably cheated on him with this man, and Baxter had turned around and blackmailed her about that. He didn't have any proof, but instinct told him it was the likeliest possibility.

He felt sick to his stomach. This wasn't like the sinking feeling he'd had when his mother had sat him down and told him that Jo had worked as a prostitute. *That's none of my business,* Cal had told her at the time.

*What man would be willing to date a woman like that?* she had asked, clearly astonished.

*She's not perfect. I'm not perfect. Whatever we did in the past shouldn't matter,* Cal had argued. *What we do going forward matters.*

He'd felt proud of himself, magnanimous even. He'd longed for the day Jo would confess her dark past to him; he knew exactly how he would console her and convince her it didn't matter. He admired himself for being open minded, unlike his cold, status-obsessed parents. His illusion had been shot to hell in a second. The moment in court when the assistant district attorney said Jo had gone to Andray Baxter's apartment had blown it apart. In that instant, Cal realized he had no trouble believing that Jo had been cheating on him. *With her history, why would I be surprised?* he thought.

In the next heartbeat, he wondered how much of the truth his godmother knew.

Annabelle hadn't set them up, exactly. Almost eighteen months earlier, she'd called Cal to tell him about the upstart company—already punching above its weight class—she was thinking of investing in; Annabelle asked him to go over its financials with her. It hadn't been an unusual request—Cal had done that for her before—but Cal wondered why she hadn't asked her own son to do it. Zachary had been away in Europe, studying and then working for a bank in Zurich, but he'd definitely come home by then. *Maybe Annabelle already knew some things about Jo's past,* Cal thought. Maybe she wanted to make sure Jo didn't get her hooks into Zachary.

Cal shook his head. That was a stupid thought, he told himself. Was he so consumed by bitterness that he was blaming Annabelle for introducing him to Jo? When his father's fraudulent schemes had finally been exposed, the man had implicated everyone around him, as if his own greed and cupidity weren't to blame. Cal remembered how his father had claimed that his wife and son had pressured him into his misdeeds with their grasping ways. He felt as if he were standing on a slippery slope; at the bottom was his father's ugly example, and Cal felt as if he were sliding toward it. It wasn't Annabelle's fault for introducing him to Jo; he'd fallen in love with her as soon as they'd met.

He was aware he needed something else to focus on. On his computer, he opened a file on a real estate project. Asmodeus owned retail storefronts in multiple cities, and it liked to shut shops down. Most landlords would weep at the thought of losing their rent-paying tenants and having buildings lie empty for years on end, but Asmodeus liked taking the loss to offset their profits in other divisions. For them, losing money actually made them *more* money.

Cal wasn't sure how long he had clicked through the file before his eyes glazed over. At some point, he realized that his boss, Rory, was standing in the doorway. Cal hadn't heard the door open, but he hadn't heard a knock either.

"Finally decided to make an appearance, huh?" Rory said in that arch way of his that suggested he thought he was being clever.

"I ran out of interesting places to go."

"Now that you're here, you can tell me why your girlfriend shot that guy."

"It was for asking stupid questions," Cal answered. "Nobody likes that."

"Har, har. I saw it on the news. I knew Jo was one of those crazy broads when I met her, but I didn't know she was psycho. I get it, though."

Cal stared at him impassively. He'd always suspected Rory was dropped on his head as a baby and that his wealthy parents had papered over that fact.

"Psycho chicks are the best in bed." Rory grinned wolfishly. "My wife would never do the shit they do."

Cal shrugged. "Who knows what your wife is like with other guys."

That wiped the smirk off Rory's face. "You've got a big fucking mouth, you know."

When Cal had started working for Asmodeus Capital earlier in the year, he'd figured it was a job that would help set him up for life. The money was good; there was no doubt about that. But there was a hidden cost to working in an office headed up by a bully: the culture was toxic. The last time Cal had spoken to his father, he'd said something that had always stuck in Cal's craw. In that moment, it came into Cal's mind.

"Somebody once told me that I liked money, but I didn't like what I'd have to do to get it," Cal said. "It's true. I hate dealing with morons, and you're at the top of that list."

Rory's jaw dropped. "What did you say to me?"

Cal felt weightless. He was used to the burden of putting up a front at work, day in and day out, and this exercise was liberating. "I told you you're stupid," Cal said. "What are you going to do about it?"

His boss stared at him with his mouth wide open.

"You look extra ridiculous like that, you know," Cal said.

"You," Rory said. It was the only syllable he uttered; it was as if he'd run out of words.

"I'm going to make this easy for you," Cal said. "I quit."

# CHAPTER 36

## SHERYN

When Sheryn returned to Manhattan North and walked into the squad room, she heard her lieutenant's booming voice announce, "There she is. Detective Sterling cracked the Baxter case in less than twelve hours."

There was an instantaneous round of applause from her brothers and sisters in blue. She froze for a moment, half fearing she'd walked into one of her nightmares and wasn't wearing any pants. Applause wasn't rare at the precinct—whenever they solved a case, there was often a moment like this to celebrate—but Sheryn knew this particular victory lap was premature. Her lips tightened, and she gave her lieutenant a look, but he was beaming at her and clapping in that precise way of his, where his left hand never moved while the right batted it like a flipper.

Rafael stepped toward her, balancing with a gold-topped cane. "You should've warned me," she said, raising an eyebrow.

"And miss out on the fun?" he asked. "It's not like anyone clapped for me when I hobbled in."

"Thanks, everyone," Sheryn said. The clapping died down as she made her way to her desk.

"Thank you, Detective Sterling, for your dedication and determination," the lieutenant said. Stiff and formal as he was, there was an emotional intelligence about him that Sheryn had long appreciated. With one cool nod of his sleek silver head, the cops went right back to work.

"I've gotten quite the earful about your tremendous work, Detective," he said. "You've met Assistant District Attorney Vedika Iyer, I'm sure."

"I have." Sheryn shook hands with the ADA. She didn't know her well, but they'd crossed paths a couple of times since Iyer had transferred from Houston to New York. "It's been a while."

"It's good to see you," Iyer said. She was petite but didn't look small with her lustrous black hair fanned out like a mane, a sharp red suit, and towering heels. Sheryn had long ago adopted a uniform that was meant to communicate her authority without giving away much of her personality: dark pantsuits, tall boots, her hair pinned into a large bun. She was comfortable with that, but Iyer's look was making her think maybe she needed a red suit jacket in her rotation.

"You too," Sheryn said.

"Great work on the case. You're wanted at One Police Plaza," Iyer said.

"For what?"

"For the press conference."

For a nanosecond, Sheryn was flattered. It was a rare occasion to get an invitation like that; her old partner would've been thrilled. *Play the game,* Sandy liked to say, and there was nothing more career boosting than enhancing your profile in the department. At the same time, Sheryn knew it was a terrible idea. "It's way too early to be taking any bows on this. We're still investigating."

The lieutenant turned to the ADA. "I thought you said you'd filed homicide charges this morning."

Sheryn stared at Iyer. "You did *what*? We are nowhere near done. Not by a long shot."

Iyer's smile evaporated. "We've got the murder weapon, DNA, fingerprints, and an eyewitness. We've got the blackmail letters. We've got Baxter's laptop. Seriously, you got everything except the video Baxter was using to extort money out of his killer. I know you haven't had the chance to put in the paperwork, but you've built a solid case. You've done great work, and I appreciate it."

"I thought you were just filing charges regarding the firearm," Sheryn said. "We were still hoping to get Jo Greaver to talk to us."

"Not after the forensics lab found that it was her gun that killed Baxter," Iyer said. "What would be the point of letting his killer go free?"

"Like I say, we're still putting together the case." Sheryn's mouth felt dry. "We're nowhere near done. Andray Baxter's landlord was harassing him, and Baxter had been suing him for the past couple of years. There was a woman who got him fired from his job. There are some strange inconsistencies. I want to get justice for Andray Baxter. I can't do that if we rush on this."

"Detective, I don't need to tell you that the NYPD has a fraught relationship with certain communities in this city," Iyer said. "It's essential that we build trust going forward."

Sheryn stared at her, incredulous. "We're not going to *build trust* by racing to conclusions. Right now, the evidence suggests Andray Baxter was blackmailing Jo Greaver. I had to relay that news to Mr. Baxter's mother this morning. To say she did not take it well would be an understatement. Do you want to see her staging her own press conference about the NYPD defaming her son? Think about the optics of that."

"Sheryn's judgment is solid," the lieutenant said. "If she says it's a poor idea to charge ahead, I have to agree."

Iyer turned to Rafael. "What's your opinion on this?"

"I can tell you my partner's absolutely right about Ornelle Baxter," Rafael said. "She'd go off like a land mine. We don't have enough about Andray Baxter right now. Laying out a case where he's a blackmailer who got killed by a woman he blackmailed is only going to stir up sympathy for Greaver."

"How's that?" Iyer demanded.

"Imagine how many people in this city have been filmed naked or having sex," Rafael said. "Now imagine how they'd feel about being blackmailed."

The room was silent for a moment.

"Thank you for stopping by," the lieutenant said to Iyer. "Clearly, there's work on this case still to be done, and my detectives need to get back to it."

"You should know there's a lot of interest in this case upstairs," Iyer said carefully. Sheryn took it to mean that Iyer was under pressure from her boss, the district attorney, but she knew there was no point in asking for details. "I'll be in touch," Iyer said as she walked away.

The lieutenant looked at his watch. "Want to wager when I'll get a call from a very angry district attorney?"

"I'm sorry, sir," Sheryn said quietly. "I know it's a tough position to put you in."

"You have nothing to apologize for," he answered. "I meant what I said about you and your work. But the pressure from on high isn't going to stop. If there's an alternative theory of the case, we need to come up with it quickly."

After the lieutenant was gone, Sheryn sat down and met Rafael's eyes. "Thanks for having my back," she said. "I know you don't agree with me about the case."

"I don't disagree with you," Rafael said. "And I'm contrary as hell. If the DA's office is in a hurry now, that makes me want to slow down."

Sheryn smiled inwardly at that.

"By the way, in case you think I'm some kind of malingering slug, I was busy while you were out," Rafael added. "I hunted down the detective who investigated Lori Fielding's death. And I use the term *investigated* loosely."

"What did you find?"

"Detective Reich at the Thirteenth Precinct laughed at the idea that there was any foul play involved," Rafael said. "He told me—and I quote—'Junkies OD all the time.' No autopsy, no nothing. Not even a body—it was cremated almost immediately."

"What made you call?"

"Peyton Chin told me Greaver thought there was something suspicious about her sister's death, but the police ignored her," Rafael said. "At least now I know I can trust her on that subject. Greaver got that door slammed in her face."

"I'm glad you followed up, even if it was a dead end," Sheryn said. "I had better luck."

"Do tell."

"At the health club, I found out it was a woman named Sofia Severight who got Andray fired," Sheryn said. "We need to find out what Jo Greaver's connection is to Andray Baxter. Let's see if she'll even talk to us now."

# CHAPTER 37

## Jo

As the hours passed without Cal showing up with bail money, Jo started to panic. If he didn't return, she'd be taken to Rikers. Her sister had been arrested several times, landing in prison for a week here and there, normally for drugs, prostitution, or some combination thereof. In spite of her fraught relationship with Lori, Jo had felt compelled to rescue her every time. *Not by choice,* Jo thought ruefully. *If I hadn't, there would be enough money in my savings account to bail me out right now.*

She wasn't good at waiting. Jo liked to take action, come up with plans, direct outcomes. She felt powerless sitting in a cell, waiting to be rescued. That was prison, Jo realized. It made time a burden. Your life screeched to a halt, and there was nothing you could do about it.

It was almost a relief when she was told the police were there to see her. One of the guards took her to a private room. Mike Nakano was waiting there, along with the two cops who'd accosted her in the hospital.

"We have a strange situation," Detective Sterling said. "Our case looks like a slam dunk from the outside. We have plenty of evidence that shows you were in Andray Baxter's apartment yesterday. We've got the gun . . ."

"Not my gun," Jo interrupted.

"Okay, but we've got a gun, the one that shot Mr. Baxter dead," Sterling continued. "The point is, there's a mountain of evidence against you, yet we're questioning some of it."

Mike sat up straighter. "You think Jo is being framed," he said.

"Let's not overstate this," Mendoza said. "My partner has doubts. I have . . . some questions. I think the evidence is convincing, but some of it's been a little convenient."

"And you're looking for help from Jo?" Mike said. "I mean, my client. Since anything she says in this room can be used against her in court, I don't see why she should talk to you at all."

Jo felt a surge of affection for Mike. He was a clueless guy who'd thrown up on her shoes while drunk, but he was trying his best.

"Honestly, I want to help you," Jo said. "I also want to get out of here. Can you arrange that?"

"I stopped the ADA from filing a murder charge," Sterling said. "But you'd need another hearing to adjust your bail."

"What do you want to know?" Jo asked.

"Let's start with this," Sterling replied. "Who would have the means and ability to frame you for a crime?"

Jo closed her eyes for a moment. She'd been thinking about that since she'd been handcuffed to a hospital bed the night before.

"I have no idea," Jo said, opening her eyes. "I wish I did."

"Okay. Do you know anyone named Severight?"

"Like, the name on that building on Forty-Second Street?" Jo asked. "I wish. I would've made bail already."

"Specifically Sofia Severight," Sterling said. "Does that name ring a bell?"

"No." Jo had expected them to try to ambush her for a confession. It was odd to have them asking about someone she'd never met.

"Maybe you've worked for a company the Severight family owns," Mendoza suggested. "We've been researching them, and they seem to own a lot."

"I started my company when I was twenty-one," Jo said. "I was still in business school at Baruch. It's not like I've worked for a bunch of places. Unless these people own a cosmetics company I'm competing with?"

"Not as far as we can tell," Mendoza said.

Jo glanced at Mike, who was tapping his pen against his hand. He was frowning, which was a new look for him. Jo couldn't figure out what was wrong; these questions seemed innocuous enough to her.

"We would like to go through what happened on Monday with you," Sterling said. "We want to understand it from your perspective."

"There's only one reason I agreed to meet with you," Jo said. "I want to see his photograph again."

"Andray Baxter?" Sterling pulled it up on her phone and set it on the table.

Jo pulled the device toward her, cupping her hand over the top of his head.

"What are you doing?" Mendoza asked.

"Trying to figure out what he'd look like in a ball cap," Jo said.

"That's right," Sterling said quickly. "In the hospital last night, you told us the man you saw was wearing a cap."

"It had a broad brim," Jo said. "I didn't get a good look at his eyes. He was well tanned, but he was white. And his mouth was drawn in this thin, grim line. There's no way it's the same man. I think his name was Tony."

"Did he introduce himself to you?"

"No," Jo said. "That's what the other man in the hallway shouted after I . . ."

"After you shot him?" Sterling asked.

"Don't answer that," Mike said quickly.

182

"Let's speak in hypotheticals," Sterling said. "If a man in that apartment got shot, was it in the chest?"

"No. The stomach."

"This theoretical man didn't die immediately?"

"Definitely not," Jo said.

"Did you see the second man?"

Jo glanced at Mike, but since he didn't object, she responded. "No. I heard a door slam and footsteps in the hallway. He shouted at Tony, asking if he was okay, then he put two bullets through the door."

"Where did this second man come from?"

"I have absolutely no idea," Jo said. "I didn't see anyone when I came in. He must've been in one of the apartments."

"Or he followed you into the building," Mendoza suggested.

Sterling stared at her silently, as if attempting to divine the truth.

"Let's start from the beginning," Sterling said. "You received some hateful messages via email from someone using the handle . . ." She glanced at her phone. "123ABJG666 . . ."

"I know who you mean," Jo said.

"When did that start?"

"The first one was a month ago," Jo said. "I was creeped out, but I ignored it."

"The second message from that account came in a few days later," Sterling said.

A chill ran through Jo. She still remembered how she felt when she'd seen it. She hadn't been able to breathe.

"Do you remember what it said?" Sterling asked.

"It said I was never a successful model like my sister. It asked if my boyfriend and other people would like to see . . . certain photos of me."

"Did you think about going to the police?" Sterling asked.

"No," Jo said softly. "I thought that would make everything worse."

"Did you sense that the person knew you?" Sheryn asked. "He mentioned your sister."

"There wasn't anything personal about what he said about Lori. You could do a ten-second internet search and know she was a model," Jo said. "It was the pictures that were attached that got to me."

"You looked very young in them," Sterling said.

"I was," Jo said softly. She turned to Mike. "Would you mind stepping outside for a bit?"

"I have to be here," Mike said. "It's my job to make sure the police don't . . ."

"It's okay," Jo said. "Really."

"Okay." Mike got to his feet. "Knock on the door when you want me to come back in."

When he was gone, Jo said, "Mike is a friend of my boyfriend's. They went to high school together. My boyfriend doesn't know about this, and I'd rather he never hear about it. Especially not from a guy he knows."

"We'll keep this confidential," Sterling said.

That was the moment of truth for Jo. There was no way to tell them the entire story, but she could reveal a part of it.

"I came to New York after my mother died," Jo said. "I was fourteen. I knew my sister, Lori, lived here, and I thought she had this great career. She was always talking about being a model. Only, when I got here, I found out that it wasn't like she described at all. She had this cute apartment and a boyfriend who paid for it, but things were a little off. She would vanish for days at a time. She let me sleep on her sofa, but after a couple of weeks, she told me I should be a model." Jo shook her head. "Even I knew that I was too short to be a model, but I went along with it because I didn't see how I could say no. The photographer wanted me to take off my clothes, but I wouldn't. When Lori found out, she got so mad she slapped me. She told me I'd have to leave if I didn't . . ." Jo could feel her face flame. "So I did it. The photographer came back, and I took my clothes off."

"I'm sorry," Sterling said.

"Things went on like that," Jo went on. "When I turned sixteen, Lori said it was time for me to *start* working. She brought me to the place where she was working. By *working*, I mean prostitution. You probably figured that out already."

"We suspected you'd been trafficked," Sterling said. "When we saw the photos."

All three of them were silent for a moment, absorbing the weight of that.

"I've worked hard to build a good life for myself, Detectives," Jo said. "I always stayed in school, even when my sister forced me into pornography and prostitution. I graduated early. I attended CUNY and Baruch. I wanted to make a life for myself. I wanted to be more than people thought I could be. I wanted to prove myself." *Prove that I wasn't just a whore,* Jo thought, but she didn't say those words.

"Do you remember any of the people who worked with your sister?" Mendoza asked. "Any of the photographers, any of the other girls?"

"People went by first names, and I don't think a lot of them were real names," Jo said. "In the brothel, I was Suzanna."

"But somebody had these pictures," Sterling said. "All this time, someone's been holding on to them, and only recently did they decide to use them."

Jo bit her lip. She had to be careful diving into this part; she was afraid where it could lead. "My sister had them. Lori would hold them over my head. She made me give her money."

"Your own sister blackmailed you?" Mendoza asked.

Jo nodded.

"So there's a strong possibility that your blackmailer got this material from your sister," Sterling said.

"I don't see how," Jo said. "Lori was not the kind of person to share what she had. She wouldn't have given this away. There would've been less money for her to take if someone else was blackmailing me."

Both of the detectives were staring at her, and Jo sank down a little in her chair. She was ashamed of her past, but far worse was the fact that she was related to a demon like Lori. Much of her sister's DNA was the same as her own, which suggested that she was a monster too.

Mendoza cleared his throat. "On a practical level, your sister had this information stored somewhere. It's possible somebody took it."

"My sister didn't have a will when she died," Jo said. "The police gave me her stuff. The . . . blackmail material was on her computer."

"You still have it?"

"No. I destroyed it," Jo said. "I mean, I literally erased it, poured acid on it, and burned it. The remains of the hard drive are in my safe. No one got anything from it."

"There are no other copies that you know of?"

"None. I don't know how my blackmailer got it." Jo swallowed hard. "That was the first thing I asked that man yesterday. He laughed at me and told me what a hot little bod I had."

"We should bring your lawyer in for the rest of this, if that sounds good to you," Sterling said.

"Yes, please."

When Mike came back in, he sat down and looked at Jo. "Everything okay?"

"As much as it can be right now," Jo said. She looked at the detectives. "You have more questions?"

"Yes, about your blackmailer," Sterling said. "We've seen the emails that he sent you, and your responses to him. Was there any other contact, besides the emails?"

"No. He never tried to reach me any other way."

"There was a reference to a video he sent you," Mendoza said. "But there wasn't one attached to an email."

"There was an online storage service he put it in. I think it vanished as soon as I watched it," Jo said.

"What was on the video?"

"It was a . . . sex tape," Jo said, cursing herself mentally for pausing. "It was something I was forced to do. As a teenager, I mean." She gulped.

Fortunately, the detectives left that alone. The suggestion that there was particularly brutal sex she'd been subjected to when she was underage was enough to steer them away.

"We've got video of you on your way to 631 West Forty-Ninth Street on Monday with a big black duffel bag. What happened to it?" Sterling asked.

"That was my bag of cash. I dropped it when I got shot in the arm," Jo said. "I left it behind when I ran. I thought I was going to die. When I went out the window, I wasn't thinking about anything except getting away."

"Was your gun in that bag?" Mendoza asked.

"Don't answer that," Mike said. He stared at Mendoza. "It sounds like you're trying to trap my client in a statement."

Mendoza put up his hands. "I'm not."

"We need to get to the truth," Sterling added. "Can we speak in hypotheticals?"

Jo watched Mike give her a grudging nod. "Okay."

"We found ammunition in your safe," Sterling said. "What kind of gun would that be for?"

"Beretta BU9 Nano," Jo answered. "If I had one, in theory, I might've gotten it at a gun show in Virginia."

"That's not the gun we found in your bag," Sterling said.

"I threw it in the Hudson, a pier up from the *Intrepid*," Jo said.

"Hypothetically speaking," Mike added.

"In broad daylight?" Mendoza asked. "Seems like a risky move."

"I didn't know what else to do. I couldn't put it in a trash bin. A kid could find it."

"Ms. Greaver," Sterling said, "I want you to think about this hard. Who had access, even for a second, to that bag?"

"I left it in my office while I went out," Jo said. "Anybody in my office, anyone who walked in, could've touched it. When I came back, Annabelle Davies was in my office—she's my principal investor, and there's no way she dropped a gun in my bag. When I left the office, I went straight home."

"Was anyone else there?"

"Just Cal," Jo said. "And his mother, Priscilla. She hates my guts." Jo froze for a moment, turning that thought over in her mind. What had Cal's mother been doing at her apartment anyway? It seemed too strange to be a coincidence. It was true that Priscilla had sent Jo a lawyer, but all that lawyer had wanted her to do was plead guilty to the gun charge. "Detectives, if anyone snuck a gun into my bag, it was her."

"You're not serious?" Mike said. "Mrs. McGarran wouldn't do that."

"She's a shark in a Chanel suit," Jo said. "She would do anything to get me out of Cal's life."

# CHAPTER 38

## SHERYN

"Hello, I'd like to speak to Sofia Severight, please," Sheryn said. While she and Rafael had been interviewing Jo Greaver, some details about the heiress had come in, and Sheryn was making calls as her partner drove them north.

"Who, may I ask, is calling?" asked the chilly, vaguely English voice on the other end of the line.

"It's Detective Sterling of the NYPD," Sheryn said.

"You're with the police?" There was a note of surprise in his voice. "One moment, please."

There was a long hum and a pause, and then a phone rang. "Casper Peters McNally," said a crisp female voice. "How may I direct your call?"

"I was being transferred to Sofia Severight."

"Severight?" the voice said. "Of course. Let me take your name and number. Someone will call you back."

"Sorry if I wasn't clear," Sheryn said. "I'm looking for Sofia Severight. I'd like to speak with her."

There was a light sound, almost a chuckle. "No one speaks directly to the Severights," she said. "Everything goes through their lawyers."

Sheryn left her name and number, but she was sure it was going straight into a circular file.

"That's twenty minutes of your life that you're never going to get back," Rafael muttered when she hung up.

"It's insane. They don't even know why I'm calling."

"Rich people like to put as many layers as possible between themselves and the real world," Rafael said. "Think about it: Is there any reason she'd want to talk to you? No. What's in it for her?"

"Being a good citizen?"

Rafael shook his head. "Listen to yourself, would you? She got a guy fired from his job. Maybe he deserved that, maybe not. Either way, why would she want to talk about it if she didn't have to?" He eased the car into a spot on First Avenue and parked. "I really hope Priscilla McGarran's building isn't a walk-up," he added.

It turned out there was an elevator, but it was a creaky old contraption they had to wait several minutes for, watching its progress down to the lobby via old-fashioned clock hands and numbers.

"This was probably a state-of-the-art place in 1929," Rafael said.

"The bloom is off that rose," Sheryn said. "I figured Cal McGarran for someone born with a silver spoon in his mouth. But if he ever had one, his family pawned it."

"Appearances can be deceiving. Everyone knows that, but when you live in LA, you really see it up close," Rafael said. "All of these perfect-looking people who are basically living out of their cars, hoping for their big break. You get people in designer clothes at soup kitchens."

Upstairs, Sheryn knocked on the door. Priscilla McGarran answered a moment later. She was tall and slender, with silver hair and intelligent blue eyes. She wore an elegant shift dress in a dark leopard print, but her stockinged feet were shoeless. It wasn't immediately clear to Sheryn if she had just come home or was getting ready to go out.

"Priscilla McGarran?" Sheryn asked. "I'm Detective Sterling, and this is my partner, Detective Mendoza. We're involved in an investigation that concerns Jo Greaver. I believe she's involved with your son."

McGarran sighed. "She is, unfortunately. Do you want to come in?"

"Thank you," Sheryn said, stepping inside.

The apartment wasn't large, but it was magnificent, decorated with fine antiques—or possibly replicas, Sheryn couldn't be sure. Either way, it was beautiful.

"Can I offer you something to drink?" McGarran asked, picking up a Persian cat from the sofa and depositing the creature gently on the carpet.

"No, thank you," Sheryn said. "We have a few questions. Ms. Greaver told us that you were at her apartment yesterday afternoon when she came in. Can you tell us what you were doing there?"

"I wasn't feeling well," McGarran said. "I'm a personal stylist, and I'd dropped off a few things for a client downtown. After that I . . . I started feeling sick, as if I were having a heart attack. I called my son in a panic, because I couldn't find my medication."

"Did your son meet you?"

She nodded. "Yes. Cal found my medication in my bag and calmed me down. I wanted to go home, but he insisted that I lie down for a bit at his apartment. He's incredibly kind."

"Do you remember Ms. Greaver coming in?"

"Yes. I was lying down on the sofa. Cal was in the kitchen, I think. Jo screamed when she saw me. She made it very clear she was unhappy that I was there. Obviously neither of us was expecting to see the other."

"You don't get along?" Sheryn asked.

"We're not close," McGarran said. "Early on, I had concerns that Jo was attempting to use Cal, that she was a social climber. Since I've come to understand that they are serious about each other, I've attempted to make overtures to Jo, but she isn't interested. She's always telling Cal that I said or did something mean to her."

Sheryn tried to keep her face neutral, but she felt her eyebrows rise. "She told us that you don't like her. That you'd do anything to break her and Cal up."

"Hardly. Cal was dating a really lovely girl before Jo came along," McGarran said. "Unfortunately, she moved to Korea for work. I wish he'd find someone else, but it's not really my business."

Sheryn shot a quick look at Rafael. "Did you know that a gun was found in Ms. Greaver's bag last night?"

"Yes. My son told me about it."

"Ms. Greaver suggested to us that you put it there."

Priscilla McGarran stared at them for several seconds, clearly astonished. "That little . . ." Whatever word she was about to utter died on her lips; Sheryn noted her self-control. McGarran shook her head, and her cheeks flushed bright pink. "Obviously, that's not true. My son went through my handbag before I even got near the apartment. Of course, you're not going to trust my son as an alibi . . ." She stood up. "Do you want to examine the bag? It's a Birkin, and it's worth a small fortune."

"I don't think we—" Rafael started to say.

Sheryn interrupted him. "That would be really helpful, Mrs. McGarran."

After McGarran retrieved the handbag, she handed it to Sheryn. "Please promise me you'll be careful with it," she asked, clearly worried about its care. "I hate letting it out of my sight."

"We'll have an officer return the bag to you before the end of the day." Sheryn glanced at the bag in her hands. "I've never seen one of these up close. It is beautiful. I promise we'll take good care of it."

McGarran sat down again. "I can't believe Jo would accuse me, but then again, Jo is *not* the nicest person. I'm not talking about her background; I mean her own nature. Did you know that I hired a lawyer for her this morning? Jo turned around and fired him immediately."

"What lawyer was that?" Sheryn asked.

"Jon Urraza from Casper Peters McNally," McGarran said.

"Hold on," Sheryn said, feigning innocence while a frisson of excitement crackled down her spine. "I just came across that law firm's name. How did you find them?"

"They were recommended by an old family friend," McGarran said. "They represented me over a decade ago when I divorced my husband."

"Who was the family friend?" Sheryn pressed.

"Malcolm Severight."

Sheryn felt like her head was spinning. Priscilla McGarran seemed completely unaware that she had put her finger on a pressure point in the case. *Keep it casual,* she reminded herself. *And don't drop the fancy handbag.* "Oh, do you know his daughter, Sofia?"

"Only a little," McGarran said. "She's several years younger than her brother was. Serge and my son were best friends in elementary school. I haven't seen Sofia in ages."

"Her brother . . . was?" Rafael asked. "Did something happen to him?"

"Yes, he died in an accident a few years ago."

"That's very sad," Sheryn said. "We really appreciate your time, Mrs. McGarran. We won't trouble you any further." She looked at the handbag she was holding. "We'll have this back to you in no time. The case seems to be wrapping up quickly."

McGarran smiled. "Thank you, Detective. I know I should feel pity for Jo, but she's brought all of this on herself."

Outside the apartment, Sheryn and Rafael waited for the elevator in silence. Only after it arrived, and its ancient iron doors had creaked shut like skeletal limbs, did Rafael speak. "What, exactly, are you doing with her purse?"

"The lab can swab it for gunshot residue," Sheryn said. "But I also want to get it printed."

"You don't really think she planted the gun, do you?"

"She handed over the bag with a minimum of fuss," Sheryn pointed out. "So, no, I don't think we'll find anything at all."

"You like being mysterious, don't you?" Rafael asked.

"It has its uses."

On their way out of the building, Rafael asked, "You don't really think somebody planted the gun, do you?"

"Call me crazy, but I believe Ms. Greaver on that." Sheryn caught Rafael's dubious look. "I know she had a gun, but the ammo in her safe doesn't match the gun we found. I think she's telling the truth about there being a second man at the scene."

"You think Andray Baxter was allowing the blackmailer to use his apartment? And he somehow got shot in the aftermath?"

"I keep trying to work up a theory, but the facts don't support anything that makes sense," Sheryn admitted. "Let's say Ms. Greaver met her blackmailer in the apartment, and they had their shoot-out. Both get shot. The man in the hallway tries to get in and shoots through the front door. Jo Greaver goes out the window, and presumably the man in the hallway comes in . . ."

"And then?" Rafael prompted.

"What if the blackmailer shot Mr. Baxter? That way, he could keep the money for himself and cast blame elsewhere."

"Okay, except the blackmailer has a slug in him," Rafael said. "Double-crossing your partner is harder when you're bleeding out."

"You're saying he needed Mr. Baxter—or anyone, really—to get him help." Sheryn nodded slowly. "See what I mean? Things don't add up."

They got into Rafael's Mercedes. "What do you want to do now? It's getting late."

"I need to see the crime scene again. Ms. Greaver said she didn't see another man in the hallway. He had to be hiding somewhere."

"We still haven't gotten a list of tenants from that weasel Westergard," Rafael pointed out.

"If we can find some kind of evidence—even a drop of blood in the hallway—ADA Iyer would be able to get us a warrant for the building."

"Dammit," Rafael said. "I hate those stairs."

"Fair enough," Sheryn said. "I can check out the hallway and stairs without somebody holding my hand."

"Okay," Rafael said. "Let me see what I can wring out of Westergard."

# CHAPTER 39

## CAL

Once Cal started thinking about his godmother's connection to Jo, questions multiplied in his brain. Annabelle had never explained why she'd taken an interest in Corvus Alchemy; she had described it to Cal as *the upstart company everyone is talking about,* and Cal had accepted that. But since he'd met Jo, he knew that her struggling company had only hit it big because of Annabelle's extensive investment. That made him wonder about how Jo had ended up on Annabelle's radar. It also made Cal even more curious why his godmother had asked him, rather than her own son, to go over the financials.

It had been a long time since he'd stopped by Annabelle's apartment. When he was young, it had been like a second home to Cal. His godmother lived across Gramercy Park from his parents' place but in a loftier, airier space. He didn't recognize the doorman who opened the door for him and rang up to the apartment, but the wood-paneled elevator with its brass hardware was exactly as he remembered it. Cal was expecting to find Annabelle at home, but it was her son, Zachary, who opened the door.

"Hello, Cal," he said, sounding delighted to see him. "No sightings for a year, then twice in two days. What's new?"

"I just quit my job," Cal blurted out. "And my girlfriend is in jail. I was hoping to speak to your mother," Cal added.

Zachary stared at him. "She's out, but you need to come in."

As he stepped inside, Cal realized Zachary had said something similar the last time he'd turned up unannounced, years earlier. Cal had been seventeen years old and was dressed in an ill-fitting suit to visit Annabelle after her husband had suddenly passed away. Nothing in the apartment had changed; it looked like a movie set, except for the framed photographs on the end table, including one of Annabelle, her husband, and her son basking in sunlight.

"My mother should be back soon," Zachary said. "I made coffee, but I think we need something stronger. Bourbon?"

Cal nodded. He walked around the room while Zachary went to the kitchen. He found his way to the window, with its spectacular view of downtown Manhattan. He was standing there, taking it in, when Zachary returned and handed him a crystal highball glass.

"I don't even know what to say." Zachary took a drink. "I'm sorry, Cal. Poor Jo."

"Have you met her?" Cal asked.

"No. But my mother talks about her. Why is she in jail?"

"Long story." Cal drank some bourbon; it burned on its way down. "I wanted to ask your mother how she got involved with Jo's company in the first place. Do you have any idea?"

"My mother's always looking at potential investments," Zachary said.

Cal felt like Zachary was sidestepping the question, as if he knew more than he was saying. But before he could ask, Zachary went on.

"I still feel bad about telling her Jo's company wasn't a good bet. I really got that one wrong."

"Annabelle had you look over the financials?" Cal asked. "She never told me that."

"Probably because she didn't want to bias you," Zachary said. "I noticed that Jo dipped into the company's reserve fund for reasons unconnected to the business. I thought that was a bad precedent, and that's what I told my mother."

"What did she say?"

"She said thanks and proceeded to ignore my advice." He took another drink. "I guess I should be used to that by now."

"I'm sorry—I haven't even asked how you're doing," Cal said, prompted by Zachary's glum expression. "How's work?"

"Mr. Severight hired me to run his family office, but the job has been taking over my life," Zachary said. "He's brilliant, but he's an oddball. He also keeps crazy hours and expects me to be at his beck and call when he's up."

"He used to tell me he did his best thinking at three in the morning," Cal said.

"His butler and I have a secret support group. He says everything went to hell after Serge died. It changed Mr. Severight for the worse. He's angry all the time."

"A tragedy like that always changes people," Cal said. "How could it not?"

"I don't know," Zachary said. "I don't think my father's death affected my mother much at all. She just went on with her life. I mean, she married that imbecile Montana Bob less than a year later."

"I felt weird about missing her wedding," Cal said. "You remember what was going on with my family at the time. I guess part of me wanted to be happy for Annabelle, but I missed your dad and couldn't understand how she could get married again so soon."

"You and me both," Zachary said. "It was a nightmare. I went from Horace Mann to living on a ranch. Montana Bob didn't think you were a real man if you couldn't rope a steer. Living with him was torture. 'Real men don't talk so much, boy. Real men don't need books.' He kept telling my mother she'd raised a fairy." Zachary shook his head. "The happiest day of my life was when my mom ditched him."

Cal realized that when he looked at Zachary, he still saw him as the bespectacled boy he remembered, the one obsessed with Dungeons & Dragons and superhero comics. Zachary was now sharply dressed and smooth, but Cal realized he hadn't changed much under the skin. Did anyone?

There was an odd ringtone, and Zachary reached for his phone. "Sorry, Severight hotline," he said, looking at his screen. "Ugh, I have to go back to work."

"No problem," Cal said. "Thanks for the drink."

Zachary was still scanning his screen. "He's really angry this time." He put the phone away. "I should get up there."

"I'll wait for Annabelle downstairs."

"She's not far away," Zachary said. "She's at Corvus."

They took the elevator down together and shook hands. Cal hurried west. It took him all of five minutes to reach Jo's office. He didn't recognize the receptionist at the front desk when he walked in. She was grumbling as she packed things up.

"I hope you're not a reporter," she said.

"I'm not. My name is Cal McGarran. I'm looking for Annabelle Davies."

"You just missed her," the receptionist said. "If you want to leave a message, I can write it down on paper. Don't call. The phone's been ringing off the hook."

"Cal?"

He turned and saw Peyton Chin standing there. He'd met her several times, and her hair was always a different color. Today it was navy, but it was pulled back in a simple headband. She wore a black dress and ballet flats. Her expression was serious.

"Hi, Peyton," Cal said. "I was looking for Annabelle."

"We need to talk," Peyton said. "Why don't you come into my office?"

Cal felt uncomfortable, as if he were in middle school and being called out by the principal. Still, he followed her into her cubbyhole of an office and sat in a chair. Peyton stood over him, glowering, with her arms crossed.

"Why haven't you posted Jo's bail?" she asked.

Cal was taken aback. "I was going to. But . . ." His voice faded out.

"But what?"

"I was in court when Jo was arraigned. I hadn't heard the evidence against her before."

"You think Jo murdered that actor?" Peyton demanded. "Are you for real?"

"I don't know," Cal said. "I can't imagine Jo killing someone. But she went to his apartment . . ."

"So what?"

"She was involved with him." It was tough for Cal to get the words out. "She was cheating on me."

Peyton opened her mouth to speak, but she stopped and took a deep breath. She walked around her desk and sat in her chair, exhaling loudly. "Fuck you, Cal McGarran."

"What?"

"Fuck you and your hurt feelings," Peyton said. "Your girlfriend is on an express train to hell right now, and all you're capable of is wallowing in self-pity. I don't know what Jo did or didn't do. But I know she's a good person, and she's my friend. I also know if the shoe were on the other foot, and *you* were under arrest, she'd be supporting you right now."

"Nobody knows what they're capable of," Cal said quietly. "Not until they're in a bad situation."

"Where's your sense of loyalty?" Peyton asked.

"That's exactly what my father said when the police arrested him. He thought my mother and I should lie for him. I guess you think we should have, out of loyalty."

"No. I'm saying you don't walk away when someone you care about is in trouble," Peyton said. "Whether or not Jo stepped out on you is a different issue. Work that out between you later. I'm telling you that you're being petty. You're not going to feel good about this later."

Cal looked away. He already felt bad. Guilt gnawed at his stomach like a beast. But he believed Jo deserved to suffer for betraying him.

"Things haven't been going well the past few weeks," Cal said. "Jo's been lying to me. She withdrew the money out of our joint account. I even caught her watching some violent porn on her computer. She tried to blame that last one on you. She said you sent it to her."

"Jo told you I sent her porn?" Peyton looked incredulous. "That's insane."

"She's not herself. I don't know what's going on. She won't tell me. How am I supposed to help her if she won't be honest?"

"Maybe you need to convince her she can trust you," Peyton suggested. "But that begs the question: *Can* she trust you?"

"Yes," Cal said. There was a hard lump in his throat.

"Do you want to help her?"

"Yes."

Peyton pushed a folder toward him. "Take a look at this."

Cal opened it. There was article after article about teenage girls who'd killed men who'd sexually abused them. He recognized a few of the names, including Cyntoia Brown, who'd been sold to the man who abused her, and Sarah Kruzan, who'd been convicted at seventeen of killing the man who'd trafficked her for five years.

"I know Corvus Alchemy donates money to help girls and women who've been trafficked," Cal said.

"Jo started doing that as soon as she started the company," Peyton said. "But this is different. The police took her computer away, but I was able to get her search history off the server. She's been obsessing about teenagers who killed their abusers."

"Why would she . . . ?"

"You know her better than I do," Peyton said. "Or at least, you're supposed to. What do *you* think?"

# CHAPTER 40

## Jo

After the detectives left, Jo sat in the interview room with Mike Nakano for a few minutes. "I'm really sorry for everything you went through," Mike said.

Jo tried to remember how much he'd heard. The cops had made a reference to the photographs before he left the room, and to the video after he came back in. "Thanks."

"I didn't know you had it so hard," Mike said. "You always seem so confident. Like someone who has it together."

"I'm good at pretending I do."

"You should tell Cal." Mike looked at her seriously. "He would want to know."

"I don't think Cal wants to be in this picture anymore, as evidenced by his failure to bail me out."

"He'd feel differently if he knew," Mike insisted. "Look, I don't know how much he told you about his dad, but Mr. McGarran blew Cal's life up after he was arrested. He was trying to take other people down with him. Mr. McGarran didn't care who he hurt, and that included his own family. He was a sociopath."

"Cal probably thinks I am, too, at this point."

"No, he doesn't. But he has fears about being betrayed."

Jo looked at him. "You're supposed to be the crazy party animal who drinks and snorts his days away, not the sensitive guy."

"I was always the sensitive one," Mike said, with a rueful grin. "That's why I started drinking until I threw up. I never belonged anywhere I went, and I couldn't stand it."

*That gives us something in common,* Jo thought. *Even before this nightmare started, I knew people would figure out I was a fraud.*

After he left, a guard took Jo back to her shared cell. She retreated to a corner and cried so hard that the other women in the cell, whatever they were or weren't guilty of, took turns comforting her. "It can't be that bad, honey," one of them said. *But it is,* Jo thought; *it is so much worse.* She had loved Cal, but she had lost him anyway. That wasn't the worst thing, though: talking to the police about her sister had made Lori loom large in her mind.

*JoJo, you won't believe it, but I saw a ghost today. He looked exactly like the man I loved. The one you destroyed.*

Thinking about her sister always broke Jo's heart. She'd grown up idolizing Lori, who was nine years older than she was and had fled to New York City when Jo was seven. Technically, she was Jo's half sister, since they had different fathers; no one, including her mother, seemed to be sure who Jo's was. That technicality hadn't mattered to Jo, though; she had put up photographs of Lori on the wall of the trailer whenever Lori sent one home. Jo had wanted to be exactly like her, until she'd found out what Lori really was.

*Don't be a useless crybaby,* Lori hissed, but it was too late, because Jo was sitting in the holding cell, weeping. One of her fellow prisoners slipped her a pill that Jo accepted gratefully. Jo didn't ask what it was; she simply took it and let her mind drift away from her body. It made her feel as if there were a pane of glass between herself and her feelings, and she was grateful for it.

When the guard finally came by to tell her that her bail had been posted, Jo was sitting quietly by herself, wondering how she could ever tell Cal the things she needed to say to him. She loved him, but at heart she was a cynic, and she didn't believe there was any way she could explain the choices she'd made. She believed that Mike was right about Cal's sympathies for what had happened to her as a teenager; she didn't doubt that. However, the decisions she'd made afterward would be another story.

She was forced to sign a series of forms, and the possessions that had been confiscated from her the night before were returned. Then she braced herself to face Cal, but when she was taken to the atrium, she discovered Annabelle Davies waiting for her.

"Jo!" Annabelle hurried over to hug her. "I'm so glad you're safe."

Jo felt frozen in place, so startled and upset that she couldn't even move her arms to hug Annabelle back. "What are you doing here?"

"I saw the news." Annabelle let go and stepped back. She was wearing an elegant violet suit with a nipped-in waist; strands of pearls hung around her neck. "I couldn't believe it. I *don't* believe it, of course. The idea that you're guilty of a crime is ridiculous."

Jo knew she should be touched, but she was horrified that the woman she admired most in the world had been dragged into her personal drama.

"Thank you," Jo whispered. She wanted to say more, but she couldn't choke the words out.

"I have a car waiting," Annabelle said. "Let's go outside."

When they did, Jo discovered a black SUV idling at the curb. The driver got out and opened the door for them. Jo got in first, sliding across the leather seat, and Annabelle followed her, elegantly crossing her legs at the ankles but ignoring the seat belt.

"Let's get you home," Annabelle said. "I imagine that's where you'd like to go."

"I'm desperate for a shower," Jo said.

Annabelle gave the driver Jo's address and then raised the glass partition so they'd have some privacy.

"Someone is trying to frame you, and I'm going to make sure that doesn't happen," Annabelle said. "You need a really good lawyer, of course. That's got to be the first priority. But I've got your back, Jo. You know that, right?"

Jo couldn't understand why each kind word seemed to cut her a little deeper. "I'm guilty," she said in a soft voice. "Someone was blackmailing me, and I shot him. Not the actor, but . . . I don't know who the man was. All I know is that he fired at me, and I fired at him."

Her words didn't seem to register on Annabelle. "You're a good person, Jo. Whether you know it or not."

"I don't think I am." Jo realized she sounded as miserable as she felt. "I think there's something wrong with me, with the way my mind works. Maybe it's in my DNA."

"Jo, you are absolutely nothing like your sister."

Annabelle's words were like a shock of electricity between them. Jo saw that her mentor was trying to look nonchalant, gazing out the window of the car, but she also noticed a vein pulsing in her forehead. "You never told me that you knew my sister," Jo said.

"I didn't know you were related until after I started investing in your company," Annabelle said. "Your last names were different, and you didn't look anything alike. After I realized it, I . . . well, I didn't want to say anything about it."

"Why not?"

"I disliked your sister," Annabelle said. "Immensely. I crossed paths with her and foolishly believed her words of praise and admiration. I invited her to a party and—" She stopped speaking abruptly. Her normally serene face was scowling.

"And what?"

"Your sister threw herself at my husband," Annabelle said. "Not the horrible second husband with the ranch in Montana. I wouldn't have minded someone taking that wretched man off my hands. My first husband. Zach's father."

"I'm so sorry. I had no idea."

"First, don't apologize for matters that aren't your fault," Annabelle chided gently. "Second, your sister was a horrible person who was awful to everyone. I'm sure she was a monster to you, my dear. Living with her must've been a nightmare."

Jo felt her heart fluttering in her throat. "How did you know I lived with her?"

"She's your sister," Annabelle said simply. "I assumed you must've lived with her, growing up. Didn't you?"

"Yes, but she left home early. I was still pretty young."

"Oh, I see. You probably didn't get to know her at all. Truthfully, that was a very good thing."

The SUV pulled up in front of Jo's building in Hanover Square. "Thank you, Annabelle. I promise I'll pay you back. For everything."

"You don't need to worry about that," Annabelle said. "You need to focus on yourself and your defense. I'll have a short list of lawyers for you to speak with by tomorrow morning."

"You don't have to do that."

"I do. I owe it to you." Annabelle was calm, but Jo saw anxiety behind her eyes. "There are stories circulating about you. About men and about . . . photographs of you. This is red meat for the tabloids right now. Believe me—I know what that's like. You're a lovely young woman who's got a successful business, and that's like painting a target on yourself to the bottom-feeders. I think you should sue anyone who defames you. I have a lawyer to suggest for that too."

Jo didn't trust her voice. She only nodded. The driver opened her door, and she ran out of the vehicle and into her building. She really did want a shower, but she wished she could take one that would scrub her brain and clear her memory. Normally, she moved fast enough to out-pace the bad feelings and awful memories. Now, she felt as if she were sinking into them. The past was a black hole that was pulling her apart. The first thing she did once inside was call the shop around the corner.

A while later, the doorman rang up, telling her there was a delivery. The man at the door handed her a bag. She looked inside: there was a bottle of champagne and one of whiskey.

# CHAPTER 41

## SHERYN

The building at 631 West Forty-Ninth hadn't changed since the day before, to Sheryn's eyes. She knew that the CSU crew had been thorough on Monday, she knew they were solid, and she trusted them. But on Monday, the case had looked deceptively simple to everyone: there was a murdered man and killer to be found. Twenty-four hours later, the world had been turned on its head; Sheryn was now looking for evidence to string together a new working theory for the crime. As far as she was concerned, the case against Jo Greaver was coming apart at the seams, even if no one else saw it. At first, she'd been taken in as well, but that was only because she had looked at it in low light; in the harsh light of day, its cracks were fully on display, much like the building itself.

Climbing the stairs, she felt a sense of déjà vu: there was a television blaring on the third floor, just as there had been the day before. Otherwise, the building was quiet.

The door to Andray Baxter's apartment was closed, with the yellow police tape crisscrossed in front of it. It was locked, but that was a silly formality with a chunk of the door missing. She reached inside and turned the lock. As she stepped inside the apartment, the first thing that hit her was the smell. The blood hadn't been cleaned up; it had congealed on the floor, and the stink of it made her eyes water. It was a little odd that it hadn't been removed, but she could understand why: the owner of the building was responsible for hiring a private company to decontaminate the apartment.

*He probably looks at this horror show as a blessing,* Sheryn realized. Westergard wasn't going to pay anybody to clean anything. He'd leave this nightmarish scene as it was to chase away the few remaining tenants he had.

She pulled plastic booties over her shoes and stepped in farther. When she'd first seen the apartment, she'd been struck by how bloody the kitchen floor was. Jo Greaver hadn't actually come out and said that she'd shot a man in the apartment, but she'd come awfully close. She'd admitted she had a gun, and that she'd thrown it away afterward. If she had encountered a white man—and Sheryn believed her on this point—where had Andray Baxter been? The timeline was tight; he had to have been killed immediately before or immediately after Greaver had shot the other man. What wasn't clear was why.

*The money he was giving his mother,* Sheryn thought. *Where was that coming from?* Had Andray allowed a shady friend to use his apartment in exchange for cash that would pay for his mother's cancer treatments?

No matter how Sheryn looked at it, the idea that Andray Baxter was Jo's lone tormenter was unlikely. Jo had been ordered to be at that apartment at a particular date and time. Sheryn didn't believe Andray had orchestrated that; someone else was involved. Sheryn had been frustrated by her inability to find any link whatsoever between Baxter and Greaver. What if there was no direct link between them, only a third party who knew them both?

Greaver had told her that a man had come running down the hallway shouting the name Tony. Had that been Baxter in the hallway? Was he the one who'd put two bullets through his own front door? That idea didn't sit right with Sheryn. For starters, Andray was house proud, with his well-ordered, lovely little oasis in that decaying building; for another, that meant he'd had a gun, and Sheryn had a hard time believing that.

She went through the apartment carefully but found nothing useful. She stopped in front of the painting of the Holy Family. It was beautiful, and not unlike an image on the wall of her childhood home. As she gazed at it, she remembered what Jo had said the first time they'd met. *I got scared because I thought I saw blood.* She had been talking about the painting. Sheryn peered at it. Mary wore a simple blue robe, but Joseph's long cloak was woven of kente cloth that was red, gold, and green, and it swept around the bottom of the frame. The longer Sheryn stared, the more she noticed tiny flecks of rust that she wasn't sure belonged on the canvas. Could that be blood? She moved her head closer, trying to decide. It was impossible to tell.

But not impossible for everyone, she knew.

She pulled out her phone and called Florian.

"Hello, Detective," he said when he answered. "I was finishing up for the day."

"Florian, I have a huge favor to ask. Could you come back to the crime scene? I think I may have found more blood here."

"Detective, your case is rather boring, and I have a lovely bottle of Nieto Senetiner Bonarda waiting for me at home."

"Is that wine?"

Florian's sigh dragged on for several seconds. "Nieto Senetiner was founded in 1888, and Bonarda is *only* grown in Argentina, Detective."

She was glad Florian wasn't in the room, because she wanted to strangle him. "This is important, Florian. This case is anything but boring. We thought it was a straightforward homicide yesterday, and we were wrong. There was a second man shot at the scene, and we don't know if he's alive or dead."

"Hmm," Florian said. "That *is* curious."

"We're starting to think our main suspect was framed." Sheryn knew she sounded melodramatic, but she was aware that Florian couldn't resist a complicated case. "That would mean some of the evidence was planted to deceive us, and the real evidence . . ."

"Is still to be discovered." There was an edge of excitement to Florian's voice. "You win, Detective. I'm coming over."

After she hung up, she used her phone to take a couple of shots of the painting, including a close-up of what she was hoping really was blood splatter. Then she turned around and looked at the hallway.

*There are only two routes in and out of the apartment. The hallway and the fire escape.* Sheryn knew the fire escape had been thoroughly investigated, because that was how Jo Greaver had gotten out. The hallway had been largely ignored. She stepped closer to it, turning her head to look left and right. There had once been a carpet running down the center of the hallway; there were still studs in the wood marking its position, like a forgotten landing strip. The wood was pockmarked and stained.

The man Jo Greaver heard in the hallway hadn't materialized out of nowhere. Did he live in the building, or was he only there to ambush Greaver? Sheryn stepped into the corridor. Could Greaver tell the difference between footsteps coming from the hallway or up the stairs? Maybe, since the stairs creaked and groaned out an unholy symphony. Greaver had only heard footfalls on the wood in the hall. Sheryn turned to the right and tried the door of the next apartment; it actually rattled on its hinges when she knocked. She listened for a minute, but no one answered. The obvious thing to do was wait for a warrant, because if the apartment was a private home, she'd be in a huge amount of trouble for breaking in. On the other hand, the city marshal's notice on the door made it virtually certain that the apartment *had* no legal tenant. There was a dark stain on the floor in front of it that *could* be blood. Sheryn was looking for a man who'd been shot. Was that moan she heard coming from the building or inside? She took a minute to pick the lock and opened the door.

The apartment was a mirror image of Baxter's in terms of its layout, but it was empty and bleak. When Sheryn stepped across the floor, she realized she was leaving footprints in the dust and grit. *I should've brought a face mask,* she thought ruefully. Who knew what she was breathing in? The kitchen was worse: there were shards of glass and china on the countertop and on the floor. Sheryn had the feeling that the tenant who'd moved out had left that as a final *Screw you* to the landlord.

In the midst of that mess, a giant rat sitting on the counter stood up on its hind legs when it saw her, then leaped into the air and hurried toward her. Sheryn ran to the door and slammed it shut.

"Freaking rats," she hissed, her heart beating frantically. "I hate you so much."

She was grateful that Rafael wasn't there to laugh at her. She made a mental note to have somebody else open *that* door when they got their warrant.

There were a total of six apartments on the floor, and none of the others had city marshal's notices, meaning that any of them could be occupied. There was no way she could justify picking those locks. Instead, she tried the handles to see if any were unlocked; none were. The door on the other side of Andray Baxter's apartment was different from the others, though. As Sheryn grasped it, electricity shot into her hand, making her jump backward. She stared at her palm. It hurt like hell, but there wasn't a visible injury. It was like a practical joke, maybe one designed to jolt a landlord from hell. Sheryn examined the floor in front of it; there were stains there, too, but nothing that was obviously blood.

She heard groaning sounds from below and noticed Florian's sleek head as he came up the stairs, carrying a black briefcase.

"I've decided you owe me a bottle of wine," Florian announced. "I suppose Malbec will do, since it's easier to procure in this country, with its dead taste buds."

"Thanks for coming," Sheryn said. "You are a prince among men."

"This case better be as interesting as you promised. Now where is this mysterious blood?"

"On the painting in here," Sheryn said, darting into Andray Baxter's apartment again. "There are tiny specks that don't look like they belong."

"Hmm. I doubt it."

"I was looking at the hallway floor too," Sheryn added quickly. "Our second suspect was shot in the stomach, according to the woman we have in custody."

"That's a messy wound," Florian said. "It's hard to imagine there's no trail down the staircase."

"Be careful," Sheryn said. "I got an electric shock from the door-knob next to this apartment. I'm starting to feel like the place is booby-trapped."

Her phone rang, and she didn't recognize the number. She didn't recognize the gentle voice on the other end of the line either.

"Is this Detective Sterling?" a woman asked. "My name is Audra Baxter, and I need to talk to you as soon as possible. It's about my brother, Andray."

# CHAPTER 42

## RAFAEL

Rafael had mixed feelings about not returning to the crime scene. He was genuinely glad to avoid the walk up inside a death trap, where there wasn't a banister to hold on to. But the fact that his partner had instantly agreed made him feel like Quasimodo, as if she was ashamed to be seen with him in public. He knew she wasn't shallow like that, but he also knew that Sheryn gave her all to the job and expected everyone else to do the same. The truth was, he wasn't capable of that at the moment. He wondered if he ever would be again.

He double-parked his car in front of a nondescript building on West Thirty-Eighth Street. From his perspective, it was in some kind of wasteland between Pennsylvania Station and Times Square, with all the charm that implied. Rafael was a recent transplant from Los Angeles and still homesick for his hometown; winter's early approach in New York wasn't helping to ease that. He planted a flashing light on the dashboard and walked away with a tiny sliver of guilt. Sheryn hated cops who did that, but that was too bad. He was stuck limping everywhere with a cane, so he wasn't making any extra steps.

He took the elevator up to the fifth floor. The place reeked of perming solution, which made him wince. He'd always been sensitive to smells. Everybody said that if you dulled one sense, the others got stronger; that had been true for him ever since he'd woken up in a hospital with a nonstop buzzing in his head. It wasn't that he couldn't hear people; it was that he had to work to hear them, to tune them in. Meanwhile, his sense of smell hit him like a sledgehammer all day long.

He was about to open the door for Westergard Real Estate Holdings when his phone silently vibrated. It was a pair of texts from Brett, and the messages made him smile.

> Not bothering you at work. Just checking that you're okay.

> PS I still hate your job, but I love you.

Rafael rested his shoulder against the wall and pulled his gold wedding band out of the inside pocket of his jacket. He had issues about wearing it at work; cops were generally a conservative bunch. Brett had had the bright idea to inscribe their rings with PIBO, which stood for *Put It Back On*. Rafael slipped it on his fourth finger and texted back an emoji heart. As he did, Rafael caught Elliott Westergard's voice inside the office, loud and agitated.

"No, I won't hold." Westergard's voice was heated. "I've been holding all day! This is the tenth time I've called."

Rafael froze in place.

"It's Elliott Westergard. W-E-S-T-E-R-G-A-R-D. Mr. Severight *knows* who I am."

*Severight?* Rafael hoped he'd heard that right, that his faulty senses weren't playing with him. There was a long pause, and Rafael started to feel self-conscious about standing in the hallway. It was a small building, and the floor was quiet. *Maybe everyone else passed out from huffing the perm solution,* he thought. He didn't want someone to materialize and ask what he was doing. He figured he could always grab his cane and play the injury card, but that idea hurt his pride. He'd never had trouble recovering from a wound before. The fact that this had been going on for so long scared him.

"What do you mean he's never heard of me?" Westergard's voice was heated. "He made an offer on my building at 631 West Forty-Ninth. No, I don't have that in writing. Put him on the phone. Now."

A moment later, there was a long string of curses. Rafael figured it was time to chat. He turned the door handle, but it was locked. There was no bell to ring, so he knocked.

"Who's there?" Westergard called out.

"Rafael Mendoza. We met yesterday afternoon." *No percentage in reminding him I'm a detective,* Rafael thought.

"Why are you here?"

"To talk about the case," Rafael said. "There've been some developments you should know about."

There was a pause, but Westergard turned the locks and opened the door. When Rafael saw him, he hoped the shock didn't register in his face. Elliott Westergard was wild eyed in a crumpled suit. Rafael recognized it as yesterday's and figured Westergard had probably slept in it. The landlord's hair hadn't been combed and stood at odd angles.

"Is everything okay?" Rafael asked. "When I was coming down the hall, I thought I heard a shout."

"I fell over a box," Westergard said.

"Damn, that's pretty bad. You don't want to end up like me."

Westergard stared at him blankly.

"With a cane, I mean," Rafael clarified. *What the hell is this guy on?* he wondered.

"What did you want to tell me about the case?" Westergard asked.

Rafael hadn't been invited in, but he nudged his way in the door. He barely resisted the urge to whistle when he saw the disaster inside. The suite was small: there was a tiny reception area with a cheap desk that had a fake wood-grain pattern on it that let you know no trees had been harmed in its creation. There were three small offices behind it, and their doors were open; from what Rafael could see, there had been some kind of paper bomb that had detonated inside and covered every surface.

"What happened in here?" Rafael asked. "Did someone break in?"

"No. Why would you think that?" Westergard frowned.

Rafael took his measure in a nanosecond. Westergard was one of those people who masked their inner chaos with a meticulous act. For whatever reason, it was crumbling. Rafael took that as a sign to press harder.

"We need details on which apartments are occupied. You were supposed to send that to us yesterday," Rafael said.

"You think I can find anything here?" Westergard asked. "Everything's on paper. My father never trusted computers. He thought the internet was a giant scam and refused to digitize anything. When I inherited the business, I had no idea what I was getting into. It's a nightmare."

"Really?" Rafael tried not to sound skeptical.

"What did I get? A few crumbling buildings inhabited by scheming gutter rats who won't leave." He shook his head sadly, obviously feeling sorry for himself. "All I want is to sell the bricks and go anywhere else."

Rafael noted how easily the insult rolled off the man's tongue. In spite of his act yesterday, he hated his tenants. "Was Andray Baxter a scheming gutter rat? Is that why you were spying on him?"

"I never did that." Westergard drew himself up to his full height. "I know Andray claimed I did. He even came to my office and threw this thing at my head—some kind of computer charger. I didn't even call the police!"

"I'm sure he appreciated that," Rafael said.

"He didn't believe me," Westergard said sadly. "I swear on my life, I never spied on anyone. I don't have cameras in the building! Why would I put them in Andray's apartment?"

"Maybe it wasn't you," Rafael said. "Maybe it was one of your employees?"

"I wish he *would* do something, for a change," Westergard muttered darkly.

Rafael tried to keep his eyebrow raise to himself. "You wish *who* would do something?"

"My driver. He's supposed to be a security expert, but he's useless. He never does anything."

"This is your driver who you told us is on vacation this week?"

"Florida. He's in Florida. He's a moron who can't do anything right, and now he's gone and he's left me with this mess, and I don't know what to do."

Rafael took half a step back. It wasn't surprising that an entitled douchebag was angry at his employee for going on vacation, but Westergard's vehemence caught him off guard. "Is this man your *only* employee?"

"Yes."

"What's his name?"

"Mardiks."

"That a first or last name?"

Westergard shrugged. A little alarm dinged, and he sauntered to a desk, opened a tiny golden pillbox, and popped a couple of tablets.

"Those are legal, right?" Rafael asked.

"Of course. I have anxiety. You're not helping. None of this is helping."

"Yeah, it's been a stressful week, and it's only Tuesday," Rafael said. "I need to talk to Mr. Mardiks. What's his number?"

"Who can find anything around here?"

*That excuse is getting old,* Rafael thought. "Your phone just pinged. I bet it's in there. Unless you want to be charged with obstruction, you should get it."

Westergard glowered at him, but Rafael was unfazed. He watched the man slowly retrieve it; the name Mardiks flashed on the screen, with an address in Queens and a phone number. Rafael also noted that whatever Westergard was on wasn't helping his reflexes; maybe that was why he was getting a glimpse behind the shiny mask. Westergard was like a puzzle permanently missing a piece.

"There's another issue that's come up," Rafael said. "There was a bag of cash delivered to Baxter's apartment right before he died. It's nowhere to be found."

"Cash?" Westergard looked flummoxed. "How much cash?"

"Fifty thousand or so."

"The woman who killed Andray must've taken it."

"Nope. The more we look at her, the less guilty she seems," Rafael said.

"If there was cash, I should be paid," Westergard said. "He was holding back rent from me."

"That's not how this works." Rafael was surprised by the man's reaction. He clearly wanted to get his hands on the money. Up close, there was an unmistakable air of desperation floating around Westergard like a dark cloud.

"You think someone took it, someone in the building?" Westergard chewed his lower lip nervously. "There's a tenant on the second floor who might . . ."

"What about the fourth floor?"

"No. None of them are occupied."

"Are you for real?" Rafael asked. "You know which apartments are occupied and which aren't, and you're holding out on us. That's textbook obstruction. You'll be spending the night in some great accommodations we have downtown."

"I only know the fourth floor because it's empty! It was hell getting people out. I have to find the tenant agreements for the other floors. Half the units on two and three are occupied."

Rafael considered pressing the landlord harder, but he didn't think there was much more to get. His real temptation was arresting the man; he recognized Westergard as the type who couldn't take much adversity. But he knew that was premature, and anyway, the guy was zoned out; it would make sense to come at him again fresh the next day.

On his way out of the building, Rafael pulled out his phone and called Vedika Iyer. "We need a search warrant," he said. "For 631 West Forty-Ninth."

"Your crime scene? Which apartment?"

"Not for one apartment," Rafael said. "For the whole building."

"Is this a joke?" Iyer asked. "You've got how many housing units in there, twenty or more? You need a separate warrant for each one."

"I just received verbal confirmation from the landlord that all of the units on the top floor are unoccupied," Rafael said.

"It would be better if you had it in writing," Iyer said. "But at least there's no Fourth Amendment violation if they're empty. What are you even looking for?"

"We had a talk with Jo Greaver today after we saw you," Rafael said. "She told us there was another man in the hallway. She didn't see him, but he was the one who fired the bullets through the door. He was in the building. Either he lives here or was hiding here."

"We're taking her word for this?"

"We are."

"I might—*might*—be able to get a warrant for the unoccupied units." Iyer let out a frustrated sigh. "Okay, let me work on it. This is going to take a while."

"Thanks," Rafael said. "I appreciate it."

When he hung up, he sent a text to Sheryn with a brief update. Then he arranged for a couple of uniforms to drop by Westergard's driver's apartment in Queens. He knew it never hurt to double-check a story. The landlord was involved in Baxter's death; there was no doubt in his mind at all. *Knowing it isn't the same as proving it,* he reminded himself. He looked at his watch, remembering that he had to take his own dose of medication when he got home. He was sore and exhausted and glad it was only a short drive. The case wasn't coming together yet, but he had the feeling it was about to. Just give it a day.

# CHAPTER 43

## SHERYN

It was getting late, but at least Hamilton Heights was on her way home, Sheryn figured. The young woman who answered the door looked a great deal like her brother, with her expressive brown eyes, high cheekbones, and generous mouth. Her relaxed hair tumbled loosely over her shoulders. She was dressed simply, in jeans and a red Stanford University T-shirt, with a black cardigan for warmth.

"Audra?" Sheryn asked, dropping her usual formality. The woman nodded. "I'm Sheryn. I'm so sorry for your loss."

"Thank you. Please come in."

The apartment was lovely and yet melancholy. The curtains were drawn, and photographs of Andray were spread over every flat surface. One table had a burning pillar candle behind several framed images; it looked like a shrine. Sheryn paused to look at them, taking in the progression from laughing child on a tricycle to middle school graduation to actor on stage.

"How's your mother?" Sheryn asked.

"She's having a really hard time with this," Audra answered. "That's why I wanted to talk to you as soon as possible." She lowered her voice. "She's struggling with what you said about Andray. I wanted her to talk to you again, but she's holed up in her room right now, refusing to come out. But she baked some peach pecan bread 'for company,' as she put it."

"That was kind of her."

"Let's talk in the kitchen."

Sheryn understood her suggestion as soon as they stepped into the room. The walls were painted a sunny yellow, and there were no sad mementoes. The scent of cinnamon and cloves hung in the air.

"My brother wasn't a criminal," Audra said. "This idea that he blackmailed anyone is flat-out wrong. I know you never met him, so you're probably thinking this is just how his family talks about him, but that's not it. He was a really special person."

Sheryn nodded. She *was* thinking that Audra was looking at her brother through rose-colored glasses.

"But at the same time, I have to admit that my brother was very secretive in some ways," Audra continued. "He cared what people thought of him, and he felt like it was his job to make people happy, to lift their mood. He never got a break from that. If he was sad, he couldn't show it, because that would be letting people down, to his way of thinking."

Sheryn nodded again, but she felt a little ray of hope; maybe Audra had some real perspective.

"This last year had been hard on Andray," Audra said. "He fell in love with a white girl who was one of his clients at the studio where he worked. Used to work, I mean. He was crazy about her. She was from a rich family, but she was totally down to earth. I met her one time, when I came home last May."

"What was her name?"

"Sofia. Sorry, I don't know her last name."

*That's okay, because I do,* Sheryn thought.

"Things went bad, though," Audra said. "First, Sofia's father had Andray fired from his job. Inappropriate fraternization with clients, they called it. He knew what it was, of course. He said it didn't matter, but . . ."

"What?"

"Then he broke up with Sofia a little while later," Audra said. "He told me it was the hardest thing he'd ever done. I asked him what happened, but he wouldn't say. A couple of times after that, he talked about how he missed her, but when I said he should call her, he said he couldn't."

"Couldn't?"

Audra shrugged. "It made no sense to me at the time, and it still doesn't. It was like he'd decided they couldn't be together. I don't know what else to call it. My brother dated a lot of girls, but he wasn't really serious about anyone. Finally, he got serious, and then he ended it? I don't know."

"I appreciate your telling me this. Does your mother know?"

"Uh-uh, and I'd like to keep it that way. Andray never talked to her about his girlfriends. My mom is kind of old fashioned."

"Sure. Do you know about Andray having any conflicts with anyone?"

"Only his landlord. That guy sounds like such a creep," Audra said.

"He is," Sheryn said. "I've met him."

"You meet his bodyguard?"

"His what?" Sheryn leaned forward.

"He's got this guy with some quasi-military background who acts like his shadow," Audra said. "Andray called him GI Joe."

"A couple of people mentioned that guy. One tenant referred to him as Westergard's henchman."

"Oh, that's GI Joe. Andray was positive that was who put the spyware in his apartment. They never got into it directly, but GI Joe liked to glower at him."

"Did you ever see this guy? Could you identify him?"

"No, but Andray snapped a couple of photos of him, but they were at a distance. You want to see?"

"Absolutely."

Audra scrolled through her phone. "This is GI Joe."

Sheryn stared at the screen. The image was taken from across the street. The man was standing ramrod straight, his arms crossed in front of him. He was dressed in a black shirt and jeans. Sheryn couldn't make out his face, but one detail hit hard: the man's face was in shadow under a gray ball cap. It didn't mean anything in and of itself. It wasn't even exactly the look Jo Greaver had described. But Sheryn felt a chill run down her spine. *Now we're finally getting somewhere,* she thought.

"I need you to do something for me," Sheryn said. "I've been trying to get in touch with Sofia. Could you reach out to her and ask her to meet with you?"

"Okay," Audra said. "But I don't know what I'd say."

"That's okay," Sheryn said. "I'll be the one doing all the talking."

Sheryn's phone rang, and she glanced at the screen; it was Florian. "Would you mind if I took this?" she asked.

"Of course," Audra said.

"Hi, Florian," Sheryn said when she picked up. "How's it going?"

"When are you coming back, Detective?"

Sheryn glanced at her watch. She wanted to head home to spend some time with her family, but she'd pulled Florian away from his cozy night with that fancy bottle of wine, and she owed him. "I'm speaking with the victim's sister, but I can be back down in twenty minutes. Why?"

"The forensics here are a mess," Florian said. "What you found on the painting? That was blood. I can only do a Kastle-Meyer test here, but it's definitely human, type A. That would be a potential match for Andray Baxter."

"He wasn't shot in the kitchen?" Sheryn said.

"It appears as if he was shot in what I will call his vestibule," Florian said. "Of course, this is a one-room flat, but you know what I mean. But I found . . . something else."

"What?" Sheryn asked.

"I don't want to say on the phone," Florian whispered. "Please come back as soon as you can."

# CHAPTER 44

## Cal

While Cal was still at Jo's office, he called about her bail and was informed that it had been taken care of, though the officer wouldn't tell him by whom. Cal felt guilty, but there was nothing he could do. There was no way he could go home; Jo had every right to kick him out on the street. Instead, he trudged east to his mother's apartment, literally bumping into a woman on his way into the building.

"Mom?" Cal was startled. His usually elegant mother was wearing a puffy black jacket with the hood up.

"Cal?" She blinked at him in surprise. "What are you doing here?"

"Would you mind if I slept on your sofa tonight?"

"Of course!" His mother paused. "Does this mean Jo kicked you out?"

Cal didn't answer that. "Could we go upstairs?"

Inside the apartment, Sukie was stretched out on the sofa, licking her paws.

"I'm sorry to interrupt you on your way out," Cal said.

"I was just running an errand. I couldn't go out earlier because I was waiting for the police to bring back my Birkin bag."

Cal was startled. "The police were here?"

"They came by this afternoon." His mother didn't seem perturbed by this fact. "They were perfectly nice, but they had to talk to me because your girlfriend claimed I planted the gun."

"I had no idea."

His mother fluttered over to the sofa. "You are well rid of her. Sukie, move over." She sat down. "Tell me what happened today."

"Mom, you never told me why you hired a private investigator," Cal said. "What made you do it?"

"Once burned, twice shy. I had my suspicions about her from the beginning. Jo is one of those people who's disconnected from everything—no family, no proper education, no breeding—yet she had money. It all seemed rather dubious to me. And this story of hers of putting herself through school . . . I knew she was hiding something."

"Did you tell the police about the investigator?"

"Of course not. They wouldn't understand."

"I'm planning to talk to the police tomorrow," Cal said. "I'm going to tell them everything I know, which, I admit, isn't much. You can either tell me about the investigator you hired, or you can tell them."

"Cal, don't do that. I may have . . . stretched the truth a bit. I never *hired* an investigator."

"Then how did you know about Jo?" Cal asked.

"It was Annabelle," his mother answered quickly.

"What was Annabelle?"

"She's the one who dug up dirt on Jo and told me about it. That was why I stopped speaking with her for a while. I was so angry that she'd introduced the two of you."

"Why would she investigate Jo?"

"She was considering investing in her business," his mother said. "Annabelle didn't want any surprises."

Cal couldn't even begin to imagine Jo's reaction. She adored Annabelle, and she would be heartbroken, but she had to know the truth. He pulled out his phone.

"What are you doing?" his mother asked, visibly alarmed.

"I'm calling Jo," Cal said. "She needs to hear this."

His call went to voice mail. That wasn't a surprise; he knew Jo didn't want to speak with him. Emergency, he texted her. I need to talk to you.

The message went through as delivered, but she didn't open it. He waited, knowing Jo always kept her phone close at hand. Maybe she was asleep. But that didn't seem likely.

"I have to go," Cal said.

"But you told me you wanted to stay here . . ."

"Good night, Mom."

He hurried out the door and down the stairs. His steps got quicker as he approached Union Square Station. There was an uncomfortable pressure in his chest, as if his heart were beating in double time. He was lucky enough to get an express train, which dropped him off at Wall Street. He checked his phone again as he surfaced on the sidewalk; Jo still hadn't read the message.

Cal ran to their building. On the elevator ride up, he checked his phone again. Nothing.

When he opened the door of the apartment, the lights were on, but everything was quiet. "Jo?" he called, but there was no answer. Jo wasn't in the living room. Their bedroom was empty too.

That was when Cal noticed that the yellow police tape had been pulled off the entryway to Jo's office.

He eased the door open. All the photos on the icon wall had been pulled down. The frames lay on the rug, with the backings pried off. Then Cal saw a pair of bare feet at the far side of the desk and realized that Jo herself was curled up on the floor. When he crouched beside her and said her name, she didn't move. There was a bottle of whiskey on her desk, and it was almost empty. Scattered on the floor were several photographs Cal had never seen before. He picked one up and gaped at a naked teenage girl. It took him a moment to realize he was looking at a much younger version of Jo.

# CHAPTER 45

## SHERYN

When Sheryn returned to 631 West Forty-Ninth Street, it was almost ten p.m. In the cold relative quiet of the night, the falling-down building looked like a set for a horror movie. Her stomach lurched, but she realized it was more from hunger than fear. She texted Florian—Parking on W49, you still at the scene?—and rooted around in her glove compartment, looking for something, *anything*, to eat. She came up with a small bag of salted peanuts, which she poured into her hand and devoured in one shot.

It only took Florian a moment to respond. YES COME UP.

Sheryn shook her head. She knew Florian from working with him many times, but it wasn't like they socialized. Still, it was out of character for him to be so skittish. The CSU crew tended to have nerves of steel; they'd seen every conceivable nightmare at least once.

She gave up on foraging for food and grabbed her flashlight, knowing that the lighting situation inside the building would be grim. Inside, she trained the beam on the stairs, which creaked and groaned, as they had every visit up. The building was remarkably silent otherwise; the loud television on the third floor was off. She shone the light on every step, praying there would be no rats to greet her this time around.

Her phone started to ring, and she stopped on the third-floor landing. "Hey," Rafael said casually. "ADA Iyer came through. We've got a partial warrant. The empty units on the fourth floor can be opened up."

"You shook that list out of Westergard?"

"I did my best, but he was tripping on something. He let it slip that the fourth floor is uninhabited. The rest of the building, we have to wait."

From the landing above, Sheryn heard Florian's voice. "Detective," he stage-whispered, his voice strained.

"Good work," Sheryn told Rafael. "I'll get a squad car in front of the building, and we'll go into those units first thing tomorrow morning."

"Define *first thing*," Rafael said.

"Seven-thirtyish?"

"I'd rather come over now," Rafael grumbled.

"Shhhh!" Florian hissed.

"I better go," Sheryn said. "Florian's trying to get my attention." She hung up her phone. "We've got the warrant," she told Florian.

"Did you not read the email I sent you?" Florian asked tersely.

"I drove straight here from Hamilton Heights," Sheryn pointed out. "I didn't get to read any emails. Why?"

"I bet you didn't read the ME's report either," he snapped.

"I read Pola's summary. Everything was consistent with a single bullet being the cause of death."

"True. But Pola noticed livor mortis on the victim's buttocks and legs."

"I don't follow," Sheryn admitted.

"Red blood cells are heavy, and they sink postmortem," Florian said. "Your victim was found lying on his back. There should be livor mortis on that side of his body, except where he was touching the floor, because that compresses the capillaries."

"And there wasn't? Why wouldn't Pola call . . ."

"Pola thought the back of his lower extremities was perhaps darker than his upper extremities, as if he had died sitting up or was placed in that position afterward," Florian said. "But she wasn't certain, because livor mortis is harder to see in a dark-skinned person."

Sheryn stood silently, turning that over in her mind. "In other words, Andray's body was moved after he died."

Florian sighed. "Come inside."

Sheryn paused to put on the plastic booties again.

"You don't need those," Florian said. "The entire scene is contaminated."

Sheryn was alarmed. "What are you talking about?"

He flicked off the ceiling fixture and shone a purplish light over the floor. Sheryn stared in horror. It lit up as if the floor were stained from wall to wall with blood. "It looks like a bloodbath," she whispered.

"Certain types of bleach interfere with luminol by mimicking it," Florian said. "I can't tell you conclusively until I go back to my lab, but someone treated the floor with bleach so that it would react this way."

He turned on the light again. "I also found blood from your second suspect or victim or whoever the person is."

"It's not from the two we know about?" Sheryn asked.

"No. They're blood types A and B," Florian said. "We have someone else who's type O. Again, I can't tell you more than that without my lab. The field kit is only to make sure we've found human blood, not animal blood or ketchup."

"Where did you find it?"

"In the hallway," Florian whispered.

"Why are you whispering?" Sheryn asked.

"There's surveillance equipment in the hall," Florian said.

"The landlord said there weren't any cameras on-site."

"I can't tell you who put it there," Florian said. "It's plugged into the wall and looks like a small charger made of black plastic. It's not. It has a camera and it's transmitting remotely."

Sheryn frowned. "How can we find out where?"

"You need TARU for that," Florian said. "I can tell you that the maximum range would be to a wireless receiver less than two hundred feet away. Half that is more realistic inside a building."

"So, an apartment in this building or maybe next door," Sheryn said. "Good thing we got that search warrant."

There was a low boom, and suddenly everything in the apartment rattled. Sheryn heard the sound of breaking glass, though she didn't see its source.

"What the hell was that?" she asked.

"That was an explosion." Florian walked calmly to the window and opened it halfway, as far as it would go. He stuck his head out the window and immediately recoiled. "Did you tell me that the apartment next door had a booby-trapped handle? Because it's on fire."

Sheryn ran to the window to look. Flames were swallowing the black garbage bags that had been taped over the window.

"We can go out the fire escape," Florian said. "It will be safer than the stairs in the dark. This whole place will go up like a tinderbox."

"There are people on the other floors, and there's no alarm," Sheryn said. "Knock on the windows. Break them if you have to. Call 911."

She ran to the doorway. There were flames licking the edge of the apartment next door, but they hadn't made it to the stairwell. Sheryn caught sight of the black transformer Florian had ID'd as spyware, but it was on the other side of the flames. She couldn't risk grabbing it, not if she wanted to get everyone out of the building. The air was already heavy with smoke, and that made her eyes water and her throat raspy.

She rushed down the stairs shouting, "Fire! Get out of the building!" On the third floor, she banged on the door of the one apartment she was absolutely positive was occupied. Wilbur Bowen didn't answer, but all that meant was that he was saving the battery on his hearing aid again. She pounded on the door with the end of her flashlight, then rushed around each door, hitting them all and shouting. An elderly woman with her hair in foam rollers answered. *"Que pasa?"* she asked fearfully.

"Fire," Sheryn said. *"Fuego.* Run."

The woman grabbed a coat and pulled it on. Her feet were already in running shoes.

"Wait," Sheryn said. "The others. *Otros . . ."* She couldn't remember the word she wanted. *"Occupado?"* she asked, pointing at a door.

"No, no," the elderly woman said. She pointed at Bowen's door. *"Occupado."*

"Okay," Sheryn said. *"Gracias."*

As the woman hurried down the dark staircase, Sheryn looked at the door. She didn't see how she had any choice if she was going to get the man inside out of the building alive. She only prayed that he wasn't standing behind the door. She marshaled every ounce of strength she had and kicked the door, aiming her black boot just to the side of the lock. The door swung open.

"Who's there?" Bowen called out. He was sitting up in bed, his eyes scrunched as if the light had woken him up.

"Fire!" Sheryn shouted at him.

He put his glasses on. "Are you that lady cop from yesterday?" he asked.

Sheryn grabbed him by the shoulder and put her face up to his. "Fire!" she shouted.

Bowen flinched. "Fire?" He reached for his hearing aid to turn it on.

"Run," Sheryn said. *"Now."*

She hustled him out of the apartment barefoot but in a bathrobe. Upstairs, the fire was roaring as it fed itself. The air was murkier now, and Sheryn found it hard to see. The flashlight was almost useless from the gray ash and black soot filling the stairwell. Sheryn had nothing to cover her nose and mouth with. *Stay low,* she reminded herself.

There was a commotion on the second floor. In spite of the acrid air, people seemed unsure whether they should leave. "Fire!" Sheryn shouted again, her voice completely hoarse. That made a young man run down the stairs, his arms wrapped around a laptop and what looked like a gaming console. An elderly couple gazed at her dubiously. When Sheryn tried to speak, a raging cough erupted from her throat. Her lungs felt heavy, as if they were being weighed down by soot.

She tried to grab the couple by the arms, but the woman resisted. She pointed at an apartment door that was still closed. "Okay," Sheryn croaked. "Go." The couple still regarded her curiously. Then there was a terrible crack, and part of the staircase came tumbling down from the third floor. The couple scurried down the stairs before it became impassable.

Sheryn had no time for second thoughts. She was doubled over in front of the door, trying to find air to breathe. Even though she was well trained about the effects of smoke inhalation, she was surprised by how dizzy she felt. *You've got no time,* she reminded herself. She didn't have the energy to kick this door down; there was no option but to aim her gun downward at the lock and fire a shot. She felt less steady on her feet with every second that ticked by. *I can't do it,* she thought, her eyes swimming in tears. In the next heartbeat, her resolve hardened. *I can do all things through him who strengthens me,* she prayed. She stood upright, shot the lock, and shouldered her way in.

When she turned on the overhead light, she saw a woman with a halo of silvery hair sitting up in bed. The woman was in her sixties, younger than most of the other occupants Sheryn had seen, but she looked thin and frail in her pale nightdress.

"I broke my hip," she told Sheryn. "I can't walk."

"Don't worry," Sheryn rasped. "I'm going to get you out of here."

There was no going back to the staircase. The fire was on the second floor now, the flames leaping high in the hallway and starting to make their way into the room. Sheryn grabbed a pillow, pulled it out of its covering, and handed the fabric to the woman. "Cover your mouth and nose," she croaked.

Sheryn opened the window. The fire escape was in reach. The tough part would be getting the woman to it. "Sorry," Sheryn whispered when she tried to pick her up, knowing that she wouldn't be able to keep her from feeling pain. She half-carried, half-dragged her to the window and hoisted her onto the ledge. A firefighter had jumped up and was waiting for her. "Reach for me," he told the woman. "Put your arms around my neck." She did as she was told, and he carried her down to safety.

Exposure to the cold, crisp air made Sheryn cough even harder, but it cleared her mind. She jumped out the window, landing on the metal slats of the fire escape. She could feel the searing heat of the fire behind her, and when she looked back, she saw the tongues of flame licking the open frame. With her last ounce of strength, she grabbed the bar at the end, somersaulting over it and hanging on for a moment over the sidewalk before dropping the last couple of feet down. She spotted Florian on the street, watching her.

"Everybody out?" she rasped.

"Everybody," he said.

Sheryn nodded at that and fell into another coughing fit. When the EMTs hurried over to her and pulled her into an ambulance, she didn't even try to resist.

# WEDNESDAY

# CHAPTER 46

When Sheryn woke up on Wednesday, the first thing she noticed was that it was eight o'clock in the morning. She blinked at that, trying to remember the last time she'd slept in.

"Good, you're up," said a delighted voice.

"Am I in the hospital?"

"We were going to keep you here for observation for a little while overnight, but you really just needed sleep." The man was short and slender with an unruly mop of brown hair. "I'm Dr. Kaplan, by the way. It's an honor to meet you. I heard about what you did last night."

"Did you give me a sedative?" Sheryn asked suspiciously.

"No, that's the aftereffect of smoke inhalation. We gave you oxygen, but that was it for treatment. I can send you home if you want to take some time, but it's okay if you want to get back to work. I have the feeling you'd prefer that." He smiled. "Your family's here to see you. They're pretty eager. Is it okay if I send them in?"

"Please do," Sheryn said, sitting up.

In a moment, Douglass, Martin, and Mercy came in. Mercy ran to her, jumping up on the bed to give her a hug. "You saved everybody, Mommy!"

"Did I, baby?" Sheryn said.

"You did." Mercy let go a little so she could study her face. "But tell me how *you're* doing."

Sheryn fought the urge to laugh. Mercy had taken to quoting her grandmother, who'd changed careers in midlife, going back to school and switching from nursing to psychology. "I'm fine now that I see you and your brother."

"What about Daddy?"

"Yes, Daddy too." Sheryn smiled at Douglass. Mercy never liked to leave anybody out.

Douglass stepped forward to kiss her, resting his head on top of Sheryn's for a minute. "You're amazing—you know that, right?"

"A lady could get used to this," Sheryn said.

"I can take today off school to help you, Mommy," Mercy volunteered.

"Oh, no, you don't," Sheryn said. "You're going to make Mommy feel better by doing your best in school, you hear me?"

They hugged a little more; then Douglass left to take Mercy up to her school in Harlem and to drive to work himself. Sheryn noticed that Martin had been hanging back, but then he came over and sat on the bed.

"I couldn't sleep after Dad told me about the fire," Martin said.

"You really did inherit my genes, didn't you? The worrywart ones, along with the early-bird ones."

"I don't know if I'd ever run into a fire to save people," Martin said.

"You have the same instincts. I think that's why I get so upset with you," Sheryn said. "I run headlong into things, and I worry you're going to be like that too."

"It's a good way to be," Martin said. "You saved lives."

"But it's also hard on the people you love."

They sat quietly for a minute.

"I'm not going to hold you back from doing what you know to be right," Sheryn said. "You care about justice. There are different ways of achieving it. What I want for you is to always be aware that you're risking more by stepping forward than a lot of other people are. I don't see that fact changing in my lifetime."

"I think it can in mine," Martin said. "But only if people keep stepping up."

"You know I'm proud of you, right?" Sheryn said, hugging him.

"Yeah. Even when you yell at me."

After Martin left to take the subway uptown to his Upper East Side high school, Sheryn checked her messages. Her phone was blowing up, but the person she was most interested in talking to was Xavier Torres of the FDNY.

Keeping this off the news right now, but we found a body, he'd texted her. Come to the scene when you can.

That made Sheryn's blood freeze. She thought she'd saved everyone last night, but she'd been wrong. She changed into fresh clothes Douglass had brought her, brushed her teeth, and pinned up her hair. Then she grabbed an egg wrap from the cafeteria and got into a taxi.

To Sheryn, the building at 631 West Forty-Ninth didn't actually look a hell of a lot worse than it had the first time she'd laid eyes on it. The facade was still crumbling, but the brickwork had held its own against the fire. She could see that it was charred black around the windows, and under a cloudy, forbidding sky, it looked cursed.

"Where's Xavier Torres?" she asked the first firefighter she saw, flashing her gold shield.

"On the phone with the commissioner," he answered.

"He told me there was a body."

The firefighter nodded slowly. "Yeah. It's . . . really something. Xavier wants to show it to you himself."

"All right," Sheryn said. "While I'm waiting, can I see what's left of the building?"

"There's not a lot of floor left," the firefighter told her. "There's some terra-cotta in the walls, which is why the whole building didn't fall down, but it's just a shell now."

"Gimme one of those hats," Sheryn said. "Let's go."

Once she stepped inside, the smell made her eyes water, and some of her bravado left her.

"We can walk halfway up this staircase," the firefighter said. "There's not much left of the second floor anymore."

He wasn't lying. Sheryn stood halfway up the staircase, taking it all in. The wooden banister was gone. The carpet had vanished. The wooden floorboards had disintegrated to the point where the skeleton of the building was exposed. The ceiling had been devoured by flames, and she could see a patch of sky through a hole in the roof if she craned her neck.

"Which apartment was the body in?"

"It was on the top floor."

Sheryn would've bet her life that it was the apartment next to Andray Baxter's. *The damn door that shocked me,* Sheryn thought. *What horror was hiding behind that?*

They returned to the sidewalk. "You know you're lucky to be alive, don't you?" the firefighter said. "We found the device that started the fire. It was remote detonated, but most of it didn't go off. Idiot who made it didn't know what he was doing."

"Remote detonated?" Sheryn asked. "How?"

"With a phone, probably. It's been taken off-site for examination. If it had worked the way it was designed to, it would've taken out the fourth floor."

Sheryn gulped inaudibly. She remembered that moment, standing with Florian when the blast went off next door. It could've killed them; it was supposed to kill them.

"There was some surveillance equipment on the floor. Is there any way to trace it?"

The firefighter shook his head. "Florian told us about the spy cam, but the plastic turned to liquid. There's the remains of a computer, but it'll be a miracle if TARU can extract anything."

After he left, Sheryn studied the building. Then she looked down the street, wondering where Elliott Westergard was. He'd shown up immediately after Andray Baxter's body was discovered. Where was he now?

"Detective Sterling?" said a voice behind her.

Sheryn turned around. She recognized Xavier Torres, who was built like a wrestler; he had one brown eye and one green, a fact that always caught Sheryn's attention. But her gaze wandered past his shoulder, because Rafael was there, leaning on a mahogany cane.

"I tried to get him to make a bet with me," Rafael said, jerking his head toward Xavier. "But we both wanted to wager that you'd come to work as usual today."

"Thought I could put something over on the new guy, but he already knows you." Xavier reached out to shake hands with Sheryn. "You did real good last night."

"Thank you." Sheryn took a breath. "You said there was a body. Your message was cryptic."

"Because it's really bad," Torres said. "Not what you're thinking. Ten times worse."

"This guy didn't die in the fire," Rafael added. "He was long gone before that."

That was awful news, but it made Sheryn feel a little better; when she'd learned there was a body, she'd thought there was someone she should've saved but hadn't.

"Follow me," Xavier said.

Sheryn started to, but she noticed that Rafael wasn't following. "You coming?" she called.

He raised his eyebrows. "I got the tour. I'll be seeing that body in my nightmares for a while."

Xavier led Sheryn to an ambulance. "I knew you'd want to see it before they take it to the morgue. Brace yourself, Detective."

"I've seen plenty of dead people in my time," Sheryn said.

"Not many like this," Torres warned her.

The form under the tarp was large. Torres lifted an edge of the fabric gingerly to reveal a hand. Only, it didn't look right to Sheryn. At first, she assumed it was because it was burned—what was left of the skin was gnarled and black—but that wasn't it. Every finger on that hand was missing the segment above the top knuckle.

"The other hand's the same," Torres said while Sheryn stared at it in horror. "Because it's burned, it's hard to say definitively, but each fingertip was deliberately cut off. This didn't happen in the fire."

"You're telling me someone didn't want him to be identified," Sheryn said. She squared her shoulders. "What about his teeth?"

Torres pulled the tarp farther back. There was no semblance of a face anymore, only shards of bone sticking out in all directions. The jaw was smashed to pieces.

"Someone took a hammer to him." Sheryn swallowed hard.

"You want to hear my theory? I'd guess that the fire was started to get rid of this body," Xavier said. "Whoever did it couldn't get the corpse out of the building, or they had nowhere to take it."

"I'm surprised this much of him survived," Sheryn murmured.

"You might've been told this already, but the incendiary device didn't go off the way it was intended," Xavier said. "Also, this body was left in a bathtub, which was the one thing that survived the fire in the apartment where it started."

"We had just gotten a warrant . . . ," Sheryn murmured. She remembered Florian's paranoia. Had someone been watching them—or listening to them—and set off the device? Or was there another reason it had been triggered at that moment? Sheryn cleared her throat. "There's no way to tell how much of this was done to him while he was alive, is there? Or if he was shot too?"

"Not from here," Xavier said. "The ME's office will know, but it might take a while."

Sheryn nodded absently. The more she saw of the case, the more it seemed like Jo Greaver was telling the truth. But every piece of the puzzle was putting together an increasingly disturbing picture.

"I don't know much about the case you were investigating, but I can tell you this," Xavier said. "Someone was willing to murder everyone in the building to get rid of this guy."

# CHAPTER 47

## RAFAEL

"You know who my money's on," Rafael said. He was fighting to keep his cool. As soon as he heard about the arson, he knew he'd made the wrong call in not arresting Elliott Westergard.

"You really want to win a wager today, don't you?" Sheryn answered. "Elliott Westergard seems like the type to try a Hail Mary pass. He also seems like the type who would bungle it. But to be cold blooded enough to blow up everybody in the building . . . I don't know."

"I told you I went to see him yesterday, after you went back to the crime scene," Rafael said. "He was coming apart at the seams. He looked like he'd slept in his suit. He popped pills for anxiety. It's not impossible that he was trying to psych himself up to set that device off."

"We don't know he did that."

"He calls his tenants 'scheming gutter rats,'" Rafael said. "I think he would."

"Someone went to a lot of trouble to disfigure the body." Sheryn frowned, deep in thought. "That wouldn't be an easy thing to do, not with his manicured hands."

"In LA, there was one case I worked . . . ," Rafael started to say, then immediately regretted it. His partner was looking at him expectantly, and he felt compelled to tell her. "There was a whole family that was murdered. We thought it was gang related because the bodies . . . well, the bodies looked like this. Burned. Scarred. Chopped. Gangs do that as a warning to rivals and snitches, so we took it for a professional hit. The family had a drug connection that made it seem vaguely possible."

"But it wasn't?"

"It was one man who did it, and he did it to his own damn family," Rafael said. "His father, older brother, the brother's wife, their kid. He killed them over an inheritance."

There was more to the story, but he could see that his partner's head was drooping, her head shaking sadly. He felt bad for mentioning it. They saw terrible crimes in their daily work, yet there were some that stood out for their brutality. That one haunted him.

"Elliott Westergard's got no conscience," Rafael said. "I'm not saying he's bold enough to be a killer—he's an anxious, wormy guy—but if somebody would do the work on his behalf, he'd take it."

"All this is going on at the same time his assistant has gone AWOL," Sheryn said. "You know what I say about coincidences."

"Yeah. That's why I had uniforms go to his driver's place last night. Basement apartment in Flushing. It was empty. It made me think the driver really was in Florida. But when you said they'd found a body . . ." Rafael shook his head. "I figure either the driver did this—and went into hiding—or else got himself killed. Westergard said the guy couldn't do anything right."

"I've got something on that," Sheryn said. "While I was at the crime scene, I got a call from Andray Baxter's sister. She wanted to talk, so I met with her. Her brother had made jokes about Westergard's driver-slash-assistant. He called him GI Joe. I even got a snapshot." She held up the photo.

"He looks like the kind of guy who would join a paramilitary organization."

"I'm asking myself if this was the guy Jo Greaver met in Andray's apartment. He fits the general description. But if it is . . . that's the guy she shot."

"In which case, he's not running around burning down buildings," Rafael said.

"Or chopping off his own fingers."

"We need to look at how much insurance Westergard's got on the building," Rafael said. "By the way, remember my text from last night? He was trying to contact a certain Mr. Severight, who was ghosting him."

"What do I keep telling you about coincidences?"

"Let me put it this way," Rafael answered. "If I had a T-shirt printed up for you, it would have a photo of Captain Avery Brooks on one side and the words *There are no coincidences* on the other."

Sheryn smiled. "You mean Avery Brooks *as* Captain Benjamin Sisko. But damn, partner, you *know* me."

"Which is why I won't waste time arguing about the random nature of the universe," Rafael said.

"Sofia Severight got Andray Baxter fired from his job. Her father happens to be the guy Elliott Westergard is planning on selling his building to? What are the odds of that?"

"How do you want to play this?"

"The Severights aren't returning my calls. It's time we paid the mysterious Mr. Severight a visit."

Rafael shook his head. "You're dreaming. Remember, we looked this guy up. He lives in a huge town house on the Upper East Side. Place is a fortress, and we are not getting in. ADA Iyer isn't getting us a warrant, and Severight's got an army of lawyers between us and him."

"When did you become such a defeatist?"

The question, coming from his partner, didn't bother him, but it was an odd counterpoint to something his mother had said to Rafael since he was young. *Where do you get this strange optimism from?* His mother was a hard-core cynic, one who used disdain as a shield against the world. *Life has no meaning the moment you lose the illusion of being eternal,* she liked to say, quoting Jean-Paul Sartre.

"I'm not a defeatist," Rafael said. "I'm just honest about how hopeless this world really is."

"I don't know how much they'll be able to tell us about the device that started the fire, but they should have some idea of how close a person had to be to set it off," Sheryn said. "We can pull all the footage from cameras on the surrounding blocks. I don't see Jo Greaver or her boyfriend doing this, but I'm not ruling anyone out yet."

"Greaver ended up in the hospital last night," Rafael said. "Some medication they gave her didn't mix well with booze. From what I heard, her boyfriend has been there the whole time. So far, Greaver hasn't regained consciousness."

# CHAPTER 48

## SHERYN

There was no answer at the door of Elliott Westergard's brownstone on East Thirty-Eighth Street. It was the nicest house on the block, Sheryn thought, a minicastle festooned with stone garlands and cherub faces. It was entirely the opposite of the ramshackle monstrosity he owned across town. Deep down, Sheryn wanted Westergard to be forced to sleep in one of his falling-down buildings, to see how he liked it.

"At what point do we admit we were too slow on the draw with this guy?" Sheryn asked Rafael quietly. "We got distracted by all the red herrings pointing us toward Jo Greaver. Meanwhile, the landlord has been tormenting Andray for two years."

"We knew something was off with Westergard when we met him," Rafael said. "And he was definitely in a crazy headspace yesterday. But what were we going to do? Bring him in for being squirrelly?"

"Maybe we should've done that."

"You didn't like it when Iyer jumped the gun on the Greaver case," Rafael pointed out. "Bringing Westergard in early would've resulted in a wrongful-arrest lawsuit. You know that."

"What kind of man starts a fire in an occupied building. And at night! Everyone could've died."

"They didn't because of you," Rafael said.

Sheryn brushed that off. "We've got an arrest warrant," she said. "You want to break this door down?"

"Are you kidding me? I learned my lesson from the Traynor case," Rafael answered. "I'm still recovering from it."

"I know I could pick the lock," Sheryn said. "But let's do it the old-fashioned way." She smashed the glass in the door and reached inside to unlock it.

"Why do you always get to be the badass?" Rafael asked as they strolled in.

The interior of the brownstone was beautiful. Sheryn took in the high ceilings and crown moldings. The furniture was Victorian antique. A laptop was open on a walnut writing table in the front room, but its screen was dark. Sheryn touched a key, and it came to life. She read it silently. "Rafael?" she called.

He limped over to her, his cane tapping on the wood.

"You've got to read this," she said.

I can't live with myself.

Tony killed Andray by accident. We didn't know that a woman would be coming over with a bag of cash. She killed Tony.

I didn't know what to do. I left Andray's body in his apartment. I hid Tony's body next door.

Tonight, I burned it. But everything caught fire.

I didn't mean to hurt anyone. I was desperate.

I'm so sorry.

"That's either a suicide note or a really bad poem by a freshman student," Rafael said.

"I don't believe this," Sheryn murmured to herself. She stared at the screen. "Every time we think we've found the bad guy, we find an even worse guy waiting in the wings."

"I'm not sure I get what you mean," Rafael said. "But I'm pretty sure we're going to find Westergard's body in this house, aren't we?"

"I'd bet you anything we will," Sheryn said. "And I'd double down on it looking like a suicide. But it won't be. The same monster who played us before with Jo Greaver is playing us again."

"Who?"

"Severight," she hissed.

Rafael sighed. "I'm calling for backup. And a bus. We know we're going to need it. Why wait?"

"You do that," Sheryn said. "I'll take a look around."

She walked to the kitchen at the back of the house, pausing only to take in a photograph on the bookcase, which showed Westergard next to a tanned, grim-mouthed man Sheryn now recognized as GI Joe. Nothing looked out of place except the door to the basement, which was open, with the lights on. Sheryn took five steps down the stairs before she spotted Elliott Westergard's body. It was crumpled in a heap on the concrete floor, a rope noose still around his neck and a metal folding chair lying flat beside him. She continued down until she stood on the floor with the unfinished ceiling in view. There were pipes and beams in plain sight; one of the pipes was broken and dripping water. It suggested a scenario: Westergard had hanged himself, and the pipe had given way afterward, dropping his body to the floor. Sheryn gazed at the pipe, which was narrow; she had the feeling it had probably given way the minute Westergard's full body weight was applied to it. She'd need a CSU team and the medical examiner to prove that theory, but she didn't need anyone to tell her that Westergard's death scene had been faked.

# CHAPTER 49

## Jo

When she finally came to, Jo opened her eyes and stared at an endless blank expanse. It took her some time to realize that it was a ceiling and she was in bed and that there were beeps and footsteps and other sounds in the not-far-off distance. She realized that she wasn't dead, and that disappointed her. It wasn't that she'd tried to kill herself, but she'd given up on finding a way out of this mess.

"I thought I saw your eyes flicker," Cal said. "How are you feeling?"

"Rode hard and hung up wet," Jo said. "When did you get here?"

"I was the one who found you."

Jo closed her eyes. "I thought you were leaving me in jail to rot."

"I'm sorry about that," Cal said. "There's no excuse for it. I was upset, and so I acted like an idiot."

Jo smiled a little at that. But her smile faded as she remembered her conversation with Annabelle on the way home from jail. "Did you know that Annabelle was . . . acquainted . . . with my sister?"

"No." Cal sounded surprised. "She never said anything about that to me. Are you sure?"

"Definitely. My sister threw herself at her husband." As she said the words, her chest squeezed, as if there were a lead weight holding her down. *All my life, Lori has dragged me into the mud,* she thought. *Even from the grave she's pulling me down.*

"Not Montana Bob?" Cal asked. "That wouldn't be terrible. Annabelle despises him."

"No. The first one." Jo closed her eyes. She wanted to cry, but not with Cal in the room. There was nothing in her life that Lori hadn't ruined. Jo wondered if it would finally stop when she died. *Just my luck: there will be an afterlife, and Lori will have poisoned everything in it,* she thought.

It was ironic that Lori had blamed Jo for ruining her life. In a way, Jo understood it, no matter how grossly unfair it was. She didn't want to think about that anymore; last night, she'd drunk until she'd obliterated the memory. She'd almost obliterated herself in the process.

"Why did you go out and buy whiskey?" Cal asked.

"This is New York. I called the shop and had it delivered to my door," Jo said. "I just . . . I wish I could blot out the past. All of it, really. I used to be so good at blocking it, but it feels like it's catching up with me."

"Detective Sterling called me this morning. She was worried about you. You should know that the police are looking at you less like a criminal and more like a victim in all of this," Cal said.

"Why? They have all the evidence they need to put me away."

"The building you went to on Monday was set on fire overnight," Cal said. "I don't think it actually burned to the ground, but it was arson."

"Who did it?"

"They don't know," Cal said. "She wouldn't say much about it. She wants to meet with us later today."

"I don't know what else I could tell them," Jo said, swallowing hard. "My head still feels like I've got a murder of crows nesting in there."

"Rest up." Cal leaned forward to kiss her. "You're going to need it."

"Maybe I'll nap now," Jo said, because she didn't want to talk anymore. There was a heaviness weighing on her that she couldn't escape. If the police met with her, they'd manage to extract more of the truth out of her. She was already wondering how she lived with herself; if everyone knew the truth, life would be unbearable.

# CHAPTER 50

## SHERYN

"You two brought me another body already?" The medical examiner, Pola Ostrowska, peered through her cat's-eye glasses at Sheryn and Rafael. "I had a kitty like you once. It was dead mouse after dead mouse on my doorstep. It's how she showed me she really cared."

"Next time, it'll be roses, I promise," Sheryn said.

"Unless you prefer mice," Rafael added.

"At least this one isn't barbecued," Pola said. "You have no idea how difficult you make things around here."

"We try."

"Your charred corpse was shot in the stomach," Pola said. "It took him a while to die, and it wouldn't have been pleasant. There's no evidence that anyone tried to treat the wound. Because of the state of the corpse, I can't tell what was done to stanch the bleeding, but the bullet was still inside him."

"You've got the slug?"

Pola held up an oval silver bowl. "It's from a 9 millimeter, if that's useful to you. The forensics team will have to figure out the details."

"That's helpful, actually," Sheryn said. "I'm pretty sure I know who fired that bullet."

"Was it the same person who gave him the head wound?"

"That I don't know," Sheryn admitted.

"There's a hairline fracture of his skull," Pola said. "He would've had a concussion for sure. I can't tell you how bad it was because . . . well, I can show you what's left of his brain."

"Hard pass," Sheryn said.

Pola looked at Rafael.

"Hell no."

"Humph. Between the gunshot and the head wound, this guy was having the worst day of his life," Pola said. "And that was *before* somebody chopped off his fingers."

"I was going to ask you about that."

"His fingertips were removed by some type of device."

"What kind of device?" Sheryn asked.

"Think of a meat slicer," Pola said. "All of the cuts and edges are identical. There's no way a person could do that with a knife. You need a machine to get a clean cut like that."

"Disgusting, but interesting," Sheryn said.

"What about a cigar cutter?" Rafael asked.

"That would work. Small, compact, efficient," Pola said. "We're lucky, because even though the body was doused in gasoline, we managed to extract some DNA. Your victim is in the system." Pola walked to a counter and grabbed a sheet of paper.

"Anthony Wayne Mardiks," Sheryn read. "Arrests for domestic violence, no convictions. Nice."

"Note that he's a Florida Man," Rafael said. "I've heard about those on the interwebs."

"Is there anything you can tell us yet about Elliott Westergard's body?" Sheryn asked.

Pola shrugged. "Until I do the autopsy . . ." She turned to it. "The marks are consistent with the manner of death."

"The marks?" Rafael asked.

"You'd be surprised how many times I see a corpse that's been strangled, but someone's trying to pass it off as a suicide by hanging." Pola sighed. "Everybody thinks they can beat the system."

"This guy was pretty high when I saw him yesterday afternoon," Rafael said. "I don't know what he was on, but he claimed it was anti-anxiety meds."

"That's good to know," Pola said. "The toxicology report takes weeks. There might be some data earlier, but you guys know how long this process takes."

"Thanks, Pola," Sheryn said. "Whenever there's news, give us a shout."

On their way out of the medical examiner's office, Sheryn turned to her partner. "We subpoenaed Andray Baxter's cell phone carrier," she said. "Has that even come through yet?"

"Unless it's shown up this morning, no."

"It's frustrating," Sheryn said. "And it's the tip of the iceberg. We've got subpoenas out on his email addresses, to the apps he used, to Apple itself. Nothing's come through yet, and we probably are missing a bunch of targets because we don't have his phone."

"It used to be so easy," Rafael lamented. "You got the landline records, and that was it. Now it's separate records for FaceTime and Skype and WhatsApp . . ."

"Those were the good old days, partner," Sheryn said. "Now we need to dive in fifty different directions."

"It's interesting that our perp made off with the phone, and that never turned up," Rafael said. "Think about it. The laptop vanishes, but it surfaces soon after, and it's used to plant evidence against Greaver. The cell phone and the bag of cash are gone for real. Why?"

"Bag of cash, obvious answer," said Sheryn. "But the phone . . . you think there's something on the phone that would change the trajectory of this case?"

"What do I know?" Rafael shrugged. "But someone keeps telling me there are no coincidences. If that's true, there's a reason it's gone."

Sheryn looked at her watch. "Maybe I can find that out from Sofia Severight."

"Excuse me? When did you get your foot in that door?"

"I didn't, but Andray's sister did," Sheryn said. "I'm just taking advantage of that opening."

# CHAPTER 51

## SHERYN

"I'm not sure what you need me to do," Audra Baxter said.

"Chat with her for a minute," Sheryn said. "I don't want to spook her. If she sees me sitting with you when she walks in, she might run."

They were standing together outside a café on Seventh Avenue in Chelsea. Sheryn had expected Sofia to want to meet somewhere near her family home on the Upper East Side, but Audra had already explained to her that Sofia had been a student at the Fashion Institute of Technology and that she really liked the neighborhood. Sheryn figured it had a certain scruffy appeal if your frame of reference was Daddy's town house.

"Okay. I don't think she knows about Andray," Audra said. "She asked me what I was in town for, and I told her family stuff."

"There's no reason to believe Sofia's directly involved with any of this," Sheryn said. "We thought she had Andray fired from his job, and it turned out it was her father." Sheryn sighed. "Thanks again for doing this."

Audra nodded at her and walked into the café. Sheryn waited outside, pretending to scroll through email. Sofia Severight showed up maybe five minutes after Audra had stepped into the café. Sheryn had been expecting her to pop out of a hired car, but she came out of the subway station, conspicuous because of her blonde hair, which was center-parted and framed her round face. She wore a puffy black coat and black suede boots. She didn't appear to have any kind of security. Sheryn noticed a couple of guys checking her out, but they weren't with her.

She looked through the glass of the café's front window and saw Sofia and Audra hug hello, then stand in line together for coffee. As soon as they sat down, Sheryn decided there was no time like the present.

Inside, the café smelled good. The only seating was a long wooden bench built into one wall of the café, with a row of small tables and upholstered stools facing it. Either by accident or design, Audra had gotten Sofia to sit on the bench. *Good girl,* Sheryn thought. *That'll make it harder for her to run away.*

Sheryn walked up to them. "Hi, Audra," she said. She turned to Sofia and extended her hand. "We haven't met before. I'm Sheryn Sterling."

"Pleased to meet you," Sofia answered in a quiet voice. If she recognized her name, there wasn't any outward indication of it. "I'm Sofia."

"Severight?"

The young woman looked a little nervous. "Yes."

"I've been trying to reach you," Sheryn said, taking a seat. "It's about Andray Baxter."

"I haven't seen him in a while," Sofia said. "I was surprised when Audra texted me."

"No one told you that Andray passed away this week?"

The blood ran out of Sofia's cheeks. "What?" She looked at Audra. "Is this some kind of . . . some kind of . . ."

"It's true," Audra said quietly. "He was murdered."

"No," Sofia said. "No. This can't be happening."

She started to sob. Sheryn looked at Audra and saw that she was crying too. She went to the counter and grabbed a bundle of napkins.

She'd been expecting—or maybe hoping for—a different reaction. This felt like genuine sorrow, and it squeezed at her heart.

"I'm sorry to have to do this right now," Sheryn said. "But I'm with the NYPD, and I'm investigating his death. I need to ask you some questions."

"I can't believe it," Sofia said. "I don't know how I can help, but I'll try."

"I went to the health club where you used to work out with Andray. Why was he fired?"

"That was my father's fault," Sofia said. "He found out that Andray and I were seeing each other, and he told me that I was making a terrible mistake, that I was embarrassing myself by sleeping with 'the help.' That's what he called Andray." She blew her nose into a napkin. "My father's been married and divorced three times. I told him I didn't need relationship advice from him."

"So he disapproved because of Andray's job?" Sheryn asked.

"He disapproves of me dating, period," Sofia said. "He thinks I'm still ten years old. I get why he's protective, but it's too much."

"What happened after Andray lost his job?"

"We kept seeing each other," Sofia said. "But a couple of weeks later, Andray called me and ended it. He wouldn't explain why. Even at the time, I thought, *Why are you saying you can't see me anymore?* He never said he didn't want to; it was *can't.*"

"Could your father have threatened him?"

"I doubt it," Sofia said. "Andray's such a gentle guy, but he wouldn't put up with shit like that."

For some reason, Sheryn was a little surprised when Sofia swore. That was silly, she knew, but the girl had the face of a doll, and her voice was so soft. "Did you see Andray after that?"

"I tried to, a couple of times," Sofia said. "I went to a play he was in. I went to his apartment one time. I thought if I could talk to him, he'd explain what happened."

"What about your father? Did he know?"

"Yes, and he gloated about it," Sofia said. "He was all, 'I wonder where Prince Charming went?' He can be the most infuriating person on the planet."

"Do you know a man named Elliott Westergard?" Sheryn asked.

"That's kind of familiar." Sofia chewed on her plump lower lip, and her eyes widened. "The shitbird slumlord!"

"That's the one. Did you ever meet him?"

"No, but Andray told me stories."

"Mr. Westergard indicated that your father was going to buy the building where Andray lived," Sheryn said. "Do you know anything about that?"

Sofia shook her head. "No. And I would if it were true."

"Why's that?"

"Because my brother died a few years ago, and my father is counting on me to take over the business," Sofia said. "It's not what I want to do, but it's what he expects."

"You wanted to be a fashion designer," Audra said.

"I still do," Sofia said. "But that's only going to happen if I clone myself. Which is something one of my dad's companies is working on."

"Do you know a woman named Jo Greaver?" Sheryn asked.

Sofia shook her head. "Who is she?"

"She was . . . well, she was framed for Andray's murder," Sheryn said, realizing that she believed what she was saying. "Someone went to a lot of work to make it look like she did it. We're still trying to figure out why."

"You think my dad's involved in this, don't you?" Sofia asked.

Sheryn nodded. "His name keeps coming up."

"My father is an obsessively competitive person," Sofia said. "He likes to win at all costs. But he's never been violent. He wouldn't have harmed Andray."

Sheryn watched the girl, understanding why she'd want to think that. She was acutely aware that parents had secret lives that they hid from their children. A daughter's defense wasn't going to convince her that Severight was innocent.

"Andray had started coming into money around the time he was fired from the health club," Sheryn said. "He was getting thousands of dollars every month. Do you think your father was involved in that?"

"You think he was giving money to Andray? For what?" Sofia's soft features hardened into a frown. "You're saying he paid him to stop seeing me? No. Even he wouldn't stoop that low."

# CHAPTER 52

## RAFAEL

"It's not that I don't understand tech," Rafael said. "I totally do. I just need some help interpreting what the report says, because it's written in the usual TARU gobbledygook."

"It's reasonably straightforward." The tech TARU had sent over looked like a stereotypical nerd to Rafael: underweight and overopinionated. He wore round glasses that reminded Rafael of the kid in those wizard books and movies his nieces and nephews were so crazy about, and he looked to be about the same age. He'd introduced himself as Chuck, and he wore a close-cropped afro and a very bored expression. "What part don't you get?"

"All of it," Rafael said. "How about you start from the top?"

He sensed that Chuck wanted to roll his eyes, but to his credit, the TARU tech did not. "Okay, the laptop is a gold mine," he said. "It's got a lot of information sitting right on it. It was password protected, but the password was *My Password*, so it took us a nanosecond to open it. When we did, this is what we found."

He typed rapidly on the laptop he'd carried in with him, then turned it so that Rafael could see it.

"This is cloned, obviously—the real laptop is in evidence," Chuck said. "But the first thing that comes up is web-based email. It looks like it was created only to send email to one person, Jo Greaver. Literally all the correspondence is with her."

"Yeah, you guys gave us that on Monday. It's how we knew she was being blackmailed."

"Right. Okay, the guy has more tabs open. One is this company called Corvus Alchemy—I like that name, by the way. I was born in Kentucky, and it's the land of the crows. They're everywhere. Anyway, it's on the 'About' page, where you read about people at the company. There's Jo Greaver again."

"Okay," Rafael said.

"There's a tab for a search engine," Chuck said. "Search term: 'Jo Greaver.'"

"This is getting predictable."

"There's a little variety. There are a couple of other tabs open on porn sites. GILF porn, specifically."

"What's a GILF?"

"Grandma I'd like to . . ."

"Got it, thanks," Rafael said. "Moving on."

"Right. Next, we have the calendar. There you have, at one o'clock on Monday, Jo Greaver. Basically, this computer is a trail of bread crumbs to Jo Greaver." Chuck shook his head. "There are photos, too, but they're really bad."

"We saw them already," Rafael said. The humming in his ears got louder for a moment, as if it were influenced by the beating of his heart. "I'd rather not see them again."

"The point is, the computer is like a big flashing arrow that points at one person," Chuck said. "It's not like everything on the laptop was about her. We found two complete screenplays and some short stories; there's e-books and music and all kinds of stuff. What I'm saying is, the laptop you found belonged to Andray Baxter. It's legit, but the stuff pointing to Jo Greaver is not."

"This is the part I don't get."

"Someone erased the search engine history and cleared the cache," Chuck explained. "When we're looking at a computer, we're really interested in history. We've been rebuilding the history, and there's no record of Andray Baxter ever accessing that web-based email before. He never went to Corvus Alchemy's site before. Even the GILF porn was bullshit. Someone had literally gone in and put that there for you to find."

"We really were being played."

"Even the calendar entry is questionable," Chuck said. "It was added at twelve forty-nine on Monday afternoon. I'm not saying it's fake, but I have questions."

Rafael remembered something the elderly witness across the street had said. *I thought maybe it was a car. Because nothing happen. Pow! But all quiet.* She had told them that she thought she'd heard a single shot half an hour before the five shots that had made her call 911. At the time, it hadn't seemed like a big deal—her apartment was practically next to the West Side Highway; there had to be all kinds of sounds from cars—but in an instant, it made sense to Rafael.

"Whoever did this murdered Andray Baxter first," he said. "Then they waited for Jo Greaver to come in." He looked at Chuck. "Can you figure out if and when that web-based mail account was accessed?"

"Not on our own. We need a certain giant tech company to respond to our subpoena."

"Can you harass them, please?" Rafael asked. "We really need this. Now that the frame job is obvious . . ."

"Sure," Chuck said. "You good right now?"

"Thanks for coming by," Rafael said. "That was a big help."

Chuck closed his laptop and got to his feet.

"Is your name really Chuck?" Rafael asked. "Because you look about forty years too young for it."

"It's Chukwuemeka, but there's almost nobody in the NYPD who can pronounce that," he said.

After the tech left, Rafael picked up the phone and called the ADA.

"I've got proof that Jo Greaver was set up," he said.

"What kind of proof?" Iyer asked, her voice suspicious.

"TARU's figured out that the stuff about her was planted on Baxter's computer. He never even logged in to the account the blackmailer was using," Rafael said. "We need to get to the bottom of this, but that's not going to happen unless you give Greaver immunity."

# CHAPTER 53

## SHERYN

"My partner and I asked all of you to come here because we'd like to update you on the case," Sheryn said. "And because we've got a new problem."

They were seated around a conference table: Sheryn, Rafael, Vedika Iyer, Jo Greaver, and Cal McGarran. Greaver's lawyer, Mike Nakano, had been in to set things up for his client but had left after that.

"It's imperative that we get to the bottom of this case," Sheryn said. "First, I'd like to acknowledge the elephant in the room. Andray Baxter was murdered, but not by Jo Greaver. The charges in that case have been dismissed. We now believe that Mr. Baxter was murdered by a man employed by his landlord, Elliott Westergard. That man's name was Anthony Wayne Mardiks."

"Tony," Jo said swiftly.

"Mardiks was Westergard's assistant, chauffeur, and bodyguard," Sheryn said. "His body was burned in an arson at 631 West Forty-Ninth Street early this morning. When we went to arrest Elliott Westergard, we found his body in the basement of his brownstone with a noose around his neck."

"He killed himself?" Cal asked.

"That is certainly what the scene was staged to look like," Sheryn said. "The medical examiner is investigating right now. We're waiting on toxicology reports to find out whether he was drugged, but we're not going to get those for a while. In the meantime, we're proceeding as if Westergard were murdered. We've got officers going through his home and office right now."

"Who'd kill him?"

"We'll get to that," Sheryn said. "But first, we need a clear understanding of what happened to Andray Baxter and his killer. We can't proceed without that. To that end, I've asked Assistant District Attorney Vedika Iyer to join us. That's not just because she has a swankier conference room than we do over at Manhattan North. We've also arranged for an immunity agreement for Ms. Greaver."

"What does that really mean?" Jo asked. "I thought you said the charges were dropped."

"The charges regarding Andray Baxter," Iyer explained. "The immunity agreement means you won't be prosecuted for gun possession for the gun you actually had. Nor will you be prosecuted for shooting Anthony Mardiks with that gun."

"Which is what we are ninety-nine percent sure is what happened," Sheryn said. "In other words, we want you to tell us everything about what happened on Monday, and what led up to it. You have to tell us the complete truth, but nothing you say will be held against you."

"Okay." Jo nodded.

"Let's start with Monday," Sheryn said. "Tell us exactly what happened."

"The email told me where to go, what time to be there, the denominations of the bills," Jo said. "I went from my office to my health club, because it allowed me to change and because it was closer to the address."

"Why did you bring a gun?"

"I was afraid," Jo said. "The blackmailer sent photos, but he also sent a video, and I . . ." She gulped. "I knew he wanted money, but I also felt threatened. It was a last-minute gut decision to bring it."

"We need to talk about what's on the video."

"Can we talk about it later?" Jo asked. "I want to go over Monday first."

"Sure. Go ahead."

"I went to the building," Jo said. "When I pressed the buzzer, the man who answered gave me a hard time. He asked what my name was. He seemed determined to get me to say my name, but I wouldn't. When I went upstairs, the building was pretty quiet, except for one very loud TV. I think that was on the third floor. No one else seemed to be around. I got to apartment 402, and I knocked. A man answered the door. I was wondering if my blackmailer would be someone I knew, but I'd never seen this man before."

"For the record," Sheryn said, sliding a photograph across the table to her. "This is a photo of Anthony Wayne Mardiks."

"It looks like a mug shot," Cal said.

"It is. He was arrested several times in domestic disputes, but those cases never made it to court. Have you seen him before?"

"That was the man who answered the door," Jo said. "That mean, cruel mouth. There's no doubt at all."

"Okay, what happened after he opened the door?"

"I walked in, and he double-locked it behind me," Jo said. "That made the hairs on the back of my neck stand up. I thought I was going to be raped or murdered or maybe both." There was a moment of silence in the room. *You were about to be murdered*, Sheryn thought. *If you had been, we never would've gotten to the truth.*

"I had the gun in my jacket pocket, and I kept my hand on it, just in case," Jo said. "He offered me a drink—he said he had scotch but no ice. I said no. Then he started asking weird questions. He wanted to know if I felt guilty. He didn't say about what. It was creepy."

"What did you say?"

"I wanted to know where he got the video," Jo said. "He never answered that. He handed me some photographs that were taken when I was fourteen and said what a hot little bod I had." Jo gulped.

"What happened next?"

"He had a gun on the counter, but I didn't see it until he grabbed it and pointed it at me. I'd had my hand in my pocket, ready to shoot him if I had to. We fired at each other. He got me in the arm, but my shot hit him in the stomach. He fell backward. I heard his head slam on the counter on the way down."

"He had a head wound?" Rafael asked.

"I don't know for sure," Jo said. "I thought he was dying. He was twitching on the floor, trying to talk, swearing at me. Suddenly, there was a guy in the hallway. He was shouting, 'Tony, are you okay?' That guy shot at me through the door," Jo said. "That's why I went down the fire escape. I knew he would kill me if he got the chance."

"I can't believe you went through this," Cal said.

"I wanted to tell you, but I couldn't. I didn't know what to do."

"But you know you can tell me anything . . ."

"Mr. McGarran, could you please simmer down until we're done?" Sheryn said. "Someone's trying to frame your girlfriend for a murder."

"Sorry," Cal murmured. His cheeks flamed red.

"Did your blackmailer try to contact you afterward?" Sheryn asked.

"No. I haven't heard anything from him."

"Does the name Elliott Westergard ring a bell?"

Jo thought about that. "Never heard of him."

"He owns the building. He also had an ongoing dispute with Mr. Baxter that was in the courts. He was the one who hired Mardiks." Sheryn passed a photograph of Westergard to Jo.

Jo shook her head. "I've never seen him before."

"We need to talk about the video," Sheryn said. "I know it's a painful topic for you, Jo. But we have to be on the same page here. We need to understand why you were being blackmailed. You told us that you were forced to make the tape."

"I didn't know it was being recorded," Jo said.

"Okay. You described it as a sex tape."

"I did, but that doesn't really describe it," Jo said. She took a couple of deep breaths. "I was raped."

The room was silent for a moment.

"Do you know who raped you?" Sheryn asked.

"My sister's boyfriend." Jo lifted her eyes, staring straight at Sheryn. "There was something else I held back. I didn't tell you that I killed him."

# CHAPTER 54

## Jo

"Before you say another word." Sterling looked at the assistant district attorney. "This is already covered by the immunity agreement, right?"

"Correct," Vedika Iyer said. "Ms. Greaver was being blackmailed, which pertains directly to the crime we're investigating."

Jo nodded, trying to calm down. Cal reached for her hand. She squeezed it but let go.

"There's a lot you don't know," Jo said. "I told you I came to New York after my mother died."

No one said anything. Jo paused, wondering if Cal would reach for her hand again, but he didn't.

"My sister made me earn my keep," Jo continued. "I told you about the photographers she made me take off my clothes for." She glanced at Cal. "I guess you saw them last night."

Cal nodded.

"Lori had a boyfriend, but she didn't let me meet him. I didn't know, for a long time, that he ran the brothel where she worked. I never actually met him until Lori decided it was time for me to start working there. Any time he wanted to come over, she'd kick me out of her place."

Cal looked astonished. "Where would you sleep?"

"He never came over at night. It would be maybe an hour in the evening or on a weekend morning," Jo said. "Even being totally green, I knew he was married."

"She wanted you to work for him?"

"Yes. He always needed girls. He ran a brothel stocked with former and aspiring models. Lori recruited for him. But she also worked in the brothel." Jo's mouth felt so dry as she tried to explain. "It was in a building at 110th Street. It actually looked pretty nice, if you didn't know what was going on inside. Lori told me it would be like having my own apartment. I was in junior year then. She said it wouldn't interfere with my schoolwork."

"I am so sorry," Sterling said. "I can't even begin to imagine what that was like."

"That was when I started drinking a lot. Sometimes taking pills," Jo said. "The pictures . . . that bothered me, but it wasn't like having strangers lay hands on me. That was . . ." She struggled to find a word that could encompass how she'd felt back then, and how she still felt now. It stuck like a stone in her throat, choking her. "That was too much," she croaked.

"We can take a break if you need to," Sterling said softly.

"No. If I don't get this out now, I won't be able to do it." Jo tried to calm herself. "Lori made sure she was there when I was working, in case I ran into trouble. I think it was also because Dom was so handsy with all the girls. She was his girlfriend, but that didn't mean he didn't play around, and anyway he was married. One evening, Dom came into my room. He told me he needed a back rub. I asked him where Lori was, but he said she was busy. He took off his shirt and made me massage his shoulders. He told me I was really bad at it and then said maybe that was why so many customers were complaining about me. He took off all his clothes and told me he was going to give me a lesson. I tried to run out of the room, but he grabbed me and threw me on the bed. I screamed and he punched me in the face." She wiped a stray tear, angry that it had materialized at all.

*Don't be a useless crybaby,* Lori's voice taunted her.

"He forced himself into me, and I . . . I lost it," Jo said. "I had a pair of scissors in my bedside table, and I grabbed them and stabbed him as hard as I could."

"Where did you stab him?"

"In his side." Jo touched her waist with her left hand, indicating the spot. "He howled like an animal. He jumped off me, but he was bleeding a lot. That was when Lori came running in. She screamed at him, and then she screamed at me. Dom was kind of crying. I told him I was sorry, but he kept calling me a stupid bitch. Lori told me to get out and never come back. I pulled on my clothes and took my book bag and ran out of there."

"Where did you go?"

"I went to Lori's place. She didn't come home for days. When she did, she told me Dom was dead."

"He died from the stab wound?"

"I think so. She said Dom was dead and it was all my fault." Jo gulped. "I asked if the police were going to arrest me, and she said they would. I was terrified. She also told me I couldn't stay with her. Now that her boyfriend was dead, she wouldn't be able to stay in that nice apartment. I ruined everything for her. That was what she told me."

"What did you do?"

"I rented a room in Chinatown from a woman who didn't care about anything except cash up front," Jo said. "I finished high school. And I found a job with an escort service. It wasn't what I wanted to do. It was what I knew how to do."

It felt to her as if a shock wave had hit the room. Everyone was silent.

274

"I didn't find out until later . . . a lot later . . . that there was a video," Jo said. "Lori had the tape. She used it to get money out of me. I have no idea how the blackmailer got it."

"That was what you were watching," Cal said softly. "That morning I walked in on you in your office . . ."

Jo nodded. She could feel her head drooping forward, and she didn't think she had the energy to lift it again. Jo couldn't even tell what the worst part of her story was anymore; all of it caused her so much shame and pain. She didn't want to meet anyone's eyes, but when Cal reached over to take her hand again, she let herself feel a little bit of hope.

# CHAPTER 55

## Rafael

"I can't tell you how sorry I am. Or how awful this is," Rafael said. "I just want to be clear on the technical aspect of this. Did Dom start filming you when he came into your room?"

"No," Jo said. "I had no idea any of it was being recorded. When my blackmailer contacted me, he uploaded the file. It was shot from above. There was a ceiling fan in the room. All I can think is that the camera was hidden inside that. It makes me think that *everything* that went on in that room was recorded."

"But you've only seen this one video?"

"That's right."

"What was Dom's full name?" Rafael asked.

"I don't know," Jo admitted. "Dom wasn't even his real first name. Lori told me it was short for Dominus, Latin for 'master.' He thought it was funny to have all these girls calling him master."

"What a peach," Rafael said.

"I know I'm not supposed to say this, but I feel like you did the world a service," Sheryn added.

"Do you remember the date this happened?" Rafael asked. "We could do a search of deaths around the date."

"I remember," Jo said. "It was a month before my seventeenth birthday."

"We'll get the date and start searching," Sheryn said. "We should probably expand it to New Jersey and Connecticut, too, in case his primary residence was outside the city."

"The police never questioned you about him?" Rafael asked.

"Never. For a long time afterward, I expected a knock on my door," Jo said. "After a year went by, and then another year, I stopped worrying so much. Or maybe I was drinking so much then that I don't really remember."

"This is going to sound crazy," Rafael said, "but are you *sure* he's dead?"

"Lori said he was."

"With all due . . . I mean no offense, but your sister dragged you into a really awful situation," Rafael said. "Are you *certain* Dom died?"

"I've been wondering about that since the day my sister died," Jo said. "She called me and said she'd seen Dom's ghost. I went to her apartment, but she'd overdosed and wasn't breathing. I started to wonder if he might be alive. I know it sounds crazy. There's never been any evidence of it, but . . . I still wonder."

"Do you remember any of the other women—or girls—who worked at the brothel?" Sheryn asked.

"I didn't talk much to anyone except my sister," Jo said. "I really kept to myself."

"I can't believe you were keeping it together at school while you were living this hell," Rafael said.

"I kept telling myself I had to get through it, that one day I'd be free," Jo said. "I would tell myself it wouldn't always be like that."

"Do you remember any of the men who paid for sex?"

"Sure," Jo said. "I used to worry I'd run into one of them again. Then I realized they had more to fear about running into me."

"Any names?"

"I don't think anyone around there was using their real identity," Jo said.

"I'm wondering if there's a chance that you encountered Severight at the brothel," Sheryn said. "Not by that name, of course. I've been trying to find a photograph of him and haven't been able to come up with anything in the past twenty-five years."

"Severight?" Cal McGarran asked. "Not Malcolm Severight?"

"The one and the same," Rafael said. "Why?"

"I'd never claim he hasn't used a prostitute, because he may well do so," Cal said. "But he hasn't left his house in the past twenty years."

# CHAPTER 56

## CAL

Suddenly, every pair of eyes in the room was on him. Cal felt oddly exposed.

"Hold on. *You* know Malcolm Severight?" Sterling asked. She put her hand to her mouth. "Your mother mentioned that you'd been friends with his son, but she made that sound like it was just in elementary school."

"Serge and I were close all through school. His sister, Sofia, is four years younger. I know her a little as well."

"Where's the brother now?" Mendoza asked.

"He died in college," Cal said. "A car wreck. Serge loved fast cars and cocaine. The two didn't go well together. I think their father was in the process of divorcing Sofia's mother when we were in high school. He's a . . . difficult man."

"How do you mean?"

"Sofia's mother wasn't allowed to see her daughter anymore," Cal said. "Just like Serge's mother wasn't allowed to see him. That's Malcolm Severight. He likes to control people."

"Let's talk about Sofia," Sterling said. "Her father got Andray fired from his job because he was in a relationship with her."

"I haven't seen Sofia for years," Cal said. "She was a good kid. Her father was overprotective of her. He wouldn't let her go to school. She had private tutors. All of her friends had four legs and fur. She hung around her brother all the time because she was lonely."

"When was the last time you saw her?"

"At graduation. She was a sweet girl. I guess she was thirteen or fourteen then, but she seemed younger."

"Mr. Severight did not like his daughter's relationship with Andray Baxter," Sterling said. "When he found that getting Mr. Baxter fired didn't end the relationship, he started to pay Mr. Baxter ten thousand dollars a month to stay away from Sofia."

"That sounds like Malcolm Severight," Cal said. "He always thought he could control people with money."

"What a charmer," Mendoza said.

"At least this part of the picture is getting clearer," Sterling said. "Thanks for telling us, Mr. McGarran."

He slumped in his chair, glad not to have the spotlight on him anymore.

"Let's talk about the gun," Sterling said, turning to Jo. "It really bothers me that we haven't figured out who put it in your bag. We talked to Cal's mother yesterday, but there's no evidence that she did it. She was oddly generous about giving us her handbag to test." She looked at Cal. "She told us you went through her bag, looking for her medication. That was the only bag she had with her?"

"It was," Cal said. "I can promise you that she didn't have a gun."

"I know we talked about suspects," Jo said. "But it's not anyone who works for my company."

"We actually can't rule anyone out, even if they've helped you in other ways." Sterling said.

"A woman named Annabelle Davies was in your office on Monday," Mendoza said. "We need to interview her."

"There's no way it's Annabelle," Jo said.

"It just might be," Cal said.

All eyes turned to him again.

"My mother wanted to break up Jo and me, and she told me she'd hired a private investigator to dig into Jo's past," Cal said. "Last night, when I pushed for the name of the investigator, she admitted that she got the information from Annabelle."

"No," Jo said.

"She claimed it was Annabelle who told her that Jo had worked as an escort," Cal said.

"Your mother is the devil," Jo said. "She's trying to throw Annabelle under the bus."

"But she knows I can check this with Annabelle, and I will," Cal said.

"Do you think this is because of my sister?" Jo asked.

"What about your sister?" Sterling asked.

Jo slumped in her chair. "Annabelle put up my bail yesterday. When she took me home, she mentioned my sister. She's never done that before, not in the year and a half I've known her." She took a breath. "I guess it shouldn't be a surprise. They both worked in modeling, and they crossed paths."

"Who is Annabelle Davies, exactly?" Rafael asked.

"She was a supermodel back in the day. She's an investor in my company," Jo explained. "I met her right after my sister died. She approached me."

"She introduced us, actually," Cal said. "She's my godmother."

"What does she get out of being an investor?" Sterling asked.

"She owns part of my company," Jo said. "If I sold it or went public, she'd get a big payout."

Sterling glanced at her partner. "Occam's razor?"

"The simplest explanation being greed?" Mendoza asked. "Maybe. We definitely need to talk to her."

"I don't understand," Jo said. "What are you saying?"

"If you were out of the picture—say, in jail—Annabelle Davies would be controlling the company, right?" Mendoza said.

"I guess . . ."

"What about her personal life?" Sterling asked. "What do you know about that?"

"She's been married a couple of times," Jo said. "Divorced twice, I think."

"No, widowed and then divorced," Cal said. "I remember when her first husband died."

"Died of what?" Sterling asked.

"He was upstate on a hunting trip," Cal said. "I'm sorry, but I don't remember all the details."

"We'll look into that," Mendoza said.

"She has a son," Cal added. "Zachary." He slapped the table. "I just remembered. He works for Severight."

"That could be very significant," Sterling said. "What does he do?"

"He works in the Severight family office—all of the family's investments, their gifts to charity and so forth—are coordinated there," Cal said. "I saw him yesterday. He didn't seem very happy with his job. He said Severight calls him at all hours, that he expects him to be up in the middle of the night."

"There's one other thing," Jo said. "About Annabelle's first husband. When Annabelle told me yesterday . . . she said Lori had thrown herself at him."

"You think she's still holding a grudge about that?" Sterling asked.

"I don't know," Jo said. "She told me she disliked her immensely. But she said I was nothing like my sister." Jo's eyes darted around the room. "I thought she was being sincere. Now I don't know."

# CHAPTER 57

## SHERYN

"Admit it. You're disappointed," Rafael said. "I am. It's like we can't get a single foothold on this case."

They had parked on a side street off Gramercy Park, since double-parking in that area would've completely blocked traffic.

"It would've been perfect symmetry, you know?" Sheryn took his phone and scrolled across Marc Lytton's death certificate. "You're *sure* this is the guy?"

"Positive. Finding out that Annabelle Davies's first husband was stabbed to death by a teenager he was sexually exploiting would've been gold," Rafael said. "Learning he actually died from sepsis on a hunting trip in the Adirondacks is a downer."

"Now we have no motive, except for a possible business takeover. I know people kill for money, but . . ."

"What?"

"Everything about this case feels personal," Sheryn said. "Whoever did this hates Jo, and they hated Andray. There's so much malice mixed up in it."

They walked into an apartment building on the north side of Gramercy Park, the tallest on its block.

"Look, an elevator," Sheryn said.

"If you thought I was walking up the stairs to the penthouse . . ."

They showed their badges to the doorman, who looked startled by them. "You're police? Has something happened?" He was in his early sixties, sharp and trim in his forest-green uniform. His eyes were a soft brown, and his accent hinted at Puerto Rican roots.

"Some routine questions, that's all," Sheryn said. "Which penthouse is it?"

"That would be Penthouse B," he answered. "Please go on up."

Inside the elevator, as soon as the door slid closed, Rafael murmured, "You know he's calling her to give her a heads-up."

The elevator arrived at the penthouse floor, twenty stories up. There were only two apartments there. Sheryn turned to the door marked with a B and rapped on it lightly.

There were footsteps inside. A moment later, the door opened. The rail-thin woman who answered stared at them imperiously. Sheryn gazed at her, fascinated. The woman's skin was pulled tight over prominent cheekbones. Her flaxen hair was parted in the middle and curled to either side. A lit cigarette burned in one hand. "Yes?"

"Are you Annabelle Davies?"

"I am."

"I'm Detective Sheryn Sterling of the NYPD. This is my partner, Detective Rafael Mendoza . . ." Sheryn could hear the overpoliteness in her own voice—she didn't like it—but she knew that people who lived in penthouses like this didn't look at police as authority figures; they were more like servants. She had to tread lightly, for now. "We wanted to ask you a couple of questions regarding a case we're investigating."

"What case is that?"

"It involves an associate of yours," Sheryn said. "Jo Greaver."

"Is Jo all right?" Davies asked, exhaling plumes of smoke.

Sheryn noted her concern, which felt like a genuine mark of warmth in an otherwise frozen statue. "She ended up in the hospital last night, but she seems fine now. Could we come in to talk?"

"No," Annabelle Davies answered calmly.

"You want to have this conversation in the hallway?" Sheryn asked.

"I don't mind answering your questions. I'm very particular about who I let into my apartment," Davies said. "Tell me what happened to Jo."

Sheryn raised an eyebrow. If this haughty woman really did care about Jo—for whatever reason—that was Sheryn's hook to keep the door open and keep her talking. There was no benefit in answering *her* question directly. "We'd like you to tell us about your visit to her office on Monday," Sheryn said.

"Why?"

"Did you have an appointment?"

"No, I dropped in. I'm an investor in the company; I often do that," Davies said. "Jo wasn't there, so I waited for her."

"In her office?"

"Yes. I love the view from there."

Sheryn remembered the view as being pretty, but it didn't seem like one that a rich woman with a Gramercy Park penthouse would find particularly memorable. "Did anyone else come into the office while you were there?"

Annabelle Davies considered that while she crushed her cigarette in an ashtray on a table in the foyer. "Peyton—Jo's assistant—came in a couple of times. She kept offering me coffee or tea. I don't remember anyone else coming in. Have you talked to Peyton?"

Sheryn felt the edges of her mouth curl up slightly. Always a good sign when a suspect tried to throw someone else into the maw of the lion; it indicated a consciousness of guilt. "How did you meet Jo in the first place?" she asked.

"I was researching businesses to invest in, and I found hers interesting. I saw that Jo was a smart businesswoman with great ideas. I knew she'd be able to expand quickly with some help."

"There've got to be a million start-up businesses in this city at any given time," Rafael said. "What, specifically, led you to Jo Greaver's?"

"That's an odd question for the police to be asking," Davies countered.

"Call us curious," Rafael said.

"I worked in the beauty business for many years. Decades, actually," Davies said. "Not that I'm admitting my age, of course. But I take a special interest in it, and I keep up with as many of the new companies as I can. I know I read something about Jo's company, but I don't remember specifically. I liked her environmental awareness, her commitment to social justice. She was already successful before I came into the picture."

"How much did you invest in her company?" Rafael asked.

"That's definitely none of your business," Davies said.

"What happens if Jo is unable to run her company?" Sheryn asked.

Davies frowned. "Why would that happen?"

"Just a hypothetical. What would happen to the company if Jo were incapacitated or, say, in jail?"

"I'm the only other shareholder, so I would run it."

Sheryn nodded at that; it was exactly what Jo had told them. But she would've expected this woman to dance around the topic; somehow, she didn't seem to catch the significance of it. "Jo told us that you knew her sister, Lori Fielding. What was your relationship with her like?"

Davies's demeanor shifted, growing harder with each moment. She checked her watch. "I'm all out of time for questions, Detectives. If you want to ask anything else, you can contact my lawyer."

# CHAPTER 58

## Jo

Jo was sitting on Priscilla McGarran's sofa when the older woman unlocked her door and strolled in. Priscilla stopped dead when she spotted her.

"Hi, Priscilla," Jo said. "I hope you don't mind. Cal let me in to wait for you, because he knows how much I want to talk with you."

"Talk? About what, precisely?"

"For starters, what were you doing in my apartment on Monday?" Jo asked.

"I felt ill, so I called my son. He dragged me back to your apartment. I didn't even *want* to go there. Ask him."

"Funny thing, you getting sick a few blocks away from my apartment," Jo said. "You're aware of how dutiful Cal is. It's not like he'd leave his sick mother on the curb. You knew he'd insist on bringing you back there to rest up."

"Cal didn't give me a choice. *Ask* him."

"Priscilla, you're tough as old leather and cold as a well-digger's ass," Jo said. "Don't think you can play me like you play your son."

"Since there's a cashbox where your heart should be, that's no surprise," Priscilla shot back. "Don't think that I don't know exactly what you are."

"Which is?"

"You're an opportunistic hustler with Olympian ambition who has climbed higher than anyone could've imagined," Priscilla said. "You've whored yourself out, and you've reaped rewards from it. But you're too much of a narcissist to see that you're about to fall. I can't think of a female version of the Icarus story, so that's the allegory I'll use."

Her words didn't hurt, exactly. They were pretty much what Jo had expected: *opportunist* and *hustler* and *whore* had been thrown at her before, and their effects had been blunted. *Ambition* Jo took as a compliment. *Narcissist* was new, and it left Jo off balance in equal measure with the implied threat.

"I've worked hard for everything in my life," Jo said. "Nothing was ever handed to me. I've earned what I have. I was never some spoiled heiress who married someone even richer for his ability to support me."

"In spite of what you've been led to believe, I didn't come from privilege," Priscilla said. "I had to work for everything I had too. Then I married a man who turned out to be a hustling opportunist himself. I had to cut him out of my life like a cancer to protect myself and my son."

"I know Cal's father was a con man," Jo said. "I'm not a crook. I never have been."

"Let me tell you a story," Priscilla said, taking a seat across from her in a Louis XV chair covered in gold brocade. "When I met Chip, he was dazzling. He was from a good New England family, he was on the rowing club at Harvard, he owned every room he walked into. He was a consummate charmer."

"Your first clue something was wrong with him was that he went by *Chip*."

"Ha! That is funny, now that I think about it." Priscilla was more animated than Jo had ever seen her. Her eyes flashed, and her hands fluttered with a nervous energy like pale, bejeweled birds. "Back in those days, it didn't seem odd at all. Chip was one of those men everyone admired. He had the world by the tail." She gave Jo a rueful smile. "It took me a long time to realize that Chip wasn't much good at anything except charming people. He bounced around from job to job, but nothing ever took. He didn't really apply himself. I think that a life as the golden boy had left him ill equipped to rise to a challenge. He was fundamentally lazy."

"Look, I appreciate your telling me this, but it has nothing to do with me," Jo said. "No one has ever called me lazy."

"You see, this is why you're a narcissist, Jo. You think every story is about you," Priscilla said. "You think it's some comment or critique of your life. You're not listening. You're missing the point."

"Which is?"

"Chip didn't start life as a con artist," Priscilla said. "He got there because nothing else was working out easily. Chip liked money. He'd grown up with it, and he expected to have it. Honestly, I think he was counting on his inheritance to fix everything. But when his father died, we discovered he'd gambled everything away and was actually hopelessly in debt. That's what pushed Chip to do bad things. He started taking people's money to invest—he was very good at separating people from their money—and it all spiraled from there."

"You're saying he wasn't a bad person; he just did bad things."

"You could argue that he did what he had to in order to survive," Priscilla said. "It wasn't for basic sustenance but for what survival means in our social class. Morality mattered less to him than saving his own skin. And in that way, you and my ex-husband are exactly the same. That's why I want you as far away from my son as humanly possible."

"Hold on. I own a legitimate business I built from scratch," Jo said. "If you want to ridicule me for working as an escort to put myself through school, you can. The bottom line is that I worked for everything I have, and I still do."

"You take enormous pride in being an industrious little worker bee, Jo. I'm not denying that you are. I'm saying that you are as amoral as my ex-husband. You wouldn't hesitate to commit a crime to save yourself."

Her words hit Jo hard. It was easy to hate Priscilla: she was a pretentious, diamond-hard monster who reveled in cruelty. But that didn't mean she was wrong.

"That's not true," Jo said.

"There's no point lying to me, Jo. I've seen the video."

Jo could hear her own heart thudding in her ears; the shock was that it was still beating at all.

"The video?" she repeated, each syllable chipping off like shards of ice. "What video?"

Priscilla smiled and shook her head. "Don't be coy—it doesn't suit you. You've never been able to pull off naive and innocent, and you should stop trying." She leaned forward. "I've seen the video you're so desperate to keep under wraps."

Jo sat in wordless horror. How many people had seen the video?

"If you're thinking about harming me to save your own skin, don't," Priscilla said. "There are copies ready to go if anything happens to me."

"You're blackmailing me?" Jo said.

"Good heavens, you're slow," Priscilla said. "I'm not your blackmailer. I don't care about publicly outing you. I only want to protect my son."

Jo was so desperate she was past all denial. "Then . . . how did you see it?"

"That was Annabelle's doing," Priscilla said. "She's the one who showed it to me. She told me all about you."

"I don't believe you," Jo said. "You told Cal this same lie. Why would Annabelle do that?"

"I have no idea," Priscilla said. "Why don't you ask her yourself?"

# CHAPTER 59

## Rafael

"You know what I keep thinking about?" Rafael asked.

"That New York traffic may actually be worse than Los Angeles traffic?" Sheryn asked. They'd made the mistake of deciding to drive to Priscilla McGarran's apartment and had gotten stuck in a traffic jam on East Twenty-First Street.

"You've never been stuck for hours on the Freeway," Rafael said. "You have no clue what real traffic is. No, I keep thinking that this case would've barely gotten a look if Greaver had died. You'd have two bodies in an apartment and a record of one blackmailing the other. It would look like they'd shot each other, and that would be it, case closed."

"I was thinking exactly the same thing when we were sitting in the meeting," Sheryn said. "When Jo was talking, it hit me how close she'd come to being murdered."

"Murdered and left there undiscovered for who knows how long," Rafael said. "Two bodies in that wreck of a building."

"You know, if Jo hadn't gone out the fire escape, there probably wouldn't even have been a 911 call," Sheryn said. "Andray's mother wasn't expecting to see him until Sunday. No one knew Jo was there.

Their bodies could've been decomposing when we found them. It's awful to contemplate."

"It makes me crazy that the clues leading us to Greaver were so stupidly obvious. I mean, a business card tucked into the victim's jeans. Really?"

"Don't forget the laptop."

"I haven't," Rafael said. "I got a guy from TARU to go over everything with me when you were out for your meeting. Literally the first time the blackmailer's account was logged in to from Baxter's computer was Monday."

"When you think about it, the original plan is kind of genius," Sheryn said. "Get two people you want get rid of in a remote-ish location and kill them both. Make up a connection between them that's sordid and trashy, the kind of thing people have no trouble believing."

"You ever watch old movies?" Rafael asked.

"Not really. It's kind of uncomfortable when the only black faces you see on-screen are maids."

"Fair point. In old movies, my people are all hot-blooded lotharios and spitfires," Rafael said. "But I was thinking of Alfred Hitchcock and *Strangers on a Train*. The whole idea is that these two strangers each have someone they want to kill, but they know they'll be tied to the deaths. So they basically trade victims. That way there's nothing tying them to the death."

"Only in this case, the victims are strangers, and we can't find anyone who has a grudge against them both."

"But we know Malcolm Severight had a grudge against Andray, and it's looking like there's something shady with Annabelle Davies and Jo." Sheryn shook her head. "I get what you're saying, but it still makes no sense. What my brain keeps circling around is that somebody came up with this big plan, only to have it fall apart. They tried to save it, but it went to shit. They're not so great at thinking on their feet, and now they're desperate and panicking."

"What, you're not buying Elliott Westergard as the puppet master behind this show?"

"That's what I mean about desperate. Plus, neither Severight nor Davies could work alone. They'd need help."

"Davies has a son," Rafael said. "He could be the connection. Or else Severight's daughter."

"I don't believe Sofia is involved, but I would definitely like to have a word with Zachary."

Rafael's phone rang, and he answered it.

"It's Chuck," said the voice on the line. "Your dreams have come true. We got a bundle of ISP data dropped on us, and it's amazing."

"What did you find?" Rafael asked him.

"Andray Baxter's ISP—sorry, that's internet service provider . . ."

"I'm not two hundred years old," Rafael grumbled.

"Huh. Anyway, your victim's service was with Verizon. Whoever set up the account was with Spectrum. I can't give you exact coordinates yet, but the user is around Gramercy Park."

# CHAPTER 60

## Jo

Jo wasn't sure how she'd stumbled out of Priscilla McGarran's apartment. Somehow, she'd found her feet and fled; the sound of her heels clacking in the stairwell on her way down echoed in her ears. She was going crazy, she was sure. Priscilla wasn't stupid; she'd zeroed in on Jo's one vulnerability with laser-like precision.

Annabelle was her investor; she was also her friend. She was warm and nurturing, and Jo felt like an utter fool for trusting her. Even before Jo's mother had died, Jo hadn't really had a parent; the woman she called Mom had looked to Jo to care for her. Afterward, Jo knew she was completely on her own, and she'd fled to New York, flinging herself on her sister's mercy. Then she'd learned that mercy wasn't a quality her sister possessed.

She didn't notice the buildings and people she passed as she walked west. She found herself in front of Annabelle's building, wondering if she was stranded inside a nightmare. "I'm here to see Annabelle Davies," Jo told the doorman.

"She's having a busy afternoon," the doorman said. When he called upstairs, Jo half expected to hear a flood of profanity in response to her name, but that didn't happen. "Go on up." The doorman smiled at her.

In the elevator, Jo started to have doubts. *I should've punched Cal's mother in the nose,* she thought. Tracking Annabelle down and tackling her seemed insane. She and Annabelle had been working together for the past year without any conflict. How could Annabelle have gotten her hands on the video?

"Jo, this is a delightful surprise," a breathless Annabelle said when she opened the door. "I was just tidying up. Would you mind waiting—"

Jo stormed into the apartment. "Is it a surprise, Annabelle? Really?" She stopped abruptly, hypnotized by the grandeur of the place. From the hallway, all she'd been able to view was the foyer; once she'd set foot inside, it was like watching a magical kingdom open up. The ceiling soared above like a church's, the floors were covered in pristine white carpet, and the walls were painted azure blue, as if Annabelle lived atop a cloud in the sky. There was a gilded mirror over the fireplace and antique furniture arrayed in front of it. There were end tables filled with gold-framed photographs. But what struck Jo the most were the mirrors. Long ago, she'd read about how they could be used to create the illusion of a bigger space. This apartment in the heavens was majestic, and the mirrors made it feel otherworldly.

"The police were here earlier," Annabelle said, trailing behind her. "Asking all kinds of questions. How are you feeling? They told me you had been to the hospital, but they wouldn't say what happened."

Jo swept through the grand room. At the end was a towering window. The view of the southern end of Manhattan was breathtaking. *From here, you can probably see my building,* Jo thought. It was an unnerving notion.

"Why don't you sit down, Jo? You don't sound like yourself."

Jo turned and saw that Annabelle had picked up one of the framed photographs from an end table. For a moment, Jo thought she was going to hit her with it, and she grabbed it from her.

"No!" Annabelle shrieked.

Jo looked at the framed photograph in her hand. It was a family portrait of a man and woman with their little boy. Jo immediately recognized Annabelle, but it was the man next to her who took Jo's breath away. "That's your husband?" she whispered.

"Yes," Annabelle said.

Jo gingerly set the framed photo back on the end table. That was him. Annabelle's husband was Dom, Lori's boyfriend and pimp. He was the man who'd raped her. He was the man she'd killed.

# CHAPTER 61

## Cal

Cal rang the doorbell at Malcolm Severight's mansion on East Seventy-Ninth Street. It was answered by an elderly butler.

"Calton McGarran?" the butler said, clearly surprised. "It's been years, sir."

"It has," Calvin said, extending his hand. "I need to speak to Mr. Severight. It's important."

"Allow me to check with him, sir. Please, step inside."

Cal did, and the large wooden door closed behind him. The grand foyer was exactly as he remembered it: dim and dark with a staircase dead ahead that split into two under a stained-glass window depicting an angel. The staircases continued up—one east, one west—but it was impossible to see exactly where they led. Cal knew that the Severights had a priceless art collection. Somewhere in that hallway, there was a Monet and a Degas, a Van Gogh and a Cézanne, but the light was so low it was hard to appreciate them.

"Please follow me, Mr. McGarran," the butler said when he returned. "Mr. Severight will see you at once."

Cal followed him. He'd found the house creepy as a child. It was exactly the sort of place he imagined as a breeding ground for monsters. There were so many alcoves for them to hide in.

Cal remembered Mr. Severight's office well. To call it an *office* was patently ridiculous. It was more like a throne room, with Severight holding court in a massive plush love seat at the far end of the room. It was what he used in place of a chair, because no chair could have easily held his enormous bulk. The last time Cal had been inside the house— when Serge was still alive—Severight had probably been closing in on four hundred pounds. He was larger now.

"Thank you for seeing me, sir," Cal said as he approached Severight to shake hands. As he got closer, he saw that one side of Severight's face hung strangely, with a half-closed eye, as if he'd had a stroke; the other side was alert, and that half of his mouth smiled.

"Young Calton, it's a pleasure to see you again."

"It's been a long time, sir."

"Please have a seat. James, would you bring young Calton a drink. What will you have?"

"Nothing, thank you."

"Brandy," Severight announced loudly. "We'll have brandy. Thank you, James."

The butler quickly exited the room.

"How is your father doing?" Severight asked. "I never thought he'd leave New York, but now that he has, I can't imagine him returning."

"I'm not in touch with him," Cal said, "though I understand I have a new baby brother down in Florida."

"I heard about that," Severight said. "I suppose it seems odd to people, but I was fifty when my first child was born, so I'm in no position to judge."

"The news sent my mother for a loop," Cal admitted.

"It's difficult to imagine Priscilla caring about that," Severight said. "Though nature plays strange tricks on us all."

"Do you still work with him?" Cal hadn't planned to ask anything on that front, but the words escaped his lips before he could catch them.

Severight's good eye narrowed at him. "You haven't turned fed, have you, Calton?"

"Of course not."

"Because if you were wearing a wire . . ."

"I'm not," Cal said, getting to his feet. "If you want, I'll strip down to my boxer briefs."

"That won't be necessary." Severight waved one bloated hand dismissively. "I should warn you, as tech averse as I am, we have fantastic technology in this house. Any recording technology won't work. Your cell phone won't either. Go ahead and look."

Cal pulled his out. "There's no signal."

"It's a dead zone by design." Severight smiled. "My neighbors aren't fond of me, because sometimes the effect seeps out. But this house is a lockbox."

"That's impressive, in a disturbing way," Cal said. "But doesn't it disconnect you from the world?"

"That assumes I want the world coming into my home. I don't. It's bad enough that the barbarians are perpetually at the gate. I'm not inviting them in." Severight sighed. "Modern life is a series of shackles people willingly attach to themselves. Do you remember your Rousseau from junior year?"

"Man is born free, and everywhere he is in chains," Cal quoted.

Severight smiled. "Exactly, young Calton. True in the eighteenth century and even truer now." He sighed. "I always wished Serge had been as studious as you were. Rousseau would have interested him only if he were a race car driver."

"Serge was smarter than me," Cal said. "He did all right without studying. I had to work hard because none of it came naturally. I always wanted to be as funny as he was."

"Natural talents are a blessing and a curse, aren't they?" Severight asked. "I've found that myself, many times."

"I need to ask you about something important."

"You're not here looking for a job, are you?" Severight asked. "Because the only opening I have at the moment is for a bodyguard."

"I remember Big Mike and Little Mike," Cal said. "Do they still work for you?"

"Big Mike retired to Arizona last year. Little Mike is still here, but his arthritis is terrible."

"I'm not here about work. I wanted to talk to you about my girl-friend," Cal said. "Her name is Jo Greaver."

"Jo, as in Josephine?"

"No. Just Jo."

"Jo was always my favorite character in *Little Women*," Severight said.

"Jo is everyone's favorite character," Cal said. "I'm here because her life is in danger."

The good side of Severight's face registered curiosity. "Why do you say that?"

"Someone took a shot at her," Cal said. "They only hit her in the arm, but they killed another person at the same time."

"That's horrible."

Cal pulled a photograph out of his pocket. "A photo I took of Jo last summer." He studied Severight's face for any sign of recognition. Instead, there was a sly smile on half his face.

"She's a beauty. Well done, my boy!"

"Thank you, sir." Cal put the photo back in his breast pocket.

"Does she have a stalker?" Severight asked. "What kind of beast would attack her?"

"That's the thing," Cal said. "Someone was trying to blackmail her with a videotape. She was told to bring money to an apartment in Hell's Kitchen, an apartment rented by a man named Andray Baxter."

That name got a reaction. "Andray Baxter." Severight's mouth twisted, as if he'd tasted bitterness.

"You know him?"

"He was inappropriately involved with my daughter. Sofia is so innocent. She has no idea that people like that will use you for your money. She was lonely, and he took advantage of her."

"What did you do?" Cal asked.

"I did what any responsible father would do," Severight said. "I got rid of him."

# CHAPTER 62

## Jo

The air in the room felt oppressive, as if the clouds in the sky were gathering to choke her. "I need to go," Jo said.

"Sit down, Jo," Annabelle said. "I think I should call a doctor."

Jo started toward the front door, but there was the sound of a key in the lock. It opened, and a man stepped inside. His head was down, but Jo caught sight of his dark hair. She choked out a garbled sound and fled down the hallway. When she found a bathroom, she locked herself inside.

The wall above the sink was mirrored tile, and Jo caught sight of her face—not pale anymore, but flushed and anxious.

*This can't be happening,* she thought. Annabelle had been married to the man who'd attacked her? The same man Jo had stabbed to death.

*Vengeance,* Jo realized suddenly. Annabelle had been out for blood all along.

Her mind was frantic. Jo remembered the first time she'd met Annabelle. She'd seemed so wise and sophisticated and kind. Had it been a setup all along? Because there was Annabelle, swanning in at exactly the right moment, investing in Jo's struggling start-up, an angel investor who provided her with cash and concern and an endless supply of advice. Because it had seemed like a dream come true, Jo had done the bare minimum of due diligence on Annabelle Davies.

She felt sick. There was a pounding in her head. She'd been set up from the start, and she finally knew it.

Jo listened at the door. Annabelle's voice was quiet, but she heard her say "out of the hospital" and then "upset." The man's voice was even softer; she couldn't clearly make out a word.

She pulled out her phone. The detectives had given her their numbers, but she couldn't find them. In her panic, she dialed 911.

"What's your emergency?" asked the woman who answered.

"I . . . I'm calling about a murder investigation," Jo whispered, afraid Annabelle and the man would hear her.

"Ma'am, you need to call the precinct directly. This line is only for emergencies."

Instinctively, she messaged Cal. I'm at Annabelle's apartment, she texted him. If you don't hear from me in the next fifteen minutes, call the police. I love you.

The message showed as delivered but not read. *Damn it,* she thought. It was hopeless.

*Go out there and act normal,* she ordered herself. *That's the only way you get out of here alive.* She pressed a couple of buttons on her phone, and it started recording; she dropped it back into her purse. If she died, at least there would be a record of exactly what had happened.

When she unlocked the door and stepped out, she saw that Annabelle was in the living room, sitting on the sofa and smoking a cigarette. "Jo?" she called when she noticed her. "Are you feeling all right?"

"Not really," Jo said. "I think it's the pills they gave me at the hospital. I'm a bit woozy."

"Please sit down. I asked my son to make us some tea."

"And I said, 'Consider it done,'" said a dark-haired man who walked in carrying a tray. "Hello, Jo, I'm Zachary. My mother said you just got out of the hospital. You probably need some real food."

Jo stared at him. Lori's words rang in her head. *JoJo, you won't believe it, but I saw a ghost today.*

Jo was seeing exactly the same ghost. He was standing right in front of her, the image of his father. The fact that he was smiling didn't put her at ease—quite the opposite, because Dom had been capable of doing terrible things while he was grinning.

"I was there overnight," Jo said, her voice as faint as her heartbeat.

"I can scramble eggs or make a sandwich," he offered. "My repertoire is limited."

"Thanks, but I'm not hungry," Jo said.

"You never mentioned why you came home early," Annabelle said to him.

"Mr. Severight has a secret meeting I'm not supposed to know about," Zachary answered. "It's better if I don't ask too many questions."

Jo had been ready to make a run for the door, but at the mention of the name Severight, she forced herself to stay put. The detectives believed Severight was mixed up in this crime; if she had the opportunity to learn more about him, she owed it to them to take it. "You work for Malcolm Severight, the zillionaire?" Jo asked, nervously perching on the sofa. "What's that like?"

"He keeps me on my toes," Zachary said. "Mostly, I handle his investments and charity, but I also research businesses and people for him. I guess it keeps things interesting."

"I bet it does." Jo noticed that the tray Zachary had carried in contained a steaming teapot and two empty cups.

"Nice to meet you, Jo," Zachary said. "Mother, I'll be in my room. Mr. Severight might call at any minute." With an absentminded wave, he disappeared down the hallway.

Annabelle poured the tea and handed her a cup, which was painted with pink roses and delicate thorny vines. Jo lifted the teacup close to her face. Its scent was delicious, jasmine blended with another flower she couldn't identify. *What are the odds that she's trying to poison me?* Jo wondered. *High enough that I am not eating or drinking a damn thing in this apartment.* She set the cup down on the table.

"I feel terrible about everything that's happened," Annabelle said, sipping her tea.

"Getting shot wasn't the worst thing that happened to me this week," Jo answered. "That was finding out from Priscilla McGarran that you hired a private investigator to dig up dirt about me."

"I never did that." The teacup shook in Annabelle's hand, as if to give the lie to that claim.

"When you approached me about investing in my business, you already knew who I was, didn't you?"

Annabelle laughed nervously. "Why would I want to invest in your business otherwise? I wouldn't invest in a stranger."

"Cut the act," Jo said. "I know who you are. And I know who your husband was: a pimp and a rapist."

Annabelle set her cup down. She didn't meet Jo's eyes.

"I recognized him in your family photo," Jo said. "He raped me. He held me down, and his forearm was over my neck, choking me. I thought I was going to die, Annabelle. I really did."

Jo couldn't read Annabelle's expression; her face was tilted downward, as if something invisible yet fascinating were in her lap.

"You knew that already, didn't you?" Jo asked. "Because you've seen the video, haven't you?"

"Yes." Annabelle's voice was almost inaudible. She rubbed her temples, as if she had a headache.

"How did you get it?"

"Marc was the one who made it in the first place," Annabelle said quietly.

The explanation was so simple that Jo couldn't take it in at first. Naturally Dom—or Marc, whatever his name was—had filmed everything that transpired in that sordid little room in the brothel. Of course his widow had the tape. The only question was why she'd decided to start using it after all these years.

"You've been playing me for the past year and a half," Jo said. "What was your plan? Cozy up to me and destroy my life, piece by piece?"

"My plan was to help you." Annabelle reached for the family photo on the end table. It was so heavy in its gilded frame that her arm trembled. "When I look back, I'm not sure what I loved most. Was it my husband, or the life I thought we had together? I don't know, but I still miss it. Part of me wishes I'd never learned the truth."

"You're saying you still love him? The pimp who raped a teenager?"

"I'm saying that I didn't know my husband was a monster," Annabelle said. "I loved him, but I had no idea who he really was. I didn't find out until after he died."

Jo felt as if there wasn't enough air in the room; maybe the atmosphere was thinner in Annabelle's world. The scent of jasmine was overwhelming.

"For a long time, I was so angry," Annabelle said. "I had no idea my husband was cheating on me, let alone . . . that there were multiple women involved. For a long time afterward I hated them. But I hated him too. I thought my marriage, my life, was one thing, and it turned out to be something entirely. It was all a lie."

Jo sat quietly, staring at her. She was certain Annabelle was about to pull a gun on her. Instead, Annabelle stared at the photo with a stricken expression.

"Do you know what it's like to be betrayed by the person you love most?" Annabelle asked.

"Betrayed by the person I admire most, yes," Jo said. She wasn't only thinking of Annabelle; at the moment, Lori's ghost was floating at the edge of her vision.

"I never betrayed you, Jo. I felt . . . a sense of obligation to you. When I understood what had happened, what Marc had done to you, all I wanted to do was help you. Investing in your business was the only way that I could think of."

"Why didn't you approach me when your husband raped me? I was almost seventeen, and I had nothing. I could've used some help then."

"I didn't know who you were back then," Annabelle said. "That was a terrible time for me. I'd learned the truth about my husband, and I didn't know what to do. I ended up running away from New York and marrying a stranger in Montana because I didn't know what to do. I was horrified by everything Marc had done."

Jo made a mental calculation. If Annabelle could be believed—and that was a big if—Jo understood her fleeing her old life and trying to forget what had happened. Jo had shed her own past like a reptile slithering out of its dead skin; she never wanted to look back. But the timing seemed too strange to be a coincidence, because Annabelle Davies had entered Jo's life immediately after Lori had exited it.

"You contacted me two weeks after Lori died," Jo said. "That wasn't an accident."

"I read that she'd passed, and it made me think about you again." Annabelle's averted gaze told Jo that she was lying.

"Why won't you tell me the truth?"

Annabelle touched her own temple again. "I hated your sister," she said. "She was the most toxic person I ever met, vicious like a cut snake."

Jo couldn't deny that. "Lori was awful," she said quietly. "I know that better than anybody."

Annabelle's expression softened, as if Jo had thrown her a lifeline. "I didn't know what I was getting into," she whispered. "I didn't know what a can of worms I was opening up . . ."

"What are you talking about?" Jo asked. "What did you do?"

Annabelle got to her feet. "My head is killing me. I need to take something for it."

Jo watched her stumble toward the kitchen. Then she reached into her purse to make sure her phone was still recording; it was. She was afraid to check her messages in case that would interfere with the recording. She set the phone down again just as something smashed into the back of her head. Everything went dark.

# CHAPTER 63

## CAL

The room started to spin around Cal. He glanced down at his brandy; he'd only had a few sips. Severight couldn't have poisoned him, could he? Cal felt certain he was going to throw up.

"You look astonished," Severight observed. "What man wouldn't protect his family?"

"But you *killed* him," Cal said.

Severight stared at him and broke out laughing. "Calton, you are such a dramatic boy. I didn't say I harmed the man. I meant that I pay him to keep away."

"*Pay* him?" Cal's voice sounded shocked to his own ears, but he realized how foolish that was. As he'd told the detectives, Malcolm Severight's modus operandi was to use money to make people do his bidding.

"I told Sofia I was going to prove to her that Andray didn't care about her, and I did," Severight said. "Of course, it broke her heart. She's been threatening to do terrible things ever since. She won't, of course, but she acts as if I'm the villain of this story." Severight shook his head sadly. "Andray promised not to tell her, and I doubt that he would. Say what you will about him, he seems to be a man of his word."

It hit Cal all of a sudden that Severight was speaking about Andray Baxter in the present tense, as if he could pick up a phone and call him at any moment. He knew that the man was averse to modern technology, that he eschewed television in favor of nineteenth-century novels. Was it possible that he was so uninterested in the borders beyond his own little planet that he had no idea what was orbiting nearby? The other possibility was that Severight was feigning ignorance, but that wasn't a pose Cal had ever seen him take. Severight never wanted to be viewed as out of the loop; that would've been weakness.

"Don't you know that Andray Baxter was murdered?" Cal asked.

Severight's one good eye reacted, growing wide. "When?"

"On Monday. He was shot dead in his apartment."

"No!" Severight's hands fumbled against the soft fabric of the love seat until he hit a bell. The butler appeared a moment later. "James! Where is Zachary?"

"He left a little while ago, sir."

"Well, call him to come back. We have to stop payment on a check immediately."

Cal opened his mouth and closed it again without uttering a sound. There was a cold horror in the realization that Severight's first impulse— upon learning of a murder—was to think of his own fortune. Ironically, it reinforced Cal's belief in Severight's innocence. If the man had already known Baxter was dead, he would've reclaimed his money.

"I will call him, sir." The butler disappeared again.

"Excuse me, but you pay Andray Butler with a check?" Cal asked.

"It's actually one of those electronic check transfers," Severight said. "I don't have to physically sign checks anymore, which is a blessing, because these arthritic hands can barely hold a pen. The payment is automatically deposited to his account every month."

To Cal, it had seemed a sordid business: paying off your daughter's lover not to see her anymore. He realized that, to Severight, it was simply another financial transaction. "You don't drop off a bag of cash?"

"A bag of cash? This is not a Jimmy Cagney movie, young Calton. There are benefits to paying Andray as an employee. If I hand him cash, I'm out the money, and there's not even proof of payment."

Cal sat back, astonished. This didn't fit with what he'd been told by Jo or by the police. "You're saying you didn't pay Andray Baxter ten thousand dollars a month in cash?"

"I wish he *had* come that cheap. It was twenty-five thousand dollars a month, and he's surely got quite the little nest egg now. It's been five, no, six months. Well, not six if we stop the latest payment." He drank the last of his brandy. "Now I suppose someone has to tell Sofia that he's dead. Oh, dear. She hates me enough already."

"Did you set up the arrangement with Andray?"

"No, I left that up to Zachary, who turned out not to be the great negotiator he promised to be," Severight said. "Twenty-five thousand dollars a month was my upper limit."

As the realization sank in, Cal felt queasy. This wasn't exactly like learning that his father was a criminal or that his girlfriend had a dark past. Those were individual cases he could look at as exceptions rather than rules. He'd known Zachary since he was a child, but he realized he was only seeing him clearly for the first time. All his life, he'd been surrounded by people raised with the best of everything, people who believed their natural position was to be leaders. They were products of a good background, one with breeding and taste, but they were con artists and grifters all the same. All their advantages had only created an unquenchable desire to take more than they ever deserved.

"Zachary didn't fail to negotiate," Cal said. "He was pocketing that fifteen-thousand-dollar difference himself."

"That's impossible," Severight said. "He'd never dare to cheat me."

"My father did, and you let him get away with it," Cal said gently.

"I couldn't let that get into the papers. It would be like wearing a target on my head."

"Zachary has access to your finances," Cal said. "If you look into it, you'll see that he was scamming you and Andray Baxter. But there's more to it than that. He's led the police to believe that you were behind the murder."

# CHAPTER 64

## Jo

When Jo came to, a chandelier swam into focus briefly, then oozed out of the frame. Jo turned her head to one side. It pounded something awful. The carpet underneath her was like a plush, cozy bed. Jo had to force herself to sit up. She reached one hand back to touch her head. The pain jolted her fully awake. There was blood on her fingertips.

Then she caught sight of Annabelle.

The older woman was lying on the carpet, too, but she didn't appear to be breathing. Her hair had tumbled over her face, so Jo couldn't see if her eyes were open, but there was a massive bloody wound on the side of her head. Beside her body was the photo, topped with shattered glass. Where was the frame? Jo couldn't see it. It was only when Jo tried to move toward the other woman that she realized the gilded picture frame was in her hand.

Jo reached for her phone to call for help but couldn't find her bag. Had it fallen on the floor? When she lifted her head, she saw that someone had placed a laptop on the floor in front of her. A video was playing on the screen.

Not just any video. *The* video.

She had a bird's-eye view of the room. There she was, almost seventeen years old, sitting in bed with a textbook on her lap and a notebook beside her. Her door—which she knew she'd locked—swung open. Dom stepped in, closing the door and locking it behind him.

"Hi, Dom," said the girl in the video, her voice a little squeaky.

"My neck is really tight," Dom said. "I need you to give me a back rub."

"Where's Lori?"

"Lori's busy." In two short words there was so much aggression and entitlement. Jo wasn't sure she'd heard it clearly the first time around; back then, she'd been terrified. Dom was big and muscular and liked to show off what an alpha male he was.

She watched herself close the books and slip off the bed, putting more distance between herself and Dom. "Okay, let me see if I've got any massage lotion."

He took a couple of steps forward, grabbed her wrist, and yanked her back onto the bed. "We don't need that." He turned his back to her and unbuttoned his shirt, then tossed it onto a chair.

In her memory, the massage felt like it lasted an hour, but on the video, it was less than two minutes.

"You suck at this," Dom said. "No wonder everyone complains about you. I have to educate you."

She flinched, watching Dom grab her teenaged self and force himself on top of her. Jo watched herself on the screen, flailing and thrashing on the bed. The camera was directly above her; she couldn't see her attacker's face, only his dark wavy hair and broad shoulders. He was pinning her down, trying to force her legs apart. She could see the gold wedding ring on his left hand; that was a detail she hadn't remembered. In her nightmares, she saw his face, cold and square jawed and cruel.

The video seemed to slow down, as if to savor her torment. Then it sped up as she opened the drawer of the night table and pulled out the scissors. Blood sprayed on her body and on the silky silver bedding. The video sped up, and the sound went off. Her sister came in. Lori had screamed and screamed while the man sat on the bed and Jo cowered in a corner. Only, whoever had made the video had covered up the man's face and his penis, placing black rectangles where they should have been. It made it seem as if he were the victim and that his modesty and reputation had to be protected.

After Jo had fled from the room, the video slowed to normal. Jo stared at it in wonder. The first time she'd seen it, when Lori had played it for her, the video had ended with her stabbing Dom. The second time, when her blackmailer sent it, the screen had gone dark, with a teenaged Jo still shivering in a corner. She'd never seen the extended cut. The camera had kept on recording, its unblinking eye taking everything in. Of course there was more.

"That fucking bitch," Dom said. "I'm going to kill her."

"I can't believe she did that to you," Lori said. "What a psycho. Are you okay?"

"I'm fine," Dom said. "Get me a bandage."

Jo watched Lori minister to Dom, cooing at him while she tended to his wound. "I told you not to bother with her," Lori said. "She's an ugly little crow."

"I thought you were just jealous," Dom said.

The video stopped without warning, and the screen went black.

"That was quite the show, wasn't it?" Zachary said. Jo wondered how long he'd been standing there.

"What are you doing?" Jo whispered.

"I'm going to do what my father should've done to you back then," Zachary said.

# CHAPTER 65

## Jo

"You attacked me?" Jo asked. "Did you hit your mother?"

"I did," Zachary said. "Frankly, we haven't seen eye to eye on things for a very long time. Certainly not about my father's murder. She found out the truth about his death and chose to do nothing about it."

"I always thought . . . I was the one who killed him," Jo gasped. "Lori told me I'd murdered him."

"You did," Zachary said. "My father walked out of that room, only to die a few days later from sepsis. He was too proud to tell anyone what had happened. He actually thought he'd caught the flu, but he took me on a hunting trip anyway. Then he died because of you and your sister."

Annabelle stirred on the floor.

"You saw him rape me," Jo said. "I know what's it's like to have a monster in my family. That's what my sister was. You don't have to be like him."

"My father was brilliant," Zachary said. "He found stupid girls who thought they should be stars and put them to work for him. Then he found stupid old men who thought they deserved sweet little girls, and he blackmailed them. Think about that for a minute. Perfect planning, perfect symmetry."

"Your father . . ." Annabelle tried to sit up. "Your father was like Dr. Jekyll and Mr. Hyde. He never told the truth a day in his life."

"Don't talk to me about what he was," Zachary said. "He made a fortune, and you spent it. Who do you think paid for your lifestyle?" He looked at Jo. "Do you know what she did when my father died? She burned his entire collection of videos and recordings. All of the material my father had assembled—gone! Just like that. He had told me about it because he wanted me to use it. She ruined everything."

"Your father poisoned you," Annabelle said. "He was a sick man, and he passed his illness on to you." She looked at Jo. "I'm sorry. I wanted to do right by you."

"Why did you tell Cal's mother about me?" Jo asked.

"I didn't," Annabelle said.

"That was me," Zachary added.

"Why did you do it?" Jo demanded.

"Priscilla already hated you," Zachary said. "She was my natural ally."

Jo turned to Annabelle. "I still don't understand why you contacted me in the first place."

"I didn't want to deal with what Marc did for a very long time," Annabelle said. "I thought I could bury it. Then your sister died, and I . . . I realized I couldn't ignore it. I'd given money to charity, but I'd never given anything directly to the people my husband hurt. I wanted to fix that."

"Oh, Mother," Zachary said. "Why don't you tell Jo the truth before I get rid of her?"

Before Jo could react, he'd uncapped a small vial and poured liquid over her legs and feet. It was only tiny droplets, but Jo screamed in agony. It felt as if he'd set her on fire.

"Sulfuric acid," Zachary explained. "You deserve every bit of punishment you get."

Jo tried to answer, but all that came out of her mouth was an agonized wail.

"You know, I'm glad you didn't die on Monday, Jo," Zachary said. "I was so angry when Tony screwed up. I still don't know how you shot him. He told me he'd been a Navy SEAL, but I suppose he was lying about that, just like he did about everything else. Still, a quick death would've been too good for you."

"I understand . . . why you wanted to kill me," Jo gasped through her pain. "But why did you kill Andray Baxter?"

"He was in my way," Zachary said. "Sofia's been completely infatuated with him, even after her father paid him to go away. Andray ditched her, and she kept running after him. Women are such fools."

"You thought Sofia . . . would be yours?" Jo asked. At one time, she'd been forced to cater to the desires of men who were openly contemptuous of women. They had blamed her when their own bodies failed to perform as they'd hoped. They called women shallow for not being interested in them. Jo realized Zachary had inherited more than his father's looks.

"Some people like to slum it for a while," Zachary said. "Look at your own boyfriend. But sooner or later, most of them wake up to reality. Sofia's too stupid to do that, apparently."

"You shot a man because you were jealous of him," Jo said.

"Tony fired the gun," Zachary admitted. "But the plan was mine. We wrapped Andray in plastic and stored him in the bathroom. Tony cleaned up while I tinkered with Andray's laptop. Everything went like clockwork until you showed up." He sighed. "I never should've listened to Tony."

"What do you mean?" Jo asked.

"I wanted to wait in the bathroom. Everything would've been over quickly," Zachary explained. "But I had to go next door because Tony wanted some time alone with you. He had his own . . . ideas."

Jo imagined Tony's hands on her and winced. "I'm glad I killed him."

"It took him a long time to die. He cried and made me promise to get a doctor."

"Did you?"

Zachary laughed. "When I finally went back, it was with my dad's cigar cutter and a hammer. I figured if the police couldn't identify him . . ." His voice trailed off.

"You started that fire," Jo hissed. "You could've killed everyone in that building."

"That wasn't me," Zachary said. "But I am going to wipe that smug expression off your face." He stormed off down the hallway.

"Did you do it?" Jo asked Annabelle.

"What?"

"Did you start that fire to protect your son?"

"No. I'd never do that."

Jo watched her closely, trying to decide if she believed her. "We have to get out of here."

"You go," Annabelle said. "I can't."

"Why not?"

"I'm responsible for him," Annabelle said.

Zachary was back before his mother had finished speaking. "This wasn't supposed to be for you, Jo," he said. "It was going to be a special treat for my mother after all of this blew over. I always plan ahead."

He uncapped the bottle as he moved toward her. Jo curled into herself like a shrimp, pulling her knees up to her chest. When Zachary was in front of her, she kicked out as hard as she could, and the bottle flew out of his hands. She turned her head away, terrified that the acid would burn through her face, but it was Zachary who shrieked. When she turned her head to see him, he was running away.

She started crawling across the floor again as she heard the sound of water running. A drop of the acid had hit her arm, and it made her want to scream. The grand apartment felt interminable as she inched through it. She was almost in the foyer when she heard the ding of the elevator bell. Someone banged on the door, and she could've wept for joy.

"Annabelle Davies? NYPD. Open your door. We have a warrant."

Jo immediately recognized Detective Sterling's commanding voice. "Help us!" she screamed. "Zachary attacked me and Annabelle. She has a head wound. I don't think she can move."

She heard the sound of a body slamming against the door, as if to break it down. But then Zachary was back.

"Don't come in here!" he shouted. "I have a gun, and I'll kill them both."

# CHAPTER 66

## RAFAEL

"Is that Zachary Davies?" Sheryn called back. "My name is Sheryn Sterling. I'm a detective. Could you open the door so we can talk?"

"It's Zachary Lytton," Zachary shouted back. "You come near my door, and I'll put bullets in their heads."

"Do you think he really has a gun?" Sheryn whispered to Rafael.

"Doesn't matter," Rafael whispered back. "He has hostages."

Rafael took a couple of steps closer to the door, feeling a terrible sense of déjà vu. The case he'd told his partner about that morning about the murdered, mutilated family had been a prologue; there was an epilogue he didn't want to remember. "Hey, Zachary," he called out, his voice crackling with nervous energy. "My name's Rafael. I'm also a detective. It sounds like you're having a really bad day. What can we do to help?"

Sheryn stared at him incredulously. "What can we do to . . . *help*?" she whispered. "Are you joking?"

"I don't need help," Zachary called back, his voice subdued. "I need to deal with this."

"I hear you." Rafael turned to his partner and whispered, "Call the Hostage Team."

"What are you doing?" Sheryn demanded.

"I was in a situation like this once in LA," Rafael whispered back. "All I can tell you for sure is that I have to keep him talking."

*That's the only thing I know,* Rafael thought, *because I got it wrong last time.*

While Sheryn backed as far away as she could from the door and made the call to the NYPD's Hostage Negotiation Team, Rafael kept talking.

"We know Jo Greaver's a criminal," Rafael said. "But that's something you need to let us deal with, Zachary. This isn't on you; it's on us."

"Did you know she murdered my father?" Zachary called back.

"I had no idea, Zachary," Rafael said. "Why don't you tell me what happened?"

"She was a prostitute," Zachary said. "She stabbed him with a pair of scissors. She murdered him, and her sister helped her cover it up, and nobody ever arrested her."

"We can investigate that, Zachary," Rafael said. "We can set things right."

"I have proof," Zachary said.

Rafael noted the oddly hopeful tone in his voice. He hadn't laid eyes on Zachary, but he already knew that this man wasn't used to being held to account for anything he did. Zachary believed he had reasons, and they could justify anything.

"I have video," Zachary added.

"That's the best kind of proof you could have." Rafael kept his tone encouraging, like a camp counselor cheering for a kid who could barely keep himself afloat in the water. "Juries convict based on video evidence."

"I can send it to you," Zachary said. "Hold on. I have to wash my hands again."

"Wash his hands again?" Sheryn whispered. "What is this, some OCD thing?"

"I don't know," Rafael said. "But I think he desperately wants to share that video."

Sheryn's phone buzzed. She held it up so that Rafael could see the screen. It was a message from Cal: I think Jo might be in trouble at Annabelle's apartment. She told me to call you if I couldn't reach her. She can't/won't answer.

"Poor Cal," Sheryn said. "Always a day late and a dollar short."

"If Zachary's the one who's been blackmailing Jo all along, she's in trouble," Rafael said. "He wanted her dead on Monday. Now's his chance."

"You think she and Annabelle are in imminent danger?"

"If he's anything like the killer I told you about, he's going to murder them both," Rafael said. "He won't break a sweat doing it."

Sirens wailed in the background, joining in a chorus with the ringing in his ears. Rafael knew the procedure: police would be blocking the streets around the building. *It's too late*, Rafael thought. *He's inside with a gun, and he knows he's exposed.*

"Zachary?" Rafael called. "I definitely want to see that video. The whole world should see it. But you can probably hear all those sirens coming. It would be really good to open the door now."

"Okay," Zachary said. "But I need to take care of this first."

There was the sound of a scream and a gunshot inside the apartment, and then everything was quiet.

# CHAPTER 67

## Jo

Jo watched Zachary pace back and forth from the foyer to the living room. She could hear Rafael Mendoza calling encouraging things to him, as if they were buddies. "We can investigate that, Zachary," Mendoza called. "We can set things right."

"I have proof," Zachary said. "I have video."

What the police couldn't see was that Zachary was struggling to load a gun. Jo watched him wrestle with it. He had no idea what he was doing, and the acid burns on his hands hobbled him. She was glad to share some of the searing pain that had burrowed into her. The acid had literally burned holes through her sweater. She looked at her legs, which were bright red and raw where the acid had devoured her skin. How deep could it burn?

Annabelle was sitting next to her on that luxurious carpet. Jo slowly turned her throbbing head to gaze at her.

"Your son is going to murder us," Jo said softly. "I understand why he wants to kill me. Why does he want to kill you?"

"After my husband died, I left New York for a couple of years. When I came back, your sister started blackmailing me," Annabelle said. "She had proof of what Marc had done, and she threatened to sell her story to the tabloids. It wasn't a lot of money at first, so I paid her to go away. But she kept demanding more."

"That sounds like Lori," Jo said. There had never been such a thing as *enough* for her sister: not with money, not with men, not with drugs.

"One night, almost two years ago, she showed up here, at my apartment," Annabelle said. "That was when I decided she had to die."

Jo found it hard to breathe, and it wasn't because of the pain she was in. All those times she'd wished Lori dead. She knew she should be horrified by what Annabelle was saying, but she understood it, deep in her bones.

"You must hate me," Annabelle said. "I'm sorry."

"No," Jo whispered. "I get it. More than you can imagine."

"An overdose seemed like the obvious way," Annabelle said. "I had drugs delivered to her, thinking she'd overdo it, but she never did. She just . . . absorbed everything. Finally I talked to Zachary. He said we'd need to add fentanyl to the heroin."

Jo couldn't breathe.

"Zachary delivered the drugs to her," Annabelle added. "She died that night."

Jo remembered her sister's call. *JoJo, you won't believe it, but I saw a ghost today.* Lori hadn't imagined a specter; she'd laid eyes on Zachary, a replica of his monstrous father.

"I can send it to you," Zachary called out to the cop on the other side of the front door. His words brought Jo out of her reverie. "Hold on. I have to wash my hands again."

He disappeared down the hallway, fumbling with the gun as if it were a hot potato.

Jo tried to stand but fell back to the ground. The pain was agonizing.

"Run!" Jo urged Annabelle. "Open the door!"

Annabelle got to her feet. She was bleeding from her temple, and her hand came away red when she touched it. "Can you stand?" she asked Jo, trying to help her up.

"Go!" Jo hissed.

Annabelle didn't listen. She got Jo to her feet. But by the time she was up, Zachary was back.

He had loaded the gun.

"Zachary?" Mendoza called. "I definitely want to see that video. The whole world should see it. But you can probably hear all those sirens coming. It would be really good to open the door now."

"Okay," Zachary said. "But I need to take care of this first."

He pointed the gun at Jo.

"You killed my sister," Jo said. "Tell me exactly what happened."

"I went to her place," Zachary said. "I charmed the pants off her. Literally."

"You never told me *that* part," Annabelle said.

"I copied everything on her laptop," Zachary said. "She didn't have that much material from the brothel. It was disappointing. But she did have that video of you stabbing my father."

"Why did you come after me?" Jo asked him.

"You killed my father. I had to do it."

"But . . . why did you wait for well over a year?" Jo said. "Were you hatching your plan all that time?"

Zachary didn't answer that directly. "How could I call myself a man if I didn't avenge his death?"

In spite of the gun pointed at her, Jo turned to stare at Annabelle. In a way, she had the same question for her; Annabelle had hunted her down, not to harm her but to help her.

"When I saw the video, I wanted to die of shame," Annabelle said. "I felt horrible. Your sister and my husband had robbed you of your childhood. You were innocent, and you deserved better." Annabelle's head drooped. "After what I did to your sister, I felt . . . guilty. I wanted to help you. It was my way of balancing the scales."

"You didn't plant the gun in my bag?" Jo asked softly.

"Of course not," Annabelle said.

"Mother, you wonder why I hate you so much," Zachary said. "Jo murdered your own husband, and you feel bad for *her*."

He fired the gun.

# CHAPTER 68

## SHERYN

After the shot rang out—while Rafael banged on the door of Penthouse B, shouting to Zachary—Sheryn opened the door of Penthouse A. The interior was musty, as if no one had been inside for a long time. She hadn't seen much of Annabelle Davies's apartment—just the foyer and a glimpse of a grand parlor—but Sheryn was expecting this one to roughly be a mirror image of the other. Specifically, she was hoping that the balcony she'd seen from the street went all the way around.

She saw immediately that it didn't. The balcony of the penthouse stretched only across the northern face of the building. But when she stepped outside, she saw that the drop down to the next level was a single story, and that looked like a garden level that ran around the entire building.

*Here goes nothing,* she thought, going over the edge and dropping down to the side. She ran around the perimeter of the building until she reached the southern side, overlooking Gramercy Park. That had to be the Davies's balcony, she knew. The question was how to get to it. It was a lot easier to go down than to leap up.

There was a startled woman in a maid's uniform cleaning the glass doors to the terrace. Sheryn flashed her gold shield at her. The woman opened the door. "I hear gun?" the woman said in broken English. "Danger?"

"Yes, it is dangerous," Sheryn told her. "Stay inside and lock the door. But first, do you have a ladder?"

# CHAPTER 69

## Jo

The bullet had been meant for her, Jo knew. But Annabelle had stepped in front of her, and it had struck her instead, hitting her in the chest and throwing her back. Annabelle opened her mouth to speak, and blood seeped out.

"No," Jo whispered. "Annabelle. No."

"Why?" Zachary raged, hurling one curse after another. "Why did you get in the way?"

Jo stared at him, but he wasn't even looking at her. It took her a moment to understand he was talking to his mother as she bled out in front of the fireplace.

"What happened?" Mendoza yelled from the hallway. "Did the gun go off? Is someone hurt?"

"Shut up!" Zachary yelled at him. "You're making everything worse."

He turned to the door while he was speaking. Jo forced herself to push past her pain and ran to the door to the kitchen. It was flimsy, and there was nothing to barricade it with, so she kept on running through the door on the other side. She found herself in a hallway. There was a door to the right, and she ran to it, slamming it shut and locking it just as Zachary was closing in behind her.

"You're going to die here," he said. Then he fired two shots through it.

Trapped in a luxurious bedroom, Jo remembered being in Andray Baxter's apartment on Monday, when bullets came flying through that door. Zachary had been the man shouting in the hallway. Less than an hour ago, when she'd met him, his voice had been refined, and she hadn't recognized it.

Jo looked around for anything to use as a weapon. Something rattled against the glass. She turned and saw Sterling standing on the balcony, gun drawn. Jo had never been so happy to see another person in her entire life. She ran to the doors and opened them. Sterling carefully pulled her outside, into the cold but farther from Zachary.

"You're not shot, are you?"

"No," Jo said. "Annabelle tried to grab the gun from him. She got shot in the chest."

"If I help you over the ledge, a couple of cops on the next terrace will catch you," Sterling said. "Can you do that?"

"I think so." Jo looked down. Her shoes were gone, and her legs were covered in furious red blotches. Even the freezing air didn't stop them from burning.

"What happened to your legs?" Sterling asked.

"Vitriol."

"Lord, give me strength," Sterling prayed. "Because I badly want to shoot this man." She looked over the balcony. "Be careful—she's covered in acid burns."

As Jo went over the side, she heard another shot. Turning back to look, she saw Zachary coming through the bedroom door.

# CHAPTER 70

## SHERYN

"Don't take another step," Sheryn said, leveling her gun at Zachary. "Because I will shoot you between the eyes."

"Aren't you supposed to pretend to be my friend?" Zachary mocked.

"That was my partner's job," Sheryn said. "I'm the bad cop."

"Don't tell me what to do," he snapped back. Sheryn noted that, face to face—even with a gun in his hand—he was too scared to call out insults anymore.

"You shot your own mother," Sheryn said. "She needs help. Are you going to let us do that, or are you going to let her die?"

"I don't care if she dies," Zachary said. "She betrayed my father and me. She deserves the worst that can happen to her."

"Put the gun down," Sheryn ordered.

"Make me," Zachary bit back, as if he were a well-armed toddler.

"You keep talking about your father's death," Sheryn said. "You orchestrate all this for him?"

"Yes," Zachary said. "No one else ever cared enough to get the vengeance he deserved."

"Jo told me he raped her," Sheryn said. "If you have the video, you know that's true."

"You can't rape a prostitute."

"Wrong. All your wiring is wrong," Sheryn said. "You know that, on some level, right? Everything in your head is twisted."

"Don't you understand? She murdered him."

Sheryn could hear some noise from the apartment behind Zachary. Clearly, he heard it, too, because he looked behind him.

Rafael was standing in the doorway, clutching the doorframe with his left hand.

"You promised to show me the video," Rafael said calmly. "You keep disappointing everyone, don't you, Zachary?"

Sheryn jumped forward and grabbed the gun from a startled Zachary. Rafael stepped closer, then lifted his cane high with his right hand and smashed it behind Zachary's knee.

Zachary screamed and dropped to the ground.

"Damn, but you know how to make a dramatic entrance," Sheryn said, keeping her gun trained on Zachary while holding his weapon in her left hand. "That was amazing."

Rafael had a wary eye on Zachary, who was howling like a wounded animal on the carpet. "One false move and I take out your other knee-cap," he warned, holding up the cane.

"I don't think he's walking away from this," Sheryn said. She holstered her gun and touched Rafael's arm. "Are you okay?"

Rafael nodded, but he didn't look at her. Zachary sobbed helplessly.

"Officers, we need some help in here!" Sheryn called.

A moment later, a pair of uniformed cops came through the doorway, secured Zachary's hands behind his back, and dragged him from the room.

Rafael set the cane on the bed and sat down. "Last time I was in a situation like this, it didn't end well," he said.

"I'm sorry." Sheryn took a seat next to him.

"Three people ended up dead. Not the suspect. His coworkers." Rafael stared at the carpet.

"That's a lot to live with," Sheryn said. She was quiet for a minute. "I thought I was going to have to shoot Zachary."

"I'm sure part of you wanted to," Rafael said.

"True. But another part knew I didn't want to live with that." She picked up the cane, feeling its weight in both hands.

"I figured this had to come in handy sooner or later," Rafael said.

"Now you're making me want one," Sheryn admitted. "Come on. We've got a suspect to interrogate."

# CHAPTER 71

## SHERYN

Sheryn wouldn't have minded depositing Zachary Lytton directly into Rikers, but she was obligated to bring him back to the precinct first. She'd expected him to cry "Lawyer!" at the first opportunity, but for a man with everything stacked against him, Zachary was surprisingly subdued.

"I can tell you exactly what happened," he announced inside the interview room. "Jo Greaver came to the apartment I share with my mother. She was planning to kill my mother. You can ask Priscilla McGarran. She called me when Jo left her apartment. She said Jo had a gun and was going to kill my mother. You can ask her."

"Priscilla McGarran has had a sudden onset of chest pain," Sheryn said. "She went to the hospital. It doesn't look like she's in any hurry to corroborate your story."

"The most interesting part," Rafael said, "is the communication between you and Priscilla. You two called and messaged each other several times a day. What was going on with you lovebirds?"

Zachary flushed when he said *lovebirds*. There was a silence in the interrogation room. Sheryn knew it was only a matter of time before he demanded a lawyer, but he hadn't yet. He was narcissistic enough to believe that he could outsmart the police.

"I'm sure Cal will be thrilled to know that you were banging his mother," Rafael said.

"All cats are gray in the dark," Zachary said. "Besides, older women are so grateful." He looked directly at Sheryn and gave her a lopsided smile.

*Do not punch him in the face,* Sheryn warned herself. *Do not punch him in the throat. Do not punch him in the groin.* Instead, she smiled back. "It's actually very helpful to know about your relationship with Ms. McGarran. We've been wondering how you framed Jo Greaver with the gun used to kill Andray Baxter. Thanks to the GPS data on your phone, we know that you were at Ms. Greaver's apartment on Monday afternoon. Please don't embarrass yourself by saying you weren't. We know it was you. But unless you were hiding in her apartment, how did you sneak the gun into her bag?"

"I don't know what you're talking about," Zachary said.

"I have a theory," Sheryn said. "Ms. McGarran wasn't supposed to go to the apartment. She was supposed to keep her son away. But after he dragged her there, she used the opportunity to move the planted gun."

"Is this what you do, come up with crazy theories all day?" Zachary asked.

"Ms. McGarran wasn't as careful as she thought," Sheryn said. "Her fingerprints are on other items in Ms. Greaver's tote bag."

Zachary shrugged. "Proving what?"

"Proving that she would be a good witness to testify against you."

Zachary laughed. "If you think Priscilla would testify against me, you're nuts."

"Why did you kill Elliott Westergard?" Rafael asked.

"Who's that?"

"Don't be coy," Rafael said. "He hated Andray, and he wanted rid of him. Westergard wasn't the kind of man who'd do his own killing, but he struck me as the type who wouldn't mind if blood was spilled on his behalf."

"Oh, I know who you mean," Zachary said. "Sounds like a coward to me."

"Westergard thought he could sell his crappy building for a mint, if only he was rid of Andray. There's a lot of calling back and forth with you, Westergard, and his employee Mardiks," Rafael said. "When did you decide to kill Andray and Jo? Was it a two-for-one special? Make it look like Andray was blackmailing Jo. You killed him before Jo got there."

"Andray was used to seeing your face," Sheryn said. "On account of you delivering cash to him every month. It must've been easy to get him to open his door. Who did the shooting, you or Mardiks?"

"I knew Andray, and I delivered his payment that day. Maybe Elliott Westergard and his bodyguard stole the money. You never know with people like that."

"People like what?" Sheryn's tone was acid.

"Grifters. Lowlifes. Whores. They'll do anything." Zachary leaned forward, his hands, roughly bandaged by EMTs, resting together on the table like mittens. "Let me tell you exactly what happened, Detectives. Jo Greaver came to my apartment and tried to kill my mother and me. If my mother ever regains consciousness, she'll confirm that. Jo shot my mother, but I got the gun away from her. Jo threw acid on me, damaging my hands, but she also spilled it on her own legs."

"You think anyone is going to buy that?" Rafael said. "You were holding hostages in that apartment. I had to negotiate with you."

"I thought you were thugs Jo hired," Zachary said. "I had no idea you were really police. I was holding Jo's gun on her at that point. I didn't know what to do."

"It's amazing, watching you spin," Sheryn said. "We know you started the fire at Westergard's building." She didn't have any evidence to back that up, but in her experience, there was rarely a downside to throwing a hook into the water.

"You have my GPS data, so you know that I wasn't anywhere near the building that night. I was at Malcolm Severight's town house," Zachary said. "Obviously, I visited the building multiple times, so my prints and DNA would be there. But being an arsonist? You obviously have a fevered imagination." Zachary smiled. "This is the best you've got? Honestly, I won't even need a lawyer. I can represent myself."

Sheryn crossed her arms. "Look at you, all high and mighty. You don't seem to understand that, in your very short career, you've made a pile of enemies, Zach."

"Do not call me that," he snapped.

"Soon I'll be calling you by your inmate number," Sheryn said. "We know you stole from your boss. He thought he was paying Andray twenty-five thousand dollars a month to stay away from his daughter. Andray was only getting ten thousand dollars. You were pocketing the rest."

"I don't know where you came up with those numbers . . ."

"They came directly from Malcolm Severight," Sheryn said.

"He wouldn't talk to the police in a million years," Zachary said.

"You are so behind the times. He already spilled his guts to Cal McGarran."

"Ah." Zachary shifted in his seat. "Let me tell you something people of your social class wouldn't know, Detectives. Mr. Severight isn't going to testify against me. It would be beyond embarrassing for him to appear in court and have everyone know that I hoodwinked him. Cal McGarran's own father ripped him off, and Mr. Severight was too embarrassed to admit it in public." Zachary smiled. "That's how this world works."

"You think some gentleman's code of silence is going to save your ass?" Sheryn rapped on the double-sided glass. "Ladies? Would you come in here for a minute?"

A moment later the door opened. Audra Baxter stepped through it, followed by Sofia Severight.

Zachary eased back in his chair, as if to put distance between them. "What is this?"

"If I had my way, it would be a firing squad," Sofia said.

"We'll settle for locking you away in jail until you rot there," Audra said.

Zachary stared at Sofia. "Please don't do this. You know I love you. Anything I've done, I did it because you mean everything to me."

"I hated my father for coming between Andray and me," Sofia said, her voice soft. "But that doesn't come close to how I feel about you. You stole from Andray, and then you murdered him."

"He never cared about you," Zachary said quickly.

"Andray was the only person in the world who really saw me for who I am," Sofia said. "But you're about to find out."

"Your father wouldn't want me telling the courts everything I know about his business," Zachary said. "I've been working for him long enough to know where his vulnerabilities are."

"That's where you screwed up," Sheryn said. "You think everybody's a coward like you, worrying about their place on the social register. You don't get that some people are going to step up and do the right thing. And it's like a cascade: one person does it, and others will too."

Zachary didn't even look at her; he kept his focus on Sofia. "You don't know how hard it is to lose everything. How impossible it is to build it up again. You have to trust me. I want to take care of you."

"This from a man who shot his own mother," Audra said. "After murdering my brother."

"I'm going to testify against you, and so will my father," Sofia said.

"You are making the greatest mistake of your life," Zachary said.

"My greatest mistake was letting other people control my life," Sofia said. "I won't make that mistake again." She started to walk out of the room but turned back. "If you think my father would've let you come near me, you're out of your mind. You're nothing but the help to him."

Sheryn's phone rang. It was the worst possible time for a call, but when she saw Jo Greaver's name on the screen, she answered immediately. Jo had been taken straight to the hospital in very rough shape, and Sheryn was fearful for her.

"Hey," she said. "How are you feeling?"

"They're patching me up," Jo said. "But I have to tell you something that can't wait. I got it."

"Got what?"

"I have Annabelle and Zachary telling me exactly what they did. I sent you the audio file from my phone."

"That's . . . really something," Sheryn said, feeling like manna had just been delivered from heaven. "Thank you. I'm going to let you go now."

"There's something else," Jo said. "I really need to talk to you, Detective. Can you come to the hospital?"

"I will," Sheryn promised. "As soon as I'm done here."

She hung up and looked at her messages. There was one from Jo, and she opened it. It started to play immediately.

"I understand . . . why you wanted to kill me . . ." It was Jo's voice, overwritten by pain. "But why did you kill Andray Baxter?"

"He was in my way," Zachary answered. "Sofia's been completely infatuated with him, even after her father paid him to go away. Andray ditched her, and she kept running after him. Women are such fools."

Zachary's face turned pale. "What is that?"

"It's a recording of everything that happened in your mother's apartment," Sheryn said. "Jo Greaver's one smart cookie. You never should've gone up against her. You were out of your league."

# CHAPTER 72

## Jo

The doctors did their best, but they couldn't save Annabelle. She died an hour after surgery, while Jo was holding her hand.

Jo watched her, at peace, her tense face finally relaxing. In a terrible way, she envied her. Annabelle had done some awful things, and she'd struggled to live under the weight of her guilt. Jo knew she'd been going through something similar, and she couldn't deal with it anymore.

While she waited for Detective Sterling to come by, Cal kept her company. Jo couldn't see the bandages on her head, but they were tight enough that she couldn't forget them. The dressings on the burned parts of her legs had to be changed frequently. Cal held her gently and kissed her. "You look like an Egyptian mummy," he said. "How are you feeling?"

"I'm okay. I thought I was going to die. Part of me is maybe a bit sorry that I didn't, because now I have to do this."

"Do what?" Cal's eyes were wide with surprise and alarm.

"I have to talk with Detective Sterling about something."

"You're the hero of the day," Cal said. "You got Zachary on tape. He killed several people, including his own mother. He'll be locked up forever."

"Do you really believe that?" Jo asked him. "People like Zachary get lawyers who find loopholes and bend the law for them. Zachary will probably go to some home for the criminally insane and be out in a few years."

Cal didn't argue. They sat in silence for a while until the detective showed up. Cal left quietly, closing the door behind him.

Sterling smiled at her. "I wish you could've been there to watch Zachary Lytton go down. The man bawled like a baby when he realized he couldn't wriggle out of the trap you set for him."

"You're giving me too much credit," Jo said. "I was terrified and desperate, because I'd recognized the photo of Annabelle's first husband. I thought she was going to kill me. Making a recording was all I could think of to do."

"It was smart." Sterling sat on the edge of the bed. "What did you want to see me about?"

"I guess I'm wondering . . ." Jo's voice tapered off.

"Take your time," Sterling said. "You've been through hell. Take a breath."

Jo nodded. "Annabelle gave me a . . . a gift today. She told me she killed Lori."

"I listened to the entire tape on my way here," Sterling said. "I heard all of it. She and her son conspired to do it."

"There's more to it than that," Jo said. "The night Lori died, my sister called and told me she'd seen a ghost. I never understood what she meant by that. She didn't explain, and when I went over . . . there was no way to ask her then. I only understood today when I saw Zachary. He's the image of his father . . . in every way, unfortunately."

"Sadly, that seems to be true."

"I told you about my relationship with Lori. How she forced me to make porn and sold me to her boyfriend. She gave me pills. I told you Lori blackmailed me too."

"I remember," Sterling said. "She was the one with the videotape of you."

"Right. Lori said she'd tell the police that I was the one who'd killed her boyfriend. I paid her off, over and over. You didn't know me then, but I was always bailing her out. It wasn't because I wanted to. It was because I felt like I had to." Jo gulped. "When she called me that night, she wanted me to come over."

"Why?"

"She'd been a drug addict for a long time, but she had a strong sense of self-preservation," Jo said. "She would call me when she thought she'd need someone to administer naloxone."

"Okay," Sterling said.

"I went over that night like she wanted me to," Jo said. "She'd left her door unlocked so I could get in easily. When I got there, Lori was passed out on her bed. She had a dozen doses of naloxone on her night table. I injected her with one, but it didn't do anything. I picked up the next one, and then I . . . I set it down again, Detective. I thought, 'Why would I ever want to bring her back?' She was evil."

"You gave her one dose of the antidote, and then you stopped," Sheryn said. "I want to make sure I'm understanding this clearly."

"You are," Jo said. "But it's worse than that. I went through her apartment and found her laptop. I told you I destroyed it. That was true. But that was later. What I didn't tell you was that I waited to call 911 until I found her computer. I erased her files before I called." Jo could feel tears trailing down her cheeks.

"Jo, when you went into her apartment, was she still breathing?"

"Her chest wasn't moving," Jo said. "I don't know how long she was like that. It took me twenty minutes to get there after she called me."

"Why are you confessing this to me?"

"My life flashed before my eyes this afternoon," Jo said. "I realized that I've been carrying around shame all my life. But ever since that night at Lori's . . ." Tears welled up in her eyes. "I know I don't deserve anything good. I could've saved her, and I didn't."

"How do you know you could've saved her?" Sterling asked.

"I'd done it before. Several times."

"It's not easy, living with guilt," Sterling said. "I know something about that myself. I had a family member who was disturbed, and he ended up hurting some people. The shame I felt when I thought about what I could've done—should've done—to prevent it."

"This isn't the same," Jo said. "I should've given her all the doses of the antidote. I should've called 911 immediately."

"Do you really think that would've changed the outcome? Especially now that you know Annabelle and Zachary added fentanyl to the drugs?"

"Not when you put it like that," Jo said. "But I know what I did. I know how I felt. I wished she would die. I don't know how to live with that."

"One of the bravest things you can do in life is to keep moving forward under the weight of that burden," Sterling said. "You don't get to put it aside. It's going to be with you every day, and you're going to have to figure out how to cope with it."

"I don't know if I can do that," Jo admitted.

"I do," Sterling said. "You're far stronger than you know."

# EPILOGUE

## SHERYN

The memorial service for Annabelle Davies was organized for the following Tuesday, late in the afternoon. Even though it was Thanksgiving week, it drew a large crowd to Grace Church on Broadway. The church was midway between Union Square and Astor Place, a French Gothic Revival masterpiece constructed of pale-gray stone. The interior was festooned with yellow roses, brightening the somber space on a rainy day. The sky was so dark that little light came through the Pre-Raphaelite stained-glass windows.

Sheryn and Rafael got there early. They were both in black suits. Sheryn kept stealing envious glances at his gold-topped cane; this one looked like a gold octopus with tentacles grappling with the wood. "It's not exactly a style choice yet, but I think it's turning into one," he admitted.

Sheryn watched Jo walk into the service with her friend Peyton. The media coverage of Jo's purported affair with Andray had died down. The tabloids were now having a field day with Zachary Lytton's murder of his mother, though none of them had figured out why he'd attacked Jo. Zachary had been charged with the murders of Andray Baxter, Elliott Westergard, and Anthony Wayne Mardiks; however, he hadn't been charged yet in Lori Fielding's death, nor had he been charged with arson. Malcolm Severight was cooperating with the police, and he'd only reluctantly provided Zachary with an alibi for that night, which dovetailed with the GPS data from Zachary's phone. The decision to hold off on pressing charges in Lori Fielding's death was a strategic one—Sheryn didn't want to shift the focus from the bodies that had piled up that week—but the fire was another matter. It was the one crime that remained unsolved.

"There's no sign of him yet," Rafael whispered.

"He'll be here," Sheryn answered. "I have no doubt."

"I'm not sure I'd trust a guy who would betray his mother," Rafael said.

"Even if his mother has the heart of a killer?" Sheryn asked.

Sheryn caught Jo's eye, and the young woman turned in her direction. As they approached her, Sheryn heard Peyton's voice. "I have the feeling Annabelle wouldn't approve of these flowers. Who decided on yellow roses anyway?"

"Montana Bob," Jo answered. "His eulogy should really be something."

Peyton shook her head disapprovingly. "There's no way your ex should be allowed to organize your memorial. That's just not right."

"It's good to see you both," Sheryn said. "How are you coping, Jo?"

"It's been intense. Everyone knows there's more to this awful story, but they don't know what it is," Jo said.

"We heard the media were camped out at your home and office," Rafael said. "We can't do much about them on the street, but there are measures we can take if they overstep." He lowered his voice. "You know Zachary is going to be here today, right?"

"I heard about that," Jo said.

"You couldn't stop it?" Peyton asked.

A judge had made the controversial decision to allow Zachary out of jail for his mother's memorial service. It wasn't unusual for a prisoner to get compassionate release to attend a family funeral, though that sympathy didn't usually extend to people who'd put their relative in the ground in the first place.

"Our ADA was going to object, but we asked her not to," Sheryn said. "I wish I could explain our thinking. There's a part of this case that hasn't come together yet."

"I trust you," Jo said. "Just make sure he doesn't come anywhere near us."

"He won't," Rafael said. "There are a couple of plainclothes officers who'll make sure he doesn't."

Jo gave them a shy smile. "I owe both of you a lot," she said. "I hope you know how grateful I am."

There was a commotion at the front of the church, and they all turned to look. Priscilla McGarran, decked out in a chic black bouclé suit, had entered the church. She was leaning on Cal's arm.

"You still don't have enough to arrest her, do you?" Jo asked.

"Not yet," Sheryn said. "We have some calls and texts between her and Zachary, but nothing proving a crime. They were both using an encrypted app, too, but knowing they were working together isn't the same as having proof."

"I can't believe Cal moved back into his mother's apartment," Peyton said. "He has to know what she did. I hate him so much."

"I guess you never really know a person," Jo said wistfully.

Sheryn wished she could alleviate the young woman's sadness; at that moment, there was nothing she could do. The fact that Priscilla McGarran was still walking around free was galling to Sheryn. From her perspective, Priscilla should've been charged with conspiracy and obstruction of justice for planting the gun in Jo's bag, and probably a lot more.

As Jo and Peyton took their seats, the organist began to play a hymn that Sheryn recognized—"How Great Thou Art"—and she and Rafael were quiet, waiting for Zachary Lytton to be escorted in.

Sheryn watched Priscilla say something to Cal, then stand and walk to the door of the church. She wanted to follow her, but there were plainclothes officers who were handling that. Instead, Sheryn strolled over to Cal. "How did she take the news that Zachary ratted her out?"

"She won't tell me much," Cal answered. "But she's in a panic."

"Good," Sheryn said, moving away quickly.

When Priscilla returned to her seat, Sheryn was next to Rafael. She was waiting for the real drama to start. At long last, Zachary stepped into the church, his dark hair combed back and his muscular body in a tailored suit. His handcuffs were in front this time, one of the provisions the Department of Corrections had agreed to for this excursion. Sheryn wouldn't have been so lenient.

She watched Zachary turn his head in Priscilla's direction, but she wouldn't meet his eyes. Sheryn stared at Priscilla's hands, believing for a split second that she saw the blade of a knife, but it was only light glinting off one of Priscilla's rings. *What are the odds of her trying something in the church?* Sheryn thought. *Low, of course. But maybe right after the service . . .*

The music picked up again, and Sheryn watched the large man in that plaid jacket walk up the aisle. She recognized him as Montana Bob—Annabelle's second husband—even though she couldn't recall his surname. Sheryn saw him pause when he got to Zachary. "That's okay; he's my stepson," Montana Bob said, pulling Zachary into a bear hug. When he let go, Zachary fell back into his pew. The man in plaid kept walking up to the front of the church.

"Thank you all kindly for coming today," Montana Bob said. "I know my dear Annabelle would've loved to know that she was appreciated by so many fine people."

Sheryn stared at Zachary. His expression was thunderstruck, as if he'd finally realized the horror of what he'd done. Was he slumping?

"Get the EMTs in here now," she hissed at Rafael before hurrying over to Zachary.

"He . . . he . . ." Zachary's eyes were glassy with fear. "Help me."

Sheryn opened his jacket. The bloodstain from the knife wound was visible on Zachary's white shirt. She'd expected Priscilla McGarran to act, but since when did that woman dirty her own hands?

"My partner's calling you an ambulance right now." Sheryn pushed Zachary to lie down on the pew, folded his hands against the wound, and put pressure on it. "Hold it like that. Harder."

People were starting to notice that something was terribly wrong. There was muttering from the pews, and the music stopped.

"I didn't do anything wrong!" Montana Bob yelled as four detectives wrestled him to the floor. "That boy murdered his own mother. He had it coming."

"Am I going to die?" Zachary whimpered.

"Maybe," Sheryn said cheerfully. She leaned closer. "We told Priscilla that you ratted her out. That was all it took for her to have you killed."

"But that was Montana Bob."

"Priscilla worked on you for a year before you decided to get revenge on Jo," Sheryn said. "You think she didn't work on your stepfather?"

Zachary gulped for air. "Priscilla started the fire."

"How, exactly, did Priscilla McGarran do that?" Sheryn asked, forcing herself to stay calm.

"I couldn't leave Mr. Severight's house," Zachary sobbed. "I gave Priscilla the code and told her she had to be a block away from the building."

EMTs were hurrying up the aisle.

"Good luck," Sheryn told Zachary. "You're going to need it."

She took a step back, turning to face a startled sea of faces. "Priscilla McGarran, you're under arrest for arson," Sheryn announced. "You have the right to remain silent. Anything you say can be used against you in court . . ."

Priscilla stormed up to her, her face bright red. "I will sue you and the entire force for harassment."

Sheryn slapped a handcuff on one skinny wrist. It rattled against the assorted bangles. "Turn around," she ordered.

"Cal!" Priscilla cried. "You have to tell them I'm innocent. You *have* to! Anything I did, I did for you."

But her son was staring at her as if he'd never seen her before. "The police told me you plotted against Jo, and I wouldn't believe them," Cal said. "Don't pretend that was for me."

"Of course it was!" Priscilla screamed. "No one else matters!"

Sheryn couldn't see Jo's face, but she wondered what her reaction would be when she found out that Cal hadn't abandoned her after all. Sheryn had been the one to ask him to stay with Priscilla; later, when Sheryn had asked Cal to deliver some information to his mother, he'd been dubious, but he'd followed through. She wanted to thank him, but she had to focus on hustling a criminal out of the church.

"Sorry for the interruption, everyone," Sheryn called out.

She handed a shrieking Priscilla over to a pair of uniforms to pack into a squad car. She waited at the church doors for Rafael, knowing it would take him a little longer to get there.

"You claim I know how to make a dramatic entrance," he said when he finally got there. "You, partner, know how to make one hell of an exit."

"You think the charge will stick?"

"You got a dying declaration out of Zachary," Rafael said.

"Zachary's going to live," Sheryn pointed out. "I expected Priscilla to make a move. The medics were around the corner."

"Damn. There I was, being an optimist." Rafael smiled at her. "You want to stay for the rest of the service?"

"Not really," Sheryn said. "It feels like a fashion parade. It's nothing like Andray's was."

"Yeah. That was beautiful."

They had attended Andray Baxter's funeral on Saturday, in a grand Harlem church packed to the rafters with people who wanted to honor a man who was truly loved. There hadn't been a dry eye in the place, and that included Sheryn's and Rafael's. They kept that fact to themselves.

"We could've let Zachary bite the dust," Rafael said. "No one would've been the wiser."

"We used him as bait," Sheryn said. "And that's harsh enough. Would you want a lowlife like Zachary Lytton on your conscience?"

"He's not worth it," Rafael grumbled. "But I hate it when you're right."

"Which is all the damn time." Sheryn laughed. "Come on. We know this dragon isn't going down without a fight. Let's do this."

# ACKNOWLEDGMENTS

Writing the acknowledgments for a novel always reminds me of how many amazing people I know. That list starts with my wonderful, witty, and wise Thomas & Mercer editor, Megha Parekh, who was the first to suggest that NYPD Detective Sheryn Sterling should be a series character. Both Megha and my developmental editor, Charlotte Herscher, were a joy to work with as I wrote this story. I can honestly say the book wouldn't be what it is without them.

The staff at Thomas & Mercer really is a dream team, and I want to thank everyone on it for their help and their support. That list starts with the production squad: I'm grateful to production manager Laura Barrett for shepherding this book through the process, to copyeditor Susan Stokes for catching my errors and for her brilliant suggestions, and to Bill Siever for reading the proof with infinite care. My thanks to editorial director Gracie Doyle for her boundless enthusiasm and support. Thank you to author-relations manager Sarah Shaw for her endlessly thoughtful ways. Special thanks to Jeff Belle, vice president of Amazon Publishing, for creating a cocktail in honor of my first book in this series (friends, it is delicious). Thanks to the appropriately named Brilliance Publishing team for all their amazing work. I'm grateful to Christopher Lin for his gorgeous cover design (my jaw literally fell open when I first saw it) and to art director Oisin O'Malley. Thanks, too, to the exceptional marketing team, especially Gabrielle Guarnero, Kyla

Pigoni, Laura Constantino, and Lindsey Bragg, for their dedication and genius. Endless thanks to publicity manager Dennelle Catlett for always going above and beyond the call of duty (and for being incredibly thoughtful about every last detail of my tour). I'm also grateful to publicity specialist Megan Beatie for her tenacity, brilliance, and follow-through.

The truth is, working with everyone on the Amazon Publishing team has been a privilege and a pleasure. Thank you all.

I also owe tremendous thanks to my agent extraordinaire, Mitch Hoffman, for his wisdom, enthusiasm, and friendship. I appreciate the support of the entire team at the Aaron M. Priest Literary Agency. Whenever I try to come up with a list of all of the amazing people I know in the crime-fiction community, I always miss a few and feel terrible. This time, let me just say that I want to thank all of the criminal types who brighten my day in person and online. It's a joy to see you, whether it's at Bouchercon, Left Coast Crime, ThrillerFest, Mystery Camp, a Mystery Writers of America meeting, a Sisters in Crime event, or on Twitter. Writing is a largely solitary profession, and you make it better.

Love to all of my friends, especially Helen Lovekin and David Slayton. I am so lucky to know you.

My family is simply amazing. I owe so much to my parents, John and Sheila Davidson (special thanks to my mom, who reads all of my books early and gives me feedback). My aunts Amy, Evelyn, and Irene are the world's best cheering squad. Most of all, thank you to my amazing husband, Daniel, for his encouragement, calmness, and boundless sense of humor; I really couldn't do this without you. Finally, thank you to all of my readers. I'm so grateful you choose to spend your time with me. Here's to more adventures together!

# ABOUT THE AUTHOR

*Photo © 2018 Anna Ty Bergman*

Hilary Davidson is the bestselling author of *One Small Sacrifice* and the winner of two Anthony Awards. Her novels include the Lily Moore series—*The Damage Done*, *The Next One to Fall*, and *Evil in All Its Disguises*—and the stand-alone thriller *Blood Always Tells*. Her widely acclaimed short stories have won numerous awards and have been featured everywhere from *Ellery Queen* to *Thuglit*, as well as in her collection *The Black Widow Club*. A Toronto-born travel journalist who's lived in New York City since October 2001, Davidson is also the author of eighteen nonfiction books. Visit her online at www.hilarydavidson.com.